GOLDMAN'S THEOREM

R. J. Stern

ISBN: 978-1-897512-22-7

Saga Books
Sagabooks.net

Dear Jesse —

Thanks for coming —

Good luck and best wishes

Ron Stern

For Judy, Sach and Adam

Do not worry about your difficulties in Mathematics. I can assure you, mine are still greater.

---Albert Einstein

To most of us, nothing is so invisible as an unpleasant truth. Though it is held before our eyes, pushed under our noses, rammed down our throats - we know it not.

---Eric Hoffer

CHAPTER 1

On campus

-1-

When Beatrice phoned, Professor Herman Melville Singleton was slumped in his chair, staring at the mountain of MATH 101 finals heaped on his desk. The course was a remedial offering called *Quantitative Reasoning Skills*, and about a third of all freshmen in the liberal arts and social sciences were railroaded into taking it---the unfortunate subset not exempted upon admission to the University of Northern Vermont. Slutnick had coerced Singleton into being czar over all six sections, because Goldman was too much of a superstar and the other instructors were too junior.

He surveyed his office. Dozens of texts on fluid dynamics and partial differential equations littered the floor, the bookshelves were in chaos, and coffee-splattered file folders buried the small threadbare sofa. What a godawful mess, he thought, and vowed to tidy up in the near future. Straightening his long, thin body, he reached for the phone, now on its third ring.

"Aitch, Beatrice Beauregard here." Everyone called Herman by that nickname. "A couple of things. One. In your capacity as 101 czar, you must ensure that all grades are submitted by four o'clock, today. Two. Come see Chairman Slutnick immediately."

Beatrice was Guillermo Slutnick's one woman praetorian guard, and 'please' was not in her lexicon. Aitch grunted an affirmative and tried to thank her, but she hung up before he could speak. The reminder about the deadline was no surprise, but a Monday morning summons from the chairman was unusual. He hoisted himself up and shuffled down the corridor.

***

Slutnick's office had few furnishings. Other than his large desk and throne-like recliner, there were only two stiff oak chairs for visitors---no bookshelves, no file cabinets, no blackboard, and the walls were bare. The only decoration in the room was a pointy marble obelisk---dark, featureless, and six feet in height. A small brass plaque screwed into its base was engraved with 'Esmeralda', and below that, 'Dr. G. Slutnick'. Guillermo was forty pounds overweight, and despite being in his mid-fifties, he had skin like a baby. Last year he abandoned his pompadour and started wearing his oily dark hair in a short ponytail, the effect of which was to accentuate his jowls.

Chairman Slutnick was transfixed and glued to his monitor. He was aware that Singleton had been admitted to his inner sanctum by

Beatrice, but he had to finish a hand of internet poker before greeting him. Without turning, he raised a finger and wiggled it in a tense request for silence and patience. He was on a $10-$20 seven-card stud table---and the money was real. Players bought into the game with their credit cards, and various options existed for cashing out winnings. Aitch slipped behind the recliner so that he could see what was happening.

All the cards were dealt, the five other hands had folded, and now it was a showdown between Slutnick and a player with the pseudonym Bigballs, whose address box said Shenzhen, China. Guillermo presented himself as El Bandido de Venezuela, and he had caught a king high flush on the river card. Bigballs was showing 5-6-7-8 on top, and the pot had $438 in it. But after Bigballs called Bandido's third $20 raise, it turned out that he did not have a straight, as any rational person would have thought, but a well concealed full house, 5-5-5-6-6.

Uh-oh. Guillermo is not happy.

There was a chat-box on the poker website. The players were nastier than at a live table in Las Vegas or Atlantic City, because in the internet version of the game, there is no casino parking lot where one might get knifed. After raking in his pile of virtual chips, Bigballs wrote a message.

> Hey Bandido,
> You idiot stupid. Bigballs fuck you again.
> Go get Mommy Mastercard.
> Have a delightful day.

"MotherFUCKER!" Slutnick erupted, followed by "*LOFAS A SHEGED BEH!*" and a further torrent of obscenities in Hungarian which Aitch was content not to comprehend. He was sure that if his chairman were holding real cards and not virtual ones, he would have hurled them across the room. Slutnick pressed the 'Deal Me Out' button, rotated in his seat, and exhibited a murderous scowl.

"It looks like I caught you at a bad moment," said Aitch, as he folded his lanky frame into a wooden chair.

Suddenly cool as a cucumber, Slutnick said, "Well, maybe. But not because of that fucking full house." He popped a Rolaids. "Actually, I'm up over seven hundred already today. Bad hands like that are as rare as rocking-horse shit."

Somehow, with his perfect diction and upper-class Caracas twang, Chairman Slutnick could make himself sound almost charming while uttering the vilest profanities. It was deliberate and done with thespian flair, whenever he felt that he required extra dramatic effect in making a point, which was always. He was like quicksilver, and his penchant for changing moods in a flash made Aitch and everyone else nervous.

"Maybe you should quit while you're ahead," said Aitch.

Guillermo wanted to get right down to business, because he intended to gamble for the rest of the day, before going home to Esmeralda and his three brats. Perhaps he could gut Bigballs and teach him a lesson. He picked up a sheet of paper and held it high.

"Maybe you should shut the fuck up and pay attention. You know what this is?"

Aitch had learned over the years that the best way to deal with Chairman Slutnick was to adopt as flat an affect as possible---sometimes you could ride out the storm, sometimes not. So he said nothing and gave an innocuous shrug, waiting for the tirade to come, even though he had no inkling what it would be about.

"This is Goldman's progress evaluation form---provided by the Horst Von Essen Foundation."

The Von Essen coat of arms was visible on the letterhead---a large ornate 'E' with two swords behind it forming a 'V'. Aitch recalled some story Guillermo once told him about a Slutnick who purchased a 'Von' during Austro-Hungarian high times a hundred years ago. He wondered if the Von Slutnicks might have a coat of arms too.

Guillermo continued, "In a few weeks I have to fill it in, sign it, and then get the Virgin Queen to sign it as well. Do you know what the purpose of this goddam form is?"

Aitch gave a slight nod, but he did not know and it did not matter, because Guillermo was going to have his rant no matter what.

The phone rang. It was Esmeralda. She was terrified that she might make a spicing error in preparing the *paella Valenciana* that Guillermo had ordered for supper.

"No, Esmeralda---*two* pinches of saffron. I know that you will do a magnificent job. I will be home around six."

She reminded him about the parenting workshop he had promised to attend that evening. He ignored her, said something affectionate in Spanish, and rang off. After pausing for five seconds to ruminate on which wine would best accompany his meal, he had Goldman's evaluation form in the air again.

"At first we thought that this fucking form was just some kind of trivial formality those fucking Nazis wanted---a slam-dunk. It *should* be a slam fucking dunk."

"They aren't Nazis and never were. The Von Essens are Pomeranian-Prussian aristocrats, members of the *Junker* class. And they are patriotic Americans."

This barrage of truth had no effect on Guillermo Slutnick---none whatsoever. Aitch recalled that it was Guillermo's erroneous belief that the Von Essens were Nazis, or at least anti-Semites, which triggered his brilliant manipulation of them a few years ago, resulting in Goldman being awarded his endowed research professorship.

"All Von Essen professors are required to provide a progress report every five years. Now I know why. Do *you* fucking know why?"

Aitch deadpanned, "Is it because the Von Essens are fascists and it appeals to their insane Teutonic sense of order?"

"Don't copy my style and I won't copy yours," said Guillermo, and he was not joking. "No, the purpose of the form is simple. The dean let me know that the Von Putzes intend to spring for *another* seven endowed research professorships next year, and they already intended it five years ago, but didn't mention it then. They told the rector last month, who told the dean, who told the department heads in Arts and Science two weeks ago. The new endowments will commemorate the eightieth birthday of Rolf, Horst's baby boy, and UNV will be in competition with the University of Burlington again, just like five years ago, when Horst turned one hundred. As you well know, last time we got four and Burlington got three---a major victory for our beloved institution. The progress forms for the first crop of Von Essen professors are intended to help the Krauts decide where to throw their dough in the upcoming competition, and will probably tilt them in the tie-breaker. It shouldn't be a fucking problem for us, now should it?"

Aitch began to sweat.

"Are you under pressure from Dean Fulton?"

"The Virgin Queen has to sign it too. And she will undoubtedly seek a third term as our deanette, so of course she wants to look good like everybody else. You know what she's like."

***

When the first Von Essen windfall was announced six years earlier in June, 1997, Margaret Fulton was nearing the end of a seven year term as the first female Dean of Arts and Science at the University of Northern Vermont, and she had already accepted and signed on for a second stint of the same duration. Her first years as dean had been tentative, cautious and conciliatory, but she was at last beginning to achieve control and hegemony over her unruly division, and to assert her particular sense of what was right on a diverse and bulging faculty.

A veritable chimera which I must tame! If it is to be the carrot or the stick, then the stick it shall be!

The Faculty of Arts and Science was comprised of nineteen departments, five of which, including Mathematics, were in the sciences. Margaret's own background was in British history under the Tudors. She belonged to a patrician Boston family that could afford to send her to Vassar for her baccalaureate, and then on to Cambridge for a doctorate. Her first academic posting was at the College of William and Mary, a position she acquired more on the basis of her Cambridge pedigree than her dissertation. But after five years there, she failed to secure tenure, and moved on to the greener pastures of northern Vermont. It was here at UNV that she found her true calling as an administrator, and she never ceased to be informed by her study of Elizabeth I of England, the Virgin Queen.

I know I have the body of a weak, feeble woman, but I have the heart and stomach of a king!

Elizabeth inherited a bankrupt realm, torn by discord. She showed judgement, determination, some luck in escaping assassination, and she succeeded in treading the line between her father Henry's Church of England and the Scottish Presbyterians, whose Knox she detested and scorned.

An intemperate, ill-educated lout!

Dean Fulton was influenced by Elizabeth's success in holding the decentralizing forces of Knox's fundamentalism at bay.

Power to the presbyteries? Never! I daresay, never!

And Margaret appreciated Queen Elizabeth's willingness to do the dastardly deed when it needed doing. Her rival, Mary Queen of Scots, overstepped the boundary and her life ended in the Tower of London.

Off with her head!

On the other hand, Dean Fulton recognized that the great monarch knew how to reward the obedient.

My faithful bootlickers!

The dean also admired how Elizabeth protected her power by maintaining her chastity.

I must avoid the intrigues of men.

Chastity, or at least the appearance of chastity, suited Margaret very well after the Baronet Mumford, her lecturer in Classics at Cambridge---the man who deflowered her and to whom she had pledged her troth---dumped her in favor of the new male groundskeeper at his Lincolnshire estate. Being jilted and disrespected in this manner, and denied entry to Britain's lower aristocracy, caused something in poor Margaret's psyche to snap.

You shall make whores of others, but you shall not make one of me!

Her present carnal proclivities amounted to clandestine relationships with a stable of married faculty members over whom she could exert sexual and administrative dominance.

In order to avoid the perception that she favored the arts and humanities over the sciences, Dean Fulton appointed Assistant Professor of Chemistry, James Carver, as her Associate Dean. He turned out to be her staunchest ally---her hatchet-man and chamberlain.

I have found my Walsingham!

It was Carver who encouraged Margaret to resist the anarchic trends that seemed to always be welling up in certain departments. The economists, for example, were in a perpetual state of confusion.

Drunk on Milton Friedman and his Chicago centurions.

And the political scientists were adopting decision theory and strategic behavior not just in their courses, but in jurisdictional fights with the administration. Worst of all, the wet science departments were in a constant struggle with the administration over the right to form corporate research alliances on favorable personal terms. Ultimately it was Carver's influence that tilted the balance in favor of Dean Fulton in her battle royal with the scientists. He convinced her to call the bluff of the chairman of the Department of Biology, who threatened to leave the university if he were not granted a course remission, so as to pursue his potentially lucrative research agenda in genomics.

You would dare to cross swords with me? I am no dunce with a blade sir, and you shall be skewered!

No such machinations were ever necessary in Dean Fulton's dealings with the mathematicians, who were hapless when it came to marketing their all too theoretical skills---even the so-called 'applied' ones. They were just a motley of awkward, socially inept theorem provers, and had never posed any challenge to the authority of the Virgin Queen.

-2-

Slutnick fidgeted, glanced down at the cuff of his black Armani shirt, and blew away a long strand of red hair.

"Singleton, the dean wants another victory over Burlington, but there's no detectable pressure---yet. I haven't signaled a problem to her or anyone else. But we need to keep our eye on the ball---it was you who recruited your pal Simon Goldman from Harvard, and it was yours truly and the dean who backed you up. Lately I've been asking Goldman what's up research-wise---just making conversation, know what I mean? I wasn't trying to pressure him---just schmoozing, right? I can't get a straight answer from the little prick---only evasion. What's his big fucking secret? Will we be embarrassed? *Is there going to be a problem?*"

So now it was *your* pal Goldman and *you* recruited him? And the others just *backed him up*? Oh brother. Aitch had the sensation of floating out of his body, and felt a numbness in his jaw. He started swaying left and right, left and right.

Guillermo was on a roll.

"You know, when we were first considering Goldman over five

years ago, I said '*This guy has accomplished so much by the age of fifty that even if he never does another fucking thing, we should still get him that endowed research professorship.*' Perhaps I should have added that I WASN'T FUCKING SERIOUS! Has he done anything these past five years except sports or take trips on Von Essen money? He went to some bullshit conference in Cannes last summer, didn't he? Nice beach there. Beautiful topless women wearing postage stamps to cover their twats. Decent restaurants right off the sand. I have spies in France. *Goldman didn't attend a single goddam talk!* What do I write on the Von Essens' form---that Goldman is still breathing and having a kickass good time on the French Riviera with their gelt? And what about his federal research grant? He's in his fifth year and he needs to reapply, right? Will he get it renewed? The reason I told you to come here is to ask you, *do you think I should be worried?* STOP SWAYING, FOR FUCK'S SAKE!"

Aitch stopped swaying, but began rubbing his wet palms on his thighs, back and forth, over and over. With conscious effort, he unclenched his teeth.

"Simon had a couple of first rank articles and a monograph on complexity theory in press when he applied, so those things came out fairly recently. One of those papers appeared in the *Transactions of the American Mathematical Society*, and it's pretty rare for an applied mathematician to publish there. But I guess that won't satisfy you, because that stuff was already in his CV five years ago. Still, he ought to get his federal grant renewed on sheer bureaucratic inertia. I mean, after all, he *is* an international superstar."

Slutnick said, "Sit still, goddammit---you're making me fucking seasick. Tell me, what has Goldman done since he came to Vermont? I'll tell you what he's *not* fucking done. He has *not* assumed the leadership role in complexity and algorithms that we were so sure he would assume. He has *not* supervised or supported a single fucking graduate student. He has *not* given a single seminar or talked mathematics with anyone here, has he? And with regard to the little teaching that he does, well, the student evaluations have been shit, and consistently so---they call him disinterested, arrogant, disorganized, late for class, and they say he doesn't respect his office hours either. There are rumblings in the department about Goldman. I could go on."

Aitch was sure that he could. He tasted bagel and for a fleeting instant thought that he might spew onto Chairman Slutnick's plush carpet.

"Listen, Guillermo---don't panic---many of the really great ones went through prolonged dormant periods."

Guillermo rolled his eyeballs to the ceiling, and only the whites showed. Aitch wondered if his chairman had high blood pressure, and pushed away the unpleasant thought that he might have to resuscitate him. But Slutnick refocused and began working on another Rolaids.

"Yes, Singleton, that's true, but it's also true that after they got past fifty, some of the really great ones saw their crazy trains run off the rails. Or their brains turned to guacamole. Andropause. Deep hormonal shifts. Dying neurons and all that good shit. Isaac Newton comes to mind."

Aitch did not completely succeed in ignoring this disturbing imagery, and felt himself wilting in the face of Slutnick's onslaught. He was agonized by moral conflict, but knew that he had to break his oath of silence and spill the beans about Goldman's Holy Grail---something he learned about only yesterday.

CHAPTER 2

Sunday squash

-3-

Aitch spent most of the previous afternoon ensconced in his attic study, which was as disarrayed as his campus office, maybe even worse. He was gazing out the window at the gurgling Trout River, pondering the physics of bubble formation in turbulent non-viscous flows, when the phone rang. It was Goldman.

"Hey, Aitch. It's me. Start marking? Having fun yet?"

"Nope, not yet, but I'm nearly psyched. If you get going on your load, we could switch off in a few hours. Fun."

The six sections of the MATH 101 had a common final examination, and it was Aitch's responsibility as czar to distribute the chore of marking its ten questions. He asked the graduate students on the instructional team, Nathan Finkelstein and Ibrahim Ibrahim, to mark two questions each. The twins, as they were known, were grateful for their subsistence level teaching assistantships, and finished on May 5, the same day the exam was held. Assistant Professors Celestine Sauvage and William Hurker, the new tenure track hires, also had two questions each, and were done the next day. Two questions remained to be marked---one apiece for Professors Herman Singleton and Simon Goldman. Now it was May 18, an exquisite, fragrant Sunday in the Green Mountains, and the deadline for submitting the grades was 4 p.m. tomorrow.

"Didn't really start yet," said Goldman. "Been spending all my time on research. You know how it is."

Aitch was surprised that Simon had broached the subject of his research. Since coming to Northern Vermont from Harvard, he never seemed ready to discuss mathematics with anyone. This was new.

"Yeah, I know how it is. So what exactly are you working on?"

Simon breezed, "Oh, a little bastard of a problem in complexity theory that I've been kicking around for a few years. I believe I've finally got it by the balls."

"Be careful---make sure it's not the other way around. So how far along are you? With your marking, I mean"

"Well, I only peeked at Celestine Sauvage's section---just three exam booklets chosen at random---but it looks like they're bombing. I wonder if she actually covered exponential decay."

Aitch knew that Celestine had taught well the previous semester, but if a pedagogical problem had surfaced in MATH 101 this term, it was his job as czar to have noticed. He felt a flutter in his stomach.

"Oh brother. Not what I need to hear."

"Aitch, I totally feel your pain. Really. I'm a sensitive twenty-first century kind of dude."

Question number 10, the one inflicted upon Simon Goldman, dealt with the decay and half-life of a radioactive substance, with a practical application to the carbon dating of a fossilized mastodon femur. According to the syllabus, these topics were supposed to have been covered during the last two weeks of classes, so Aitch worried that Celestine had to play catch-up and compress it all into a last, desperate lecture. It was a common enough phenomenon in the math department.

Simon said, "Hope you don't wind up with thirty pissed off artsie-fartsies at your door. Our esteemed chairman is sure to go ape and take a personal interest in making you suffer. And he'll inform the Virgin Queen."

A tsunami of dread washed over Aitch as he envisioned a horde of incensed liberal arts majors chasing him down, complaining about disorganized teaching in the Department of Mathematics. And Simon was right. Slutnick would detonate if there was a fiasco, and tell their dean that it was Aitch's fault.

After allowing his friend to wallow in fear for a few seconds, Goldman said, "Bumpkin, here's the fix. Just ask Celestine to mark number 10 for her own section tomorrow, and encourage her to be charitable. Piece of cake."

Aitch felt his heartrate returning to normal and his innards settling down.

"Okay Simon, good thinking. Is that what they do at Harvard? Anything else?"

"Yes, of course," said Goldman. "And no, nothing else. I'll set mathematics aside and get to work in the shit mine."

***

Simon Goldman was recruited from Harvard five years earlier---stolen, Slutnick liked to boast. During the first decade of his Ivy League career, he gained fame as an innovator in game theory, the subject of his doctoral dissertation at Northwestern University. Then, in the mid-1980's, his interests shifted to complexity theory. Goldman became recognized as a luminary of the first rank in that domain because of his algorithm for computing any specified digit in the decimal expansion of π, and he embellished this achievement with theorems guaranteeing that his method did so with a minimal number of computer flops. To some, such a quest might seem arcane and quixotic, if not utterly useless, but fallout from Goldman's efforts had profound reverberations in Number Theory, adding to his glory. There were those who thought that his achievements in getting a handle on π were worthy of a Fields Medal, but that honor, the highest a mathematician can attain, is awarded only to individuals less than forty years of age. So Simon Goldman had to content himself with a prize from the Complexity Society, somewhat akin to an MVP award in baseball.

After almost four decades of friendship going back to their undergraduate days at Cooper Union, Aitch understood how his friend was hardwired. But not all of Simon's new colleagues at the University of Northern Vermont were so accepting of his Manhattan swagger and what they took to be an Ivy League superiority complex. Most viewed him as a vainglorious interloper with an overblown sense of entitlement. Professor Felix Felspar, who was always better at pretentious prose and philology than at mathematics, summed up the prevailing departmental view a few years ago, when he addressed a gaggle of his fellow deadwoods in the math lounge.

"This Goldman fellow is a veritable Montgolfière of self-puffery, refulgent with immodesty, and it was a grotesque blunder to have hired him."

***

It was warm, and Aitch was naked. Swiveling towards the window, he stretched his long legs and placed his feet up on the sill. As the breeze played upon his toes, the backyard oak brushed against the dormer, reminding him to get up on the ladder and give it a trim, one of these days. Other chores loomed---the porch needed paint and the backyard shed had to be demolished. He was annoyed with himself for his dilatory tendencies, and even ashamed. But with Maureen gone and not there to prod him, things did not get done. He heaved a sigh, pushed his glasses higher on his nose, and reached for a red pen. But before he could begin marking the first booklet, the phone rang again.

Simon's New York accent seemed more clipped than before.

"Listen. I have an idea. We pretend to be sportsmen, right? Mathletes, yes? So I want to suggest a sporting approach to this evil drudgery."

Aitch said, "Yeah? What do you have in mind?"

But he already knew.

"How about a squash match? Loser does the winner's share. I'm making this challenge in spite of my pulled hamstring---I'm eating Vioxx like candy. I can pick you up in half an hour."

Aitch always liked to take his time and think things through, and hesitated while weighing the offer---so Simon sweetened it.

"And after we play, why not come over and have dinner with me and Mona? It's been a few months. Come on. You owe it to yourself. What do you say?"

His friend's mind was still gridlocked, so Goldman felt obliged to launch a nuclear goad. Piece of cake, thought Goldman.

"*Herman*, after we play and I win, you can sit at my dining room table and get in an hour of marking while I putz around in the kitchen. I'll make you a nice pasta so you'll have enough energy to stay awake until 4 a.m. finishing the job."

Over half a century ago, when Herman Melville Singleton was a three year old in the tiny Adirondack hamlet of Schroon, he once decorated his parents' bedroom wall with a gigantic **'H'** drawn with his mom's bright red lipstick. His schoolteacher parents loved *Moby Dick* enough to name their son after its author, but following his act of toddler vandalism, Herman Melville became Aitch---forever.

He absorbed Goldman's taunt, believing that he might have an edge. Goldman's brain might be worn out from his bastard of a problem, and that could cause his hand-eye coordination to suffer on the squash court.

"I hardly slept a wink last night," said Aitch, and it was true. "Overstressed from my bike ride yesterday---the 85 kilometer Jay Peak circumnavigation. First time this season, you know. My quads are fried and I might need ibuprofen. But what the heck. We'll play for it."

-4-

After cradling the receiver, he shot an e-mail to Celestine Sauvage, because Goldman's stratagem still made sense.

> Bonjour Celestine:
>
> There seems to be a problem with your section's performance on #10.
>
> I know you already completed your marking job, but I think it would be best if you marked that one for your own section, tomorrow morning. If some material on half-life etc. wasn't covered, please just give them their points.
>
> In situations like this, it is best to be generous!
>
> I'll be on campus tomorrow morning.
>
> Merci beaucoup,
>
> Aitch S.

He padded down to the basement and found some clean squash

clothes in the dryer. He chose the T-shirt with the logo,

NEW ENGLAND
MASTERS SQUASH TOURNAMENT
UNIVERSITY OF NORTHERN VERMONT
OCTOBER 15-17, 2002

Last year the competition was held on home territory, and in the 'Over 50' men's group, Simon lost 3-0 to some wealthy lawyer from Montreal. Aitch destroyed the shyster 3-0 before being dismantled by Dartmouth's squash coach, but since he bageled the player who bageled Goldman, he hoped the T-shirt might serve as a cruel reminder, and undermine his psyche. Of course, the mere fact that he was trying to undermine Simon might undermine him. He had never worn the T-shirt against him before---he was waiting for the right occasion, and this was it. Newton took a keen interest in things today, and tried to crawl into the racquet bag his human was packing. "Man's best friend," said Aitch as he placed the disappointed cat in a laundry basket.

On his way out, he paused in the living room to water Maureen's favorite plant, a ficus, next to her photograph on the baby grand. Dust was dancing in a sunbeam and coating the mahogany, so he made a mental note to call Mrs. Trudo and ask her if she could give the place a going over.

He went out to the flaking front porch and seated himself on a wicker chair next to a stack of dog-eared *Scientific American* magazines going back ten years. Newton climbed onto his lap, flipped over and began kneading his paws in the air, purring, living the memory of nursing at his mother's side. Aitch stroked the cat's belly and allowed his gaze to wander down the road. Just around the bend was a graceful, century-old covered bridge built by the Jewett brothers. Others were in the region, and some had given him shelter when he was caught in boomers while out spinning. His view encompassed the white clapboard Montgomery Methodist Church, whose parishioners were proud that the clock in its steeple had not kept time since 1895, and he could see miles of the Trout River Valley and its bordering verdant hills from here. He never tired of the soothing vista, an endless, undulating ocean of the deepest green. "Music for the eyes", sweet Maureen used to say.

After a few minutes, he saw Simon's vintage Volvo approaching, so he drooped his head and pretended to be napping.

-5-

Simon Goldman pulled up and took a moment to grin and admire his friend's sleeping act. Couldn't do better myself, thought Goldman.

Herman Melville Singleton was an odd specimen. At six foot three, 158 pounds, with thick dark-rimmed glasses, pronounced Adam's apple, large aquiline nose, and spiky salt-and-pepper hair, he looked just how some people thought a fifty-six year old Professor of Mathematics ought to look---a botched attempt to clone Harrison Ford. His physical appearance inspired a crack graffiti artist ten years ago:

Singleton posed for the centerfold of Nerd Magazine.

The microscopic declaration was written in the thin space between the tiles above a urinal in the men's room near his office. He did not care if people mistook him for a nerd, and the quip was long since eradicated. But to this day, he hoped that it was the work of a student and not a faculty member.

The horn tooted. Aitch faked a startle response, and Newton leaped. Yawning, he yanked himself up and limped to the car as though his walkway was the Via Dolorosa. As he collapsed into the passenger seat, he noticed that Goldman's T-shirt and baseball cap both bore the Harvard logo. So that was how Simon intended to poison his mind---Ivy League intimidation. Just wait til he sees *my* T-shirt, thought Aitch.

Today the usual good natured mind games became serious, because they were going to play for more than bragging rights and a bottle of Gatorade from the vending machine. So today guilt tripping and righteous indignation were added to the standard mix of hubris and excuse making.

"You realize you screwed me, right?" said Goldman as he put the Volvo into gear. "You gave me number 10, which is a bitch to mark ---especially the mastodon part---but you gave Ibrahim-squared a trivial one on logarithmic rules. And his twin, Finkelstein, had an easy one too."

What a little prima donna his friend could be, thought Aitch. And now he was being even more insufferable than usual, probably because he's been obsessing on a math problem.

"Simon, first of all, I hope you noticed that I gave myself the longest question---the word problem about converting Fahrenheit to Celsius and vice-versa. And the twins each had one easy question and one hard one, which only seems reasonable. And you could have volunteered to be czar, you know, so don't complain now. I have enough other stuff on my plate."

Goldman suppressed a smirk and gave his friend an affirmative nod in hopes of stifling the impending litany, but it did not do the trick.

"I'm on the Departmental Personnel Committee, the Library Committee, the Faculty Tenure Committee, Faculty Council and University Senate. And this year I got elected Departmental Caffeinator at the meeting I missed when I had the flu."

Aitch went on to point out that Simon Goldman could have

taught Calculus, a jewel in the crown of human intellectual achievement, to a semi-enthused audience of math majors. But Goldman had asked for MATH 101 because it required next to no preparation and because he was able to teach a section which met at 8 a.m., suiting his early bird biorhythms and allowing him to return home by ten. In fact, Simon came to the campus only for his two lectures per week or for a squash match. But this did not raise any eyebrows. Now that the UNV library could be accessed online, there was no longer much need to scour the stacks for reference articles and then photocopy them---most could be downloaded to a desktop computer and printed at home. So it was natural that conducting mathematical research in one's domicile, and even in one's bed, had become fashionable in the Department of Mathematics.

Goldman abandoned the moral high ground.

"Okay, don't go postal on me. It's a piece of cake to teach 101, but I just can't stand it. Students in history, literature, underwater basket-weaving---you name it---*they hate our fucking guts!* "

He steered the Volvo around a downhill curve with one hand on the wheel, turned his Harvard cap backwards with the other, and reincarnated himself as a UNV freshman, complete with a 'duh' tone.

"Sir, why do I have to take this course? I'll never need it for anything."

And then with more seriousness, "How do you respond to them? Tell me, please. Enlighten me."

"Oh, for Pete's sake, come off it, Simon. You behaved the same way in the 60's at Cooper Union when they rammed humanities courses down our throats. Remember Professor Klein? Remember *Beowulf* and the Venerable Bede? How about Quasimodo? *The Canterbury Tales*? Rose Fingered Dawn? You asked Klein the same darn question! And by the way, I never admitted it back then, but I really *liked* reading *Moby Dick*. Best darn book ever written. Call me Ishmael."

Stroking his goatee, Simon squinted and dredged his memory for Professor Klein. Tweedy little guy in his forties who reeked from pipe tobacco and had patches on the elbows of his corduroy jacket. He wondered if Klein might still be alive. Simon considered resurrecting some tasteless undergraduate Moby Dick or Rose Fingered Dawn jokes, but decided it was too easy. A grin crept onto his face.

"Well, Quasimodo rings a bell."

"Very funny," said Aitch. "To answer your question, I give them the mathematical analog of what Klein said to you when you harassed him. I point out that MATH 101 really does teach useful skills they might need one day, such as calculating approximately when a mastodon died. Just like when Klein told us,

You never know when you'll have to harpoon a demented albino sperm whale.

And then I remind them that they can't graduate without passing the course. Two realities, Simon. *Two realities!* I let them choose the one they like better, just like Professor Klein let us choose. You can turn your hat around."

Goldman turned his hat and gave his friend the slightest nod of respect for his sagacious response.

"Well, I still say we should mark the easy ones because we're senior."

"Simon---we're old pros, right, so what's the big deal? And by the way, buddy, as a reward for solving your big problem in complexity theory, I hereby appoint you associate 101 czar. Put it in your CV for the next performance review exercise, not that it matters in your case."

He was referring to the fact that Goldman was the *Horst Von Essen Professor of Mathematics* at UNV, a coveted and prestigious lifetime sinecure---a fully funded research chair awarded five years earlier, when he was lured to the University of Northern Vermont from Harvard. Aitch Singleton was credited with arranging the initial contact between UNV and the world renowned Goldman---a feather in his cap, to be sure.

Like the other three Von Essen appointees at the University of Northern Vermont, as well as those at UNV's archrival and nemesis, the University of Burlington, Simon did not carry a full teaching load. Other active researchers in the math department, Aitch Singleton among them, taught two courses per semester, and Chairman Slutnick made sure that the deadwoods all taught three. But Simon Goldman, to the envy of his new colleagues, taught only one course per semester.

Goldman had other perks beyond light teaching, adding to his image problem. For example, The Horst Von Essen Foundation's endowment guaranteed him a salary twenty percent higher than any other professor in the department. And the foundation provided a further $25,000 each year for research related travel or the support of graduate students, all this in addition to the generous government grant he already held. But to some, the icing on Goldman's cake was the fact that he was the only faculty member not put through the grueling and time consuming biennial performance review process, which involved the preparation of a gargantuan dossier. Only a brief and informal report, co-signed by the chairman and dean, was required every five years---just a single page form to be submitted to the Horst Von Essen Foundation, discussing Goldman's scientific progress and publication record over that period. The first of these evaluations was due next month---a mere courtesy to the Von Essens. Or so it was thought.

***

They followed the Trout River Valley westward on Route 118, and then at East Berkshire turned south onto Route 105. Mt. Pinnacle straddled the Quebec border to the north, and double-humped Mt. Sutton was visible as well, across the international line. To the east, Jay Peak shimmered like an emerald pyramid, its gondola port giving the four thousand footer its distinctive profile. In this borderland, the Appalachians make an incursion into Quebec. The province's other mountains are part of the Canadian Shield, and their look is different---more conifers than here, more glacier-gouged lakes, and more mosquitoes. The mountains of northern Vermont are higher, but the valleys are broader. It is the Big Sky country of the American Northeast.

Most of the land they were driving through was virgin forest, but they were also passing dairy farms and crop fields, corn for the most part. Cattle and horses were out grazing on the short spring grass, and some farmers were out working their fields, even though it was a Sunday. The majority were Franco-American, the descendants of rural Quebecois who migrated to New England during the Great Depression and earlier. As the old Volvo whooshed along, the names on their mailboxes became blurred.

"Simon, did you know that many of the family names around here have mutated or been corrupted? Fleury became Florry and Gagnon is now Gannon. I once biked past a mailbox near Eden with the name Robshaw---I bet it was once Robichaud."

"Sounds like some kind of nonlinear transformation," said Simon. "Let's prove some theorems about it and submit an article to the Transactions."

"You get a different feel for the land when you bike it. Much more intimate than when you're in a car."

"Fucking disturbing," said Goldman, still playing the wise-ass, which he seemed to feel was expected. "Looks like Klein really did get into your head."

Aitch took in a deep breath of the country air and put his hand out the window to catch the wind, like when he was a kid.

-6-

The University of Northern Vermont was situated a mile northwest of Enosburg Falls, on the heights overlooking Lake Carmi. Founded by Methodists in 1869 as a small agricultural college, it had undergone steady expansion since then. All the original buildings were still standing and in use, but more recent structures now dominated the campus. One of the grandest was the sprawling Von Essen Sports Center. Simon had phoned the front desk and double-booked a court, which was possible because most normal people preferred outdoor activities on a nice day like this.

***

Their lockers were in the same row. After he changed, Simon said, "I think I'll go upstairs and warm up for a few minutes on a cardio machine---gotta loosen up my damaged hamstring."

"Good idea," said Aitch. "I'll come with you---maybe I can wake up my dead quads."

Both demonstrated their limps on the stairs leading to a balcony overlooking the UNV swimming pool, which was in a huge atrium. People exercising on bikes, treadmills and other devices read magazines on small easels or watched the swimmers in the sun-speckled water below. Simon mounted an elliptical trainer, and began limbering his arms and legs. Aitch selected a stationary bicycle, set the timer for five minutes, and started spinning.

He noticed one swimmer in particular---a slender woman---doing fifty meter lengths, alternating between crawl and breaststroke. She slid through the water with effortless grace, and her flip-turns were a study in efficiency. The rhythm of her movements mesmerized him as he rotated the pedals of his machine. Thirty seconds before his warmup was over, the swimmer took a break at one end of her lane and stood in the chest-deep water, a sleek figure in her black Speedo swimsuit with matching cap and goggles. A plastic water bottle and Styrofoam flutter board were positioned near her at the pool's edge. She drank a few swigs, reached for the board, and began power-kicking down the lane, trailing a foamy wake. Her head remained to one side as she passed below Aitch, and he had a clear view of her face in profile. It was Celestine Sauvage.

***

Goldman materialized by Aitch's side and brought him back to the here and now.

"Let's go, Herman. Get your bony ass off the bike and save your energy for the match."

Aitch complied with a grunt, and as he dismounted, stole another glance at Celestine, who had increased her pace. Quite a kicker, he thought. The two mathematicians went down to the court, both continuing to display their faint hampettes, as the precepts of gamesmanship demanded.

***

The Von Essen Sports Center housed four squash courts and six racquetball courts. No one at UNV played both---the four-wall universe was dichotomized here. Simon's name for racquetball was 'faggotball', because in his opinion, it is insufficiently macho. He called it a pussy game because it required much less physical toughness than its British ancestor, squash. All serious squash players, especially converts from faggotball, know with certainty that this opinion is correct. But most are not as vehement and demonstrative as Simon Goldman. His childish lack of restraint led him to insult Bill Hurker, who was gay, something Simon was not aware of last September at the wine and cheese party where new faculty were welcomed. Knowing that Simon was one of the department's sports fanatics, Bill approached him and asked if he might like to play racquetball sometime. The reply was loud enough to appall all within twenty feet.

"Sorry Bill, but I play *squash*, not *faggotball*."

Simon never showed self-reproach nor did he apologize, despite Aitch's repeated urgings.

***

They dropped their bags at court side. Aitch entered first, and began driving the small, soft black ball with his backhand, up and down the left wall, tight and deep. Simon strode through the door after fussing with an elastic bandage, and Aitch told him to make sure that he had it on the correct leg. Then he noticed that Simon was wearing one green sock and one red sock. And his Harvard T-shirt was now inside-out, as were his headband and wristband---and he was again stroking his little goatee.

Aha!---the goatee is new---last week he had a full beard!

Aitch's mind reeled as he thought of those stupid puzzles in the newspaper where you are supposed to find six differences between two cartoon panels.

Sweet baby Jesus! He wants me to keep looking!

He knew that he had to ignore Simon's clever psychological assault, just as Simon dared not admit taking notice of Aitch's diabolical T-shirt.

Aitch lofted the ball over to Simon on the right, and they knocked it up together, heating it so that it would bounce properly. After two minutes, Aitch spun his racquet, and on the handle it showed 'Your serve.' A bad omen.

-7-

Some members of the UNV squash varsity were loitering about, and when the veterans' match was about to get underway, seven of them were spread out on the slatted viewing gallery behind the plexiglass backed court. One of the youths possessed the temerity to greet Aitch with, "Yo, Professor." This was Atkins, captain of the men's squad. He was a string bean, even taller and skinnier than Aitch, who had him in MATH 101 two years earlier. A linguistics major and he did okay, Aitch recalled. Atkins was wearing a sweat-soaked T-shirt emblazoned with a cartoon of a psychotic bovine with bulging eyes, a deranged toothy grin, and the words 'MAD COW' below the image. The milk cow is the unofficial symbol of Vermont, and 'The Mad Cow' had been the name of the main campus cafeteria for two years now, the result of a student referendum. Atkins worked there, twenty hours per week.

UNV's sports teams had always been called 'The Bulls', but this nomenclature had been undermined of late by the popularity of the cafeteria's new name. So this past season, whenever the UNV football team took to the gridiron, it was greeted with a hearty chorus of "GO COWS." And the games were accompanied by prodigious and enthusiastic mooing, which had replaced the traditional booing. This fan behavior carried over to other varsity sports as well, and needless to say, the incessant moos were quite distressing to UNV's female athletic teams. The UNV Bull mascot was upset too, after being dry-humped by a drunken undergraduate seeking cow companionship. Many onlookers thought this was very undignified and humiliating, even for a sports mascot. But despite the merciless derision and having "MOOO" as their fans' battle cry, all of UNV's intercollegiate sports teams had winning seasons, and all dominated their university's constant rival, the University of Burlington. This included the squashers, who made the Mad Cow T-shirt their official uniform. Cow pride.

Ordinarily this entertainment---'The Geezer Show' they called it---was held on Wednesday afternoons, and this Sunday match between Dr. Octopus and Professor Roadrunner was an unexpected treat for the squash varsity. Aitch and Simon agreed that since they were playing for something of substance, one of the squash kids should be coerced into refereeing and calling out the score. Their natural victim was Mohibullah Khan, a barrel-chested math major who grew up near the Khyber Pass.

Aitch Singleton's philosophy was that racquet skill is important in squash, not so much to end a rally with a super-accurate drop shot or rare dead nick, because a speed merchant like Simon Goldman was capable of retrieving almost anything. No, the main function of racquet skill, Aitch believed, is to control the 'T' area and run one's opponent around the court on errands of ever increasing urgency, thereby inducing cardiovascular embarrassment, or failing that, reducing him to a puddle of sweat. His style of play reflected his deliberate and patient nature, and his big wingspan helped. Goldman, on the other hand, was a little scrambler with vast stores of energy, and he was much more willing than Aitch to bounce his body off the walls and attempt a risky shot.

***

The matches between Dr. Octopus and Professor Roadrunner were always ones of physical attrition, and this one was true to form. The first four games were close, and after an hour, it was two all, with the fifth and deciding game looming. A ninety second break was allowed, and they came off the court to take water. After Mohibullah toweled the floor for the geezers and called time-in, Simon went back on. As Aitch followed, Atkins caught his attention from the front row.

"Yo, Professor. *Keep eye on ball, is most important one thing I tell you.*"

He was doing a Pashto accent as he quoted the famous dictum of Hashim Khan, the great squash champion of the 1940's and 50's. All of Atkins' teammates appreciated the performance, especially his dialect coach, Mohibullah Khan. Aitch forced a smile and nodded, communicating that he understood the Zen-like directive. He vowed to obey it even if he had no blood in his brain and could not remember his own name. If you kept your eye on the ball, the universe unfolded as it should. The gallery was filling with onlookers.

Simon made a string of high risk winners and surged to an 8-7 lead, placing him on the threshold of victory. Aitch was running on empty, but dug in his heels and won a long, blistering rally. Luring Simon to the front with deceptive body language, looking as though his intent was to feather a drop, he flicked his wrist and lobbed instead. It was pure touch and a thing of beauty, the ball hovering in the air like a hummingbird before dying in the back of the court. Applause erupted, diminishing Goldman, who looked down and shook his head in disbelief. Serving at 7-8, Aitch won a point when Simon tinned a volley-drop from long range. It was a foolish thing to attempt, and he was disgusted with himself. Now at eight all, a grim-faced Goldman held up two fingers, meaning that the game would go beyond nine points to ten. A few hard fought rallies later, Mohibullah called out to his professors.

"Nine all. Match Ball."

The gallery was hushed. Aitch got into position to serve, and Simon struggled to concentrate his mind---it was sweltering and they were both suffering. Aitch gripped the ball and rotated it until he could focus on its two yellow dots, which stared back at him like a pair of beady little eyes. Bearing down on the small rubber sphere like Hamlet contemplating Yorick's skull, he squeezed it and dribbled it on the floor with his racquet eight times, and then---for what reason, he did not know ---gazed towards the seats. He thought he saw a face at the back, through the tangle of bodies and slats.

Jesus! It's Celestine! Did she notice me scoping her from the balcony? Christ!

After another eight obsessional bounces, he was ready to serve. But he turned his head again.

Where did she go?

He proceeded to serve the ball out---two feet over the cut-line. An incredible unforced error. A choke.

Simon raised his eyes to the lights.

"*Miracle!* Thank you, God."

Aitch stood there, positive that God hated him, and young Khan announced that it was still match ball. Simon served, and ten shots later, the rally ended when Aitch struck a powerful backhand drive along the left wall---a perfect rail shot---which sent Simon hurtling into a back corner. The ball was glued to the wall and he dove, flailing and managing to make contact only with the frame of his racquet. The unintended result was a fluky three-wall dead nick in the front right corner. Game and match for Professor Roadrunner! Another miracle, and a double load of grading for Dr. Octopus, who stood at the 'T' in frozen disbelief for thirty seconds, not hearing the applause. Goldman made another show of religiosity, and the two of them shook hands.

"Never really a doubt," said Goldman. "Piece of cake."

They sat outside the court, stretching their muscles and tendons. Atkins smiled as he and his teammates ambled by, and with an upturned palm, sang the Raj ditty which Mohibullah Khan had taught him.

Keep eye on ball,
And bend the knees.
That will be fifty rupees, please!

After the students' laughter faded down the corridor, the geezers hoisted themselves up and headed for the fountain of youth, which was what they called the whirlpool.

-8-

The Goldmans lived in Montgomery Center, two miles from Aitch's home in Montgomery, in a renovated farmhouse set fifty yards from the road. Mona was on the porch watering her hanging plants, barefoot and on tiptoes, in faded jeans and an oversized Mad Cow T-shirt. She greeted them with her Londoner's lilt as she finished with the bougainvillea.

"My heroes! My hungry and thirsty goad warriors! Sweetest Aitch, how have you been keeping? How is dearest Newton? That kitty is a prodigy, as is my wonder boy."

Mona Hope Goldman was a pixie, petite and very pretty, with skin like porcelain and a mop of dark hair, which had always made Aitch, think of the Beatles. He bent to hug her and kissed her on each cheek, Montreal style. Johnny Cash was singing *I Walk the Line* from inside.

"Don't mock heroism, Mona. Simon's the only mathematician I know with a Purple Heart and a Bronze Star to go with it. Or with a tattoo, for that matter."

Simon had *Saigon, 1970* etched in blue on his left shoulder.

"Yeah, I'm a major hero. Audie Murphy and Sergeant York rolled into one."

His eyes glazed and narrowed as he scanned the darkening forest, as if searching for something or someone. He was never willing to discuss his 'all expenses paid vacation in Southeast Asia', the only topic which inspired such reticence in him. Simon was involved in an ambush and came out of it with three cracked ribs, the medals, and a promotion to buck sergeant---but that was all Aitch knew. Mona claimed to be in the dark on these matters as well. "You'll have to ask Simon about that," she would say, if anyone inquired.

An Associate Professor of Music at the University of Northern Vermont, she was hired five years ago as the second body in what mathematicians and physicists like to call a 'two-body problem'. At the University of Northern Vermont, Mona taught the same courses in musical theory as she did at Boston College, specializing in the music of the Tudor court. A tireless supporter of Green Mountain Public Television, she often manned a telephone during televised GMPTV fundraising interludes, along with other members of the UNV String Ensemble. She poured ice-water with lemon, and listened to their rendition of the squash match, managing to look interested in all the epic details.

"Oh dear, Aitch, oh dear. Dreadful Simon won with a slut nick. How utterly unfair. What ignominy. Simon, shame upon you."

It was Aitch's long held contention that only Brits like Mona and Maureen could be so sardonic and condescending without giving offense. Standing behind her husband, Mona tousled his short, sandy hair, kissed his small bald spot, and whispered, "My wonder boy," this time without sarcasm. He squinted, overcome with pleasure. Just like Newton getting a head-rub, thought Aitch.

***

February 7, 1958----Washington Heights

It is a Friday evening. Ten year old Simon Goldman and his mother Mathilda are sabbath dinner guests at the home of Uncle Meinhold, Tante Lotte, and cousins Rutie and Eva-Leah. Meinhold Mannheimer is Mathilda's brother, two years older than her. After immigrating to the United States in the late 1930's, he served in the 101st Airborne Division during the Second World War. A screaming eagle is tattooed in blue on his left shoulder, its talons holding a banner with *Bastogne, 1944* on it. He has a steel plate in his skull as a result of that battle, but he never discusses his experiences during the war, a period which he refers to as his 'all expenses paid vacation in Europe'.

The sixth floor apartment is on Haven Avenue, near 173rd Street in upper Manhattan, the high ground where the island narrows. Seated at the table, Simon gazes through the dining room window. He sees the snow-speckled New Jersey Palisades towering over the mile wide Hudson, and the mighty George Washington Bridge making its arc over the river, providing a nexus between the city and the rest of America.

He detects the aroma of Tante Lotte's *Sauerbraten*, sure to be accompanied by homemade apple sauce and boiled potatoes. *Himmel und Erde*. Heaven and earth.

They are not religious people, but traditions persist. The sabbath candles have been lit, and blessings said over the grape juice and *challah* that Simon's mother picked up at Grostern's bakery on their walk over. During the meal, the conversation is conducted in German, and the accent, like the cuisine, is that of the Rhineland. Yiddish is regarded as the language of the lower classes---impoverished Eastern European *shtetl* Jewry---and is not spoken here. Theirs was the culture that had given the world Mendelssohn and Einstein. They claim Freud as well, forgiving him for being Viennese, and Karl Marx is on the list too, but never mentioned. This neighborhood, Washington Heights, was a Mecca for tens of thousands of German Jews who fled the Nazi terror two decades earlier. It is strange to hear some of them talk about it. There is less animosity towards Germany than one might expect---it was the Nazis whom they reviled, not the Germans. One day a book will be written about these people and their culture, which was in equal parts German, Jewish, and American---*Frankfurt on the Hudson.*

Before Lotte brings in the plum pie and sour cream, Simon's mother pings on her teacup with a spoon.

"Everyone---your attention please---I have a very big announcement."

Rutie and Eva-Leah, aged five and seven, giggle and ping on their juice cups.

"I had the school test Simon's IQ. *Guess*."

No one dares.

"*ONE HUNDRED AND SEVENTY THREE.* Just like the street!"

Meinhold emits a long whistle and Mathilda says, "Simon is OFFICIALLY a genius. He is especially strong in mathematics."

Lotte and Meinhold say "*Wunderbar!*" and mean it.

They know Mathilda is not trying to make them jealous---this is just her way. After Gustav died, Simon was all she had.

Uncle Meinhold tosses a ball of wadded bread at his nephew, hitting him in the temple. The little girls are red-faced and beside themselves with glee.

Simon's mother is now standing behind him. She strokes his hair, kisses the back of his head, and whispers, "*Mein wunderkind*," just like when she sits next to him on their special park bench, gazing at the George Washington Bridge in a teary-eyed trance, or when she lays next to him at night to tuck him in.

In English, Simon says,

"Rutie is such a cutie, I bet she has a high '*I Cute'*.

Cutie Rutie and Eva-Leah hide under their chairs and everyone laughs.

***

After his stroking, Simon brightened.

"Mona, instead of calling it a slut nick, you also might say it was a dink shot, which makes me similar to Descartes."

Mona and Aitch stared.

"You know. I dink, therefore I am....not marking finals."

"I always admired Descartes," groaned Aitch.

Simon said, "Well, you're right, honey. I *am* ashamed, but mainly I'm hungry---I'd better get going on the pasta."

The last time Aitch saw Simon exhibit shame was thirty-six years ago, when Professor Klein chastised him for plagiarizing his term paper on *The Tempest* from a booklet in the Monarch Notes series.

Johnny Cash began singing *A Boy Named Sue*, about the kid who had to get tough or die. Simon snapped himself up from the cushions and headed towards the kitchen, but then pivoted towards the CD cabinet and rummaged. Cash's last words were "What could I do? What *could* I do?" before the adagio from *The Godfather* filled the air.

Then Simon changed course again, and rejoined Aitch and Mona on the sofa. There was a small teak box on the coffee table, with a seashell inlay depicting a water buffalo---a souvenir from Vietnam. Simon opened it and produced a well rolled joint. He had a lot of rolling practice over there, Aitch suspected.

"Want to share this, buddy?"

"Simon, I couldn't even if I wanted to---I have all that darn grading to do."

Mona flushed red with a blast of menopausal heat. Insouciance seemed to possess her as she fanned herself and chirped,

"I ascribe this recent deviant behavior and everything else weird about my husband to some sort of mid-life crisis that mathematicians or Vietnam veterans go through, just as he ascribes everything weird about me to menopause or being a musicologist or being British. I'm quite certain we're both right. Quite. A shame you won't partake, Aitch. Wonder Boy has become quite the gentleman farmer---he claims his one-plant harvest is almost as good as what he and his degenerate comrades smoked in the army. I do hope he's not relapsing---he went through a year's rough patch after his jungle holiday, you know."

Rough patch? No, Aitch did not know.

Simon tossed an accusatory glance at Mona, and her expression deadened. But then he morphed his look into something more benign by rolling his eyes and shrugging, communicating that his wife was speaking nonsense. And with that, Mona produced an ashtray and provided a light. She only had three dainty tokes and quit. It was too strong, and Simon was happy to bogart. After stubbing out the roach, he rose without a word and got busy in the kitchen.

Aitch said, "Maybe you're right, sweet Mona. Maybe Simon is having a mid-life crisis. Me, I don't know if I'm having one or not. Everything's been cloudy the past few years."

She placed her hand on his, and they were silent. Aitch and Simon were friends since the mid-60's, when they were students at Cooper Union in New York City. Simon was dating Mona, who was studying at the Juilliard School of Music. Maureen was a student there as well, Mona's best friend and a fellow Londoner. Aitch met her on a half-blind double-date in 1966, and ever since that first get-together, the two British girls referred to their foursome as the 'Math Brothers and Music Sisters'. Maureen died as a result of a hit-and-run while jogging at dusk, three years ago this month. There was no hope, the doctors said ---the brain trauma was catastrophic. It was the Goldmans who stood with him, little Mona inconsolable, her arms around him as he signed the authorization to disconnect. Aitch would never forget their kindness.

The aroma of oregano wafted to the porch, and Aitch said he was starving. Mona took his hand and led him to the dining room. As always, Simon's linguine putanesca was excellent, and as always, they drank too much valpolicella. A year ago it became possible for them to mention Maureen in their get-togethers---the memories now evoked more pleasure than pain. So they ate, drank, and reminisced about the good times the Math Brothers and Music Sisters shared in New York, so long ago.

***

During the drive back to Montgomery, the two mathematicians were pensive and said little. When they arrived at his home, Aitch thanked his friend for the pleasant evening, and reached into the back seat for his squash gear and the bagful of MATH 101 exams he had inherited. Then he tried to open the door.

Goldman said "Wait," and seized Aitch's left forearm in a fierce grip. "Listen---this is confidential at the moment. Strictly on the hush-hush."

He was speaking in a sped up New York whisper.

"Aitch, I'm telling only you because I know you can keep your mouth shut. I've been working on a famous problem for several years, thinking about nothing else. I believe I've had a breakthrough. I'm onto something very, very big---huge even. *The Holy Grail!* When I'm a little more sure in a few days, I'd like to bounce it off you. Can I count on you to keep this under your hat?"

Now Aitch understood why his friend seemed to have a cloud of static around him lately. No wonder---he was flying high in the mathematical stratosphere.

"Sure," said Aitch, shrugging an affirmative, trying to convey nothing. "Yeah, I could be your sounding board, and you know I can keep a secret. Mum's the word. You can let go of my arm now."

Simon released his grip.

"Thanks. I'll keep you in the loop. You *are* the loop. Stay tuned."

The Holy Grail? Jesus, what the heck is he on to?

It flummoxed Aitch that he was the loop. After all, Simon did complexity theory, and Aitch specialized in fluid mechanics. They were as far apart in expertise as two applied mathematicians could be. It did not make any sense.

"I'll have your section's packet at the department before noon tomorrow, so you can submit your 101 grades. Goodnight---and good luck with the Holy Grail, buddy. "

He patted Simon on the back and got out.

-9-

Before retiring, Aitch e-mailed the twins and Bill Hurker, reminding them of the grade submission deadline, and that he would leave their sections' exams with the departmental secretaries after lunch. It was not necessary to notify Celestine, he reasoned. She always came in early anyway.

He got into bed and lay on his back, arms extended laterally---the Jesus position, Maureen used to call it. The posture suited his twelve year old tabby, Newton, who sat purring on his chest, grinning and staring into his eyes. Some individuals, especially mathematicians perhaps, experience lightning bolts of intuition and insight just as sleep is about to overtake them---scientific epiphanies or eureka's that Aitch called 'nocturnal aha experiences'. He could spend days or weeks stalled in an attempt to prove something, and then the bolt would come out of nowhere. He never understood the phenomenon, and thought it might be a good research topic for psychologists or brain physiologists, if it was not one already. These flashes did not come as often as when he was younger, but this night, just as he began to drift off, one struck him full force. But it was not mathematical.

Aitch excused himself to Newton, lurched out of bed, and opened Celestine's envelope. He spread the thirty-odd booklets on the floor, and after a brief perusal, realized that almost all her students had aced the mastodon question. The bedroom spun---he felt queasy and flopped back into bed. Simon Goldman was self-absorbed and capable of obnoxious, anti-social behavior. Aitch did damage control in his wake many times in the past, as with Bill Hurker, and now it looked like he would have to mollify Celestine Sauvage too. Unfairly criticizing her teaching was precipitous and extreme behavior, even for Simon Goldman, and even if he was on a quest for the Holy Grail. Aitch thought about e-mailing Celestine to undo his earlier message, but decided against it. The header would reveal the time of sending, and he did not want her to think that he was some sort of old fool who bombarded his colleagues after midnight with neurotic messages.

-10-

He forgot to place his wristwatch on the bedside table when he went to sleep, and because his hand had found its way under a pillow he did not hear its alarm beeping at 6:45. Newton heard it though, and woke his two-legger by prying open an eyelid with his paw. The cat thumped downstairs, and after Aitch opened the door for him, he galloped outside to join Minipod, the calico who owned one of the neighbors. Newton fathered one of her litters, eleven years ago. Long since neutered, they still enjoyed hunting together, and now rubbed noses before embarking upon the day's killing spree.

A few minutes later, as Aitch was having his bagel and coffee on the porch, he glimpsed a flash of tawny fur rustling the high grass across the road. The movement was too robust and the color was wrong, but he dismissed it, thinking that it had to be Newton and Minipod chasing something.

***

The drive to the UNV campus took about twenty minutes. He parked his Honda Civic in his slot alongside the Fitch Sciences Building, where the Department of Mathematics had its twenty-eight offices spread over the second and third floors. The seven-story building was completed in 1990 during a period of expansion at UNV, most of it contracted to the Von Essens' construction firm. In addition to the Department of Mathematics, the Fitch housed Physics and three wet science departments. The Science Library occupied the first floor, while classrooms and laboratories filled the basement and sub-basement. Graduate students had their office space in the sub-sub-basement, packed like sardines, three to each cramped windowless cell.

Like all veteran members of the math department, Aitch Singleton was nostalgic for their old quarters in the ivy-covered, moldy old Bunt Building, which the economists and political scientists now called home. You could open the windows in the Bunt. Felix Felspar, unofficial leader of the deadwoods until his retirement, once claimed that the Fitch's windows were sealed shut not so much because of its state-of-the-art climate control, but rather to prevent suicides stimulated by the sterile architectural environment. Some members of the department were still in a white-lipped rage over the uprooting, which the administration had forced upon them, and a few expressed their grudges by never unpacking their cardboard boxes.

Aitch headed upstairs to attend to his marking, but instead wound up in his Monday morning calvary with Chairman Slutnick.

CHAPTER 3

A hard day at the office

-11-

Faced with Slutnick's imminent destabilization, and having reviewed yesterday's events during the past ten seconds of twitchy dithering, Aitch knew what needed saying. He coughed, cleared his throat, and adjusted his glasses.

"There's one *very* important thing you should know, Guillermo, and I hope you can keep a secret, because Simon asked me to be completely discreet about a certain something, and I agreed. So by telling you this, I'm in violation of that promise, but I want to calm you down."

Guillermo loved being calmed down, several times a day if possible. He expected to be told about some personal problem.

Okay, so maybe Goldman was going through a divorce, or maybe he had some fucking disease, or maybe a close relative died. Or even better, maybe he was having Vietnam flashbacks---the goddam Prussians would probably respect that. Yes, that's what we can bullshit them with.

But Aitch surprised him.

"Simon has been working for several years on a blockbuster open problem, and he expects to announce a major theorem soon. He has told this to no one except yours truly."

Chairman Slutnick was taken aback, something no one had ever witnessed. He processed the news in silence for a few seconds.

So that's why Goldman has been so evasive. The little fucker!

"Are you going to tell me exactly what blockbuster open problem we are talking about?"

"Simon hasn't told me yet," Aitch admitted. "But he said it was the Holy Grail. He's had a breakthrough and he's checking the details. He looks extremely confident, and says he wants to bounce it off me when he's certain it's nailed down."

Guillermo was staring right through Aitch, his eyes focused on some distant place.

The Holy Fucking Grail?

He was fantasizing about all the public attention and notoriety that Goldman's theorem would bring to UNV, to the department, and perhaps even to Guillermo Slutnick himself. His mind was racing and his imagination was running wild.

Perhaps there would be a PBS or Discovery Channel special---who knows? And Goldman would know how to play the media fame game, especially with me coaching him.

A camera is following Simon Goldman as he walks along the banks of the Mississiquo, hands clasped behind his back and deep in thought---pondering his Holy Grail problem. Just like Wiles taking long walks on the Princeton campus while he contemplated Fermat's Last Theorem.

And now the great Goldman is videoed at his kitchen table, piled high with math books---pondering, pondering, pondering the Holy Grail, with his cute little Brit wife dutifully plying him with tea and scones.

And there is brilliant Goldman at the blackboard in the large seminar room, being applauded, even cheered, after the official presentation of his theorem to experts in the field, just like Wiles was. Who knows, a major prize might even be in the offing.

And of course there is to be a segment where I, Dr. Guillermo Slutnick, chairman of the Department of Mathematics at the University of Northern Vermont, am interviewed and explain, ever so indirectly and subtly of course, that it was my political acumen, leadership, and eye for mathematical talent which were instrumental in hiring the one and only Simon Goldman.

Guillermo blinked and snapped back to his previous reality, as though an electrical circuit in his cerebellum had been reconnected.

"Okay, Singleton. Consider me calm for the moment, but I want you to keep me perfectly fucking informed. And I want to see something concrete as soon as possible, after we're positive that his goddam result is true---an announcement of Goldman's theorem in a well advertised and sufficiently dumbed down seminar for the masses, so that we can invite the Virgin Queen, the Von Essens, and all the other big bangers. We can schedule another seminar for experts and let Goldman show them the details---say a week after the first talk. And all this *tout de suite*."

"And you want *me* to help you orchestrate it?"

"Who the fuck else?" said Slutnick.

-12-

A shaken Aitch Singleton hustled down the corridor to the math lounge in order to fulfill his obligations as Departmental Caffeinator before facing his marking chores. There he was greeted by Isidore Fleck, who was seated in front of the blackboard and staring at some formulas. It was obvious that he had spent the night sleeping on the sofa. Eighty-one years of age, thin as a rail, with long, unkempt gray hair and a scraggly beard, he wore the same threadbare clothes that he always wore, but Aitch noticed that now his old army belt had been replaced by a length of clothesline. On the table in front of the coffee-stained sofa, next to the Chess and Go boards, there were open books on quantum theory which someone must have checked out of the library for him. His ratty knapsack was there too, and Aitch wondered if it contained all the old man's material possessions.

"How's it going, Izzy? Learning more mathematical physics?"

"Yeah. I'm polishing up on quantum theory and starting to tackle superstring theory. It's all about the nature of reality, you know. It ought to be simple, but it ain't--- hidden spacetime dimensions can make for some pretty hairy geometry."

"Izzy, you are the *man*!"

They exchanged the tiniest of high-fives, their customary greeting. Aitch was always afraid that too firm a high-five might knock Izzy over.

Anyone seeing Isidore Fleck on the streets of a big city would assume that he was homeless and possibly starving. In fact, he survived on welfare and a modest disability allowance which he received because of a leg that got damaged in December, 1944, when he was a draftee marching through northern France.

"It was a few days after Patton pivoted south. We were rushing to relieve Bastogne, and the guy next to me stepped on a mine, luckily a small one. A million dollar wound, Aitch. *A million dollar wound! Look at me! I'm a millionaire!*"

In the hospital, millionaire Izzy made his mathematical talents known to his superiors, and spent the remaining months of the war in Honolulu, cracking Japan's naval codes. He said it suited him better than the infantry, and the food was better too. Fleck once told Aitch that he used Fourier Analysis to sink a Japanese submarine in 1945, and averred that no other PFC in the U.S. Army could make that claim.

Izzy rented a basement room from a sympathetic retired mathematician in Enosburg Falls, and didn't require many calories, as he liked to say. Aitch knew little about his deeper wounds or academic history, except that he completed his education under the G.I. Bill and obtained his doctorate from Princeton in 1950. While a graduate student there, he had the opportunity to assist Albert Einstein on a problem having to do with Riemannian manifolds. Izzy once told Aitch about the sign in the great man's office.

Not everything that counts can be counted, and not everything that can be counted counts.

"I guess I took it to heart," he said.

Aitch heard that after Princeton, he held a faculty position for a few years at a Big Ten university, but did not get renewed and was never employed again. Fleck was loitering in the math lounge for as long as could be remembered, and everyone in the department appreciated his presence because he always enjoyed being pumped for mathematical knowledge and shortcuts to proofs. Izzy was welcome here, but darn it, thought Aitch, he shouldn't pass out in the lounge overnight---one day Beatrice will catch him. He promised himself for the hundredth time to read Izzy the riot act---but not today. He prepared a cup of coffee for the old monk the way he liked it, black with four sugars, and found some Oreos for him in the cupboard.

-13-

Aitch Singleton was back at his desk by nine-thirty, and checked his e-mail. The twins and Bill Hurker had responded to his earlier communication with brief okay's. Celestine had not answered his message about her section's performance on Question number 10, and he hoped against hope that she had not gotten around to reading it. He found a red pen and took a half hour to mark her section. Afterwards, in need of a break, he placed his feet up on the window sill, stared at Jay Peak beckoning in the distance, and resumed his deliberations on the mysteries of bubble dynamics.

His mathematical reverie was interrupted by a delicate but firm knock. There stood Celestine Sauvage, smiling and peeking through the crack in the door. He placed his feet back on the floor and asked her to please come in. Aitch recalled her CV, the source of everything he knew about her. Born in 1974, she was raised in Outremont, an upscale francophone part of Montreal, in the shadow of Mont Royal. She earned her B.Sc. in Mathematics *cum laude* in 1995 at McGill University, and her high grades gained her admission to the doctoral program in mathematics at Berkeley. Celestine was interested in Stochastic Control Theory, a discipline concerned with dynamical systems having uncertainty or white noise in the available information.

It was hot, and Celestine dressed for the weather. She wore khaki hiking shorts, sandals, and a tight fitting black tank-top which more than hinted at the form of her breasts. Her legs were beautiful, and her toenails were painted red, matching her fingernails. For the first time, or the first time that he noticed, she was wearing her wild, dark, shoulder length hair swept up, revealing an elegant neck and small diamond earrings. And she was not wearing her ponderous eyeglasses today. Contacts, he surmised. He detected her perfume, and marveled at the smoothness of her skin. On the male chauvinist pig scale of rating female appearance, where Bo Derek is a 10 and Eleanor Roosevelt is a 0, Aitch Singleton, if he were a male chauvinist pig---which of course he was not---would have assigned Celestine a score of 5.2. Basically okay, but nothing special. A bit nerdy with the heavy glasses, her nose was too big, and she looked scrawny. But now he knew better. When he voyeured her from the pool balcony yesterday he gained appreciation of her lithe body and supple strength, heretofore unnoticed. Today she was a 9.9 or even higher. At least that was how the sudden protuberance in his jeans was rating her. For a moment he could hear his dad explaining that it was the most sincere compliment a man can give a woman, but he drew comfort from neither the fact nor the memory.

He put his hands on the edge of his desk, leaned forward with care, and used his long arms to roll his chair forward. The wheels squeaked, adding to his self-consciousness. When he was satisfied that his tumescent tent-pole was out of sight, he motioned for Celestine to take a seat opposite him, on the other side of the desk. She sat on the front edge of her chair, body tilted forward, hands on her knees. Eager attentiveness.

"*Bonjour*, Professor Singleton."

Celestine's accent sounded more Parisian to Aitch than the *joual* dialect heard in Montreal.

"Aitch," said Aitch, smiling and trying his best not to sound avuncular. This was not the first time he had to correct her or other junior faculty members and postdocs. The unwritten rule was that if you had a doctorate, then first name familiarity was appropriate.

"Celestine, I'm sure you want to know more about the e-mail I sent you concerning Question 10."

His smile was still there, but now he was looking down. He took the opportunity to steal a glance at his engorged stiffy. Too darn noticeable. He pushed his glasses up higher on his nose.

"It was all a silly foul-up. Simon Goldman took an unfortunate random sample and drawn a false conclusion. Actually, your section did well on number ten, and by the way, I marked it myself. Their grades look high overall---maybe the best of all six sections."

He handed over her packet, making sure to keep near his desk. Celestine was communicating something to him. There was the hint of a knowing shrug, a lifting of her eyebrows, the slightest sigh of exasperation. He knew immediately and beyond any doubt that Simon had some sort of inappropriate interaction with her, and that his random sample was not random at all, but an impulsive, spiteful and stupid lashing out. Aitch allowed his own facial expression to reveal some transitory annoyance, and a flicker of shared knowledge, or at least partial knowledge, passed between them.

-14-

Because he was a perennial member of the Departmental Personnel Committee---the DPC---Aitch participated in the decision to hire Celestine Sauvage last year. At that time she was completing her second year as a postdoctoral student at the Université de Montréal, under the nominal supervision of Aitch's longtime friend and colleague, Vito de Bernardi. He and Vito had some nice joint publications in the early 1990's in *Applied Partial Differential Equations Letters*, and each had high regard for the other's strengths in both mathematics and cycling. Vito's opinions were real compliments to Aitch, because ultra tough-minded Vito de Bernardi, who was a Fellow of the Royal Society of Canada and rode as a climbing specialist for an Italian team in the 1969 Tour de France, almost never doled out respect in either domain.

Aitch thought back to the deliberations of the DPC which led to Bill Hurker and Celestine being offered tenure track positions last year.

University rules dictated that Chairman Slutnick be an *ex-officio* member of the committee. He opened the first of its hiring meetings with,

"Right off the bat, I want you all to fucking know that I had to sell my soul to the Virgin Queen just to get two shitty junior faculty slots, which that fucking redheaded nut-bar owed me anyway."

The DPC had no difficulty in deciphering this---everyone referred to Dean Margaret Fulton as the Virgin Queen, and they all knew that the positions were owed because Professors Felix Felspar and Irwin Greenspoon, both classic deadwood's, took early retirement, surprising no one.

Slutnick was a sartorially inclined man of girth, a cultured, erudite epicure and patron of the arts---well read, an accomplished sculptor and painter, a serious collector of antiques, and a connaisseur of fine wine and food. Fluent in seven languages, he could curse like a pimp in them all---and although he took great pride in his mastery of the American vernacular, he once told Aitch that Hungarian was his absolute favorite tongue because of its reliance on equine anatomy.

"English," Guillermo explained, "has no *standard* expression to rival *Lofas a sheged beh*---a horse's cock up your ass, loosely speaking. All you need know to get through the day in Budapest."

So it came to pass that Chairman Slutnick succeeded in defending the department by preventing the Virgin Queen from downsizing it after the retirements, although no one knew exactly what constituted the selling of his soul to her. Of course, maintaining or increasing the size of his dominion was a way for Guillermo to project power within the university, but there was another reason to rejoice---the two new hirings were opportunities to infuse the research groups with much needed young blood. There were four such groups in the UNV's Department of Mathematics, as well as a powerless fifth group called 'Everyone Else', consisting of a few outliers. Needless to say, each main group regarded the others as some sort of illiterate rabble, but by and large, the department was at peace. 'Live and let live' was the rule enforced by Chairman Slutnick, who oversaw the Department of Mathematics like an academic Stalin who had read up on Machiavelli and Metternich. Slutnick himself was a deadwood logician, and Logic was not one of the main groups, so he could claim neutrality in all departmental decision making, further enhancing his power. He was in his fifteenth year as chairman, and everyone in the department knew beyond doubt that he was the greatest in its history. But some years ago, when in his cups at a Christmas party, Guillermo confessed to Aitch that he only went into academia to please his mother---his father wanted him to be a politician or an executive. It showed, thought Aitch.

Each of the main groups was represented on the DPC. Slutnick let it be known that since the previous two hirings were in the Analysis and Probability groups, he was "...not about to take any fucking bullshit from them." The committee understood this to mean that the new hires this time around would be in Applied Mathematics and Number Theory ---period. Slutnick charged the DPC with drafting an announcement of the available positions, stressing the necessity of quality research and good teaching. And he was sensitive to the fact that the ad's content had to be politically correct.

"Don't forget that deaf, dumb, and blind Eskimo lepers must not feel excluded," he reminded the committee.

There was no shortage of applications---over thirty in each of the two research areas that Slutnick had identified. After a period of assessment and consensus building, the DPC reconvened. Bill Hurker was announced as the first choice of the number theorists by their representative, Bao Hoang, because not only was Hurker very good, and not only did he work on elliptic curves, an area of interest to the group, but his postdoctoral supervisor at Cornell was one of Bao's co-authors and 'in the room' when Wiles of Princeton announced that he had proven Fermat's Last Theorem. So the DPC decided without much debate that Bill Hurker was to be offered a job at UNV.

After the decision was made, Bao Hoang took the trouble to peruse Hurker's personal statement, and was delighted to learn that Bill was a fifth degree black belt in Shotokan Karate. Bao held an eighth degree black belt in that discipline, and outranked everyone at the local dojos by a wide margin. For years he had been hoping for a high level training partner close to home, and at last his wish was coming true.

On the applied side, besides Aitch Singleton and Simon Goldman, there were two others in the group---a mathematical biologist and a chaos theorist, both on sabbatical leave. Simon could not be bothered, but at least he admitted it, saying that he deferred to Aitch's judgement---that is, he did not care. So it was all up to Aitch. And even though he was tempted to hire a good numerical analyst with whom he could collaborate, Celestine Sauvage emerged as number one on his list.

In the end, it was not only her impressive credentials, but Aitch's faith in the unequivocal recommendation provided by Vito de Bernardi.

-15-

Celestine rose from her chair, thanked Aitch for his kindness, and headed for the door. He had to say something, but could not find any words. In a panic, he flashed back a half century to *The Honeymooners* and to a guilty and embarrassed Ralph Kramden, so tongue-tied that all he utter was, *"Hamena-hamena-hamena-hamena-hamena,"* while Alice stood there pouting, arms crossed in exasperation. He blinked hard and refocused on Celestine's pleasing form, now viewed from behind.

His mind hummed for a few seconds more, and then he recalled the morning last month when he went to the lounge for coffee, and found her in a mathematical discussion with Izzy Fleck. She was at the blackboard, wearing a baggy, hooded McGill sweatshirt, and her hair was a disaster area, something like the Bride of Frankenstein. Izzy was sitting on the sofa, rocking back and forth and holding a mug of his over-sweetened brew with two frail claws while she expounded at the blackboard. On the table lay a book she was talking about, a yellow one on Nonsmooth Analysis. She had drawn graphs and sets that were nonsmooth---that is, with corners and cusps. One sketch looked like a pizza with a slice removed. When Celestine finished, she surprised Aitch by asking if he might be interested in looking at nonsmooth theory with her sometime. Out of politeness, he told her sure, it sounded like a good idea.

Now he was very glad that he agreed to her study proposal, because when she was halfway out the door, he was able to fib convincingly, something at which he had little practice.

"Oh, by the way, Celestine, I ordered that Nonsmooth Analysis book by Clarke et al from Amazon. I should have it soon."

"Oh, good," she said, flashing her dimples. "I've managed to study it a bit, and I'm optimistic that it will be useful. So you're still interested in looking at it with me and my grad students, Ibrahim Ibrahim and Nathan Finkelstein?"

He did not know that she had taken on the twins.

"Of course, of course---very much so. Listen. How about joining me for lunch so that we can discuss it further? Say around 12:30?

"*Bien sur!*"

She offered to lend a hand with his marking, but chivalry dictated that he refuse. She would wait for his knock.

***

Aitch worked like a demon, managed to finish all his marking by 12:25, and made his way to the departmental office. The new secretary, Drew, was gone for lunch, and only Beatrice Beauregard was on duty. As always, Aitch was polite and even obsequious with Guillermo Slutnick's factotum and henchwoman. He put the packets belonging to the twins and Bill Hurker in their mailboxes, and wished Beatrice a nice day with all the sincerity he could muster. He would hand-deliver Simon's packet later.

***

Celestine Sauvage was at her desk studying the yellow book, with her door wide open. The office was cluttered but tidy, with a ficus and cactus competing for space on her desk.

"Celestine, thanks again for the great job you did in the course." He placed her exams on a side table. "I hope you won't mind doing lunch in the Mad Cow, because I don't think I'm dressed well enough for the Faculty Club."

She laughed. "Aitch, I've never even *been* to the Faculty Club."

'Been' sounded like 'bean', the way she said it.

"And to be honest with you," said Celestine, "I don't have a clue where it is. Besides, I'm brown-bagging."

She pointed to her lunch.

Aitch confessed, "Well, to be honest with *you*, the last time I was in the Faculty Club was four years ago when Guillermo Slutnick forced me to take a Bulgarian visitor to lunch. And the food was terrible."

She slapped her knee and laughed again.

-16-

The Mad Cow was in the Student Union Building. The walls of the vast, crowded dining hall were festooned with announcements of events such as the recent end-of-term beer bash and a public lecture on the true meaning of Fellini's work in a postmodernist context. But nothing political. Two years ago, the Dean of Students decreed that all political displays be relegated to the mezzanine area. Otherwise, she reasoned, interest groups and activists would plaster every available space on campus.

It was the height of the midday crush, so Celestine offered to find a table and asked that he buy her an orange juice while procuring his lunch. He agreed, and upon entering the food court, he was confronted by a half dozen counters offering different choices. And there was skinny Atkins, ladling out lasagna.

"Yo, Professor. Good carb's."

Aitch waved him off---he had Italian just last night. The Mad Cowburger enticed him, as did the Cow Pies, but he was tired and too big a lunch might slow him down. He was not young any more like Atkins, who required five thousand calories per day just to keep from flatlining, so he joined the oriental queue and chose the Pad Thai.

He paid his bill, added cutlery to his tray, and scanned the cacophonous, jam-packed cafeteria. Celestine was not in sight, so he decided to look for her in a rational way. He would employ a 'binary search', as taught in MATH 101. It was a first exposure to algorithms, and it illustrated the concept of limit in a gentle, heuristic way to the angry and math-phobic humanities students who were shanghaied into the course.

He recalled his lecture on the subject last month.

***

"Suppose you have a rectangular swatch of jungle, and you want to find a tiger hiding in there. Binary search is a logical method for finding the tiger."

Knowing that Professor Singleton had a gentle and tolerant nature, one student raised her hand.

"Sir, is there only *one* tiger? What if there are *two* tigers?"

It was a challenge to teach mathematics to the unwilling, so Aitch played along, congratulated the student on her excellent question, and said that only one tiger was hiding in the jungle.

Other hands shot up.

"Professor, why does it have to a tiger? Couldn't it be a hippopotamus? Or an iguana? Or a paramecium?"

"Sir, why does it have to be a jungle? How about a desert or a roller rink?"

When the outburst was over, Professor Singleton continued.

"What you do is search half the jungle. If the tiger's in that half, good for you---you've found him. And if he's not, then you search half of the half that's left."

He accompanied this explanation by erasing a rectangular chunk of a rectangular chunk of an original rectangular jungle. Formulas, more complicated examples and variations on this theme would come later, as would the idea of a limiting process, which the model exemplified.

"And then eventually, if you haven't found the tiger yet, he is trapped in a piece of jungle the size of a doormat and he's standing on his hind legs."

A comment emanated from the back of the room.

"Yeah, then you can kick him in the nuts."

This was enunciated by a blindside flanker on the UNV ladies rugby team, who had a black eye and a bandage covering an ear which was nearly bitten off in a scrum---although otherwise she was quite pretty, and actually looked a bit like Audrey Hepburn. She accepted the physical abuse as part of her chosen sport, but her sensibilities were in an uproar because she was robustly mooed during a hard fought victory over the University of Burlington the night before, not realizing that the moos were actually appreciative cheers.

-17-

Aitch scanned the near half of the dining hall, and no Celestine. And half the remaining half---but still no luck. One more halving and he saw her, waving and jumping. He weaved through the maze of tables and took a seat opposite her at the table she had claimed for them. Having already finished her peanut butter and jelly sandwich, she started working on a Granny Smith.

"Sorry for starting ahead of you, but I was starving. *Je m'excuse.*"

"*De rien.*"

"I love the name of this place," she said. "And the crazy cow imagery."

"Yeah, it kind of grows on you. I spent my last sabbatical at the University of Colorado at Boulder. The students there voted to name their cafeteria in honor of Alferd G. Packer. Alferd. Not Alfred. He was convicted of murder and cannibalism in the 1870's."

Celestine convulsed and slapped the table three times, struggling not to choke and spew her half-chewed apple. She regained her composure, and was not the least bit embarrassed. Most unladylike, thought Aitch. Better get back to business.

"So Celestine, if you don't mind, I'll eat while you talk math. Can you explain Nonsmooth Analysis to me some more? Got pen and paper?"

"Only a pen. Hope you won't mind a *serviette* lecture. It was good enough for Banach."

Students of the great Polish mathematician were known to retrieve beer stained tablecloths upon which he doodled during mathematical discussions held in taverns. Celestine dug a pen out of her hiking shorts, took a napkin from the dispenser, and reseated herself next to him. Her bare shoulder was touching his arm as she spoke and sketched. He banished all carnal thoughts and kept his concentration.

"Nonsmooth, abrupt behavior is normal---even intrinsic in nature---so calculus based techniques are not at your disposal. You need the kind of generalized calculus which is covered in the yellow book by Clarke and his co-authors. I've been looking at how this stuff has been applied recently. Mainly in the design of discontinuous feedback laws."

"Let me guess," said Aitch. "You want to understand how all this generalizes to stochastic systems, where there is some white noise present in the dynamics or in the detection of the state."

"*Oui.* Exactly. And it's far from obvious how to do it. I've got Ibrahim Ibrahim and Nathan Finkelstein reading up on what's been done in standard deterministic models, and I hope we can move on to some stochastic cases."

She never referred to them as 'the twins', and he resolved not to either, at least not in her presence.

"Sounds like a terrific project, Celestine."

She showed him some basic formulas on the napkin.

***

Sonya Jorgensen appeared, holding her tray and in need of a seat. She was a Professor of Psychology with a joint appointment in Philosophy---a fifty-ish Viking from North Dakota with a long braid of blond hair---very sturdy, outdoorsy and rosy-cheeked. Sonya often took part in bicycle rides with Aitch and other members of Il Gruppo, Vito de Bernardi's cycling club---the only female to do so. A few years ago, she won the 'Best Costume' prize at a Halloween party hosted by the Slutnicks, when she showed up as a Valkyrie in a brass breastplate and a horned helmet, carrying a battle-axe. Simon Goldman, who came as a very convincing Mozart complete with powdered wig, claimed that he had nightmares for weeks afterwards.

"Mind if I join you? I'll be a good girl and just sit and listen. Not that I'll understand a single frigging word you say."

Aitch introduced Celestine and added,

"Sonya lives in the no-person's-land where philosophy and psychology meet. She is, among other things, an authority on the work of Eric Hoffer, the 'Longshoreman Philosopher', who wrote *The True Believer*. Did I get it all right, Sonya?"

"You did, and I can't deny any of it. But enough about me and my personal problems! What you're talking about must be much more interesting. Please go on while I make a pig of myself. I'll try not to use all the napkins."

"I have never heard of Eric Hoffer," said Celestine. "What's *The True Believer* about?"

The question was directed at Aitch.

"Well, Hoffer was a self-educated dock worker---auto-didactic---interested in analyzing the types of people who participate in mass movements. Again, Sonya, did I get it right?"

"You did, indeed. What intrigues me most in my research on Hoffer is the idea that if you look at individuals on opposite extremes of any important conflict, they tend to be more alike in their thought processes than different. For example, a fundamentalist Jewish settler in Hebron and his Palestinian neighbor might have more in common, psychologically speaking, than either would care to admit."

"Aha," said Celestine.

Sonya dug into her Mad Cowburger, and by means of theatrical hand gestures, urged them to continue.

"I know that you work on vortex stability and bubble formation," said Celestine. "But the channels you study always have smooth boundaries."

Sonya raised her eyebrows in exaggerated curiosity, and the physical contact with Celestine ended.

"That's right," said Aitch as he finished off his noodles. In my models of non-viscous turbulence, I can't avoid that hypothesis. Otherwise, I'm dead meat."

"Ummm, dead meat," said Sonya, in a passable imitation of Homer Simpson. She chomped into her burger again.

Celestine said, "Well, I don't pretend to know much about fluid dynamics, but that book I'm studying shows how some classes of nonsmooth sets have nicely behaving normal maps. Worth studying, I'm pretty sure."

Sonya said, "I like normal. I like normal Norman too."

Her husband, Norm, was an accountant. Sonya sometimes said that she liked to conform to the Norm, but everyone knew that it was Norm who did the conforming.

Aitch said, "Okay, I'm turned on to the idea. How should we go about learning what we need to learn?"

Polishing off her Cow Chips, Sonya nodded with grave seriousness, now parodying an approving parent. Then she arose and made ready to leave.

"Well," said Celestine, "We could meet once or twice a week over the summer with Ibrahim and Nathan. They have a library copy of Clarke et al and they're studying the material. I could have them present it to us."

Sonya twitched as though an ice-cube had been dropped down her panties.

"Ibrahim Ibrahim and Nathan Finkelstein? I've seen them at their tables in the Mezz. People call them the *twins,* right?"

She got no response, thanked them for the table space, and left.

Celestine and Aitch agreed to schedule the twins' first lecture in two days, on Wednesday morning. He pocketed the napkin and made a mental note not to use it if he had to sneeze. They paused at a coffee kiosk on their way to the mezzanine, and she bought them cappuccinos to go.

-18-

In order for an interest group to set up a display table in the Mezz, permission of the Dean of Students was required, as was approval by the

Student Council. Many causes had strong followings on campus, and permits were issued for only a one-week period, with two exceptions. In order to maintain peace between the university's Arab and Jewish students, it was decided to provide these groups with space where they could vent in perpetuity. Hence there would always be tables for the Palestinian Rights Society and the Jewish Justice Committee.

The Mezz could accomodate over a dozen tables, but at present the only three in use belonged to the PRS, the JJC, and the Deaniacs. It was unlikely that any other organizations would mount a display before September---not even the anti-globalizers. The 'Howard Dean for President' display was between the Arab and Jewish ones, and manned by a black doctoral student in history who was riveted to S. E. Ambrose's *Undaunted Courage*, feet up on his pamphlet strewn table.

This afternoon, the PRS table was the responsibility of Ibrahim Ibrahim, and the JCC table was under the stewardship of Nathan Finkelstein. Both were twenty-three years old, of medium height and slender build. Their noses were large but not Semitic. Each had deep set dark eyes framed by thick glasses, and black hair and beard, cut short. They always wore dark slacks and light colored wash-and-wear shirts---today Ibrahim wore his white one, and Nathan his light blue. Neither of them owned any footwear other than a single pair of heavy black leather shoes. Ibrahim always had his checkered *keffiyeh* around his neck and shoulders, the one with his mother's hand-stitched embroidery, while Nathan always had the *kipa* his mother knitted bobby-pinned to his hair. Otherwise, it was difficult to tell them apart.

The twins both had middle class backgrounds. Ibrahim grew up in Amman, the son of an expatriate Palestinian engineer from Jaffa, and obtained his undergraduate mathematics degree at the American University in Beirut. Nathan was born in Smolensk but raised in Brooklyn, where his parents ran a dry cleaning store, and he had attended Yeshiva University for his baccalaureate. The level of religiosity of each could be described in similar terms---orthodox, but not ultra-orthodox In other words, even though Ibrahim was a devout Muslim, he would set the Koran aside so that he could study mathematics. And Nathan had for years resisted the proselytizing entreaties of the Lubovich Hasidim back in Brooklyn, because he wanted to be a devout Jew on his own terms, leaving time to concentrate on his mathematical development.

Among the dozen members of the PRS who took turns manning their table, Ibrahim Ibrahim was recognized as the ablest presenter of what detractors called 'The Palestinian Narrative'. And it was known that what Alan Dershowitz dubbed 'The Case for Israel' was never better defended than when Nathan Finkelstein was in charge of the JJC table. So there was a tacit understanding between the PRS and JJC. In order to neutralize each other, the twins always manned their tables at the same times. The scheduling was easy for them to arrange, because they spent a lot of time together in the cubicle they shared in the sub-sub-basement of the Fitch, along with a Chinese graduate student named Yu Wong.

Celestine and Aitch positioned themselves in front of the Deaniac table, equidistant from the PRS and JJC displays. The history grad student was freezing his butt off with Lewis and Clark in the Bitterroot's at the moment, and did not react to their presence. Perhaps he also sensed that they were standing where they were only to achieve neutrality in addressing the twins.

Celestine said, "Hi Ibrahim---hi Nathan."

The twins rose and mumbled their hellos while gazing down at their clunky shoes. Never having seen Professor Sauvage dressed in such a revealing way, they could not look at her as she gave her directives.

"Professor Singleton will join us in our Nonsmooth Analysis seminar. Can I ask that you each give an hour-long talk on Wednesday morning? Between the two of you, I hope we get the main ideas of Chapters 1 and 2 under control. There obviously isn't time to do all the details, so you will have to decide what the essentials are. I will advertise the talks on e-mail, both here and at nearby universities, in case there are others who might want to attend."

The twins glanced at each other for an instant---then indicated their understanding by producing something between a nod and a bow.

-19-

When Aitch returned to his office, he went straight to his computer and placed a rush order with Amazon for the Nonsmooth Analysis text. Then he looked out the window and spied Simon's Volvo in the parking lot. He must have come in to submit his grades.

***

Simon Goldman had a corner office, the only one in the department with two windows, other than Slutnick's. Aitch knocked, and entered when he heard a grunt. Chalk dust hung in the air---the blackboard had just been erased.

On most occasions, Simon had a well groomed appearance, at least for a mathematician, but today he looked like hell---an unshaven, unwashed little monkey with bloodshot eyes. He was wearing the same clothes he wore last night at supper, and there were dried coffee splatters on his polo shirt.

Aitch tossed Simon's packet of exams onto his desk.

"Simon, I wanted to talk to you about Celestine Sauvage's performance."

With a small smile working at the corners of his mouth, Goldman straightened his arms, presented his palms, and adopted an

Arkansas drawl.

"I did not have sexual relations with that woman."

He returned to his normal Manhattanite patter and raised an eyebrow.

"Oh, you mean in MATH 101. What's up?"

He's in gloat- mode. Jesus! He's found the Holy Grail!

"Well, just that there really isn't a problem---you must have pulled a few bad booklets and come to the wrong conclusion."

"No harm done, Aitch? The laws of probability weren't violated?"

Aitch could not find enough aggression to lambast Goldman, which was his original intent. Nobody likes a killjoy.

"No, no harm done. So did you crack whatever it is you're trying to crack? I'm trying to read your mind, but only getting static."

Goldman laughed.

"Still checking---you know how it is---but right now it's looking good---maybe even great. Piece of cake. You'll be the first to know."

"I understand," said Aitch, even though he did not. "We're on for Wednesday, right?"

"I booked us a court for one o'clock."

Perhaps Simon would divulge his big secret in the fountain of youth.

***

As he made his way down the hallway to his office, Aitch saw the twins ambling ahead of him. Ibrahim was on the left, holding the yellow book in his right hand, and Nathan was leaning over it, pointing at a formula. They were in a quiet but intense discussion, heads close.

Nathan spoke Brooklynese with a Russian accent.

"Ibrahim, this is intuitively obvious to even the most casual observer, and completely analogous to the smooth case."

"Of course it is, Finkelstein. Of course. Completely trivial, Finkelstein."

Nathan's finger moved down the page to the next key idea. They were not looking where they were headed, and Nathan slammed into a water cooler, sending his glasses flying. Ibrahim bent to scoop them up for his twin, and they continued down the hallway---but now Nathan kept his right hand on the wall like a blind man. Still gripping the book, Ibrahim drew a diagram in the air with his left index finger. To the twins, it was as real as if it were written on a blackboard.

Nathan said, "No, no, no, Ibrahim."

He reached across so that he could erase and correct the air-picture.

A smile creased Aitch's face as he felt a glow from his grad student days in the late 60's and early 70's at New York University, in

Greenwich Village.

"Different world," he whispered.

***

After submitting the grades for his section electronically, he checked his e-mail again. In addition to the usual spam, there was a message from Vito de Bernardi. It was addressed to the members of Il Gruppo, the road biking club which he founded twenty-seven years ago.

> Dear Il Gruppo:
>
> Our first official ride of the season will be this Saturday, May 24. We will meet as usual:8:30 a.m. in the Sutton post office parking lot.
>
> Long-range weather forecast is good. It will be very warm.
>
> Ciao,
>
> Vito

Aitch scanned the list of over twenty e-mail addresses. About half were from Montreal, and the rest were Vermonters. The UNV math contingent had grown since last season. It now included *sauvage@math.unv.edu* in addition to the regulars---himself, Simon, and Bao Hoang. And Bill Hurker was now on the list as well. Vito must have convinced Celestine to participate, and she must have told him that Bill would ride too. Glad that he had gotten through the day without an energy crash, he locked his office and headed home.

CHAPTER 4

Aitch tries to relax

-20-

At the wheel of his Honda, Aitch was slipping into a bad mood. He was feeling guilty for having violated his promise of discretion concerning Simon's quest for the Holy Grail. But what was stressing him even more was the fear that he had been naïve regarding Simon Goldman these past five years. He tried to push it all aside.

Okay, so maybe Simon gave himself a vacation when he came here from Harvard, figuring that he could just goof off a bit and then get back to business. But more likely, he's been working on the Holy Grail for many years, not bothering with anything else in the mathematical world. The Von Essen endowment gave him the freedom to do just that. That must be it---he's too serious a scientist to just drop out. And too darn egotistical. My best friend Simon Goldman is about to announce a tremendous advance in mathematics. He doesn't really need a sounding board. He just wants to honor our friendship by showing it to me first.

He resolved to never tell another lie, to never lose faith in Goldman, to figure out a way to have sex with Celestine Sauvage, and to relax for the rest of the day. He turned on the car radio, and a naturalist was talking about the mysterious return of the catamount to Vermont. In the Rockies, the cats are known as mountain lions, cougars or pumas, and they are called panthers in Florida. The naturalist was a native of California, where they are simply referred to as lions. To biologists, the name is *felis concolor*, the cat of one color.

A stocky tom can weigh 200 pounds, much burlier than any African leopard. Females are somewhat smaller---the size of a wolf, but many times stronger. Teddy Roosevelt shot a male in Colorado in 1901 when he was Vice President elect, and it tipped the scales at 227 pounds. In Vermont and the rest of New England, they were called catamounts, and none had been seen here for the better part of a century. It was thought that they were hunted to extinction in the Appalachians and everywhere east of the Rockies, except for the haggard clan of panthers clinging to survival, deep in the Everglades.

But now there was irrefutable evidence of one in north-central Vermont---tracks, scat, and DNA evidence left at deer kills. Two local dogs were victims as well, and one was a large Pit Bull. It all pointed to a male catamount on the loose in the Green Mountains.

The naturalist was explaining that the powerful, tawny cats are solitary stalkers, fantastic leapers, and that they kill from ambush. Like the formidable leopard, they are able to take down prey many times their own size, even elk or moose. They always go for the throat, and death could come from strangulation, cracking of the neck, or the insertion of a fang between the vertebrae, severing the spinal cord. These furtive, intelligent felines avoid humans, and sighting one is a rarity---a real privilege, she said.

Aitch knew all this already, because during his sabbatical year at the University of Colorado, he saw the cougar warning posters along his favorite jogging route skirting the Flatirons, in the Rocky Mountain foothills just west of Boulder.

"It is not possible at this stage to ascertain how this fellow made his way to northern Vermont. There are various possibilities. Of course, he may have been deliberately inserted, or perhaps he is an escapee exotic pet. But in my judgement, those contingencies are unlikely, because such an animal would not have possessed the skills required for survival in the wild. What intrigues me most is the likelihood that this dude comes from an undiscovered remnant population in some remote part of the northeastern woodlands. He may be the sole survivor of his tribe, because it appears that he has come from afar and that is he alone. My colleagues and I have named him Chingachgook, because he might be the Last of the Mohican's, so to speak."

Aitch turned up the volume.

"If you encounter a catamount, chances are it will leave you be, unless it perceives you as a threat or a meal---then even a seventy pounder could kill a man with little effort. In California, there were only about a dozen people killed by lions in the past century, but the circumstances were typically quite gruesome. In most cases, the victims would be almost surgically eviscerated, their intestines pushed aside, with only the heart, lungs, and liver consumed. Carcasses were sometimes dragged to a remote location, covered with leaves or pine needles, in case the cat wanted a snack later. And it seems that deranged catamounts, or aging ones with faded powers, pose a special kind of threat, because they sometimes make errors of judgement or act out of desperation."

***

Aitch parked in his driveway and sat stone still, reflecting on the fact that Nature had come up with a basic design for a predator, which worked in diverse habitats, and on many scales, from a nine-pound house cat to a nine hundred pound Siberian tiger. In his mind's eye, they blended into one.

He got out, walked across the lawn and called for Newton, who materialized out of nowhere and bolted across his path, missing him by inches. Minipod was an accompanying blur, and both emitted pigeon-like vocalizations as they sped past. Aitch knew it was a hello. Then they whizzed into the woods behind the backyard shed, re-emerged a few seconds later, and blitzed past him again. He noticed that the small, shabby structure's window had fallen in. Must have been the wind.

The cats got to the front door before he did, and perched with perfect symmetry on opposite sides of the welcome mat, facing one another, on their haunches, regal and proud. Dead center on the mat lay a sparrow and a field mouse, both dispatched with no obvious signs of violence, because they were intended as gifts. Probably the fang insertion technique, Aitch guessed. He pulled out some kleenex and picked up the kills.

"Thank you, Newton. Thank you, Minipod."

Eleven years ago, Maureen reacted with a shriek of revulsion to a similar show of feline generosity, and ordered Aitch to pick up a dead vole by its tail and bolo it into the woods. Newton was insulted, and disappeared for over a week. The Singletons never made that mistake again, and thenceforth showed proper gratitude when their pet brought them a token of his love. Aitch tossed the offerings into the trash, after checking that he was not being observed.

***

He finished his supper of Kraft Dinner and Budweiser, and phoned Annie, his only child. She was twenty-six years old, a psychiatric intern at a Boston hospital.

"Hi, Daddy. How's the math-in-attics going?"

It was her childhood name for what her father did for a living, and he was glad that she no longer kidded him by calling it 'a pathological form of obsessional rumination', as she did earlier in her medical studies. His mind brimmed with the memory of little Annie at the piano playing 'Chopsticks' with Maureen. He said everything was great with him, and before saying goodnight, she promised to visit soon.

He was tired, and more affected than usual by the beer. Unable to do mathematics and not in the mood to read, he was in bed by ten, glad to be in the Jesus position, with sphinx-like Newton vibrating on his chest. His last wakeful thoughts were about Horst Von Essen and his gift.

-21-

Horst Von Essen celebrated his 100th birthday five years ago, in May, 1998. A year before that milestone was reached, his son Rolf and grandson Ludwig approached him and asked what sort of gesture he thought should mark the event. Still sharp as a tack at 99, old Horst had anticipated the question and said that he wanted to give something back to Vermont, where he built his construction empire. The targets of his philanthropy would be the two universities where his firm made a fortune and where his heirs were educated---Rolf studied civil engineering at the

University of Northern Vermont, and Ludwig obtained his law degree at the University of Burlington. So Horst bade Ludwig create the Horst Von Essen Foundation, the financial instrument which was to finance, in perpetuity, seven endowed Horst Von Essen Professorships at UNV and UB.

It was with considerable fanfare that the endowments were announced in the spring of 1997, and the salient details were made public. The annual commitment of the Von Essen Foundation would be two million dollars, with built-in adjustments for inflation. Horst decreed that seven positions be awarded, with the admissible academic areas being Applied Mathematics, Biochemistry, Business, Engineering, German Culture, German History, German Philosophy, and Physics. Horst and his family would not meddle in the process by which UNV and UB each chose three endowed research professors. But since there was to be a seventh position, the Von Essens insisted upon making the final choice. The competing universities would present their intended fourth research chair to the Von Essen family. In addition to a standard CV, the two battling candidates would have to supply a McCarthy-esque 'Personal Statement and Family History', and deliver an expository lecture about their research interests. Then they would be interviewed in private by the Von Essens, who were to be the tiebreakers in this game.

The endowments were quite newsworthy, at least in the northern part of Vermont, so in addition to merely reporting on the details, the Green Mountain Sentinel ran a full-blown illustrated biography of old Horst. It was authored by his great-granddaughter Brunhilde, a high school sophomore who wrote like one. Her piece was so stiff and detailed that almost no one was willing to wade through it---but the prescient Guillermo Slutnick intuited that doing so might be worthwhile. This proved to be the case a few months later, when he would use what he had gleaned from Brunhilde's bio-epic in devising a sequence of artful maneuvers for securing Goldman's endowment.

***

In June 1997, the University of Northern Vermont and its archrival, the University of Burlington, began deliberations by which each would appoint three Horst Von Essen endowed professorships, and propose a fourth. At UNV, the bureaucratic particulars were determined at a meeting of the Board of Governors---the BOG---a body which included all the academic deans and higher administrator's as well as a dozen elected individuals including faculty, students, and community VIPs. It was clear to all of them that winning the extra Von Essen endowment would constitute a tremendous victory over the University of Burlington. This was due to the sad fact that the University of Northern Vermont had an academic inferiority complex and a huge chip on its institutional shoulder. UB had higher undergraduate admission standards than UNV, its faculty earned higher salaries and tended to get bigger research grants, it was three times larger in both enrolment and campus acreage, and it had schools of law and medicine while UNV did not. And UB offered more generous athletic scholarships. So victories over the University of Burlington mattered very much, in sports and all other ways.

It was natural that the rector of the University of Northern Vermont, seventy-two year old Dr. Peter Friend, should supervise the process. Although the title 'Dr.' was applicable to anyone with a doctorate---and nearly all the full-timers at UNV had one---it was almost never used, except in the case of Rector Dr. Friend. This is because he was a medical doctor, a fact somewhat belied by his three hundred pound bulk. Prior to his taking on the rectorship of UNV in 1995, Friend was a Professor of Psychiatry at a university in the California system, where he also directed a think-tank called the Division of Ethics. His academic credentials and repute as a peacemaker perfectly suited UNV, where political discord was a tradition.

As happened at all meetings of the BOG, there was a rancorous debate among the academic deans, who presented themselves as victims of history, and felt obliged to dredge up previous slights against their faculties. It was a bit like the Balkans. The Serbs might kvetch about a 15th century massacre at the hands of the Croats, but the Croats could always counter with some town of theirs which was torched by the Serbs in the 14th century, implicating the Bosnians and Herzegovinians for good measure.

At the present meeting, disgruntlement was being expressed due to the skewing of the Von Essens' list towards Dean Margaret Fulton's Faculty of Arts and Science---all the subject areas except engineering and business were in her division. And the Dean of Engineering was also livid because there was only a single general engineering category on the list, when in fact there could have been several---electrical, mechanical, civil, and so on. The Dean of Business had an analogous gripe---accountancy, marketing, and finance were unjustly lumped together. And naturally, there was a chorus of complainers whose disciplines were not even mentioned on Horst's list. They were led by the Dean of Computer Science, who was apoplectic because the Von Essens apparently considered his field to be a part of engineering, an unbearable insult.

After the initial round of acrimony abated, the engineering and business deans raised the ante and ganged up against Dean Fulton, because the university's most recent construction project, the climate controlled atrium, state-of-the-art Fitch Sciences Building, was built for the science component of her faculty, and now it was their turn to receive privileged treatment from the BOG.

Tall, buxom yet slender, the Virgin Queen was a commanding

presence in a black brocade pantsuit. She was wearing an elegant diamond necklace with matching earrings, and her long red hair was piled high, festooned by a sparkling tiara. Margaret was smiling and serene for the half hour during which the enemy deans were on the offensive.

Noble sirs, you have thrown the gauntlet.

When at last she spoke, she explained that often the best graduate students in her faculty transferred to engineering and business---seduced, she said, by the higher paying scholarships and fellowships obtainable in those disciplines.

"This intellectual pillage of my faculty must cease, forthwith," whined the indignant, wounded, and maligned Virgin Queen, an innocent victim who had been patient and trusting for far too many years. She droned on and on to the BOG with fact after fact and figure after figure, reading from crib sheets which Carver was feeding her like an automaton.

Rector Dr. Friend sensed that the entertainment value of the debate was waning after forty minutes of Margaret's righteous incantations---some eyelids were beginning to droop. So as everyone hoped would happen, his talents as a mediator and compromiser came to the fore, and he determined a fair and balanced approach to divvying up the Von Essen pie---an approach that would have been obvious at the outset of the process, even to a simpleton. Margaret had already put the BOG into a zombie-like trance, so his deep, dulcet voice of reason easily mesmerized all present.

"My dear, dear friends and colleagues. Please, please let us not squabble so divisively and squander our energies. In unity there is strength. *E pluribus unum.* The solution to our conundrum is clear. The Schools of Engineering and Business shall of course each receive one position endowed by the Von Essen Foundation, as will the Faculty of Arts and Science. But for better or for worse, the latter division contains more categories valued by our esteemed benefactors than do the others. So Dean Fulton, I propose that in addition to your faculty's guaranteed Von Essen Professorship, you have the opportunity to compete for the extra one against our rivals at the University of Burlington. And I believe all three faculties should have complete *carte blanche* in deciding how to choose their people."

Hands-off management was very much Rector Dr. Friend's style.

"You have the wisdom of King Solomon, Rector Dr. Friend," said Margaret.

His suggestions were made into a formal motion by the mayor of Enosburg Falls; seconded by the proctologist who headed the Alumni Association, and passed with no dissenting votes and a single abstention.

This was by the undergraduate representative on the BOG, a communications major who said could not in good conscience support the motion, because it made no mention of gender or race considerations. So it was agreed that Engineering and Business would each appoint one Von Essen Professor, while the Faculty of Arts and Science would appoint one such position and generate a candidate for the competitive one. There was no rush---the choices were to be confirmed at a meeting of the BOG in February, 1998, several months hence. A few weeks after that, the Von Essens would decide which university was to obtain the seventh endowed professorship.

CHAPTER 5

A bagel run and other activities

-22-

Aitch stumbled into the shower at 9:30 on Tuesday morning, a late start for him, and as the warm spray washed the cobwebs from his mind, he decided not to visit the campus this day. No one would miss him, and besides, he felt compelled to attend to some domestic chores which had been neglected far too long. So after completing his morning rituals, he phoned Mrs. Trudo, his occasional cleaning lady. She said yes, she was free on short notice to clean his place, and she would wash the windows too. Aitch told her that he planned to run some errands, but would return before she finished, so they could settle up. He would leave the key for her, under the welcome mat.

After driving five miles north to Northton and buying a can of green paint, he remembered that he was down to his last two bagels. So he decided to journey a further five miles across the border to Sutton, where he could obtain the Montreal variety---boiled in honey-water and baked in a wood fired brick oven.

Soon he was passing a humble granite monument which always had mathematical charm appeal for him. It was in a small park next to a seedy, rundown gas station, and next to it there was a small American flag fluttering.

THIS IS THE 45th PARALLEL
HALFWAY BETWEEN
THE EQUATOR
AND
THE NORTH POLE

He recalled using it to introduce polar coordinates four years ago, when he was teaching advanced calculus.

***

Professor Singleton was addressing a class of fifty math sophomores.

"Let's say you're trying to specify the location of a point on the surface of the earth. One way to do this would be to use our familiar three-dimensional Cartesian coordinate system---that is, we can locate the point using *x, y,* and *z* in the usual way, with the center of the earth as the origin."

On the blackboard, Aitch drew a sphere with the three coordinate axes meeting at the origin, which he labeled *(0,0,0)*.

"Suppose, in particular, that you want to locate Northton,

Vermont."

He waited for the snickers to die down, because this was a wild supposition. The students knew that no one in their right mind would ever want to locate decrepit Northton, which English literature majors who were into Chaucer referred to as Vermont's Nether Eye, because they believed it to be a degenerated and impoverished backwater where it was illegal to copulate with anyone other than a close relative.

"One way to do this would be to first specify ϕ, the angle down from the North Pole, which is always between 0 and 180 degrees, with 180 degrees giving the South Pole. Well, there's a monument in Northton which tells you that ϕ is 45 degrees there."

He described the monument, and then drew the 45th parallel around his sphere and indicated the 45 degree angle down from the North Pole.

"I just drew what is called a circle of latitude."

He marked an 'N' for Northton on it, explaining how longitude must also enter the picture for specificity, and how this is given by an angle θ in the equatorial, or (x,y)-plane.

"Note that unlike ϕ, the angle θ can take values between 0 and 360 degrees. And also note that since this is advanced calculus, we really shouldn't work with degrees, but rather with radians."

He paused, and challenged the class with a question.

"But whoa, Nellie---something doesn't seem right here. Have we somehow succeeded in representing our three dimensional universe with only two spatial dimensions? Any takers?"

Yu Wong, a recent arrival from China, shot up his hand.

"Third coordinate is necessary. It is distance from center, same value on whole surface of earth, but you not say so yet."

Professor Singleton said, "Correct. This distance is called ρ."

He posed another question for the class to ponder.

"So, what do you think are the main mathematical issues regarding this new spherical coordinate system, (ϕ,θ,ρ)?"

After a few seconds, Yu Wong again offered his insight.

"Question is how we transform back and forth between Cartesian (x,y,z) and spherical (ϕ,θ,ρ) systems. And how we do triple integrals in spherical coordinates. Maybe change of variable idea important, like in single variable calculus course, but three variables now, so not obvious how we do it. Maybe we use Jacobian matrix."

This kid is good, thought Professor Singleton.

***

A Canada Customs agent at the Abercorn checkpoint waved him through, and five minutes later he was in the parking lot of Sutton's only market. This part of Quebec, which abuts the New England border, is known as 'The Eastern Townships' or *'Les Cantons de l'Est'*. Almost all the population here is bilingual and accentless in both official languages, and many are of mixed Anglo-French ancestry. French Canadians began settling this region in the early nineteenth century to farm, but the original white settlers here were United Empire Loyalists---those citizens of New England who remained true to King George III during the American Revolution and fled north, often in fear for their lives. Known as 'Tories' in American textbooks, they are reviled as despicable traitors to a noble cause. But Townshippers, with even a drop of Loyalist blood, are more than willing to disabuse ignorant American tourists of this notion. And some are also quick to mention that their Loyalist forebears participated with understandable enthusiasm in Canada's victories over the United States in the War of 1812, including the torching of Washington. But no hard feelings, eh?

***

He bought two dozen frozen Montreal bagels---the 'all dressed' kind, rubbed with onion, garlic, and sesame---and headed home. At the Northton crossing, a young U.S. Customs agent waived him forward to his booth. Aitch hoped that he was not too gung-ho.

"Hello, sir. How long have you been outside the country?"

He spoke with the peculiar accent of the border region. Although there are still many old stock Yankees in the area, some even claiming kinship with Ethan Allen's Green Mountain Boys, it is not a New England accent at all, as one might expect. French is echoed in the flat drawl heard around here, and some linguists say it resonates with the way Cajuns speak English.

"About a half hour," said Aitch

"Sir, did you make any purchases while you were on the other side?"

Aitch told him about the bagels, and pointed to them on the front seat.

"Sir, did anyone other than yourself have access to those bagels since you bought them?"

Aitch said no.

"Sir, I want you to concentrate and tell me if this individual was at any time near your bagels."

He held up a small wanted poster featuring Osama Bin Laden straddling an overburdened, depressed looking donkey. All Aitch could do was grin and look into the agent's eyes, now crinkled with mirth. He waved Aitch through and ordered him to have a nice day.

-23-

He got back home to Montgomery a little past noon, and saw Mrs.

Trudo's battered pickup parked out front. Perched atop her extendable ladder with a bucket, she was cleaning the attic dormer with a squeegee. She was about Aitch's age, round as an apple but solid as a rock, with a red bandana controlling her shaggy gray hair. She worked a small dairy farm east of Eden with her husband---their children had long since moved out. Clippers hung from her work belt, and oak trimmings were piled twenty feet below.

"Hi, Mr. S. Ya really oughta trim this big fella more often. I left one branch long so's little Newton can come in through the window."

He could not recall her first name---perhaps it was Eloise---but he was not sure enough to attempt it and felt shy about asking her, because he was certain that he ought to know it after all these years. But it was Maureen who had dealt with her in the past, and it was Maureen who always got him organized on domestic chores like painting the porch, which he busied himself with. At four o'clock he was done, and went inside to find Mrs. Trudo in the attic, finishing up. It was still a mess, but now it was a clean one---she never touched any open books or scattered file folders, but worked around them. They went downstairs and he handed her seventy dollars for her six hours of labor. "I'm only due sixty, Mr. S.," she protested---but he insisted.

***

Aitch had a squash match booked with Simon tomorrow, and knew that he needed rest. But he felt good and it was a beautiful late afternoon, so he decided to go for an easy spin.

He kept his bicycle in the hallway, near the front door. It was a jet-black carbon fibre beauty. Custom made six years ago in Montreal by an Italian craftsman to whom he was introduced by Vito de Bernardi. The machine was his only luxury---his fiftieth birthday present to himself. Very light, very fast, with stiff aerodynamic rims and bladed spokes, high-end components all around, and it had just as soft a feel as the heavier steel model he used to ride. There were two chain rings in front and a nine-cog cassette in back, so only eighteen speeds, but he had the full range of gears he needed, from steep climbing to all-out blasting.

Now Aitch transformed from his nerd-like mathematician persona into the long limbed, powerful and fierce road biker who was his alter ego. He donned padded black cycling shorts and a triple back-pocketed red jersey into which he put five figs, some kleenex, and a tiny hand pump. Then he put on short black biking socks, fingerless gloves, and stiff, carbon-soled cleated biking shoes. His helmet was canary yellow.

A few times over the past fifteen years, he managed to finish in the top ten of the three-day North American Masters competition held every August out of Sutton---a 10 kilometer prologue on day one, a time trial as well as a brutal ten-loop criterium on day two, and a mountainous

160 kilometer road race on the final day. But he never placed ahead of the inhuman Vito de Bernardi, who always won his division, toying with the opposition. Aitch was in perpetual awe of the little man's cycling abilities.

Tending to the machine, he lubed the chain and inspected his small saddlebag to make sure there were two spare tubes and the toolkit he would need in case he got a flat. Then he checked the slick, thin tires and brought them to 130 p.s.i. with his stand-up double action pump. He put on his wrap-around prescription shades and set the computer's beeper to go off every 20 minutes, to remind him to eat a fig and to take a few swigs from the bottle of diluted apple juice that he mounted on the down-tube. By five o'clock, after a bit more fussing, Aitch was clicking into his pedal clips, ready to ride.

His sabbaticals were always taken at universities with good cycling nearby---his last two were at Turin and Boulder. But in his heart, he felt that the Greens offered the best rides. This evening, he was going to do a gentle and pretty one, the 'Berkshire loop'---only 52 kilometers door to door. On average, it took him about an hour thirty-five, but this evening he expected it to take longer, because he intended to not push himself. Just going out for a light spin.

***

For the first 10 kilometers he followed the Trout River west to East Berkshire, on Route 118. It was a rolling ride through the farmland between the forested hills defining the valley of the river, which was really little more than a stream. Like all the country roads in this region, it was not traveled much and had a paved shoulder where a cyclist could find safety. He passed the small cairn he maintained, marking the spot where Maureen was struck. It looked to be in good shape. Last year it became disarranged when the Trout spilled its banks, but it needed no attention since then. Aitch focused his eyes on the road ahead, resisting the temptation to think about fluid dynamics. Doing math on a road bike was dangerous.

After twenty minutes there came a gradual eight kilometer climb. He stayed on the small front ring and maintained high revs, keeping the tachometer reading around one hundred turns per minute. He down-shifted to save his legs for tomorrow's squash match, and whizzed past a rifle range to his right---the Ethan Allen Sportsman's Club. Its parking lot was full of beat up old cars and trucks---no Beemer's or yuppie SUV's here. The owners were up the hill on the range, getting together after work to have a few brewskies and practice their marksmanship.

A pickup came towards him in the opposite lane, moving fast. There were two occupants, bearded and wearing baseball caps, adherents of the Willie Nelson school of fashion. The driver threw a crushed beer can at Aitch, missing him by five feet, and then shouted something as the truck whooshed past. The Doppler Effect prevented Aitch from understanding it, but he knew that the tone was hostile. Around here, "Get off the fucking road!" was a common redneck greeting for cyclists, whom they assumed were all homosexual millionaires, with their fancy machines and faggy spandex outfits. They called them *Flatlanders*---them and anyone else who was intruding upon their bucolic dystopia, which most of them referred to as the 'Northeast Kingdom'. Glancing back over his right shoulder as he continued his climb, Aitch saw the truck turning into the parking lot. There were two decals in the rear window---the stars and stripes on the left, and, defying logic, the Confederate stars and bars on the right. A sudden crackling fusillade from the range caused him to duck closer to the handlebar, and he pedaled on.

Ten minutes later came the reward for his ascent, a long downhill spin heading northeast from the Berkshire Center crossroads, with spectacular views of Jay Peak and Mt. Sutton lolling in the distance. With a flick of his finger on the shifter, he threw the chain onto the big ring. He could hit speeds in excess of 100 kilometers per hour like this. Body position was the key---on the downhills it was all about aerodynamics and a good tuck.

As he flew along, he noticed a large wolf-like dog, one he had never encountered before, in front of a ramshackle farmhouse about a hundred yards ahead on the right. The heavyset bruiser dashed to the edge of the road. Over the years, Aitch was often set upon by dogs during rides, but it was always canine bluster---the worst they ever did was run alongside him, yelping and pretending to nip at his heels. But this guy had Aitch worried, so he veered left, hammered down, and blasted past him, woofing through the maneuver. The dog didn't move a muscle, but showed his teeth and snarled at Aitch, who could read his mind.

One day you're going to be passing here on the uphill, Barking Man, and then your ass is mine.

Aitch grinned like a wild man, regained his line, woofed again, and kept pounding. A minute later, safe on the flats, he tried his mooing technique on a cluster of grazing cows and was very pleased when one of the Bessies bellowed an amorous response. The rest of his loop took him through Northton, over its rusting cast iron bridge, then back along the Trout to Montgomery, and home.

He checked his time. Ninety minutes---five minutes faster than usual. He thought that he must be in the zone---at a temporary physical peak---what Simon Goldman would have called a 'relative maximum subject to constraints'. But Aitch knew it was illusory. It was not a true spike in strength, but only an adrenalized reaction to stress.

-24-

It was Taco Tuesday at Kerouac's Bar and Grill, half a mile down the road from his home. He was tired but always enjoyed the walk, especially on a warm evening like this, with crickets singing and fireflies dancing. Newton bounced along next to him for the first quarter mile, beeping now and then, but turned back as he always did, when he reached the limit of his territory.

Aitch tried to think about bubble dynamics and vortex stability as he made his way along the shoulder, but his thoughts kept returning to Celestine's metamorphosis from math-chick sloven to hottie, his mind brimming with images of her churning down the pool in her tight swimsuit, and later in her revealing warm weather clothes. By the time he got to Kerouac's, he was so hungry and horny that he was lightheaded. He looked around for some of the regulars, but didn't see any, so he ate alone at the bar. The bowling trophy on the shelf made him think of Simon Goldman's Holy Grail, and he made his last quaff of Sam Adams a silent toast to his friend's success.

***

During the walk back, he fixed his gaze on the Milky Way, and the celestial show put him in the mood to do mathematics, so he spent some time in his attic study. The window was open, and Newton leaped in from the oak. With his purring cat in his lap, Aitch contemplated Celestine's napkin, and posed some questions out loud.

"What sorts of properties would nonsmooth objects have to possess so that my smooth methods could be generalized? Can we identify and characterize classes of nonsmooth geometric sets that possess these properties? Newton, what do you think?"

Answers were not obvious to him, and delirious, dribbling Newton could not be bothered. There was a gap in his basic knowledge here, and he hoped to start bridging it in tomorrow's seminar.

***

He got into bed, flicked on the lamp, and resumed his reading of Umberto Ecco's medieval murder mystery, *The Name of the Rose.* Aitch rented the video a few months ago and enjoyed it, but became angry at himself after Izzy informed him that he had missed the brazen joke that Ecco had played upon him. The English monk, William of Baskerville, was in actuality Sherlock Holmes, and his assistant, Adso, was Watson. He had always hated being fooled, so now he was reading the novel as a sort of penance, even though there was no longer any mystery. But he was sleepy and it was late, so he placed the book on the night table. Newton took this as a cue to climb onto his chest.

Aitch picked up the remote control and flicked to GMPTV---Green Mountain Public Television---and lo and behold, was greeted by

Mona Hope Goldman on fundraising duty in the St. Albans studio. And tonight she was not just manning a telephone, but addressing the viewing audience in the garb of an eighteenth century redcoat---and a very adorable one---complete with tricorn, brass buttons, epaulets, powder horn, and a toy musket slung over her shoulder. It was her job to solicit financial support for GMPTV while introducing a movie.

Mona's playful, lilting British accent was pitch perfect.

"In a few moments we shall be treated to a special GMPTV cinematic extravaganza, the 1992 remake of *The Last of the Mohican's* starring Daniel Day Lewis as Nathaniel slash Hawkeye and Madeleine Stowe as Cora Munro. This version is not completely faithful to the James Fennimore Cooper classic, but it is quite accurate in its depiction of the various forces that were in play during the Seven Years War, 1756 to 1763. Oh dear, oh dear---pardon me! To you colonials, this conflict is known as the French and Indian War. Much of this terribly bloody affair occurred in our region, around the shores of Lake Champlain, when France and England were vying for control of North America."

Aitch grew up on the other side of the lake, in New York's Adirondack region, where the story unfolds. His late parents were both high school teachers---his mother taught math and his father, American history. His dad was a French and Indian War buff who took his classes to Fort Ticonderoga for the tour. So Aitch was well read on the war, and he agreed with Mona's comment about the film's basic accuracy---in particular, regarding the massacre at Fort William Henry. Four years ago, he and Maureen had the Goldmans over, and after dinner they watched the movie on a rented DVD. The ethereal Madeleine Stowe was even more beautiful than usual, and during the scene where Hawkeye is making it with her, Aitch whispered to Maureen that she and Cora looked like sisters. He was rewarded with an instant elbow to the ribs, delivered with more force than was intended---but later that night in bed, his reward was much, much sweeter. He smiled at the memory.

Mona, the cute little redcoat said, "Oh dear, oh dear! I'm afraid *The Last of the Mohicans* shows that we Brits did not always behave very well."

The director barged on camera, and put a beefy arm around Mona. He was a big, bearded ex-hippie.

"That's 'we' with only one 'e'. Just to be clear."

He made his exit, and after she stopped giggling and regained her self-control, effervescent Mona continued.

"In addition to taxing you colonials unfairly, we forced a war upon you in which you had no interest. Nor did we protect your frontier settlements or our Mohawk friends' villages from marauding bands of French and their Huron allies very effectively, now did we? And the French and Hurons did not behave very nicely either, to be sure---

especially that dreadful General Montcalm. Oh well, let bygones be bygones, I say! Especially because it is through the generous donations of GMPTV viewers like you here in the colonies, as well as our Loyalist and French Canadian viewers in Quebec, that presentations such as this are made possible. And hello also to our Mohawk viewers in the Kahnewake and Kahnesatake reserves near Montreal. I hope you don't believe that King George *deliberately* abandoned you up there! So please, all of you, reach into your pockets and purses for an utterly worthy cause! We survive only with your support!"

The camera panned to the bank of six telephone operators handling tonight's calls. The number to dial was shown on the screen, and Mona's detached voice explained that all major credit cards were accepted as were pledges, and that donations were tax deductible on both sides of the border.

Mona returned to view, and now she had an arrow through her hat and head---the novelty item type. Aitch heard the studio crew guffawing in the background.

"Oh dear, dear me! I had nearly forgotten something! Common decency and network rules dictate that I pass on a word of warning. This movie is extremely violent. One of its deeper messages is that a tomahawk is a more effective weapon than a single shot musket---a point that will be hammered into you viewers, so to speak. And while mentioning violence, watch the great Cherokee actor Wes Studi, who portrays Magua, the twisted, vindictive and bloodthirsty Huron---well, it is a travesty that he was not at least *nominated* for a Best Supporting Actor Oscar. Shivers! Hold onto your scalps---and enjoy the film!"

It was late and Aitch had already seen it twice before, so he only watched for half an hour. As the hapless British platoon winds its way through the forest primeval with Magua as their scout, Cora glimpses a catamount---something Aitch did not notice in his previous viewings. Then, after Magua reveals his true colors and the Hurons appear poised to annihilate the British party, Hawkeye and the Mohicans arrive just in time to stop the butchery with some butchery of their own, and a remnant is spared.

He wondered what Simon's ambush in Vietnam was like---whether there was a treacherous Magua who led his unit into it, and whether a Hawkeye came to the rescue. Simon was never willing to discuss it, which always struck Aitch as out of character for someone who never displayed a hint of verbal restraint.

CHAPTER 6

Seminar

-25-

Aitch was on campus at 8:30 on Wednesday morning, leaving him time for odds and ends before attending the twins' seminar at ten. He checked his e-mail. Besides the usual spam, there was a message from Simon. The header showed that it had been sent at 3:37 a.m.

> Aitch,
>
> Sorry, Big Guy, but I must cancel out on our squash match today. I wouldn't be able to give you much of a fight. Use the court if you can.
>
> I've been checking and re-checking my result and not sleeping, partly due to obsessively going over it again and again, and partly out of tremendous excitement. I'm confident that all is ok and that my breakthrough is holding up, but I'm not ready to relax yet. The result is too important and I've been working on it for too long---I don't want to end up with egg on my face. A mathematician's worst nightmare.
>
> I'll show you the whole business soon, and thanks for agreeing to be my sounding board.
>
> I will show up for Il Gruppo on Saturday, come hell or high water.
>
> Simon

Aitch pressed 'reply'.

> Hi Simon:
>
> No problemo---maybe one of the squash team kids would be willing to run me around a bit.
>
> I was thinking. I am honored to be your sounding board, but we work in such different areas. Maybe

you should invite Joe Malone from the applied math dept. at UB to be a co-sounding board. We both know him from Il Gruppo and I think he can be trusted. He works on complexity theory like you---and he gets respect.

So what's with the Holy Grail? This better be good.

Try to put in a few kilometers and some hills before Saturday, and try to get some rest. I don't want you dying on me before the secret is revealed.

Aitch

P.S. I watched GMPTV last night. You have the best wife in the world.

He attended to a refereeing job for *Letters in the Physics of Fluids*, one that was past due. Vito de Bernardi was the editor handling the article, whose bold authors titled it "Near-Optimal Blowing". Because it was in the realm of bubble dynamics, Vito fingered Aitch to be the anonymous referee. Vito was a friend, so he could not decline. And besides, as Simon Goldman once opined,

"You don't want to piss off Don Vito, because it isn't much fun waking up with a gory horse's head in your bed."

-26-

It was 9 a.m., and five floors below Aitch, Ibrahim Ibrahim and Nathan Finkelstein were at their desks in the sub-sub-basement dungeon they shared with Yu Wong, who had not yet come in. Nathan had affixed a *mezuzah* to the door frame some months ago, which did not seem to bother Ibrahim. And Ibrahim had placed his prayer rug on the floor next to his desk, above which hung a portrait of Yasser Arafat. None of this seemed to offend Nathan, just as Ibrahim was not offended by the poster above Nathan's desk, depicting Ariel Sharon strolling on the Temple Mount.

There was a tiny fridge on a rickety table in a corner of their cell, with an even smaller microwave oven above it. A hotplate and an electric kettle sat atop the microwave, completing the stack. Finkelstein was dunking a used teabag in a cup of hot water as he reviewed his material, and Ibrahim-squared was drinking sweet cardamom flavored Arab coffee which he had reheated on the hotplate in his rusty *kum-kum*.

Between sips, Ibrahim looked up from his notes.

"Tell me, Finkelstein, do you believe that God created Mathematics?"

Months ago, the twins had come to agree that Allah and Yahweh, whose name Nathan was not allowed to utter, were with certainty one and the same, and should simply be referred to as God or the Entity in their discussions. The arguable issues involved determining exactly what were the intentions of this being; the creator of the universe. And even though they were political adversaries in the Mezz, their theological discussions were always carried out in an atmosphere of the greatest intellectual respect and courtesy.

"Ibrahim, God created the entire universe, but the Torah only speaks of *material* creation in Genesis, the First Book of Moses, the great Hebrew prophet who Muslims refer to as Moussa. Mathematical theories like Nonsmooth Analysis are the creation of Man. But on the other hand, the Entity created the physical laws of the universe, which led mankind to discover universal mathematical concepts. So, for example, God incorporated π when He created the fabric of spacetime, and humans invented mathematical theories where π is important. So it follows that Man created Mathematics with God's help."

"Finkelstein, exactly---I also believe this. And I therefore believe that by studying Mathematics, a man can become closer to the Entity."

"Ibrahim, I believe this as well. It might be in agreement with certain concepts of Cabala, a system of Jewish mysticism, which I intend to study one day. It incorporates mathematical ideas."

"Yes, I have heard of this Cabala," said Ibrahim. "It is quite interesting. You know, it was developed under the protection of Islam, when the Jews lived as *dhimis* in Spain---safe from the primitive and crazed Christian mobs. Arabs were developing algebra and other mathematical ideas during this same period, while the followers of the prophet Jesus were living in filth and eating their own children."

Nathan nodded, indicating at least partial agreement, and Ibrahim continued in his guttural way.

"Your choice of π as an example of the Entity's creation is intriguing, Finkelstein. It is a transcendental number, and therefore unknowable in certain ways, as we learned in Professor Goldman's complexity theory course last year."

"Yes, Ibrahim. Exactly. Ibrahim, have you read the science fiction novel *Contact* by Carl Sagan? In this book, the Entity encoded a message for humanity in the decimal expansion of π when He designed the fabric of spacetime. The idea was that once mankind becomes intelligent enough to go sufficiently far out in the expansion, the message presents itself."

"Yes, Finkelstein, I have read this book. And I have been told that the mystical π theme is largely absent in the movie, which is truly unfortunate."

Nathan was about to signal his concurrence when Yu Wong entered the cubicle, offering a smiling nod of greeting to the twins. He was dressed like them---dark pants, white open-necked wash-and-wear shirt, and he wore thick, dark framed glasses just as they did. But unlike his cell-mates, who wore dark shoes and socks in all conditions, Yu Wong preferred flip-flops on warm days like this.

As usual, he went straight to the refrigerator, which had three racks, and placed three Styrofoam containers on his shelf, the middle one. Today his lunch would consist of vegetable fried rice, steamed chicken dumplings in peanut sauce, and a spicy broccoli stir-fry. On the shelf belonging to Nathan, there was a boiled egg and a Jurassic apple, while Ibrahim's held a piece of stale pita and some moldy hummus.

Out of respect for the dietary customs of the twins, Yu Wong never brought pork or shrimp dishes, even though Ibrahim and Nathan had each accepted the fact that the laws of *halal* and *kashrut* could not be observed with any degree of exactitude in this corner of the Appalachians. Compromises were made---they would on occasion eat beef or poultry, even if it was not blessed by one of the Entity's representatives. And yesterday the twins sampled the cuisine of the Mad Cow cafeteria for the first time, as Professor Sonya Jorgenson's guests. She spent a minute at their display tables on Monday, to hurriedly introduce herself and ask if they were interested in participating in a study she had designed. She would pay them thirty dollars apiece from her research grant---a significant amount of cash to starving graduate students. All her study required was their filling out a basic personal information form and a personality assessment questionnaire. So they agreed, and Sonya invited them to lunch yesterday, when she handed them the forms.

It was a mystery to the twins that someone so puny as Yu Wong could consume such enormous quantities of food---and such mouth watering, healthy and aromatic food. For a year now, a group of entrepreneurial Chinese graduate students from Shenzhen had been running a clandestine take-out restaurant from their dormitory, and were parlaying their earnings by playing internet stud poker as a team, which they had dubbed Bigballs, after a democratic vote. Clustering around the PC in the dorm's communal kitchen, they used probability calculations to decide when to hold 'em, fold 'em, raise or bluff.

Since Yu Wong was one of the restaurant's organizers, his meals were free, but for two dollars, anyone could have a repast like the one he brought today. He knew that the twins were going to cave in one day, and become customers.

Nathan said, "Yu Wong, I think you must have a hollow leg."

Neither Yu Wong nor Ibrahim understood this, and after Nathan explained the function of such a leg, the three of them shared a laugh.

Ibrahim said, "Yu Wong, you have the storage capacity of a large camel, but I do not see your hump."

More laughter, and then Yu Wong brightened and flashed a huge buck-toothed smile. He repeated what he had been telling the twins for months.

"You gentlemen eat even more than me, after you try Han People's Take-Out. I can arrange first meal free for you. Then we see who has hollow leg and who has hump."

Nathan and Ibrahim looked at each other. It was going to be both or neither, and with a mutual Levantine shrug of indecision, they communicated to Yu Wong that the answer was, "No, not yet---but maybe another time---we'll see".

"Gentlemen," said Yu Wong, never abandoning his grin, "I think I attend your Nonsmooth Analysis seminar. Subject sounds delightful, like Han People's egg roll."

-27-

At 9:45, Aitch checked his e-mail again. His firewall was not working and he knew that he needed to download an upgrade one of these days, because he was continually getting spammed. Today there were only two unwanted messages---one offering a rapid weight loss plan and another advertising a penis enlarger. He required neither. There was also a message from Simon, written in interspersed reply mode.

> No problemo---maybe one of the squash team kids
> Would be willing to run me around a bit.
> **************************
> You are a masochist. I always suspected it.
> *********
> I was thinking. I am honored to be your sounding
> board, but we work in such different areas. Maybe you
> should invite Malone from the applied math dept. at
> UB to be a co-sounding board. We both know him from
> Il Gruppo and I think he can be trusted. He works in
> complexity theory like you---and he gets respect.
> ********************
> I phoned Malone and he agreed. So I'll let you both
> know when I am ready.
>
> By the way, Joe mentioned that he will do the Il Gruppo

ride on Saturday, and that you will see him today at the twins' semen hour. I already learned basic nonsmooth calculus a few years ago when I discovered that I needed it in analyzing sensitivity to data perturbations in a certain nonlinear programming problem that I was studying. Good stuff. Maybe I'll kibitz at later talks, after the dust settles.

****

So what's with this Holy Grail? It better be good.

****

Better than good. The Virgin Queen will have me dipped in bronze and mounted atop the Castle. You'll be bragging that you know me.

****

Try to put in a few kilometers and some hills before Saturday, and try to get some rest. I don't want you dying on me before the big secret is revealed.

****

I've been out to Eden a few times. Maybe I'll do a spin toTroy or Smuggler's Notch tomorrow, if my brain allows.

****

P.S. I watched GMPTV last night. You have the best wife in the world.

asterisk asterisk asterisk asterisk asterisk

The entire shtick was my idea, I want you to know. Including the arrow.

Simon

Aitch quit the e-mail program at 9:59, hustled to the lounge to get a coffee, and strode down the hall to the seminar room.

-28-

Celestine and the twins were already there, as were Yu Wong, Izzy Fleck, and Joe Malone from the Department of Applied Mathematics at the University of Burlington. She was wearing tight jeans and a loose fitting T-shirt, and her hair was still up, like the other day. The earrings and contacts were still there too, and she flashed a big smile in Aitch's direction.

The twins were shuffling their notes and Nathan looked to be a minute from starting, so Aitch had time to scamper to the rear of the room and high-five Izzy. The old man always sat in the last row at talks in case he dozed off, despite the hyper-sweetened, strong black joe which he imbibed nonstop. Aitch took a seat in the second row, beside Celestine.

Each department in the Fitch Sciences Building had its own seminar room, but the mathematicians had the grandest. This was due to some successful lobbying of the administration in 1989 by Guillermo Slutnick, then the new departmental chairman. At a meeting of the senate, he argued with great eloquence that it was only fair that some extra space resources be given to the mathematicians, since unlike the wet scientists, they required no laboratories, and also because advances in mathematics relied on the seminar medium to such a great extent. He thought that one day the room would be named after him. Before he died, Slutnick hoped.

The large carpeted room had a capacity of 150 and had the feel of a small theater. Speakers could utilize a motorized retractable screen for use with an overhead projector, and there were plug-ins for laptop driven slide shows. But over the years, none of this technology mattered very much, because many mathematicians prefer chalk talks. For this purpose, it appeared that there were three large blackboards. But in fact there were nine, because in front of each of the three visible boards there were two hidden ones. Each blackboard was on a track which could be slid upward so that all nine could be made visible at once, obviating the need to erase. Aitch thought about why he was so paranoid about such multi-layered contraptions. A thirty-eight year old memory swept him back in time---he was transported, and his eyes became moist.

***

April, 1965---The East Village

Aitch Singleton has just taken a seat next to Simon Goldman in the large classroom on the ground floor of the Hewitt Engineering Building, where Professor Leibgott's chemistry midterm is about to be inflicted. They are physics majors at The Cooper Union for the Advancement of Science and Art in lower Manhattan, near the Bowery. One hundred twenty nervous students are in the room, fidgeting, chatting, and doing their last minute cramming---the entire sophomore class, consisting of the various engineering options, as well as the new major at Cooper Union, Physics. There are only two girls in the room. Many of the physics students, like Aitch and Simon, would have preferred to study mathematics, but that option is not offered at Cooper. Yet, even though they could have majored in math at excellent universities and obtained generous scholarships, the prestige of being accepted by Cooper Union was irresistible. And acceptance here came with a *full* scholarship.

Students of art or architecture exist in an alternate universe, across the street in the venerable Foundation Building, where Abraham Lincoln gave a historic address in 1860 while campaigning for the presidency. Since the beginning of the twentieth century, engineering students at Cooper Union have referred to their academic cousins as 'artsie-fartsies', who in turn call the engineers 'weenies'.

What all Cooper Union's artsie-fartsies and weenies have in common is that they are among the best students in the United States, tested and screened before starting their cost-free education here and savoring the fruits of locomotive inventor Peter Cooper's brilliant vision and generous endowment. Superb high school grades and astronomical SAT scores are not enough to be accepted here. The Cooper Union administers its own battery of aptitude and intelligence exams, and it is harder to gain admission here than to any Ivy League university. These gifted young scholars are members of the nation's intellectual elite---*la crème de la crème*. Most of them are from the New York City area, but there are exceptions like Herman Melville Singleton. By and large they have blue collar or middle class backgrounds, and many are first generation Americans, like Simon Goldman.

Professor Leibgott makes his entrance. He is a tall, thin, bespectacled fellow with a kindly visage. Everyone thinks he looks and acts like Jack Benny. He holds a doctorate in chemical engineering from Stanford, but his undergraduate degree was earned at Cooper Union in 1941. Leibgott has a reputation as an excellent teacher, and is known to be a tough but fair grader. He understands the institution and loves it and its students with all his heart.

The professor strides to the blackboard---a triple stack job---and even though everyone knows the drill, he says,

"Before I hand out the question sheets and answer booklets, let me remind you of a few things."

Professor Leibgott picks up a piece of white chalk. Aitch looks to his left, and notices that Simon Goldman is bug-eyed, quaking with anticipation and what looks like barely controlled glee. And two seats over, next to Simon, Albie Petrocelli is twitching with similar symptoms, and trying hard to suppress a demented grin. Further down the row, Jimmy Bingel and Aitch's roommate, Tommy Matsumoto, also look like they know something is up. Simon Goldman leans towards Aitch and whispers.

"Bumpkin, watch what happens."

Professor Leibgott writes on the first blackboard.

MATERIALS ALLOWED:

1. **PERIODIC TABLE OF ELEMENTS**
2. **FORMULAS (one sheet only)**
3. **SLIDE RULE**

Every weenie in the room is an expert in the use of the slide rule, a device soon to be rendered obsolete by the advent of the electronic hand-held calculator. A typical slide rule is about a foot long ---it resembles three ordinary rulers bracketed together in such a way that the middle section can slide back and forth. By positioning the slide and making judicious use of the logarithmic and trigonometric scales etched on the instrument, a great variety of calculations can be carried out with efficiency and accuracy.

Professor Leibgott pauses because he knows that item 3 is Tommy Matsumoto's cue to launch into his famous routine, created when he was a student at the Bronx High School of Science, and perfected over the past two years here at Cooper Union.

Tommy rises and holds his slide rule in front of him in a two-handed grip, with the sliding section fully extended and pointed at his stomach. He has tied a white silk cloth around his head with a red rising sun in front---what souvenir collecting U.S. Marines fighting the Japanese on Pacific islands called a 'meatball scarf'.

Applause erupts and someone calls out,

"SAYONARA, TOMMY!"

Tommy cries, "BANZAI!"

He plunges the instrument into his midsection, and as the sliding part moves, the illusion is one of penetration. Tommy acts out his *hara kiri* with great gusto, grimacing and groaning. There is loud applause and foot stomping when the performance ends, and Tommy makes four ritualistic bows, one towards each wall.

The professor has politely joined in the applause, and then gestures to Tommy Matsumoto that the show is over and it is time to sit down. Tommy bows stiffly and deeply towards his honorable teacher, and sits. However, he does not remove his *kamikaze* bandana, because it brings him luck on the divine wind.

Professor Leibgott slides the first backboard up to its highest position, exposing the second board, upon which he writes further information.

ANSWER ONLY 5 OUT OF THE 6 QUESTIONS.
KEEP THE QUESTION SHEETS.
ROUND OFF ANSWERS TO 3 SIG. FIGS.

The professor now rolls this blackboard up so that it and the first one are still visible, with the third slate board newly exposed. He intends to write on it, but there is something scrawled on it already, in bright yellow chalk.

FUCK YOU, PROFESSOR LIEBGOTT.

Instant bedlam! Fists pound on tables. Shrieks of hysterical laughter fill the room. The two girls are in a screaming contest. Some students cover their eyes but peek through their fingers---some shake their heads left and right, moaning with delight. Jimmy Bingel is convulsing, with his head on his table. But innocent, pure hearted Herman Melville Singleton, a.k.a. Aitch, a.k.a. Bumpkin, stares at the obscenity in numb, slack-jawed disbelief, a solitary island in a sea of pandemonium.

Professor Leibgott faces the vulgar message with his arms crossed, and then he brings one hand up and cups his chin, the way Jack Benny does. He exclaims, "WELL!", and begins to shake his head with disapproval. The fools have misspelled his name! He picks up some yellow chalk, makes the needed correction, and adds further information.

FUCK YOU, PROFESSOR LEIBGOTT.
EXAM ENDS AT 3 PM SHARP !!!

The students cheer him wildly, lustily---even louder than they cheered Tommy Matsumoto, and Aitch has now joined in. The professor distributes the answer booklets, but holds on to the question sheets.

"I'll pass these out and you can start the exam as soon as everyone quiets down."

They have to somehow police themselves and regain a measure of decorum so that Professor Leibgott will allow the exam to begin---otherwise, they will lose precious time and their grades will suffer. After one minute, the only student still hysterical is Jimmy Bingel, but he is jabbed, smothered and threatened by Albie and Tommy until he is under control. The exam begins four minutes late, so the pressure is even greater than before. But when he receives the question sheet, Aitch feels calm, as though all his adrenaline has been used up. He glances over at Simon, who is serene and smiling as he begins to answer the questions. Aitch wonders if the spelling error was deliberate, and entertains the thought that perhaps he is not among earthlings.

***

Aitch returned from his reverie just as Nathan Finkelstein was about to begin speaking. He felt disoriented for a moment, as he sometimes did when awakening from an office catnap, and it took him a few seconds to ascertain his spacetime coordinates. He blinked hard a few times, took off his glasses, and wiped away an escapee tear.

Ah, sweet Jesus. Crying in public.

-29-

Celestine turned in her seat and announced that Nathan and Ibrahim would each speak for one hour, with a five minute coffee break between.

Nathan Finkelstein's exposition was a pedagogical gem. He followed the reference text on Nonsmooth Analysis, but he had the intellectual courage to keep the focus on intuitive explanations in finite dimensions, as opposed to rote transcription of the infinite dimensional Hilbert Space theory. Izzy stayed awake and smiled with pleasure, and Aitch was glad that all nine boards were exposed, with no surprise messages.

***

At the break, the students remained in the seminar room, but Aitch, Joe, Celestine and Izzy headed to the lounge for coffee, and if they were lucky, cookies too.

On their way down the hall, Joe Malone's Texan voice boomed.

"Aitch, the Gold Man phoned me, as y'all probably know. Tell me the truth. Do y'all have any fucking idea what he's babbling about?"

Joe grew up on his family's ranch in the hill country near San Antonio, and he came off like a big knuckle-headed hayseed, which is what he was in many ways. But in the world of mathematics, appearances can be deceiving. He was thirty-seven and a rising star in complexity theory---a top gun---and he knew as much about Simon Goldman's history of accomplishment in that field as anyone in the world. Aitch was taken aback by Malone's lack of discretion, but he knew he had no right to criticize him. Not after the way he caved in and told Chairman Slutnick about the Holy Grail.

"Honest to God, Joe---I don't have a clue. I'm willing to take a polygraph. Wheel it in here."

Izzy turned towards them and cocked his head in a mischievous way, eyebrows arched and looking like a gargoyle, parodying his own curiosity about what he had just overheard. Celestine had no noticeable reaction, but as she poured coffee for Aitch, she smiled with what he took to be secret knowledge that she assumed he also possessed. It was the same look that she gave him in his office two days ago, when Simon's misjudgement about her section's performance was brought up. Aitch felt stupid that he could not read her mind, but not so stupid as to say anything. Twenty-five years of happy marriage had taught him that.

He located a started bag of Oreos in the pantry and passed it around. He knew that mathematics graduate students always appreciated free food, so he wrapped half a dozen in a napkin.

***

Aitch distributed the cookies to the students, just outside the seminar room, and went in. Yu Wong ingested his on the spot, and washed them down with a long haul of water from the fountain. The twins gripped their Oreos and looked at each other.

Ibrahim whispered, "Finkelstein, I pray that the Entity will forgive me. I am very hungry, and I am afraid that I might pass out during my talk. So I will eat these Oreo cookies even though they may not be strictly *halal. Allah akhbar!*"

And eat them he did, unsure of whether or not they contained pork by-products, such as lard. Nathan was awed by Ibrahim's courageous act, and drew inspiration.

"And I too may lose consciousness during your talk if I do not eat something immediately. Ibrahim, may God show mercy to us both. *Baruch ha shem.*"

And now Nathan's cookies were history too. He used to eat kosher pseudo-Oreos back in Brooklyn, and was amazed at how much better the real ones tasted. Everyone went back to their seats, with Nathan sitting in front because of his terrible eyesight. Ibrahim began his talk.

"For the first half-hour, I will simply continue from where my friend stopped. Then, in the second half-hour, I will skip ahead to Chapter 4 and preview how the theory applies to dynamical systems. At our next meeting, we will go back and continue reviewing the theory in the earlier chapters."

Aitch noticed that after Ibrahim had uttered the f-word, the back of Nathan's neck blushed red. He was aware of the twins' political rivalry in the Mezz, but was positive that Ibrahim did not mean it in a barbed way. Perhaps he was not even aware that he had said it.

***

It was past noon when Ibrahim finished. Everyone had left except for Yu Wong, who was having another lengthy glug of water, and Aitch, who wanted a word with him.

"Yu Wong, would you be interested in looking at some problems in fluid dynamics and partial differential equations, where nonsmooth methods might apply?"

Aitch knew that Yu Wong was the hottest property in the department, as far as grad students were concerned, and that he still did not have a dissertation topic or a supervisor. Yu Wong, on his part, had approached Simon Goldman last winter, asking if he might have a nice research problem for him to work on. Goldman was by far the strongest mathematician in the department---a great and famous mathematician---so Yu Wong wanted very much to work under his tutelage. He knew that a doctorate earned under the supervision of such a renowned figure would be the ticket to a prestigious postdoc or tenure track position. Indeed, this was the case with every Ph.D. student supervised by Goldman during his years at Harvard. But he did not seem interested in Yu Wong, saying that he could not take on a graduate student at this time. Maybe later, he said, and Yu Wong was wounded. But now he was very pleased that Professor Singleton had approached him. He knew that this professor had a good character and was a good mathematical scientist, so he took the plunge.

"Yes, Professor Singleton. I see possibilities for Clarke's nonsmooth approach to be applied to some fluid flow problems. It sounds like very delightful topic area."

Yu Wong made his name sound like 'Singer-ton', but Aitch did not mind and knew that he would get used to it.

"Tell you what. How about meeting me at around 9 a.m. on Friday---my office? I'll give you an overview of what I have in mind, and provide you with some reading material."

"Yes, excellent time for me. Thank you, Professor Singleton."

***

Thursday was foggy, and Aitch spent the whole day in his attic, studying nonsmooth theory from his newly arrived textbook. Around 8 p.m. he went down to the kitchen to pop a frozen lasagna into the microwave. Gazing outside, he observed Newton and Minipod in the middle of the back lawn. They were on their haunches, furry little sentinels with perked, twitching ears, tails sweeping, as they focused on the old shed with its caved in window, and the deep, breeze-rustled woods beyond.

-30-

After his Friday morning meeting with his new advisor, Yu Wong felt buoyant as he took the elevator down to the sub-sub-basement. Upon entering his shared cubicle, he found the twins at their desks scowling, filling out some sort of bureaucratic forms in pencil. He put down the bagful of mathematics which Professor Singleton had just given him.

"Gentlemen, how are you today?"

The twins kept their heads down, seeming not to notice Yu Wong's presence. This upset him, because Ibrahim and Nathan had never failed to be polite and respectful before. So in a gesture that was for him very aggressive and impolite, Yu Wong looked over their shoulders to see why they were in such a foul mood.

The twins had already each filled out a ten page form called the *Standard Personal Data Profile*, which asked for every biographical detail imaginable, including their birth weights and shoe sizes. Now they were working on a thirty page monstrosity called the *American*

Psychoanalytical and Psychological Society Personality Assessment Protocol. They were ticking dozens of boxes 'yes', 'no', or 'not applicable', and agreeing or disagreeing with dozens of bizarre and invasive statements like 'People think I smell bad', where a score of '0' indicated complete disagreement and '5' connoted the opposite extreme.

***

Yu Wong left in silence, and headed for the Han People's Take-Out in his dormitory's kitchen. It was not yet noon, but ten salivating graduate students were already queued up, ready to pay their two dollars and consume enough calories to get through the rest of the day and part of the next. Two of Yu Wong's colleagues from Shenzhen were manning the woks, while three others were gathered around a PC set atop the dishwasher. They were playing no limit Texas Holdem', and doing all right---Yu Wong saw that Bigballs had a two thousand dollar stack of virtual chips in front of him. The member of the poker triad controlling the mouse turned his head and spoke up in Mandarin.

"Hey Yu Wong, good news. El Bandido de Venezuela is playing---betting too much and losing."

***

Yu Wong returned to his cubicle in the sub-sub-basement of the Fitch, carrying four large Styrofoam containers, and a jumbo bottle of black cherry soda.

"Gentlemen, no charge. This is Han People's delightful introductory sample."

The twins exchanged a mutual consultative look, and speaking with one voice, thanked their friend. Together, they cleared some space on the small table near the chalkboard, and the three of them feasted on beef with broccoli, General Tao's tofu, ginger chicken with vegetables, and mountains of steamed rice.

CHAPTER 7

Il Gruppo

-31-

At 8:30 on Saturday morning, Aitch pulled into the Canada Post parking lot in Sutton, just off Rue Principale. About a dozen cycling clubs were forming up, and after a brief binary search, he spied a four man contingent of Il Gruppo in the far corner. They were Montrealers, and he had not seen them since October's final ride---a beauty, with the Green Mountains awash in their fall colors.

He nosed his Honda into the bushes and exchanged greetings with the quartet, all of whom were about his age, and lean, decent riders. Two were mathematicians---Pierre Desjardins was a number theorist from the Université de Montréal, and Bruce McAllister was a topologist from Concordia University. Bob Donnelly taught biochemistry at McGill, and Morty Zeffman, an ER physician at the Jewish General Hospital in the Côte des Neiges district, owned the van they arrived in. Morty only lasted ten minutes behind the wheel, however. He was susceptible to eyestrain, and became sleepy on the Champlain Bridge while crossing the St. Lawrence River. So as usual, he pulled to the side of the autoroute and turned the driving over to Bruce McAllister, his longtime doppelganger. Morty dozed off right away, and never heard Bruce accuse him of being a narcoleptic or ask whether he had ever fallen asleep while administering a colonoscopy.

At the moment, the four were applying sunscreen, fiddling with their equipment, and getting themselves ready to ride. Bruce was peeing in the bushes, and Morty reminded him that his prostrate was enlarging with age and in all likelihood putting the squeeze on his urethra, so he should take care not to dribble on his expensive Shimano biking shoes.

Bao Hoang's van announced its arrival with a toot---he had brought Sonya, Celestine, Bill and Drew. And right behind Bao, Mona's shiny twelve year old Mercedes pulled in too. She parked next to Aitch, who was taking his bike down from the roof rack and munching on a pre-ride fig. Since the Mercedes had no rack, Simon's bicycle was stowed in the trunk with its wheels off. It was a model Lance Armstrong favored, and for understandable reasons, very popular these days---a carbon fibre Trek with U.S. Postal Service markings. Simon took the Armstrong theme to the limit, with his helmet and spandex jersey also bearing the USPS logo. Aitch went to Mona's window, leaned in, and began probing her temples with his index fingers. Laughing, Simon got out and began assembling his bike. Mona had Hank Williams singing a song about loneliness on the CD player, and turned down the volume.

"That feels good, Aitch, but please inform me what on earth you're doing. Some sort of shiatsu massage, perhaps?"

"Why, I'm probing for the holes where the arrow passed through, sweetest Mona. You've healed remarkably well."

She put her head against the steering wheel.

"Oh God!---I should have understood. I am a naïve and gullible fool, am I not?"

Simon came around and kissed her. She couldn't tousle his hair because of his helmet, so she reached out and tugged on his goatee instead. He leaned into the caress.

"Wonder boy," she said, and drove off. She was going to spend the day with Vito's wife and mother at the de Bernardi chalet on Lac Kelly, four kilometers up the road flanking Mt. Sutton.

Celestine was prepared before Bao's other passengers, and already straddling her eight-year-old road bike. Her helmet was bright yellow just like Aitch's, and he thought that she looked great in her tight green outfit.

"Nice bike," he said. "I used to ride a Marinoni too, but it wasn't pink like yours."

"That's a relief!" she laughed. "I know I'm a bit out of date, riding steel. But it's very comfy---like my papa's old Buick."

He wondered whether he was older than her father, and hoped that she did not notice him flinch.

Everyone else had carbon fibre or aluminum frames. Everyone except their commandant, Vito de Bernardi, who flew into the parking lot on his steel Gitane, the one he rode in the 1969 Tour de France. The bicycle was state of the art in those days, but now it was an antique---a vintage clunker, painted ten times. It stood out from the other machines, with its outmoded shift levers mounted on the diagonal tube of its heavy frame. For more serious riding and racing, he used a newer and lighter titanium machine with modern shifters housed in the brake assembly on the handlebars. Vito braked only when he was among Il Gruppo's members, leaning on one foot, keeping the other clipped in. He was five foot one and weighed 110 pounds soaking wet, a little spider of a man with toothpick-thin limbs, and a tiny torso housing a pulmonary apparatus of freakish power and efficiency. He was now sixty-two years old.

Simon Goldman, who was a small wiry man himself, looked like a giant next to Vito de Bernardi when he took hold of his hand. He always made a point of tweaking Vito. During a ride last year, Simon subjected him to the light-hearted theological claim that, as even a cursory reading of the Gospels shows, it was the Italians who killed Jesus---not the Jews. The theme was different this time.

"Godfather, how good it is see you."

It was a terrible try at an Italian accent. Goldman bowed, kissed one of Vito's rings and said "Godfather" again, this time *sotto voce*, before engaging in a normal handshake. Aitch could tell that Simon was feeling his oats. The Holy Grail must be firmly in his grasp.

"Hello, Simon Goldman," said Vito in his heavy Palermo accent, with a tight crease of a smile not very different from the way his features normally arranged themselves into a kind of scowl. Vito de Bernardi would not tolerate such behavior from many people without going ballistic, but as always, Simon's high academic stature protected him. Lance Armstrong could have gotten away with it too.

"Still no brain-bucket, Don Vito?"

Vito never wore a helmet. Only a small, faded cloth cap upon which 'Italia' and 'Sicilia' were printed---something like a housepainter's hat, which he always wore backwards, covered his little shaved cranium. Simon knew that Vito's attitude towards helmet wearers was akin to his own regarding faggotball players, albeit a less rational one. With his wrap-around mirror sunglasses, dark olive skin and beak of a nose, Vito gave the impression that he was moving at high speed even when he was standing still.

Aitch and all the occupants of Bao's van lined up single file to shake Vito's hand and show their leader the respect which he demanded of them. Celestine also kissed both his cheeks, if the leathery desiccated skin covering his cheekbones could really be called cheeks.

After another minute of fussing with equipment, the riders all gathered beside Morty Zeffman's van, and Big Joe Malone was now there too. Aitch counted heads, and announced to the group that there were thirteen riders today. It was important to know this, so that quick tallies could be taken.

"It is a prime number," Pierre pointed out. As a number theorist, it was his wont to do so.

***

The four Montrealer's and Joe Malone had Morty's map of north-central Vermont spread on the hood. They were waiting for Vito to describe today's route.

Big Joe said, "Vito, the forecast is for a hot day and the air will be heavy with humidity, so breathing could get tough on the uphills. I hope y'all don't plan to bust our asses too hard."

In his deep Sicilian baritone, minuscule Vito said, "Well, *amici*, I do have a nice season opener in mind, but perhaps some of you have special places that you want to visit today?"

This was quite out of character for Vito de Bernardi, and Aitch thought that it might have something to do with Celestine's civilizing influence on her former postdoctoral supervisor. Vito had never offered options before, because leadership, even tyranny, gives comfort to cyclists engaged in a group ride. His absolutism had always been accepted by all, Goldman included. And everyone in Il Gruppo felt fortunate to ride alongside a Tour veteran, even if their outings were merely short, restful spins for him.

No opinions were offered for ten seconds, but then Bill Hurker spoke up in his soft Georgia accent.

"Well, I kind of always wanted to see Lake Carmi from the north side."

He was a blond, well constructed thirty year old who resembled renderings of Alexander the Great on ancient gold coins. And there was something in his genteel demeanor and bearing which suggested that he grew up with wealth. Bill and Drew had been a couple for half a year now, and were living together in a UNV-owned faculty-housing complex near the campus. Celestine rented a small apartment there too.

Morty had a pencil, and drew a circle around East Franklin, just north of the lake. Now Dr. Zeffman, an unredeemable fitness freak who, to his wife's eternal chagrin kept a treadmill in their bedroom, made his own request.

"Well, I for one would be disappointed if we didn't visit the town of Jay. We can restock on Gatorade and power bars there, so it's convenient."

It was Morty's obtuse way of trying to get the group to agree to two long, murderous climbs---up Jay Peak before dropping into Jay, and then up again from Jay before dropping into Montgomery Center, or the other way around. Contrary to his calling as a healer, Dr. Zeffman's goal was that everyone except him, Vito and Aitch should be in a world of pain at the conclusion of today's outing. This was how Morty liked to vindicate himself athletically, after a childhood spent labeled as a four-eyed spaz. No one had the courage to object, so he drew a little circle around Jay.

Bruce said, "You want to kill me, don't you, Morty? You know I always try to keep up."

"Bruce, nothing could be further from the truth. I don't want to kill you. I just want to hurt you a little."

Bob Donnelly added, "Remember, Bruce---what doesn't kill you makes you strong. And don't let Morty make you feel bad. You're a totally excellent cyclist---just a tad on the slow side."

Bao Hoang chimed in.

"Actually, I have a couple of places in mind. I'd like to see the memorial to President Chester A. Arthur at his probable birthplace near Bakersfield."

Aitch, the other history buff in Il Gruppo, was compelled to interject.

"I've been there, Bao, but on a fat-tire. The access is on a rough dirt road, so Il Gruppo can't do it today."

Bao was disappointed but undeterred.

"Well, I'd also like to go to Sheldon to see the roadside plaque commemorating the most northerly combat during the Civil War."

So Morty marked Sheldon on his map. Then others voiced their touristic preferences, and Morty circled all the locations they requested. Bob Donnelly was very interested in the Fenian raids---attempts by Irish nationalists to invade Canada in 1866 and 1870 which were eventually repulsed near Cook's Corners and Franklin, where there were small monuments. His request was heartily seconded by Bao, because of the historical significance of the locale. Pierre Desjardins wanted to see what his favorite ski hill, Smuggler's Notch, looked like when there was no snow. And this too interested Bao, because of the Notch's history as a rum-running route from Canada into the U.S. during Prohibition. Morty liked the choice too, because the Notch was a brutal, body numbing climb---long and steep and sure to put Bruce into a state of cardiac embarrassment. And Drew heard that there was a really nice antique shop in West Berkshire, so if Il Gruppo could pass through, he wouldn't mind taking a gander.

The discussion went on for another five minutes, until Dr. Zeffman's map had fifteen points of interest marked.

-32-

Vito did not join the cluster of bodies around the van, staying off to the side and straddling his heavy Gitane, with his arms crossed. He was impatient to start the ride, and getting steamed. I should never have offered them options, thought Vito. His color was darkening---he had reached the limit of his patience.

"*Attenzione*, everyone," little Vito boomed. "Let's start the bloody ride today and not tomorrow, okay?"

Aitch, the second strongest rider in Il Gruppo and Vito's *consigliore*, saw that his friend was about to blow his lid.

"Vito, please tell us the route you have in mind. We'll have opportunities to visit all those places later in the season."

To everyone's relief, their diminutive leader brightened somewhat, and then laid it out for them in his inimical way. His bony finger traced a route on Morty's map.

"Nice easy warm-up spin to Pinnacle Road, where we make a *formazione* until the Abercorn-Northton border crossing. *Tutto* make sure you have two flattering photo ID's with you, and don't make any jokes with the American *carbinieri* unless you're in the mood for a cavity search, okay Brucie? For the rest of the ride, we make a line if and when we can, on my commands, and every ten kilometers we make sure everyone is accounted for. In Shitville---*scusi, prego*---Northton---turn right and don't cross the bridge---then left up the hill to the Berkshire Center crossroads, near the school. Left again and we drop down into East Berkshire. Continue along the Trout to Montgomery where I pee on Aitch Singleton's lawn. On to Montgomery Center, where we stop for a cappuccino at Trout River Traders, and then my bladder is full again and maybe I also pee on Simon Goldman's lawn. Then Dr. Morty has an orgasm because we do the up and down into Jay. We reload *liquidi e carboidrati* there, and then do the up and down into East Northton. Everyone be careful and put on your brakes *before* the bottom, unless you want a case of road-rash like Dr. Morty got last year---try not to leave too much of your skin on the asphalt today, okay, Dr. Morty? Then we go right, follow the Mississiquoi and cross back into Canada at Glen Sutton. We finish by climbing Mt. Glen and dropping into Sutton along Scenic Drive. One hundred twenty kilometers and you don't need that goddam map."

"Now, that's an offer we can't refuse," said Goldman as he clicked into his pedal clips.

-33-

The 6 kilometer stretch of Route 139 to Pinnacle Road was a gentle roll, and there was a wide shoulder reserved for cyclists. Vito led, keeping his speed at a steady 30 kilometers per hour. He commanded everyone not to exceed this because he wanted them to have a gradual warm-up until they reached the intersection with Pinnacle, where he would put them into an approximation of a proper cycling formation. But until then, it was to be easy spinning.

Celestine, Aitch, and Morty rode three abreast on the wide shoulder, with Bruce and Simon tucked in behind. They were about a bowling alley behind Vito, and the others were scattered further back as they rolled south. Because he had a captive audience, Bruce decided to hold court as they pedaled.

"I just thought of an interesting applied math problem. Morty, I'm just being a good scientist now, so don't take this personally, okay? You are a hazard to my health. Not only do I take my life in my hands when you're driving, and not only do I risk heart failure if I try to keep up with you, but there's also the chance that you'll knock me over if you crash, and you have a notable history in that regard."

Morty loved this, because he considered it an invitation to abuse Bruce later in the ride.

"On the other hand, Morty is an ER doctor, so if I fall off my bike or need someone to administer the Heimlich maneuver or pump my stomach, as he once did, I want him around. So my question is this: On balance, is Dr. Morty a plus or a minus from a health slash safety point of view?"

Simon was amused.

"Bruce, you need to think in terms of a 'utility function', a basic tool in the decision sciences. Then you can get your answer. I'll explain it to you another time. And regarding your model, as you of all people should know, one should also consider *mental* hazards, not just physical ones."

Aitch popped in a fig, passed one to Celestine, and they both swigged some liquid. No one spoke until they reached the Pinnacle Road intersection, where Vito announced his next directives. It was review material for the veterans, but there were new people today, and the little Sicilian wanted to be sure that everyone was on the same page.

"*Attenzione, amici.* It is another 5 K to the border, and it is the best road surface we're going to see today, so let's ride in a line *formazione*, okay? We'll keep it tight on the flats, not more than one foot apart, and steady at 35 K per hour. Not more and not less. After ups and downs, if there is separation, we put it back together. Stay at the front for only twenty seconds. If you see broken glass or a hole, point and everybody passes the signal down. After your turn in front, slide out to the right and slip to the back of the peloton. If the rider at the rear detects a car coming up, he or she calls out 'CAR'. If two of you touch wheels, *don't brake*! Keep pedaling and usually nothing happens, unless your name is Dr. Morty. Okay?"

Il Gruppo pleased its leader by carrying out his instructions without a hitch. Riding in line is a very efficient way to defeat air resistance, even with a bit more than the one foot of following distance specified by Vito.

***

Soon they were at the U.S. border crossing. Two cars and another cycling club were in line ahead of them, so they would be delayed before entering Vermont. Everyone dismounted and got their ID's ready for inspection.

During the wait, Pierre asked, "Bao, what was that business about Sheldon? I never heard of it."

Bao was always ready to give anyone an American history lesson.

"It's really very interesting, Pierre, and not that well known. I was referring to a force of about two dozen Confederates who were trying to make it to Canada after doing some mischief in St. Albans in 1864, if I'm not mistaken. They wanted to rob a bank in Sheldon on their way to safety in Montreal, but the aroused local citizenry forced the rebels to retreat---and the plaque I wanted to see is on the site of a covered bridge which caught fire during the battle."

Aitch knew that Bao's lively interest in American history sprang from his intense patriotism---the particular brand of patriotism born of the gratitude that only refugees seemed to possess. He had seen it in *Refusenik* mathematicians, and when he lived in New York City during his Cooper Union days, he saw it expressed by Simon Goldman's relatives, who escaped Nazi Germany in the late 1930's.

Bao Hoang was born in 1964 into a wealthy Saigon family with Chinese origins, which fled Vietnam in 1976 in a leaky sailboat. They were intercepted in the South China Sea by Thai pirates who shot his father and cut off one of his mother's fingers for her gold wedding ring. They raped her and Bao's sister while he was forced to watch, following which he was beaten and kicked to the edge of death. Left adrift for ten days with neither food nor water, the three survivors were rescued by an American frigate. Like thousands of other boat people, they claimed refugee status and became U.S. citizens in California.

Two years ago, when Aitch told Bao's story to his daughter Annie, she suggested that his expertise in the martial arts might represent a 'reaction formation' to his trauma. Now he wondered if she would say the same thing about Bao's training partner, Bill Hurker, who grew up gay in the South.

CHAPTER 8

The traveling salesman

-34-

At the start of the Berkshire uphill, Vito boomed that everyone should go at their own pace and regroup at the top, near the school. They headed up through an appealing stretch of intermingled forest and farmland, which Maureen once said reminded her of the wine growing regions of Tuscany, where the Singletons had honeymooned. Only here it's cows and corn that they grow, she pointed out at the time. It was a seven kilometer ascent, and the grade was gentle except for a steep stretch about halfway up. Vito wanted Il Gruppo to do this moderate ascent first, to build confidence and prevent panic during the more harrowing climbs around Jay.

As he cranked, Aitch worried about the dog that lived three kilometers up the hill, on the steep part, but managed to put him out of mind. He was riding next to Celestine in front, with the others spread behind. Vito was flitting among his charges, mothering them---providing encouragement even though it was not yet needed, critiquing body positions, insisting that they keep their shoulders relaxed, and reminding them to hydrate. Aitch and Celestine were silent, mesmerized by the hum of their spokes and absorbed by the view of Jay Peak, 40 kilometers to the east, as the crow flies. When the grade steepened, Aitch stood up for added power, an acceptable technique here. It is called 'dancing', the idea being to let one's own weight help transfer force to the pedals. Celestine kept up with him by sliding back a bit in her saddle, remaining seated and spinning her grannie gear.

Still dancing, Aitch scanned the brush ahead on the left side, and felt a knot in his stomach when he saw the big dog, snarling and flashing his teeth. Aitch hoped against hope that nothing would happen, but thirty meters later, he was badly disappointed, and the chase was on.

"*CELESTINE!* Slow down! He's after *me*!"

He hammered, putting Celestine behind him, but the beast was right on his rear wheel. Terror made time distend, and reality became a bad dream. Although he was in mortal terror, Aitch stole a glance at his speedometer---38 kilometers per hour on a steep uphill grade. He knew that at this level of output, lactates would build up quickly and his legs would spasm. Amazed that the heavy-set animal had the lungs to keep up with him, he kept cranking for all he was worth. And then he was even more amazed. Vito de Bernardi, who was at least one hundred meters back a minute before, had caught up and was just to his left.

"MIN CHIA DI UN CANE DI MERDA! VAFANCULO

BASTARDO!"

Vito's idea was to become the target and lead the dog to an oblivion of exhaustion. But it was not to be---the *cane di merda* did not understand Italian, and Aitch was still the prey. So tiny Vito reached into a back pocket with his left hand, pulled out his hand pump, and began fiddling with the device, using both hands to telescope it to its full length and open its locking lever. The result of his exertions was a small tomahawk. All the while, he maintained perfect balance and continued to crank his heavy Gitane uphill at over 40 kilometers per hour. Placing his left hand back on the bar, he leaned and began slashing at the dog's head with the weapon in his right. It looked like a backhand swing in polo.

"TIE', ROTTINCULO STRONZO FIGLIO DI TROIA, TIE', TIE', PEZZO DI MERDA!"

After ten swipes, Vito must have struck something important, because the dog yelped in pain, and with shocking suddenness turned tail and ran home along the shoulder. They slowed down, and Aitch hunched over his handlebar, struggling to take in air.

"Thanks, Vito---I owe you one. But jeez, did you have to be so vulgar?"

Vito emitted a rare laugh and muttered, "*Bastardo,*" in reference to the dog, Aitch hoped.

Celestine soon caught up.

"Allo Geezer! *Embarras cardiaque?*"

A tractor rumbled towards them in the opposing lane, and the farmer driving it glared with an expression not much different from the dog's angry snarl. Aitch felt a jolt of *déjà vu* and was sure that he had encountered him before.

-35-

Il Gruppo reconvened at the Berkshire school crossroads, and Morty's tally confirmed that all thirteen riders were accounted for. Everyone took a drink and some reached for snacks stowed in their back pockets. All were pleased that gravity would be on their side for the next few minutes, during the freefall into East Berkshire. They took off together, with their miniature leader's orders ringing in their ears.

"*Attenzione!* Everyone keep a good distance apart and stay extra clear of Dr. Morty. If you need to slow down, be sure to engage the rear brake before the front one, unless you want to do a somersault over your handlebar and get brain damaged like Dr. Morty. Put your weight on the outside leg on downhill turns, lift the inside knee---lean your bicycle, not your body. And keep spinning lightly or you might cramp."

"Hey, I'm not dain bramaged," said Morty.

Descents like this were always a hoot, and as he started rolling downhill, Simon announced to no one in particular,

"One of the last cheap thrills left."

Everyone had a rest at high speed and enjoyed the scenery, although a certain degree of vigilance had to be maintained in scanning the road surface for dangerous imperfections. Aitch glanced at Celestine and saw that she was very proficient at maintaining an aerodynamic body position, using her flexibility to tuck down so low that her chin was almost touching the handlebar while she stood on her pedals and raised her well formed caboose high, pinching her knees together. He was ten feet behind her, and could not help but smile at the suggestive posture. She was such an efficient glider that he had to crank hard a few times in his highest gear just to keep up, his motivation purely lascivious.

About a kilometer from the bottom, they passed the Ethan Allen Sportsman's Club. With a jolt, Aitch realized why the angry looking tractor driver looked familiar. He was the moron who threw a beer can at him near here a few days ago. For no reason at all.

***

At the bottom, Vito reformed them into a riding line, because for the next ten kilometers they would be on the gently rolling road following the Trout to Montgomery. As they passed Maureen's cairn, Aitch was touched when Vito and Pierre crossed themselves as they zipped past it. A few minutes later, Vito pulled out of formation, sprinted to the front, and signalled for everyone to pause at the tiny triangular park in Montgomery, near Aitch's house.

"This is the moment of truth, *amici*", he said to his disciples. "If anyone wants to take the short route back, you turn off here. There is only one climb, and you can shave 40 kilometers off today's ride."

Vito pointed towards a century-old covered bridge built by the Jewett Brothers, beyond which was the South Northton Road, known to Il Gruppo as the 'Coward's Cut-off'. They were only 45 kilometers into the ride, but Joe Malone was already suffering---he was carrying an extra thirty pounds, it being early in the season. But neither he nor any of the other riders chose the abbreviated route. Big Joe said that the defenders of the Alamo, near where he grew up, did not skedaddle after Colonel Travis gave them permission to bug out, and by God, neither would he.

Bao was the last to mount up because he wanted to finish reading the inscription on a small memorial surrounded by flowers. He was enthralled because it honored Montgomery's fallen soldiers, all the way back to the War of Independence. It was just the sort of arcane ephemera that Bao Hoang loved, and he decided on the spot to visit the nearby cemetery to see how old the headstones were. Maybe his wife and kids would agree to make a picnic of it.

Aitch pointed out his house to Celestine as they rolled along. She murmured, "Aha," and nodded as though confirming a prescient notion concerning its appearance. They were soon passing the old church with its broken clock, and there was a sign in front advertising a concert at 6 p.m. by a Montreal group called 'The Klezmer Mavens'. It was the first performance in this season's 'Music on the Methodist Meadow' series.

Celestine pulled up next to him.

"The Mavens are from Outremont. I once heard them play in a Montreal bistro. They have a fanatic following back home. Great musicians. Even though Klezmer is Eastern European Jewish music, except for the founder of the band, all the rest are French Quebeckers---and they sing in Yiddish."

"Sounds like an interesting ensemble," said Aitch, as he passed her a fig.

He knew that he was being presented with a clear opening to ask her out, but he dithered, distracted by the sparkle of her sunglasses and the depth of her dimples.

"Let's go tonight," she said. "It will be a beautiful evening."

It sounded more like a promise than a weather forecast. She accelerated and he had to push hard to stay with her.

-36-

After a ten minute spin down the valley of the Trout, Il Gruppo arrived in the tiny hamlet of Montgomery Center. Along the tree-lined main street there were a few inns and restaurants catering to the Jay Peak ski crowd in the winter, and to cyclists in the off-season. They leaned their machines against the porch of Trout River Traders, and left their gloves and helmets to air out on the railing. A sign on the door required them to leave their shoes outside, because biking cleats tended to scratch the polished oak floor. The establishment occupied a renovated century-old farmhouse. Its lower level consisted of a soda fountain and coffee shop, while upstairs there were antiques and collectibles. Il Gruppo riders had been stopping here to refuel and shoot the breeze for many years, too many to remember.

They entered and placed their orders for snacks and speciality coffees at the counter, and then took seats around the large pine table by the front window. Morty spread out his map so that all could see how far they had come and how much distance remained. After some discussion, it was ascertained that over fifty kilometers had been covered, with about seventy to go. The fifteen markings on Morty's map were no longer of interest after Vito specified today's route, but Joe Malone noticed something. Being an expert in combinatorics and complexity theory, he realized that he was being stared in the face by a very famous mathematical problem.

"Well, I'll be a blue nosed gopher! Back in Sutton, y'all came up with a real-world *Traveling Salesman Problem*---a symmetric TSP."

All the mathematicians nodded, except for Bruce McAllister, who was perplexed.

"Dude, I'm only an ignorant topologist. Which means that I can't distinguish between a bagel and a teacup. So take pity on me and remind me what a TSP is, eh?"

Ever the competitor, Morty said, "I bet I'm even more ignorant than you, Bruce. But a lot fitter. Better looking too."

Bruce had to agree one hundred percent, but reminded Morty that he was a body nazi who worked out an abnormal amount and that he had his beauty sleep during the drive, so no wonder he felt that way.

Sonya Jorgenson refused to be outdone.

"Sorry boys, but I'm more ignorant than all of you laid end to end."

Aitch thought she blushed a little.

"Oops---not that I'm suggesting anything. Failed metaphor. I just meant to say that I'm a veritable *diva* of mathematical ignorance."

"I'm a diva too," said Drew. He winked at Bill, who winked back.

Joe said, "I could explain it to y'all, but Lance Goldman here is one of the world's leading authorities on TSP's, among other things. So go on and tell 'em about it, Gold Man."

Simon was serene and smiled. With an impresario's sweep of his arm, as though introducing a guest speaker, he beckoned Joe to give the explanation.

"Okay, Gold Man. Well, y'all want to visit each intermediate location, or 'node', *exactly once*---and end up where y'all started, right here," he said, pointing at Sutton and making it sound like 'rat cheer'.

"Y'all know the distance between each pair of nodes, and y'all want the *total* distance of the tour to be as *small as possible*."

Bruce McAllister interrupted him with an observation.

"Joe, the requirement of visiting each node only *once* is utter horseshit, because in real life we could always double back now and then during the ride to shorten the overall route. But please, do go on."

"Thanks, brother Bruce. That's very ass toot. Now put a sock in your word-hole, accept the hypotheses, and allow me to continue. If y'all don't mind."

Having cancelled out his ignorance with his intellectual and pragmatic point, Bruce was able to force himself to remain silent.

"We've got fifteen nodes," said Joe, "not counting Sutton. The problem is called 'symmetric' because the distance from node X to node Y is the same as the distance from node Y to node X for every pair of nodes (X,Y). A non-symmetric TSP can be formulated if, for example, y'all want to consider wind direction or the elevation of the nodes---then traveling from X to Y could be easier or harder than Y to X---but the problem is tough enough if there's no wind and the road is flat. That's all she wrote. That's your TSP."

Bob Donnelly said, "Well, how hard can it be to solve the problem, even with your unrealistic requirements? I mean, there are *only* fifteen places to visit."

Celestine jumped into the breach. The TSP was not very near her domain of research in applied mathematics, but she was familiar with the problem because of a graduate course on networks she took at Berkeley.

"*Really* hard, Bob. In this case, the number of possible tours is 15 factorial---that's 15 times 14 times 13 and so on, all the way down to 1. But you can divide that by two because for every tour, there is a reverse tour of equal total distance, due to the symmetry---so you only need to consider half the total number of possibilities. You see, with symmetry, a tour like a-b-c-a has the same length as a-c-b-a."

Big Joe Malone, being a closet nerd, had a mini-calculator on his wristwatch, and after a few seconds of pushing tiny buttons with his huge paw, he said,

"That's 653,837,184,000 possible network tours to consider. Over half a *trillion* possibilities with fifteen nodes. And believe it or not, with only a few hundred nodes, the number of possibilities is greater than the number of atoms in the universe."

"No shit?" blurted Sonya.

Joe said, "I shit you not. It takes huge brains to find a shortest route. Listing all the tours and searching for a best route is too big a job ---like trying to find a needle in a haystack. Y'all need a sequential procedure---an *algorithm*, for finding one, or for at least narrowing the problem down and determining a near optimal tour."

Simon said, "Big Joe has done some very nice work on this narrowing down aspect of the problem---by applying artificial intelligence techniques and genetic algorithms to an important class of problems which include TSP's."

Joe was not about to be out-humbled.

"But seventeen years ago, Professor Simon Armstrong here devised an algorithm which *exactly* solved a randomly generated TSP with *thousands* of nodes."

Simon shrugged.

"Okay, I have to admit the $500 prize was nice, but the record was soon broken, and I haven't pursued it since. As computational power never keeps increasing, there will always be people chasing the record, just like the numerical analysts and number theorists who chase after the umpteen-zillionth digit of π. I used to do that too, you know---a fifteen minutes of fame kind of thing---although I admit such endeavors have generated some powerful and important mathematics. I'm still interested in the TSP, but not in setting a record for the size of the problem that can be solved. There are other, much *deeper* issues. I've been looking at one in particular, for the past few years."

There was slyness in the way he said it---smug, teasing, sending a message, but also coy and holding something back. Joe started to speak, but his words caught in his throat. He yanked himself to his feet and froze. Thirty seconds passed before he came back to life. He gripped the table, and locked a ferocious gaze on Simon.

"Like the *P vs. NP problem*, Gold Man?"

Joe was leaning towards him, threatening and pointing a finger.

Simon held his smile, hesitated, and then gave the slightest nod.

Yes.

The big Texan fell back into his chair.

"*Don't fuck with me, Simon!* Is *that* the breakthrough in complexity theory y'all wanted to tell me about? *Did y'all find an algorithm which solves the TSP in polynomial time?*"

Simon had not intended to reveal his discovery today. His plan was to corner Aitch and arrange to show it to him on Monday morning. But Big Joe was a clever cowboy and on to him. Simon had also approached Celestine and asked her to be his sounding board, several days before he made his request of Aitch. He told her that he thought he had made a major advance in complexity theory, but she shocked him by refusing to be responsible for checking his work. She said she was too junior, and that combinatorial optimization and complexity were not really in her bailiwick anyway. But the real reason for the rejection was Celestine's firm belief that Simon Goldman was an arrogant, unreformed and unrepentant serial asshole, an opinion reinforced by her witnessing the faggotball fiasco which hurt her friend Bill Hurker, and the pedagogical horror stories told by desperate MATH 101 students who transferred out of his section into hers. She tried to be diplomatic with Simon, but feared that she had insulted him. In her mind, this fear, as well as her opinion about Goldman's character, was confirmed by his ridiculous impugning of her teaching. Such an impulsive and stupid act, she thought---something a spiteful child might do for a moment's gratification, even though it was obvious that in the end no grown-ups would be fooled.

Faced with Joe Malone's imploring interrogation, Simon allowed a trace of his usual cockiness to show.

"Actually, I didn't invent a *new* algorithm, Joe. I just discovered a way to prove that my old one had the goods."

Pierre Desjardins was the first to react. He felt a shiver run down his spine, looked to the ceiling and crossed himself.

"*Sacre fils*! You solved a Millennium Problem!"

Joe Malone was processing the fact that a mathematical nuclear bomb had just been dropped, and that this was ground zero. Staring down at the table with wet eyes, he declared,

"*Goldman's Theorem: TSP is P*. I always believed it was true, Simon, but I didn't think I would live to see it proven."

Aitch understood. Fifteen minutes of fame would never do for the likes of Simon Goldman. It was to be immortal glory for solving one of the Millennium Problems---his name would echo through the ages. And then there was the million dollar cash prize offered by the Clay Institute. Six other unsolved problems were on the Millennium list, including the Poincaré Conjecture and the Riemann Hypothesis. And there was also one involving the Navier-Stokes equation of fluid dynamics, but Aitch had neither the confidence nor the intellectual chutzpa to tackle it. He was no Simon Goldman.

The waitress brought their orders, and as always, Vito de Bernardi ate nothing, having only his usual unsweetened cappuccino, chased by a glass of water. Of all the mathematicians gathered round the table, he was the least congratulatory. Just as he did not get excited in the Tour de France when there was a breakaway from the peloton, he was not about to give Simon a pat on the back until his putative result was vetted by experts, and that was not going to happen today. Vito knew that almost always, the peloton catches a breakaway rider, envelopes him, and sometimes spits him out the back of the pack and leaves him behind---broken and punished for unwarranted confidence. And he also knew that even Wiles' proof of Fermat's Last Theorem was found to contain a serious gap after the initial announcement a few years before. Vito had tremendous admiration for the incredible courage and steel nerves which the great Princeton mathematician displayed in making the needed repairs, not buckling under the unimaginable pressures created by his proof's initial shortcoming. In Vito's eyes, Wiles was a true hero, on a par with Lance Armstrong.

"Hey Simon," said Morty, between bites of his second blueberry scone. "What was that business about 'polynomial time'? 'P' is for polynomial, eh?"

"That's right," said Goldman, glowing like a light bulb. "Once again, I'll ask Joe to do the explaining."

Joe said, "Celestine, can y'all take over? I've got to go to the little boys' room. The coffee is working its magic."

He rose from the table and clambered up the stairs, leaving the pedagogical chore to her. She borrowed a pen from the waitress and began to write on a napkin.

"Very roughly speaking, Morty, it goes something like this: If the computer time needed by an algorithm to solve a TSP with N nodes is bounded by a polynomial function like the quadratic N-squared, then it works in 'polynomial time'---where time is interpreted as the number of basic computer operations required."

She drew a network of nodes and linking paths, and wrote N^2 next to her doodle.

"Doubling N only multiplies the solution time by 4 in the worst case, when you have that quadratic bound. But the best time-bound known is *not* polynomial, but *exponential*---think of 2 to the power N as an example."

Celestine scribbled 2^N next to the network and went on.

"This is not nearly as good, because increasing your computing power by a factor over a *thousand* will only allow you to add another *ten* nodes. This explanation is too simple and not exactly accurate, but I could use calculus to show you that in the limit, *every* exponential bound eventually becomes worse than *any* polynomial bound, as N gets bigger and bigger. It's very fundamental---in a way it's all about finding limitations on what computers can actually do."

Bruce said, "Morty doesn't use calculus too often in the ER, so that was just perfect, Celestine."

"Hey, I sort of understand," said Morty. "And Bruce, I *do* remember the product rule from calculus after thirty-five years of never needing it. *Dee hi ho equals ho dee hi plus hi dee ho.*"

"I see," said Aitch. "The Holy Grail is to find an algorithm which solves the Traveling Salesman Problem in polynomial time."

Pierre said, "Yes, no one has accomplished this until now---it is a monumental achievement."

Celestine added, "And the TSP is the flagship for a whole class of problems---they would all then be taken care of as well. It is of profound significance in the theory of computation and complexity, and there are important connections to other areas of mathematics too. Yes, monumental. Congratulations again, Simon."

Simon addressed Aitch and Celestine.

"Thanks. I'd like for us to meet with Joe Malone on Monday morning."

Aitch said, "How about 9 a.m. in the lounge? I'm sure Joe will drop anything he might have had planned."

CHAPTER 9

Revenge of the nerds from Flatland

-37-

Vito told Il Gruppo to be ready to resume riding at 11 o'clock sharp, allowing them another ten minutes at Trout River Traders. Celestine and Aitch meandered onto the porch and sat on a swing, savoring the shade. Simon, Vito, Bruce, Bao, and Bill went outside too, and took seats on a long pine bench, while the others followed Drew's lead and went upstairs to peruse the antiques and doodads. Aitch was about to initiate some smalltalk with Celestine when a battered Dodge Ram and two beat-up sedans squealed into the parking lot, raising dust. The Ram was driven by the bellicose farmer Aitch saw on the Berkshire hill. He got out and walked toward Vito, with seven friends backing him up---three in a Ford and four in a Chevy.

The farmer, who looked to be around forty, had a wild bush of red hair and beard to match---like an extra in *Braveheart.* He was wearing a baseball cap stitched with 'Wally', filthy denim overalls and a sweat-stained sleeveless shirt with the Boston Red Sox logo---the type of singlet called a 'wife beater' in his social circle. Wally was a six-footer coated with a layer of flab, but there was a lot of muscle underneath---a physique resulting from a lifetime of physical labor in the fields and too much Sam Adams. He placed himself at the foot of the porch steps, and the four occupants of the Chevy took positions twenty feet behind him. The three in the Ford stayed put. Aitch was hoping very hard that Big Joe would emerge from the men's room. He would know how to deal with these rednecks, being one himself.

Wally's voice did not match his appearance---alto-tenor, almost feminine.

"You put out my dog's eye, fuckface. I *seen* you do it."

He was pointing at Vito, who maintained his relaxed posture, leaning back on the bench with arms and legs crossed, not moving a muscle. Reptilian.

"Your dog was out of control, my friend," said Vito, with icy gravel in his voice. "You should keep him tied up. I am sorry to have wounded him, but he was attacking one of my riders."

Wally said, "I ain't your friend, so don't give me none of your Flatlander bullshit. I want payback."

There was a thunderous silence, and then Bruce spoke up.

"Did you say *Flatlander?* You're not referring to the classic book, *Flatland, by* Edwin A. Abbott, written in late 19th century, are you?"

Aitch knew that Bruce should shut up, but he had momentum. Bruce McAllister was very proud to be a topologist, despite the fact that he nearly lost his mind and family ten years earlier, when his proof of the Poincaré conjecture fell apart. It was such a painful matter that no one ever ribbed him about it, not even Morty, who first befriended Bruce in the ER after pumping half a bottle of Valium out of his stomach. Bruce had a lot of company in his misery. Over the years, many mathematicians claimed to have proven the Poincaré, which deals with the fundamental nature of three-dimensional space, but they all crashed and burned. And now the jury was out yet again, because some reclusive Russian was claiming to have a proof. We'll see, thought Bruce and all the others who failed at both the conjecture and at suicide.

Wally stared at Bruce McAllister as though he were an alien life form.

"I guess not," said Bruce. "I recommend it highly---it's one of my very favorites. A topological farce which shows what life would be like in a two-dimensional universe. Fascinating stuff---highly imaginative. A tour de force of mathematical humor. I think you might be a circle. No. You are probably a triangle."

Wally hesitated because no one had ever called him a triangle before, and he was confused as to whether or not he was being insulted. He looked over his shoulder at his four associates.

"Yo, Triangle Wally!" one of them called out.

Knowing he had to act, Wally picked up one of the helmets placed near the steps---it was Simon's---and hurled it into the frame of Vito's beloved Gitane.

Vito moved quickly, but Aitch was quicker. The little man had to uncross his limbs before he could launch himself at Wally, and this gave Aitch the split second he needed to grab the back of Vito's jersey as he passed.

"GRANDISSIMI FIGLI DI MIGNOTTA, ROTTINCULO STRONZI, VE LA FACCIO VEDERE IO!"

Aitch got a grip on Vito from behind, holding him under his arms and lifting. Vito's fists were flailing.

"MINCHIONI, TANTO SO DOVE TROVARVI! VI SPACCO IL CULO, A VOI E IL VOSTRO CANE DI MERDA! BASTARDO!"

His legs were churning too, and it appeared that he might twist free. But Celestine took hold of his ankles just in time, while Aitch maintained a tenuous grip around Vito's little chest. Celestine spoke to him a hyper-calm voice, shushing him, imploring him in French to calm down, telling him that it was not worth it. Bruce, who was quite pale now, went inside after announcing that he was going to call the Vermont State Police.

Once it was clear that the homicidal Dago midget was at least temporarily restrained, Wally looked back at his friends for further assurance. Then he picked up Simon's helmet and threw it again, this time into the Trek's front wheel. Perhaps some grudge against the U.S. Postal Service caused him to choose it as his new target.

Simon was still wearing his math glory smile when he rose and planted himself on the top step of the porch, a few feet from Wally. Only Bao and Bill were still seated, and Simon turned towards them.

"Bill, this seems like a particularly opportune time to apologize for what I said to you at the wine and cheese last September. Sorry. I truly meant nothing by it."

"Apology accepted," said Bill Hurker, with a tight little smile of his own.

Now Bao Hoang whispered to Bill.

"Standard four-on-two---*no blood if possible.* Let's get on the sides."

Bill nodded, and the two of them hopped off opposite ends of the porch. They moved the same way---light footed, arms seeming to dangle from their shoulders as they maintained sideways stares at Wally's four friends. It was the Bruce Lee glide, resulting from decades of martial arts training. Three seconds later, Bill stood ten feet to one side of the four-man line, with Bao mirroring his position on the other flank. Both were taking deep, deliberate inhalations through their noses, and they were only in their socks, which was good. The rednecks had no inkling that an ancient, purified and perfected form of violence was about to descend upon them.

"Wally, let's all calm down," said Goldman the peacemaker, with one arm raised like an Indian saying, "How."

He took a step down from the porch.

"It's understandable that you're upset about your dog, but I'm sure we can work things out to our mutual satisfaction."

Uncle Meinhold had instructed him how to behave in situations like this. No trace of anger showed; even when Wally bent down to pick up the helmet again. Aitch was still engaged with Celestine in holding on to Vito when Simon turned towards him and tested his memory.

"Hey, Bumpkin---remember shooting hoops on Margaret Corbin Circle? Remember Murph?"

Aitch's eyes widened and he grunted, "Simon, forget it, for Christ's sake!---let's cool things down!"

"Piece of cake!" said Goldman, but he was not about to be dissuaded. He knew that he had two top class karate goons protecting him, the cops were on their way, he was going to win a million dollars for solving a Millennium Problem---and Uncle Meinhold's presence was tangible.

***

May 21, 1966---Washington Heights

It is a warm Saturday afternoon. Simon and Aitch are playing two-on-two half-court basketball against Vinnie Ricci and Norbert Kissinger at the upper end of Fort Washington Avenue, at 193rd Street. They are near the main entrance to Fort Tryon Park, home of The Cloisters---an annex of the Metropolitan Museum of Art devoted to medieval works, including the fabulous 'Unicorn Tapestries'. The view is similar to that from Meinhold's apartment---the Palisades and the George Washington Bridge are in sight, but from up here the steel span is to the south. The courts are just off Margaret Corbin Circle, near the sites of old Fort Tryon and Fort Washington---important to General Washington because the Continentals could bombard the king's river traffic from The Heights, three hundred feet above the Hudson. But both rebel bastions fell to a force of British and Hessians in late 1776, leaving all of Manhattan under the Crown for the duration of the Revolution. Legend has it that Margaret Corbin participated in the battles after her husband was killed, fetching water to cool the Continentals' cannons. She is believed by some historians to have been Molly Pitcher.

Aitch stayed with Simon and his mother in their spare bedroom the night before. It was a welcome break from the dump he shared with three other Cooper Union students down on St. Mark's Place. Aitch and Simon were studying junior year thermodynamics at the kitchen table all day, and now had mastery of the material. So they decided to do some sports before getting cleaned up and meeting Simon's girlfriend, Mona Hope, and her Juilliard classmate---another British girl named Maureen Hodges, whom she wanted Aitch to meet. Not in the mood for a game of stickball in the P.S. 173 schoolyard, they took the A-Train uptown two stops from 175th Street to 190th. Then they rode the elevator up through Manhattan's bedrock schist to get to the courts.

They have been going at it for over an hour against Vinnie and Norbert, locals who attend Hunter College in the Bronx, where both are majoring in political science---good players who are regulars up here. The rivalry is over two years old. Simon, Norbert and Vinnie often remind Aitch that he is the only WASP they have ever met in their entire lives, and Norbert Kissinger has dubbed him 'Bumpkin'. Simon did not know what he was doing at first, but he was getting pretty good under the tutelage of Aitch, who started at forward for Schroon High School, a million miles upstate. Simon likes to pass the ball to himself off the backboard and then lay it up, a maneuver that Vinnie Ricci calls a 'Goldie'. Now everyone who plays B-ball here uses the term. Some games are played with Goldies allowed, and others with No Goldies.

They have quit at seven games each, and Vinnie produces a

paper bag containing four bottles of lukewarm Michelob smuggled out of his father's grocery store, two blocks down Fort Wash. They are sitting on a bench, watching another game, this one between two blacks and a couple of Micks from Dyckman Street in Inwood. Simon knows one of the blacks from his years at Stuyvesant High School---Kingsley Powell. It is a great game, but elbows are flying. One of the Inwood guys is a real asshole---his teammate calls him Murph. Hotheaded, bellicose, a dirty player and a cheat. He shoves Kingsley Powell on a jump-shot, and Kingsley says it was a foul. He looks to Simon for an opinion.

Simon says, "Foul," because it was.

Murph is holding the ball and he is out of his mind.

"Fuck this bullshit," says Murph.

He strides over to where Simon is sitting, and when he is ten feet away, throws the ball at his head, missing by inches. Simon does not flinch, and rises from the bench. Murph is now standing three feet from him, and they are staring into each other's eyes.

Aitch says, "Hey, he only made the call."

"Shut the fuck up, beanpole," says Murph.

Simon does a quick assessment, like Uncle Meinhold told him he should do when he was in a tough spot. Vinnie Ricci is already gripping a bottle, and appears ready to crack it over Murph's head. And next to him is humongous Norbert Kissinger, who despite his sleepy hooded eyes, thick glasses and doofus demeanor, is quick as a cat and knows how to project power, as he had often demonstrated in past scuffles. He would not hesitate to break Murph and his friend like twigs, if he decided it was necessary to further the cause of world peace. And Simon knows that there is no way Kingsley Powell is going to stand by and watch a fellow Stuyvestanian get stomped by this schmuck.

Simon changes the direction of his gaze, and looks over Murph's shoulder. He thinks of Uncle Meinhold and controls his breathing.

"Hey Murph, here comes a cop," says Simon, just as Meinhold had taught him---and Murph turns his head.

-38-

Simon took the last step down from the porch and stood between Wally and the Trek.

Simon said, "Whoa, there's no reason to trash my bicycle."

"My dog's eye is worth more than that piece of crap."

"Well, probably not. With all the bells and whistles, that thing is worth around three thousand dollars, and I really wish you wouldn't damage it."

Wally looked back toward his friends again, and then to Simon.

"I'm gonna kick your ass," he said, in his redneck falsetto.

A car was coming down the street---just some tourists on their way to a nearby waterfall. Simon felt invincible and intuited how to apply Uncle Meinhold's dictum on distraction in an optimal way.

"Wally, you know, you have really nice tits for a triangle."

Wally froze, not knowing how to respond. Although he could have acted right then, Simon said,

"Well, here come the state troopers, just in the nick of time."

He raised his eyebrows, lifting his gaze a bit to the right, over Wally's left shoulder---in the direction of the car's sound.

Wally turned to look behind him, saw nothing, and before he could refocus, Simon smashed him with a fast roundhouse right with all his weight behind it, aiming at a target six inches behind the nose, the way Uncle Meinhold taught him to do it. Wally dropped the helmet and went down on his knees, clutching his face. Blood spurted through his fingers and pooled on the ground.

Simon scampered back onto the porch, and now the rest of Il Gruppo was there too. Aitch and Celestine were able to release their grip on Vito after Triangle Wally went down. He was calm now.

"*Grazie*, my friend."

Vito de Bernardi knew that he owed Simon Goldman a debt of honor--- something he took with solemn gravity as a Sicilian.

Bruce announced in a whisper that the phone was out of order, and that he intended to head over to the gas station next door, to call the troopers. But he lingered to witness whatever happened, along with the others. The four man line was heading towards Simon, but never reached him.

Bao and Bill closed in on the outside two, and because he thought he might want to ease his conscience later, Bill said,

"Hold it."

But it was too late. The redneck next to him cocked his right fist, so Bill perched on his right foot, looking almost dainty, and with perfect, effortless balance, launched three short, sharp, lightning kicks---struck only with the ball of his left foot---one on a knee and two in the groin. At the same instant, Bao emitted an eardrum piercing scream which shocked his man, who never reacted to a one-knuckle snap-punch to his temple---really just a backhanded flick. He fell like a pole-axed steer, and he was lucky that the ground was soft.

The outcome would have been the same no matter what formation the four were in, but this was too easy---the inner two were forced to delay their participation because of their stupid positioning. They stood frozen in ridiculous back-to-back boxer-like poses, scared witless, staring in disbelief at their three comrades on the ground. Bao and Bill stepped closer, fists dangling.

Bill said, "Beat it---we don't want to damage you."

They skulked back to the Chevy. The occupants of the Ford were now standing beside it, thirty feet away, and one of them reached in and produced a .22 calibre rifle. He was the youngest, still in his teens, and it was obvious that he was the son of the farmer next to him. The kid looked confused and unsure of himself, and Simon Goldman sensed it.

"Put it back in the car, asshole. I'm a Deputy U.S. Attorney---a federal prosecutor. This guy is an ER doctor." Simon pointed to Morty. "He's going to check on your friends, and then you're going to go away, because neither of us needs the fucking paperwork."

Goldman was one hundred percent believable. The kid threw the weapon back into the car and got into the driver's seat. Simon had provided him with an honorable way out, another lesson learned in Uncle Meinhold's street survival school. The youngster might have been the only one with any intelligence---he shouted through the window and commanded the others to get in, including his father.

Morty went down the steps and checked on Triangle Wally, who first tried to push him away, but then allowed himself to be inspected. His nose was not dripping blood any more.

"It's clotting nicely, but it's almost surely broken. Put ice on it and go to the hospital in St. Albans, where they'll splint you. You're fortunate---a broken beak is better than spitting chicklets---trust me. And try to lose a few pounds."

The fellow who Bill kicked was no longer clutching his crotch and could now sit up and rock in pain. Morty checked him too.

"My tentative clinical diagnosis is that you've been kicked in the nuts repeatedly. Apply ice and don't whack off for five years. Only kidding. Four years. You're lucky. It looks like that's only a bad contusion above your knee. Put ice on that too."

Bill Hurker said, "I guess I missed his kneecap---he must have moved a little. You really like ice, Morty."

The third case, the fellow Bao put to sleep with a knuckle to his temple, was a tougher call, a real mystery to Dr. Zeffman. A big, robust twenty-five year old who worked at the feed plant in Northton, he was now standing, wide awake, grinning like a loon and claiming that he did not remember Bao's shriek. Morty looked him over, asked a few questions, performed some simple neurological tests, and dismissed him. One minute later, the entire three vehicle posse was history.

***

"Very strange," said Morty. "I've never seen anything like it. That fellow did *not* have a concussion---his brain, if he has one, wasn't shaken. Actually, except for the short-term memory loss, he appears to be completely asymptomatic. What on earth did you do to him, Bao?"

"Extreme acupressure," said Bao Hoang with a mad grin, and all of Il Gruppo laughed. "Hey Simon, what's the deal with Margaret Corbin? I think I've heard of her. She was Molly Pitcher, right?"

CHAPTER 10

Bei Mir Bist Du Sheyn

-39-

Vito's Gitane was undamaged, but the front wheel of Simon's Trek had two broken spokes, and the ride was over for him. He announced that he would wheel it the quarter mile to his home, and have it repaired before Il Gruppo's next outing.

"Vito," said Simon, "Please be so kind as to tell Mona that she will be driving home alone from your cottage."

Vito bowed and said, "Yes, of course, Simon."

"And Vito, please tell her what happened in as gentle a way as possible."

Vito touched his cap in a two-fingered Sicilian salute and bowed again.

"Yes, of course. I understand such matters," he said, with more respect and humility than anyone had ever seen him display.

Simon gave a V for victory sign and started his stroll, holding the Trek by its handlebar as he rolled it home. The remaining twelve cyclists mounted up. After the prolonged break, their legs felt leaden, and it took a few minutes for them to get back into the rhythm. No one spoke about the incident.

***

After nine kilometers climbing and eleven descending, Il Gruppo arrived at Jay---little more than a country store and gas station situated in a deep valley flanked by some of the steepest, highest mountains in the Greens. The day had heated up beyond what was predicted, and it was muggy as well. All their water and Gatorade were consumed during the climb out of Montgomery Center, so following the downhill run into Jay, Vito gathered his troops and ordered a twenty minute break for rest and replenishment at the store.

Aitch, Celestine and Joe did not go inside, and were content to fill their bottles from a garden hose out front. They stretched out on the grass, flat on their backs in the shade of a gargantuan oak, their helmeted heads close together.

"So what do you think?" asked Celestine, looking up into the sun-speckled leaves. "About Simon's result."

Joe said, "Well, essentially he is making a claim of sufficient speed for his original algorithm, which suprises me a little. Y'all have to understand this is just a gut feeling---but my opinion always was that if the damn thing ever was proven, it would be by somehow *transforming* the original problem."

Aitch's mathematical interests were too far removed from the Traveling Salesman for him to say anything useful, but Celestine had a bit of prior exposure to the general problem area.

"I went to a talk on that issue once," she said. "Since the late 1970's, it has been known that all LP problems are solvable in polynomial time. It was quite a surprise when it was proven."

At least Aitch knew what LP or 'linear programming' was---he had learned about it as an undergraduate at Cooper Union. It involved a simple class of constrained optimization problems---like maximizing profit when production capacity was restricted.

"The trouble is," Celestine continued, "if you try to transform a TSP to an an LP problem, you need to introduce new variables---but then the problem size increases, and rapidly."

"Exactly," said Joe. "It all depends on how much it costs in increased problem size in order to do the transformation. Clever people have tried this approach and some thought for a while that they had the bull by the balls. But there was always a glitch, and there were a couple of suicide attempts. Still, I always thought that was how it would eventually be settled---a conversion method that interacts nicely with the LP algorithm, or some tweaking of it. But Simon is claiming something different. No conversion and then application of LP or something else. Nope. Gold Man seems to be saying he can *directly* prove that his *old* algorithm is polynomially bounded, period. Audacious!"

Vito emerged from the store and whistled a little riff from *La Traviata,* his signal for Il Gruppo to mount up. Celestine sprang to her feet like an acrobat, but Joe and Aitch were slow.

"Let's go, Geezer. *Allons-y!*"

She straddled Aitch, took hold of his hands, and hoisted him to his feet.

"You're raising the dead, Celestine."

-40-

They began the climb out of Jay, the toughest they would face today---so steep that it was known as 'The Wall'. No one was in the mood to push the pace, not even Morty, who would forego brutalizing Bruce today---it could wait until the next ride. Il Gruppo worked steadily, most of them alternating between seated and standing postures, except for Celestine, who only sat. They all focused on the rugged mountain vistas to distract themselves from their uphill agonies.

With a kilometer to go before the crest, Aitch was in front, spinning next to Vito, to whom he was explaining his ideas about applying nonsmooth methods to obstacle-induced bubble formation problems, even though he usually eschewed thinking about mathematics while biking. When he turned his head, he saw Celestine two hundred meters back, riding next to Sonya Jorgenson. From the way their heads were bobbing, it was clear that an animated discussion was in progress.

Aitch was very tired. In a few weeks, after he put in another thousand kilometers, he would not suffer so much on this mountain. He popped in a fig and swigged some water. Even Morty was feeling it today, and only the superhuman Vito de Bernardi seemed immune to fatigue. But then Celestine came blasting past them all, dancing on her pedals for the first time today, grimacing and showing her teeth. Vito squinted and smiled with pleasure as he watched her stop and wait for them at the summit. Perhaps he could teach her to race.

Nearing the top, Sonya tucked in behind Aitch. She was panting, hunched over her handlebars and in pain---broken. The last rider up was Joe Malone, who arrived to a chorus of cheers, huffing and puffing, ten minutes after Celestine first got there. He had nothing left, save his Texan sense of humor.

"It's not the heat, y'all. It's the humility."

They waited until he caught his breath, and then embarked on the steep, curving descent. After crossing the Mississiquoi on a rickety bridge and passing through customs, they were back in Canada. They did the one ascent which remained---the three kilometer Glen Sutton hill ---and then took Scenic Drive into Sutton. It was a roller coaster of a road, downhill for the most part and a beautiful way to finish, with Mt. Pinnacle in view most of the way.

At 2:45, Il Gruppo, minus Simon Goldman, was back in the Post Office parking lot where they started, six hours earlier. Vito invited everyone up to Lac Kelly for drinks and a snack, but no one took him up on it. They were drained and wanted to go home. Vito said he would be sending an e-mail about next weekend's ride, and waved.

"*Amici*, it has been *un bizzarro esperienza culturale. Ciao!*"

He took off. It was only a four kilometer climb up Mt. Sutton to his cottage, and he would sprint because he craved the workout.

***

Celestine looked at her watch.

"Aitch, the Mavens play at six, and it's already almost three. Do you have a double bike rack?"

He said that he did, so Celestine climbed into Bao's van and produced a little knapsack. She had to reach across Sonya, but they ignored each other. Come to think of it, thought Aitch, the two of them did not exchange a word after the climb out of Jay.

"I brought a change just in case there was time for a to visit Vito. Do you mind if I hitch a ride with you to Montgomery and take a shower at your house before the show? That pub on the road, Kerouac's, looked nice when we passed by---maybe we could grab a bite there?"

-41-

They pulled into Aitch's driveway, and after he opened the door of his Honda, the cats hopped in. Newton climbed into Celestine's lap and began to purr, rubbing his head against her hand, leaning into it, demanding attention. She obliged while Minipod positioned herself in a sunbeam on the dash and lay there half-flipped, pretty and squinting with pleasure as Aitch held her upside down head like a baseball, stroking her throat with his index finger.

"Newton likes you," said Aitch. "He probably thinks you're a cat person."

She continued to massage her new friend.

"Perhaps one day I will introduce you to my little Minou in Outremont. Are these two both yours?"

"No, Minipod is a visitor."

"Like me?" she asked, with a soft laugh.

They left their bicycles on the car for now, and went inside. Aitch poured some ice tea and showed her around the house, which she said was very nice, especially the oak floors and trim. Thank God for Mrs. Trudo thought Aitch---no dustballs. But when they got to the attic study, she took in the mess.

"Aha! *Le vrai Professeur Singleton!* I'm just as bad." He did not believe her. "Aitch, if we want to be able to eat before the show, we'd better get moving. Why don't you go shower first?"

This was a sensible plan, thought Aitch, who intended to bide his time and see if something romantic developed after the show. He sat her down in the living room where there were coffee table books, and gave her the remote control if CNN or anything else interested her. Thank God for Mrs. Trudo, he repeated to himself.

He went up to the bedroom, stripped, and padded to the bathroom. Stepping over the tub's rim, he closed the sliding door, turned on the hot water, and set the shower head on 'massage'. He felt the strong spray loosen his back muscles as he soaped up in the steam, humming. Then, as he reached for the shampoo, the door slid open, and there was Celestine peeking in, with the same expression as when she peeked into his office the other day.

"It would be shame to use all that hot water yourself, *Cherie,* when we could share it. Do my back, *s'il vous plait.*"

Oh boy, thought Aitch. *Oh boy!*

***

Forty minutes later they were in his bed. She was on top, and as he held her face in his hands, she bent forward and they kissed, melting together again. They did not move for a few minutes, still entwined, and then she kissed his eyes.

"Cherie, it's five-thirty! The Mavens play in a half hour. Let's shower again and get going!"

He said nothing at first and twirled her dark hair with his finger.

"Yes, let's go hear them," he whispered.

She reached for his glasses on the pillow, and placed them on his face. Newton was on the pillow too, taking it all in and purring.

-42-

Aitch bagged some fruit to tide them over. They hurried to the church and Celestine paid for their tickets, insisting that it be her treat. There were already about two hundred people seated on the lawn, so they scurried to the back and spread their blanket.

Celestine whispered, "Look, there's Simon Goldman with a very pretty lady."

She pointed to the Goldmans, who were near the front on small, ground hugging lawn chairs. Aitch spoke into her ear, making it a kiss, and told her who Mona was. Celestine passed him an apple.

There were four Klezmer Mavens, two men and two women, all dressed in *Fiddler on the Roof* rags. They played a variety of instruments, sang with gusto, and even danced a bit. The audience was enchanted, mesmerized by the music and the virtuosity of the performers. And the acoustics were superb considering the outdoor venue. Aitch thought that the still air and surrounding stand of old maples had something to do with it. The Mavens finished at 8 p.m. when the stars began to show themselves, and their last number was *Bei Mir Bist Du Sheyn* done in three different styles---classical ghetto, 1940's swing, and to everyone's amazement, hard driving rock-and-roll. Celestine hoisted him to his feet, just as she did earlier in the day at Jay. Then they made their way over to the Goldmans, who were folding their lawn chairs.

"We are in mathematical celebratory mode, dearest Aitch," said Mona, as he bent to double-kiss her. "And Vito told me about the Meinhold-inspired showdown you little boys were involved in at Trout River Traders, so I am also celebrating the fact that Wonder Boy is still alive."

Aitch said, "Cutest Mona, please meet Celestine Sauvage, a new assistant professor in our department, and one, we are very fortunate to have with us."

"I'm afraid we made rather merry before coming here," said Mona. "We had the leftover putanesca and as usual, too much vino."

One thing was certain. Whatever he had, Simon was wasted and in a purple haze. Comfortably numb. He must be completely certain about his Holy Grail, thought Aitch, to let himself go like that.

Celestine said, "Simon, would it be okay if my students, Nathan Finkelstein and Ibrahim Ibrahim attended your talk on Monday morning?"

Goldman was falling off his feet, but managed a barely coherent okay.

Aitch said, "Too bad you guys have already eaten. We're walking over to Kerouac's for a bite. Care to join us anyway, maybe for dessert?"

Simon was not very perceptive at the moment, but Mona sensed that something was happening between Aitch and Celestine, which warmed her. She declined Aitch's offer on behalf of herself and her nearly comatose Wonder Boy, whom she chastised for being so out of it. Aitch gave Simon a parting bearhug, lifting him off his feet.

"See you on Monday, little buddy."

He told Mona to take extra good care of him and to not let him drive.

-43-

The stars had just come out in full and they interlocked pinkies during the walk to the pub, identifying constellations, discussing gravitation, and how Einstein made the incredible intuitive leap of realizing that what we experience as a mysterious tug is in fact a warping of spacetime's fabric. There was a twenty minute wait for a table, so they shared a Sam Adams at the bar---and before they knew it, gravitation had given way to nonsmooth calculus.

Celestine said, "We must really be fanatics to be talking mathematics here, especially tonight. But at least we're not writing on a *serviette* again."

Aitch told her about the time he and Vito de Bernardi were attending a fluid dynamics conference at the University of Chicago, twenty years ago. They were so engrossed in a mathematical discussion that they did not notice the restaurant they had chosen for dinner was actually a seedy South Side strip club. A fearsome bouncer with hair on his knuckles seated them up front, near the stage. But a few minutes later, the gorilla had to move them to the rear, because the girls were complaining. They were becoming demoralized by the tall skinny guy with thick glasses and the bald midget who were drawing pictures on a napkin like a couple of retards, not watching the show.

Aitch thought that the anecdote would get a chuckle out of her, the effect it always had on others. But it devastated Celestine, who laughed for a full minute with her eyes streaming, even as the hostess led them to their table. He kidded her, saying that he couldn't tell if she was laughing or crying. She tilted her head.

"Aitch, why were *you* crying at the beginning of Nathan's seminar? Or perhaps you couldn't decide whether to laugh or cry?"

He congratulated her on her powers of observation. Then he recalled his erectile hyper-function in the office a few days ago, and changed the subject to the menu. After a few minutes, on his recommendation, they both ordered the prime rib, rare, and agreed on a California merlot.

"Celestine, if you don't mind, can you tell me what the heck was going on between you and Sonya Jorgenson during the Jay climb? It didn't look to me like it was only a friendly competition."

"It wasn't," said Celestine. "It was pretty unfriendly. I was angry."

Aitch looked at her, drawing her out.

"It concerned Nathan and Ibrahim. You will probably think I'm an idiot."

"Try me."

"It was that Longshoreman Philosopher business. What's his name again?"

"Eric Hoffer."

"Sonya assumed I would be supportive about what she was doing, so she told me the full details. I think she is arrogant this way. While you and I were finishing lunch in the Mad Cow on Monday, she went and spoke to Nathan and Ibrahim at their display tables in the Mezz, and offered them a bit of money to participate in a study which I think she dreamt up while she was sitting with us. Of course they agreed---they can barely feed themselves. She was sure I would go along and be appreciative that she was contributing to my students' support. She told me that she took them to lunch on Tuesday and gave them forms and questionnaires to fill in, because she is interested in how strongly her predictions, based on Hoffer's work, will hold up. Actually, I think she will try to show that the two of them really *are* twins, psychologically. Like they are her guinea pigs. How will Nathan and Ibrahim feel when they read her article in a year or two? They look so tough and hard at their stupid tables, but they are delicate and gentle like lambs---sensitive, and so talented. Everyone calls them 'the twins' as if they not real people. Sonya was so proud and eager when she told me her plan. I lost my temper because it was all behind my back. Who the hell does she think she is? That's what I was thinking. I said some bad words to her and accelerated up the hill. She tried to catch me to give some bad words back. But after she couldn't keep up, she just shut up. That's what was going on. I guess I'm a hothead. That's what some people say about me."

"Wow. Now I understand," said Aitch. "I *thought* I saw her eyes light up in the Mad Cow."

"She should have spoken to me before signing them on. I'm their supervisor! I want them spending their time on mathematics, not some *maudit* psychological experiment! *Tabarnouche!*"

She banged her fist on the table, shaking the cutlery. Now Aitch realized how the tiny town of Tabernash, Colorado, up high near the Continental Divide, might have acquired its name---he used to cross country ski near there at Devil's Thumb during his most recent sabbatical. It must have been a French Canadian *voyageur* or mountain man ancestor of hers who decided on it in the early 1800's. Perhaps some Cheyenne or Arapaho were pursuing him. Who knows, maybe he was the same witty fellow who named the Big Tit Mountains in Wyoming, although *Les Grand Tetons* sounds so much classier. Might have been the guy, thought Aitch. Could be.

At first he wanted to tell Celestine to grin and bear it in the name of academic freedom, and besides, Sonya violated no rules, so why make waves? But he said nothing. Celestine was unleashing her maternal instinct on the twins, and there was no fighting it. If things flared to the point that Sonya showed up at his door carrying her Valkyrie battle-axe, then he would intervene---and only then.

"Celestine, listen. I have some grant dollars I could contribute to your students' support, and I would give Yu Wong an equal amount---it appears that he will do his doctorate with me. I have him looking at certain things---exactly the kind of issues you suggested might be amenable to a nonsmooth approach. I owe you one for thinking of it."

"That's kind of you, Aitch. *Très gentile.* Yu Wong is very good---maybe even great. Let's get him to participate in the nonsmooth seminar. Also, I will ask Nathan and Ibrahim to invite him to attend Simon Goldman's talk. When they are older, they will be able to boast that they were present when Goldman's Theorem was first presented."

"You're right, Celestine, thanks. And by the way, Simon has a lot of grant money as well as Von Essen dollars---and no grad students. I bet he could help support the three of them. Especially after his theorem is announced---he will have even more funding after that---and he's a very generous guy."

As they were finishing their salads and starting on a second basket of hot bread, the main course arrived. The food and wine removed whatever static remained in the air, and their conversation shifted to a review of Il Gruppo's ride, after which Aitch told her that for him, it was the most memorable ever.

"Yes, a lot happened on that ride," said Celestine.

He raised his glass.

"That's not what I meant."

She clinked and reached for his hand.

***

At 1:00 a.m., he was on his back, in the Jesus position, very depleted in all ways. She was curled on her side and stroking Newton. who was on Aitch's chest, squinting. Newton liked feeling his heartbeat, she told him---that was why he sat there. They spoke about Simon's breakthrough, and shared a laugh when Celestine revealed that *she* was his first choice as a sounding board.

"Logical, of course," said Aitch, with a chuckle. "That's Simon Goldman for you. Too darn vain to tell me that you rejected his request, and then he impulsively lashes out like a little kid with that ridiculous business concerning your teaching. At least I understand it now, although it seems a bit extreme, even for him. I guess he hasn't been sleeping much lately and his faults are magnified. Don't take it personally, Celestine. He's really a good guy, in spite of his egomaniacal idiosyncrasies."

"Aitch, obviously it's Joe Malone that Simon needs to convince about his theorem, not us. He is a top combinatorist and connected to others, including Chen's powerful group at Yale." Newton was purring so loudly that she had to raise her voice. "Mona really loves Simon. *Vraiment mignon*---cute, the way she called him 'Wonder Boy' when she chided him. After today, I see him differently. It's obvious he got a lot of affection growing up."

"Yes," said Aitch, as they started to drift off together. "His mother doted on him, and he had a wonderful uncle who was like a father to him."

-44-

December 10, 1965---Washington Heights

It is Friday evening, and Aitch is a guest at Uncle Meinhold's for dinner. It is the festival of Chanukah, and the menorah has been blessed and lit. As usual, everyone speaks English and not German, for Aitch's benefit. He is stuffed on Tante Lotte's knackwurst und sauerkraut, and he has had two pieces of strudel for dessert. Lotte and Simon's mom, Mathilda, adore Aitch and have made it their project to fatten him up. But after two years, all their efforts have come to naught---he is still as skinny as a stick. They tell him that they are not giving up, and are pleased that he will be staying in town for the summer, so that he can visit more often. Simon and Aitch are going to work for the New York City Department of Parks in Coney Island, starting in June. 'Shitpicker' was the unofficial job title, and that was an accurate description of what it entailed---walking up and down the beach in a green uniform, armed with a needle-nosed broomstick and a sack, spearing trash. It was a wonderful summer job, and the pay was decent too.

The women have dispatched Aitch, Simon and Uncle Meinhold to the living room, getting them out of the way so that they can clear the table and wash the dishes, with the help of Rutie and Eva-Leah. They take seats in big, soft easy-chairs, and Meinhold turns on the TV. Not for the first time, Aitch is struck by the resemblance between Simon and his uncle---the same slight yet sturdy physique, the same blue eyes and straight sandy hair. Simon and Aitch agree to join him for a little while, after which they have to hit the books again, because a mechanical vibrations exam loomed on Monday. The boys decline his offer of schnapps, and he pours a stiff one for himself. A hockey game is on, and Meinhold is a rabid Rangers fan. One of the New York forwards is covering up while getting pummeled by a Bruins defenceman in front of the Boston net, and Meinhold does not like it one bit.

"HIT HIM WITH YOUR PURSE, *ASCHLOCH!* BE A *MENSCH*, FOR CHRIST'S SAKE!"

Tante Lotte yells even louder from the kitchen and instructs her husband in German to watch his language in front of Simon's friend. Then she orders him not to sit too close to the rabbit-ear antenna, because he might spoil the reception. This has been a running joke in the family for years---the creation of Simon's father, Gustav Goldman, who died of a heart attack eleven years ago. It is a reference to the steel plate in Meinhold's skull.

***

Meinhold Mannheimer sailed for America from Hamburg in December of 1938 at the age of sixteen, accompanied by his younger sister, Mathilda. Their parents were slower than most German Jews in heeding the warning signs, but after November's *Kristallnacht*, the writing was on the wall. Their father, a well-to-do optician in Frankfurt, sold everything, bribed the right officials, and obtained exit visas for his children. There were distant cousins in New York who would take Meinhold and Mathilda in, and their mother and father would come to America as soon as they could manage it. But they never could, and all contact was severed. Mathilda and Meinhold never saw them again.

Throughout the war, the young men of Washington Heights were being drafted or volunteering for military service. Many of the German-Jewish ones, brand new American citizens, went into intelligence units because of their linguistic credentials. Staff Sergeant Gustav Goldman was one of these. He interviewed POW's with glee and filtered their documents at divisional headquarters, never near the front line.

"In the rear with the gear and chair-borne," Gustav would boast to Meinhold after the war, reminding his best friend and brother-in-law that he hit Omaha Beach on D-Day Plus 22. Gustav also liked to point out that he outranked Meinhold by one bottom stripe on V-E Day, and was therefore earning two dollars more per month when the war in Europe ended.

But Meinhold Mannheimer would have none of it. When the war began, he was enraged that his parents were taken from him. And he was still angry about the way he was shunned by his classmates in Germany, many of whom had joined the Hitler Youth. So to outdo them and get payback, he qualified for and served in the 101st Airborne Division---the Screaming Eagles. He made the jump into Normandy the night before D-Day, landing fifteen miles from the intended drop zone. He is loath to discuss his experiences during the ensuing few days, which earned him a Bronze Star, except to call this period his 'all expenses paid vacation in France'. He also made the jump into Arnhem four months later in Operation Market Garden. "Piece of cake," is all he says about it, even though the history books say it was a bloody mess.

Uncle Meinhold never told Simon anything detailed about his experiences in the war, except for one time seven Decembers ago, on the eve of Simon's bar-mitzvah, when he explained why he believed in miracles, and why he felt that every day he was alive was a bonus, which he thought was a pretty good philosophy for everyone and would make the world a better place.

***

On the bitterly cold and snow-blown Christmas Eve of 1944, twenty-three year old Sergeant Meinhold Mannheimer, Meinie to his friends, was shivering in a foxhole on the undermanned line outside the strategically critical crossroads town of Bastogne, Belgium, at the height of the Battle of the Bulge. The 101st was surrounded, out-gunned and outnumbered, but General McAuliffe had told the Krauts, "*Nuts!*" when they demanded his surrender. After that, the standing order for the entire perimeter was the same.

Hold at all costs.

Not an inch of ground could be given, because there were insufficient interior lines---it was to be a last ditch stand. There would be no reinforcements or re-supply because Patton's army was still too far away, and the weather was so bad in the Ardennes that an airdrop was out of the question.

Sergeant Mannheimer was number two in the platoon now, in charge of one of its depleted squads. Most of his friends from jump school in Georgia had been killed during the past six months, and he owed his life to some of them. He was due for his three hour sleep break off the line, but volunteered to be here this evening so that the number one, Lieutenant Riley, could attend the Roman Catholic mass being held at the battalion HQ, two hundred yards back. Riley was okay for an officer, and Meinie knew that the favor would be returned.

Lieutenant Riley had him sharing a foxhole with an eighteen year old replacement from Iowa, a strapping farmboy named Clemons, who didn't know his ass from a hole in the ground and needed mothering. They had conferred about him because Riley was afraid that Private Clemons was going to fall apart, and he needed every swinging dick up on the line. Sergeant Mannheimer called out to the four other foxholes he was responsible for. All eight men yelled back that they were okay, but indicated in various impolite ways that they could do with a bit more ammo, and that they wished Patton would get his fat ass moving and bring some armor with him.

But Private Clemons was not okay. He was lonely and desperate for friends, but nobody wanted to get to know the FNG's---the Fucking New Guys---because they were likely to get killed soon. The kid had never been under fire before Bastogne. He was green and had no time for proper seasoning, battle-shocked and ready to crack. Sergeant Mannheimer saw that Clemons had developed the shakes after the last enemy probe, an hour earlier.

There were six grenades on the lip of the hole along with two rounds for the bazooka which Sergeant Mannheimer had scavenged yesterday. They had two belts left for the .30 calibre machine gun they were manning, and each of them had only four eight round clips for their M-1 Garand rifles. That was it. They were keeping a watchful gaze on the moonlit field in front of them, their breath producing clouds of white vapor, and they were glad that the big flakes of snow coming down were covering the corpses of the dozen SS panzer-grenadiers they had scythed earlier, with Meinhold doing the shooting and the kid feeding in the belt.

Meinhold was vigilant, slowly sweeping the Kraut line with his ponderous field glasses, freezing vapor hissing from his nostrils. Clemons broke the silence and in a quavering voice, teeth chattering with fear and cold, implored Sergeant Mannheimer for some assurance.

"Sarge, we're gonna get out of this crappy mess, right? We're gonna make it home, ain't we?"

He had to be given an ironclad guarantee, or he would surely break. But Meinhold had been through enough to know the truth. It was only a matter of time before the Krauts got their shit in a rectangle and made a big push, next time with their armor in front. And it would come in this sector, judging by where they were concentrating their forces---he could hear the clanking of their tanks getting into position. The defences were spread much too thin around Bastogne---they were sure to be overrun. They were dead men.

Sergeant Mannheimer lowered the binoculars. Keeping one double-gloved, nearly frozen hand on the MG, he reached into his overcoat pocket and produced the *dredel* that his girlfriend Lotte had sent in her Chanukah package. There were four Hebrew letters on the sides of the child's toy, a small square-shaped top for spinning.

N G H S

Ness ***G****odol* ***H****ayaw* ***S****ham---A great miracle happened there.*

Meinhold told Private Clemons to keep the dredel for luck and to busy himself by spinning it on the plank of wood at the bottom of the hole. He showed him which Hebrew character was the N. If Clemons could get N for *Ness---Miracle*---three times before the imminent attack, then they would both live to be one hundred and twenty years old, he told the boy.

"Guaranteed," said Sergeant Mannheimer. "Piece of cake. Start spinning. You owe it to yourself."

So Private Clemons set to spinning the dredel as ordered, and on his first spin he obtained an N, and on his second, another N, and on the third, yet another! Meinie liked shooting craps with the other noncoms, and was good with numbers. He produced a long whistle of surprise.

"Kid, hitting N-N-N is a sixty-four to one shot."

***

A long ten minutes later, as they were sharing a Lucky Strike and a gloomy, vaporous laugh, the Krauts let fly with a salvo of 88's to soften up the American line. The fuses were timed for air bursts, and one round went off thirty feet above them, dead center on their hole. Clemons was untouched---just some ringing in his ears. A miracle. But a hot shard of shrapnel had penetrated Sergeant Mannheimer's helmet and chipped off a one inch square piece of skull bone.

Lieutenant Riley interrupted his prayers and rushed up front even before the barrage abated, and when he saw Meinie laying there in a pool of blood, he wept. He never thought Meinie would get it---the little guy seemed indestructible. But he was still breathing. Clemons was big and strong---a high school fullback---so Riley pulled himself together and ordered the kid to put Sergeant Mannheimer over his shoulder and get him back to the medics immediately, even though they were pinned by an enfilade from the pair of MG-42's the Germans had on their side of the field. Clemons did not hesitate. He hoisted him up and made his dash to the aid station with such strength, speed and agility that the German machine gunners could not get a bead on him. Men witnessing it pumped their fists and roared. It would forever be remembered as 'Clemons' run'.

The medics just barely managed to stabilize Sergeant Mannheimer, and as they worked, one of them sucked hard on his cigarette and mumbled,

"Kid, it's a goddam good thing you risked your ass dodging all that lead to get Meinie to us so fast."

Then Private Clemons completely mystified him.

"No risk at all, doc. *No risk at all!* I got three N's on my first three spins! N is for miracle! I'm gonna live to a hundred and twenty. Guaranteed! Piece of cake! *I GOT THREE N'S IN A ROW!*"

And then he scampered back to his hole, zigzagging like Jim Thorpe, bullets splattering the snow around him, with a broad grin on his face and not a care in the world. The troopers in the other foxholes were galvanized. They cheered him again and one hurled insults at the enemy, criticizing their marksmanship. Before today, that was Meinie's specialty, because he could do it in flawless German.

That medic was pretty hardboiled and thought he'd seen it all here at Bastogne, but Clemons' condition was new to him. After he hauled on his cigarette again, spat, and got back to work dressing Sergeant Mannheimer's wound, he shook his head in wonder and said to his colleague,

"Clarence, I swear, if we have enough fucking lunatics like him on the line, we just might hold out until lardass Patton gets here."

***

Meinhold regained consciousness a few days later in a hospital near London, good as new, with a piece of steel alloy replacing the missing chunk of skull.

"A miracle, as is the fact that Bastogne held," the surgeon told him, and Meinhold would never forget.

***

In 1955, shortly after Gustav Goldman died, the family learned that Mathilda and Meinhold's parents were on the passenger list of the SS St. Louis---the infamous ship which was denied entry into the United States in 1939 and forced to return to Germany with hundreds of desperate German-Jewish passengers on board, most of whom would die in the holocaust. Mathilda and Meinhold Mannheimer knew that their parents had perished---the Nazis were excellent record keepers---and the new German government informed them in 1949 that their mother and father were murdered in 1943 at Bergen-Belsen. But the cruel information about the St. Louis tore open the old wounds and devastated Mathilda. At her lowest point, soon after the information about the ship and a month after her spouse's death, she told Meinhold that if it wasn't for Simon, she would surely throw herself off the George Washington Bridge. It was a constant temptation, she said.

Meinhold assuaged her grief. He was a successful young stockbroker, and promised to help her raise Simon in all ways, including supplementing her small income as a saleslady at Wertheimer's department store. He told her that she must forgive America, because the genocidal intent of the Nazis was not known in 1939. And he said that he always wanted to have a son. Meinhold said that he would honor

Gustav's memory and take Simon places, show him things, and teach him how to take care of himself.

He was true to his word, and just as he never let his buddies down in Normandy, Holland, and Belgium, he never let his sister or his nephew down either. Meinhold's Bronze Star and Purple Heart are behind glass in the dining room cabinet, along with the menorah that Lotte brought out of Germany in 1937, and a stack of Chanukah cards going back twenty years to 1946. Meinhold receives one from John Clemons---now Congressman John Clemons of Iowa---every year, without fail. Clemons' political career was not hurt by the fact that he was a recipient of the Congressional Medal of Honor.

For conspicuous gallantry and courage under fire, at Bastogne on December 24, 1944. Under heavy machine gun enfilade and completely exposed, Private John L. Clemons carried his wounded squad leader to his battalion aid station. Upon returning to his position, still under fire, with utter disregard for his own safety, Private Clemons single-handedly repelled an armored attack, destroying two Panzer tanks with a bazooka and killing over twenty of the enemy at close quarters with miscellaneous small arms.

"Too bad he's a Democrat," Meinhold said in 1960, when Clemons was first elected to the House of Representatives. "But if he ever runs for president, I think I'll vote for him anyway."

***

Tante Lotte comes into the living room between the first and second periods of the hockey game, and plants herself on Meinhold's armrest. She hugs him hard and kisses his scar. Lotte tells the boys that in addition to causing TV reception problems, the steel plate in his skull makes Meinhold stubborn, and she raps her knuckles on his head. Meinhold flashes an impish grin and says it also makes him smart---that's why he married Lotte---and she kisses him again.

CHAPTER 11

Androcles

-45-

On Sunday afternoon, after a morning of mathematics, Celestine and Aitch went for a gentle spin to Eden and back, and in the evening, she found enough ingredients in his kitchen to put together a stir-fry. He drove her home afterwards and went to bed early---but around 3 a.m. Newton woke him by leaping from his chest to the window sill, eight feet away. The cat put his nose against the screen and gazed in the direction of the shed. Aitch got up and looked out, but could see nothing, even after his feeble two-legger night vision kicked in.

***

Monday morning came with rain and a stiff wind. At 8:20, Aitch pulled his poncho over his clothes, donned his Tilly hat, and headed out to hear Simon's talk. Recalling Newton's strange behavior during the night, he decided to first check on things out back. He poked around, and everything appeared normal---until he looked in the shed. There was just enough light for him to discern a dark, glistening puddle in a corner. Laying in it were the remains of several rabbits---three, because that was how many earless, nearly skinless heads he made out. A one foot square piece of hide from some other animal was there too, but Aitch did not know what it was. He suspected that he was looking at the handiwork of a fox, and that would represent a dire threat to Newton and Minipod. So he decided to take the shed down this evening, even if it was still raining. But twenty minutes later, as he was pulling into his parking spot outside the Fitch Sciences Building, he realized that if there was a fox in the backyard last night, then Newton would not have been so calm. And didn't foxes reside in burrows? This evening, he would investigate further.

***

He made it to the lounge ahead of everyone else, so he could get a pot of coffee dripping. Upon opening the door, he was confronted by the sight of Isidore Fleck on the sofa, snoring like a buzz saw, with his filthy knapsack serving as a pillow and his face covered by an open text on superstring theory.

"*Izzy!* Izzy, wake up! *Jesus!* There's a talk here in a few minutes! I'll make some coffee."

Izzy sat up slowly, his joints audibly creaking. He placed his hands on his knees and rocked himself awake.

"I'm sorry, Aitchie---I must have passed out studying."

He pointed to the textbooks, monographs and reprints of journal articles strewn on the coffee table.

"Witten's theory is a brain-buster. I guess I got too tired."

"That's okay. You're not exactly a spring chicken any more."

"Very true, my young friend---but I nevertheless have a lot of catching up to do. I need to hurry up and cram it all in. Not much time left. You know, when Einstein was my age, he was already dead for five years."

Aitch forced a laugh and exchanged an extra gentle high-five with the old-timer.

Izzy said, "Let me guess what's happening. Simon Goldman is going to spill his mathematical guts. Am I right?"

"Big-time, Izzy. Put superstring theory on hold for a while and stick around. You're about to be an eyewitness to history."

Izzy smiled beneath his scraggly beard, and rubbed his hands together like a child expecting a treat.

Aitch got the coffee started, and a few minutes later Celestine came in, accompanied by Yu Wong and the twins. She brought a bowl of green apples, and within seconds, the three grad students and Fleck were each working on one. Joe Malone and Simon Goldman arrived right behind them. Goldman was wearing an old Harvard track suit, and after everyone took coffee, he strode to the front to fiddle with the overhead projector. He used his first slide to make sure the device was in focus.

A NEW RESULT IN COMPLEXITY THEORY
S. GOLDMAN

It was written handsomely in blue, and underlined in red. He reached into his knapsack and produced several sets of notes, each consisting of thirty stapled sheets.

"Izzy, lucky for you I made extras."

Izzy templed his hands in gratitude sprinkled with mock worship.

Goldman explained, "What you have in your hands are photocopies of the transparencies that I'm going to show you---only those are in glorious technicolor."

***

Phil Schwartz entered the lounge. He resembled a disheveled undertaker, his black garb and dark mullet accentuating the chalk dust, which always covered him, mingling with his dandruff. Schwartz was the department's sole mathematical physicist and unofficial leader of Everyone Else. He was missing two fingers on his left hand, the result of an exploding package sent by the Unabomber in 1988. Phil was chosen at random by the deranged mathematician-terrorist and anti-modernity crusader, and this horrid luck added vinegar to his already sour outlook on life. He was the Rodney Dangerfield of the department. Not that he had a sense of humor---he did not---but like Dangerfield, Phil felt that he didn't get no respect. This was not due to a lack of accomplishment, because in the mathematical physics community he had some visibility, and his work on Frobenius manifolds was sometimes cited by mathematicians who mattered. It was just that here in his own department, he felt that nobody cared a rat's ass about mathematical physics, except for Izzy Fleck, who was not really part of the department anyway. Schwartz refused to consider a joint appointment in the Department of Physics or an outright transfer there---options that Slutnick often tried to tempt him with, because the Virgin Queen would then owe Mathematics a senior level hiring, and one of the main groups could be strengthened. But Phil Schwartz said no way, the physicists at UNV were a bunch of incompetent deadwood putzes, and he would not besmirch his scientific reputation by being associated with them.

Phil was looking for lounge-lizard Izzy so that he could pump him about the hidden, curled up spatial dimensions of superstring theory, and how the fabric of spacetime could tear. He always looked angry in an abstract way, and now even more than usual, because he was craving caffeine. Without acknowledging anyone's presence, he poured himself a cup and grabbed an apple without a by-your-leave. There was no love lost between Schwartz and Goldman, who bitter Phil viewed as a conceited, overpaid, overprivileged invader from the very day Simon took up his Von Essen research professorship. Simon called him 'Phil the Pill' behind his back.

"Hi, Philmeister. How are things on the dark side? Take a seat and welcome to my spiel. It'll take maybe fifty minutes. Treat yourself to a set of notes---no charge."

Phil took a packet, said nothing, looked at no one, and chose a threadbare armchair. Aitch got up and locked the lounge door, after hanging the 'Meeting in Progress' sign outside.

Simon said, "I trust that you all will find these notes sufficiently complete. I think the material is quite self-contained. The definitions are elementary and straightforward, and where I used existing results that you might not be familiar with, particularly in combinatorics, I gave the references. And wherever I used something that is obvious, I said so. So, without further ado, here is the first slide."

The overture of his talk was devoted to defining the Traveling Salesman Problem, discussing the history of the P vs. NP problem, and explaining that the Holy Grail was to show that every TSP was solvable in polynomial time. When Goldman put his mind to it, he was a great expositor of mathematics---a pleasure to listen to and to learn from---one of the best. Not at all like in MATH 101. His penmanship was precise and flawless, a neat combination of script and printing. Even his marginalia were legible, and he used five colors to add highlighting. It was clear that he thought of this lounge lecture as a dress rehearsal.

Goldman defined a special class of problems, which he labeled 'class G'---these were TSP's that possessed a certain combinatorial property, which he called 'property G'. Using a laser pointer to great effect, he explained how property G could be viewed as a structural attribute of the network of nodes and roads in a Traveling Salesman Problem. Then he spent ten minutes giving an overview of his seventeen year old algorithm, which he referred to as the 'G-algorithm'. After this, he introduced a preliminary result which he said was of significant interest in its own right.

Theorem 1. *Every TSP of class G is solvable in polynomial time by the G-algorithm.*

The proof was so elegant that Joe Malone oohed and aahed a few times during its exposition, prompting Simon to put the laser dot on the big Texan's forehead at one point, threatening to blind him if he did not quiet down.

"Now that I have identified my new class G of TSP's which are polynomially solvable by my G-algorithm, the next step in my analysis is to show that this class is sufficiently rich, or in a sense, 'dense' in the space of *all* TSP's, in such a way that it suits my purposes. My next theorem accomplishes this, and it includes the Holy Grail."

Everyone was struck by how egomaniacal the presentation was. In mathematical talks, it is taboo for the speaker to refer to his results with the personal pronoun 'I', just as it is a no-no to use the possessive 'my' too often---as a rule, the royal 'we' and 'our' are supposed to fulfill these functions. And labeling everything with a 'G' was also way over the top. Aitch thought that his friend must have wigged out with some form of malignant narcissism, because his lecturing style was normal during his audition for the Von Essen position five years ago. On the other hand, he had to admit that Goldman was, if nothing else, honest and accurate. But Aitch did not realize that there was something subliminal at work on the audience. The outlandish pomposity and confidence of Simon's delivery and his blatant quest for posterity mesmerized them all, even Phil the Pill, who was in a paroxysm of rage. They believed every word he said, except perhaps Izzy, whose features were scrunched in an expression resembling confusion.

Goldman flashed his next slide---the one that would make history.

Theorem 2. *Given an arbitrary TSP, there exists a class G TSP* *with the same number of nodes, whose solution time via the G-algorithm does not exceed that of the original TSP. Therefore every TSP is P.*

The proof was a mathematical tour de force involving a new technique, which Simon called 'G-interpolation'. Although the result was in the realm of combinatorics, it was interesting and curious that in an indirect way, the details involved a geometric argument and even a bit of elementary finite dimensional point-set topology.

"*Quid erat demonstrandum,*" said Goldman when he was done. "QED to you non-Swahili speakers. Piece of cake."

The room was silent for a few seconds. Izzy Fleck was sitting stone still and appeared not to be breathing---his eyes were shut and the lids were twitching. Aitch became alarmed and thought that the old man might be experiencing a heart attack or some sort of seizure, but it soon became apparent that Izzy was okay because his carotid artery was pulsing steadily. Celestine broke the ice with gentle applause, and everyone joined in, except of course, Phil.

Simon said, "Thank you all for coming and for paying attention. I hope some of you find the time to peruse these notes and go over my arguments in detail."

Joe Malone knew Simon meant him, because he was the most qualified audience member to check the proof, and in fact, as good as anyone in the world.

"For however long it takes, that's all I'll do," said Joe, with a hearty thumbs up. "An honor, Simon."

Aitch rose and said, "Thank you Simon, for the excellent talk, and for allowing the people in this room to be present when mathematical history was made."

He led a second round of applause as Phil poured himself another coffee---black and unsweetened, his morose features contorted with anger under his ill kempt mullet. He put the last apple in his pocket and stormed out.

Aitch said, "Simon, I hope you don't think I'm going to let you beat me on Wednesday just because you solved a Millennium Problem."

Simon laughed, saying that such a thought could not possibly have occurred to him, and that he had already booked the court. Izzy shuffled over to where they were standing, opened his mouth, raised an emaciated arm and gestured as though he was about to say something, but then, like an airplane stalling in mid-climb, he plopped onto the sofa.

-46-

Aitch hustled down the hall to catch up with Malone, and asked him to get in touch as soon as he was ready to pronounce his verdict on

Goldman's theorem. Then he followed Celestine to her office and closed the door behind him.

"Cherie," said Celestine. "I won't do it on my desk, if that's what you're thinking. I'm not that kind of girl."

"Actually, that wasn't on my mind, but now that you mention it..."

She poked his solar plexus.

"Celestine, I was wondering what you thought about Simon's proof."

"Aitch, I wish I was an expert in combinatorics and complexity like Joe, but there's no way my imprimatur would have any meaning, even if I took a few weeks to learn the necessary background material. I'm disqualifying myself, but I must say that it does look amazingly nice. Listen, Cherie, I'm going for a swim, and on my way I want to speak to Nathan and Ibrahim. I'd like you to hear what I have to say to them. Come join me, if you can."

***

Ten minutes later, they were in the sub-sub-basement, and she was rapping on her graduate students' door. Aitch had not been down here in years, but now that Yu Wong was under his wing, he was curious as to what the scene was. He noticed the mezuzah fixed to the jamb, detected the aroma of oriental food, and began salivating. Yu Wong stuck his head out, put a finger to his lips and whispered.

"They only take one more minute."

They watched as Nathan and Ibrahim completed their noon prayers. Nathan was sitting below his Ariel Sharon poster, reading from a small black prayer book in his hand, rocking back and forth, while chanting in archaic Hebrew and Aramaic. Ibrahim was kneeling on his prayer rug, facing Mecca, which meant that he was looking at a wall, and reciting in Arabic. Aitch observed that each had a small pile of Oreos on his desk. Yu Wong tiptoed to the microwave, removed three Styrofoam containers, and placed them on the table. He had already set it for three, and for the first time, with chopsticks. Today he would teach his friends their proper use.

The twins finished praying within seconds of each other. They stood, looked down, and mumbled their hellos to Professors Singleton and Sauvage. Celestine did not beat around the bush.

"Guys, we won't interrupt your lunch. I just want to mention something. Nathan and Ibrahim, Professor Jorgenson told me that you both will be participating in her project, and that you will fill out detailed questionnaires so that she can compare your personalities. The thing I want you to think about carefully is the fact that she will surely try to write a journal article based on this, and no one can predict what it will say. I offer no advice to you---I simply want you to think about it."

The twins glanced at each other, put their gazes back onto their shoes, and grunted their thanks.

"Well, that's all," said Celestine, "Except that Professor Singleton and I would like you to participate in our Nonsmooth Analysis seminar, Yu Wong. Perhaps starting the following week, so you will have time to prepare."

"Professor Sauvage, I can be ready this Wednesday."

"Great! So I suggest you each speak for 45 minutes on Wednesday morning. Let's see if we can finish Chapter 2 and move on."

Yu Wong asked if the professors wanted to share the food, of which there was an ample amount---Szechuan beef with green beans, Egg Foo Young, and fried rice with scallions.

The twins murmured, "Yes, yes---please, please."

Aitch and Celestine were tempted, but left.

***

Yu Wong now knew beyond any doubt that his friends required his protection. He was already concerned about their participation in Professor Jorgenson's study because of how upset the questionnaires had made them. And now Professor Sauvage implied how hurt they would be if a journal article was written that somehow categorized or humiliated them. It was too much---he had to take action. He closed his eyes and listened to his inner voice for two minutes, and an idea crystallized in his exquisitely wired brain---a scheme that was divine in its simplicity and symmetry.

"Gentlemen," said Yu Wong, with an inscrutable smile. "I know way you can feel good about Professor Jorgenson's research project."

He made a bed of rice on each plate.

"Do you gentlemen still have delightful forms you were filling in?"

-47-

At 5:30 p.m., as Aitch was unlocking the front door of his house, he heard the phone ringing. He dashed to the kitchen to pick it up. It was Joe Malone, and he was excited.

"Howdy, y'all. I've gone over the Gold Man's notes. I checked every one of his combinatorial arguments, and verified his references carefully. I'd stake your life that they are all correct. Brilliant and original stuff, Aitch. I went through the geometric arguments too. They're correct as well, and those things which he says are obvious really do appear to be obvious. I asked Simon if I could show the notes to Chen and his combinatorics group at Yale, and he said yes. Chen jumped at the chance when I phoned him, so I scanned it and e-mailed him the PDF file. He and his three compadres studied it all day, and

Chen phoned me ten minutes ago. They concur! Simon also okayed my showing the notes to one of my Ph.D. students and to my postdoc---they're both real good, Aitch---with orders to drop everything and go through it. They concur too. Good Lord, Aitch! *Good Lord!*"

***

Newton was at Aitch's feet, rubbing at his shins the way he did when he wanted something.

"What's up, Newton? Show me."

The cat ran to the front door and tapped it with a paw. Aitch opened it, but Newton did not head out, and when Aitch looked down, he saw why. There, on the welcome mat, lay a beautiful albino rabbit, which was not there five minutes before. It was dead---that was obvious ---and from the angle of the head, it appeared that its neck was broken. There were no other signs of violence on its body. Aitch picked it up. Still warm.

Now Newton galloped to the shed and leaped onto the sill of its broken window. He looked at Aitch, produced a beeping sound, and dove in. A throaty chirp came from within. Aitch went over, still holding the rabbit. The slanted evening sunlight did not provide much illumination, so he went to the door and swung it open.

There was just enough light to see him. The great cat was stretched out with his paws extended, but the rear half of his body was turned on its side in a relaxed posture. The rippling power in his shoulders and hindquarters was apparent nonetheless, and his thick, bushy, black-tipped tail was over four feet long. The catamount was not young. His whiskers were gray and white, and there was a tired sadness in his eyes. A foot long scar marked his flank---perhaps an elk's antler had gashed him long ago. Aitch sensed that this animal was always wild, never under anyone's control, and even though his heart was racing, he did not feel threatened. He intuited that he was already familiar to this fellow, and in all likelihood had been under his scrutiny for some time.

Between the catamount's paws lay a fawn whose throat he had torn open. To dismember the carcass, he held it on the floor with two-inch claws while tearing off strips of flesh with his teeth, using his sinewy neck muscles. Then he began to eat.

A few small, bloody scraps had fallen to the side, and Aitch became dizzy with wonder when Newton beeped a thank-you and started feasting on them, not more than one foot from his large cousin. And then Minipod bounded in through the window, squeaking her hello in midair. She landed on the floor with a springy thud, and with great daintiness began lapping at the puddle of warm blood seeping from the kill.

When they finished, the three carnivores began to clean themselves, licking their forepaws, rubbing them against their faces, and their combined purring made the walls hum. Aitch recalled that

Boulderites feared for their domestic cats when lion sightings were reported, and knew that he was observing cross-species feline behavior never thought possible. The catamount paused during his grooming and looked straight at Aitch, who, although mesmerized and transported by what he was witnessing, had the presence of mind to lift the rabbit to his lips, caress it, and say, "Thank you, catamount, thank you," as he backed out.

Three minutes later he returned with a large pot of water, and placed it on the shed's floor.

"You've come a long way, haven't you, Chingachgook?"

He thought about geography. If the naturalist he heard on the radio the other day was correct, and this cat was the last of a remnant tribe of eastern cougars, then Aitch's guess was that he had followed an unbroken swath of forest between here and some remote location. The woodlands of northern Quebec or Maine's Hundred Mile Wilderness were possibilities, and in either case he must have crossed many frozen rivers. The catamount rose and began to lap the water at Aitch's feet. He looked up and squinted, still purring.

CHAPTER 12

Bandwagon

-48-

On Tuesday morning, Aitch phoned Beatrice Beauregard. He told her that Chairman Slutnick would definitely want to make time for him today, to hear what he had to say concerning Simon Goldman's progress. She put him on hold, and after a few seconds, informed him that now was good.

***

Beethoven's Pastoral Symphony was playing on Slutnick's sound system. He was at his easel, working on a watercolor. It was a landscape---the panoramic view to the north from his window, centering on Lake Carmi and the lofty mountains beyond. He was wearing a stylish denim apron over his Ralph Lauren polo shirt and Calvin Klein slacks. Guillermo was barefoot, with his tassled Gucci loafers and silk socks placed on the high pile carpet, near the base of the Esmeralda obelisk. Between dabs, he employed his paintbrush as a conductor's baton, and at the moment he was leading the New York Philharmonic. The music, the painting, and his role as maestro had melded.

"Hello, Guillermo---sorry to interrupt. That's really quite good. Very peaceful."

Aitch seated himself in one of the stiff wooden chairs for visitors. Guillermo rinsed his brush in a cup of water, dipped it into emerald, swished in a bit of vermilion, and then with rapid, delicate strokes, added some magical highlights to the tops of the trees in the background, making them seem to shimmer and tremble, as though rustled by a breeze. He closed his eyes and allowed his brush to follow the music. In anticipation of a crescendo, he pointed to the string section at the precise moment it was to come in. Aitch was very glad to have caught Chairman Slutnick on a high.

"I'd use real paint---oil, preferably, or even acrylic---if one could open a fucking window in this building---but this will have to do. I understand that you have something solid to tell me about our good and great friend, Simon Fucking Goldman."

He rinsed his brush again, and began diluting part of a mountain.

"Yes, and you will be pleased, Guillermo."

Slutnick continued to dip and dab, now adding streaks which suggested dark nimbus clouds off in the distance.

"Please, please me."

Aitch laid it all out, and after a five minute explanation of

Simon Goldman's mathematical breakthrough, Slutnick had a complaint.

"Too bad there isn't a fucking Nobel Prize for Mathematics, know what I mean? What were those Swedish putzes thinking when they determined the categories? Poor Goldman will have to settle for the million dollars the Clay Institute offers for solving a Millennium Problem. That ought to get UNV a bit of attention, no? We will then be the envy of the entire civilized fucking world, will we not?"

Slutnick shut his eyes again and allowed a Beethoven flourish to enrapture him.

Aitch said, "Maybe there's a way to package Simon's theorem as Mathematical Economics. Then he might win a Nobel Prize, like John Nash did."

Guillermo did not realize that Aitch was kidding, and ruminated on the idea. But after a few seconds he deviated to reality.

"No, forget it---too much of a stretch. Goldman has a beautiful mind and possibly an invisible friend, but let's not get greedy. I can pimp him for other honors later. Okay, here's how we'll play it."

He dipped his brush and added a few streaks of sunlight to the background, behind the clouds.

"We will have Goldman give his dog-and-pony show this Saturday morning, May 31---in our seminar room---let's say 10 a.m. We want working stiffs to be able to attend, so that's why it has to be on the weekend. When you tell this to Goldman, if he tries to make some wise-ass comment about not working on the sabbath, say I anticipated he would, and that he should blow it out his ass."

"With pleasure, Guillermo. You can count on me."

Aitch did not like to cuss, but if he was only quoting Guillermo, it would be okay.

"Goldman's talk is to be fodder for the masses. A pleasant mix of 'Math for Chimpanzees' and a Discovery Channel special, know what I mean? And you make extra goddam fucking sure that it's sufficiently dumbed down so that even UNV administrators can understand it. I will contact them, the Von Essens, and various local assholes---*excusez-mois* ---dignitaries. I'll also take care of the media. That reminds me---tell Goldman to trim his goatee and wear a suit and tie---he's going to be on television, for fuck's sake. In fact, tell him to wear what he wore during his big audition five years ago---red tie, white shirt, blue suit---red white and blue for the Von Essens. We want the room to be packed---allowing for standing room and ignoring the fire regulations, we could squeeze in maybe two hundred warm bodies. I'll have Beatrice arrange a video feed into an adjacent classroom in case there's an overflow. I want you to invite the local mathematics community---our department, the Montreal universities, Burlington, maybe Dartmouth and nearby SUNY schools---but mostly this will be a lay audience. Did that expression ever seem odd to you? A *lay* audience?"

"No, not until now, Guillermo."

"To continue. Put this out immediately by phone, e-mail, fax and carrier fucking pigeon. E-mail me the announcement too---I'll have Beatrice forward it to my contacts as well."

"Okay, Guillermo---good plan. I'll get right on it."

"Wait. Tell Goldman the talk is to be 45 minutes long---not one fucking minute longer. Some of these people have short attention spans and find it difficult to attenuate the moment of the mind---know what I mean? Goldman probably doesn't need to be told, but remind him to grovel like a grateful worm in front of the Von Essens, because their generosity provided him with the opportunity to do his important research, yada-yada-yada, okay? And he should say a few kind words about our administrators too, if he can come up with something without choking on his own vomit. In the announcement, say that there will be a continental brunch at 11 a.m., courtesy of our department. I'll have the divine Ms. Double-B arrange the catering from Montreal."

"Anything else?," asked Aitch.

With perfect timing, Guillermo pointed his brush towards the horn section and let their blasts take over. He puffed his cheeks and blew on the landscape, trying to get it to dry faster.

"Yes. Also get a critical mass of top complexity mavens to come here a few days later and listen to him give the same fucking talk he gave yesterday---his full schtick with all the gory details. Besides Hopalong Malone, get Chen and his Gang of Four from Yale, Ramesh Goopta from MIT, Yuri Ledyev from the Steklov, Marco Bertoli from Padua---you get the drift. In fact, try to have Hopalong make the contacts for you--- let's shoot for a dozen combinatorial glitterati and complexity cognoscenti to be there. None of them would turn down such an invitation---to be in the room when a historic result is presented ---know what I mean? Especially if I cover up to $1000 toward their travel and accommodation. Offer it---I have some discretionary funny-money available, and I can sell my soul to the Virgin Queen and get more if I have to. Also tell them which limo to take from the Burlington airport, offer some hotel choices, and so on---actually, I think Beatrice put all that crap on our website last year. Mention that I need their original travel, hotel and restaurant receipts before they leave Vermont, or I can't fucking reimburse them. See if you can schedule this for a week after the first talk. This time of year it shouldn't be hard to get academics to agree to any day you specify. Try for Friday."

Guillermo mixed turquoise and white, and began to add suggestions of choppy waves to the lake.

Aitch said, "That's June 6. D-Day."

***

Aitch telephoned Simon and told him what Guillermo had planned, as well as the pedagogical, political and pragmatic fine points he had raised. Goldman said that Slutnick was a genius at this kind of stuff, and that since he was a loyal soldier and departmental patriot, he was willing to go along with any and all of Guillermo's machinations, short of lecturing in the nude. Aitch, who was mildly disappointed that Simon did not attempt a sabbath comment, thanked him for his professional attitude, and then set about composing an announcement for the first talk.

SPECIAL PUBLIC INTEREST LECTURE

UNIVERSITY OF NORTHERN VERMONT
DEPARTMENT OF MATHEMATICS

Saturday, May 31, 2003, 10 a.m.
Fitch Sciences Building---Room 233

"A NEW THEOREM IN COMPLEXITY THEORY"
Professor S. Goldman
Horst Von Essen Professor of Mathematics

Abstract: A longstanding and famous mathematical question has been answered. It relates to a real-world combinatorial problem called *The Traveling Salesman*, and deals with its solution speed. No formal mathematical background is required.

Continental brunch at 11 a.m. following the lecture.

Aitch generated a mass e-mailing to mathematicians at nearby universities in Quebec and New England, just as Guillermo had specified. Vito de Bernardi read the message in Montreal minutes after it was sent. He telephoned Aitch and asked him what he thought about Il Gruppo attending the talk en masse, consuming muffins and fruit at the brunch, and then riding from UNV at around noon. Aitch said he thought that an Il Gruppo carbo-load at his department's expense was an excellent idea, and that his office and Celestine's could serve as changing rooms. So Vito sent out his own e-mail message.

Dear Il Gruppo:

The attached announcement is self-explanatory.
Let us honor our friend Simon Goldman with our
presence, and then ride from UNV at noon, after

snacking. We will have facilities to change into
our stretchies.

Vito

Knowing Vito de Bernardi as well as he did, it was now even more clear to Aitch that Simon Goldman had entered the select group of personages who had Vito's respect and admiration. Avenging the little Sicilian by breaking Triangle Wally's nose, combined with the fact that he had found the Holy Grail, placed Simon in Vito's personal pantheon.

-49-

Celestine gave Aitch a swimming lesson later that afternoon. She lent him her spare goggles, and spent twenty minutes getting him to concentrate on 'swimming through the eye of the needle'. Then she set him free to do a metric mile---thirty lengths of the fifty meter pool. It took him forty-three minutes---pathetic by any standard. But she declared that there was hope for him, and next time she would work on his kick and teach him how to do a proper flip-turn. He was exhausted when he finished his laps, and suggested that they head to his house for a barbecue dinner, and then watch the tube in bed.

"Just like an old married couple," said Celestine.

***

Later, in the Honda and halfway home, he decided to inform her about the catamount---it would be immoral not to do so. But when he told her that a wild beast had taken up residence in his backyard shed, she started giggling like a little girl. So as he became more emphatic, she responded by slapping her knees and rocking with shrieks of laughter. When he got to the part about Newton gorging on Chingachgook's leftover scraps while Minipod lapped up the blood, she was hysterical and in the throes of a Grade-A, Force-10 fit, incapable of any form of communication.

He pulled into the driveway and sat with her until she calmed. Then they walked to the house, and she saw the offering on the porch before he did. It was a hedgehog, and a big one. She bent and touched it.

"Still warm."

"It's not a joke or a trick, Celestine. No visible wounds---strangled probably. That's one of their techniques. This is a gift."

"Or rent ," she said.

***

They had wakened him. He yawned, showing teeth designed by Nature to rip the trachea out of an elk---then shut his eyes, and resumed his siesta. Celestine pointed to the floor under the window, and there were

Newton and Minipod, curled up in a late day sunbeam and napping too. Aitch left her alone with the cats for a few minutes as he went to fetch fresh water, after which they tiptoed out.

Walking back to the house, Celestine said, "We are witnesses to something holy, Aitch---a miracle. That cat is the most beautiful thing I have ever seen. My heart is deeply stirred."

"I feel the same way."

"Aitch, did you see Chinnie's testicles? They look like furry tennis balls! And you should have heard him purr when I petted him! Like a motorboat."

Petted him? A shiver of trepidation ran down his spine as she took his hand and led him to the bedroom.

In their previous couplings, Celestine had been passionate and uninhibited, but always gentle and patient. But this evening she was volcanic. She stripped in three seconds and tore the buttons off his shirt to speed him along, because he lagged---and his attempts to kiss and caress were met with instant, impatient ferocity. Her breaths were loud grunts as she threw him onto his back and climbed on top, with clenched teeth and glazed, unseeing eyes. She gripped his shoulders, and as she crested, her nails drew blood. After her delirium tapered to mere panting and she lay across him semi-comatose, he found himself praying out loud, imploring Jesus for strength, pleading that his fifty-six year old body would be good for the long haul.

***

The next day's seminar by the twins and Yu Wong went well, and afterwards, Aitch, Celestine and Izzy made their way down the hall to the lounge. Aitch poured coffee for the three of them.

"Any comments on Simon's theorem, Izzy? Joe Malone and other experts have expressed faith."

The old mathematician began spooning his sugar.

"I'll be honest with you, Aitchie. I dropped superstring theory completely for the past two days and did nothing but sit in the library and study Goldman's arguments. And check his references. I had to absorb quite a bit of modern combinatorics, I must say. Can't find a bug in any of it."

Celestine said, "But your tone of voice does not reflect confidence, Izzy."

"Yeah, well, that's just me and my skeptical nature. It'll take me a few more days---then I'll feel better about it. I'll go over it one more time, but after a break. I want to relax for the rest of the day and study spatial ripping with that punk, Phil Schwartz."

***

Aitch and Simon played their regular one o'clock squash match, and Aitch won this time, 3-2. They stretched, imbibed the Gatorade that

Simon was required to purchase, and headed for the fountain of youth. As always, the near scalding, churning water made their heads feel light.

"You played well today," said Simon. "You know, it's funny---a kind of instability inherent in sports, I suppose. A one per cent change in how you feel can result in a huge difference in performance. I wonder if it's ever been mathematically modeled."

Aitch said, "Like the butterfly flapping its wings in Peking and affecting weather in the Caribbean. True, I felt good today, but who knows about tomorrow? It makes me wonder what will happen as we age and lose that first one per cent of mental ability, as is sure to happen, unless we die first. Will there be a precipitous drop in our mathematical strength, or will it be a gradual, mellow decline, as in other aging processes?"

Goldman said nothing. He pinched his nostrils and slid under the steamy foam for the better part of a minute---then resurfaced.

"So, Simon---how does it feel, being on the brink of tremendous fame and glory?"

Simon rubbed his goatee.

"I don't want fame---only glory in the eyes of those few individuals who matter."

"Well, the million bucks won't exactly hurt either, will it, buddy? Fame *and* fortune. Not bad. Not bad at all."

"It'll be nice," said Goldman. "No doubt about it. I suppose I should view it as a reward for all the years of toil I spent on that problem."

-50-

Chinnie's routine was unchanged over the next few days. He liked to stay in the shed when there was daylight, but stuck to the forest otherwise, not showing himself except to drop an offering at the door. Friday evening, before a dinner of *lapin au catamount,* Aitch followed Celestine's lead and stroked their lodger behind his ears. But he was not prepared to go as far as her in showing affection---she had graduated to hugging the beast. Aitch was happy that she was otherwise back to normal, and had not scratched him since Tuesday.

On Saturday morning, they locked their bicycles onto the Honda's roof rack, put their gear in the trunk, and headed for Simon's public lecture. Aitch was wearing decent jeans, white socks under his sandals, a polo shirt and a Boston Red Sox baseball hat. To a mathematician, this is considered dressed up. Poor Simon, thought Aitch---he would have to wear a suit and tie. Celestine Sauvage did not factor in social pressures at all, and wore her biking stretchies. She had her hair up, under a UNV brimmed cap, and to Aitch she could not have looked more beautiful.

***

The seminar room was already nearly filled at 9:50. Near the door stood an easel upon which was mounted a poster announcing today's special lecture, as well as a blown up photograph of the goateed speaker.

DR. S. GOLDMAN
HORST VON ESSEN PROFESSOR OF MATHEMATICS
SPECIAL PUBLIC LECTURE:
"A NEW THEOREM IN COMPLEXITY THEORY"

Guillermo had been banging the media drum for days, and as a result, television crews from two local news affiliates had set themselves up at the back of the room. Both the Burlington Herald and Green Mountain Sentinel had reporters, cameramen and photographers present. Aitch and Celestine located themselves near the middle of the room. The excitement was palpable.

The seats in the first two rows had name cards on them, reserving places for select personages. Aitch pointed out the Von Essens to Celestine. Horst Von Essen, who had recently celebrated his 105th birthday, was pushing a walker. He had blotchy skin, moist, glazed eyes, and his lips were moving---but whomever he was speaking to was real only to him. Old Horst clung to his stubborn pride and refused a wheelchair, even though his every step required herculean effort. He was flanked by his son Rolf, seventy-nine years old and relying on a cane, and Rolf's son Ludwig, who was in his early fifties. A fusillade of flashbulbs popped as Guillermo Slutnick led the Von Essens to the front row. All three wore dark blue suits, white shirts, and red ties, which Aitch knew was their uniform. Red, white and blue for the Von Essens. Ludwig helped his grandfather into his seat, and placed the walker in front of him.

Celestine put her mouth near Aitch's ear and whispered, "These benefactors have a very distinctive look. And Chairman Slutnick is dressed just like them."

The family resemblance between the generations of Von Essens was indeed striking and unmistakable. Each was of medium height and built like a Prussian war horse, with blue-gray eyes and a full head of spiked crewcut hair---steel gray but with a trace of the original blond remaining. They sat ramrod straight, neither smiling nor speaking, staring without expression towards the front of the room.

Slutnick exited and re-entered, now ushering in another group of dignitaries. This time he seated two state senators and the mayors of St. Albans and Enosburg Falls. Aitch recalled Slutnick's similar ministrations towards these same glitterati five years ago, when Goldman was auditioning for his endowed professorship, and he had not lost his touch. After yet another dash to the door, he returned with Rector Dr. Friend, the Virgin Queen, and her toady, James Carver. Tall, busty Margaret was wearing a navy blue pantsuit, with a frilly white blouse and red kerchief. Carver was in uniform too.

At 9:55 the seminar room was packed. Most of the UNV mathematics faculty was present, as were every one of its graduate students. The prospect of a free gorging after the talk was their main motivation---'slopping the hogs' was how Slutnick referred to the necessity of feeding them when he told Beatrice how much food to order for the brunch. Celestine waved to Vito, who like her, was already clad in his biking clothes. He was a Fellow of the Royal Society of Canada, and felt entitled to dress however he saw fit. Then Aitch caught a glimpse of the Goldmans loitering in the hallway near the door, waiting for Simon to be introduced. Something did not look right. He excused himself to Celestine, wriggled to the aisle and hustled out of the room.

He hugged and double-smooched Mona.

"Simon didn't sleep a bloody wink and threw up twice. And he spent the entire bloody night in his study, because he was too sick to sleep and felt that doing mathematics would help. Can you believe it? And no bloody breakfast, of course."

Simon said, "Bumpkin, don't listen to this ostentatious fear mongering. I'm fine. How's by you?"

He was ashen and his eyes looked as red as his tie. Aitch placed his right palm on his friend's forehead.

"I don't think you have a fever, Simon, but you sure feel clammy. Have some water."

Simon obeyed, which was unusual, and took a drink from the fountain.

Aitch said, "Morty Zeffman's probably in the room next door. Want him to look you over?"

"No, there's no time. Not enough time. I'll be fine. Nothing to worry about. It'll all work out okay. The show must go on. Piece of cake."

Aitch peeked into the classroom next door---the one handling the overflow via a video feed. He saw several Il Gruppo riders and waved to them. Everyone from last week's ride was either here or in the main room, except for Sonya Jorgenson. He squeezed Simon's shoulder, told him to knock 'em dead, and scampered back to his seat.

-51-

Guillermo strode to the podium and used a control on the dais to flick the lights. He clipped a wireless microphone to his lapel, and the room fell silent.

"Welcome, esteemed visitors and honored guests, to this special public interest lecture. For those of you who do not know me, my name is Guillermo Slutnick, and I am the chairman of the Department of Mathematics at the University of Northern Vermont. The past three decades have witnessed the resolution of two great mathematical mysteries, both of which have intrigued and confounded the greatest minds for many years. The Four Color Theorem, first conjectured about one hundred and fifty years ago, was finally settled in the 1970's by Appel and Haken of the University of Illinois. And the proof of Fermat's Last Theorem, sought for over three hundred years, was at last provided by Wiles of Princeton University. The great popular interest in these achievements stems from the fact that the statements of both conundra are so easy to understand."

Suddenly and with shocking nimbleness, Horst Von Essen reached for his walker, pulled himself to his feet, pointed at Slutnick and shouted.

"*SITZEN SIE, SCHIESSKOPF!*"

Celestine looked at Aitch, in need of a translation.

He whispered, "I think he just said, 'Sit down, Shithead.' "

She cracked up, and Aitch had an unobstructed look at her inner eight year old. But she was able to keep her hysteria private by covering her face with both hands and slowing her breathing, while others in the crowded room squirmed with that curious reaction of embarrassment which one can feel on behalf of strangers. Horst remained standing, quivering and dribbling, until Rolf and Ludwig cajoled him into sitting. They were red-faced and upset, but as soon as the old man was calm, both resumed their straight-backed, forward staring postures.

Slutnick pretended to be unfazed by Horst's outburst, and showed transparencies which elaborated on the two historic mathematical breakthroughs he had mentioned. The first slide showed a map of a fictitious island continent consisting of a dozen countries, identifiable because each was shown in one of four colors---red, blue, green or yellow. Guillermo explained that once one formalizes the reasonable blob-like properties a 'country' needs to possess, then four colors suffice to color *any* map. That was the Four Color Theorem.

Guillermo said, "At first blush, it might seem that the Four Color Theorem would require a topological proof, but in fact, the proof uses networks---that is, systems of nodes and connecting arcs. As you will see shortly, the setting of Professor Simon Goldman's own monumental theorem is also in the realm of networks."

The second transparency was devoted to Fermat's Last

Theorem, another result which Slutnick said was "...well known but true". This bit of mathematical lore, first stated by Pierre de Fermat around 1630, asserts that the integer equation

$$\mathbf{X^N + Y^N = Z^N}$$

has no positive solutions when N exceeds 2. Of course, Guillermo told the audience, if N is 2, then the equation *is* solvable, as anyone familiar with the Pythagorean Theorem knows---for example, $3^2 + 4^2 = 5^2$. He took the opportunity to say that Pythagoras was both an ancient Greek as well as an ancient geek, giving credit for the quip to an anonymous UNV undergraduate. He saw it as grafitti in the men's room of the old Bunt Building, but he wisely did not mention that. The slide also showed infamous words of Pierre de Fermat.

I have discovered a truly remarkable proof which this margin is too small to contain.

Guillermo said that Fermat probably knew that he had no proof, and his tone suggested that good old Pierre was, at least in this instance, a crapologist. He explained that Fermat's proof, if he ever actually thought he had one, was the first in a long string of false ones, and the enigma was only settled three and half centuries later.

"Lies, damned lies, and bluffs," said Guillermo, charming all in attendance with his bold humor. His explanations created quite a stir, because many in the audience never imagined that they were capable of understanding the statements of problems that had stymied and bedeviled the greatest mathematical minds for ages.

"Today, Simon Goldman---the Horst Von Essen Professor of Mathematics here at the University of Northern Vermont and arguably the greatest applied mathematician in the world, will present, for the first time, a theorem which ranks alongside the famous ones I have just described. Like those results, it is not difficult to state, and its proof has befuddled the greatest geniuses for many, many years. And like the aforementioned monumental theorems, its history includes many false starts and false proofs. Professor Goldman's result---sure to become known as 'Goldman's Theorem', is the first truly great mathematical achievement of the twenty-first century."

Old Horst reached for his walker, and before Ludwig could restrain him, rose once more.

"*WO IST MEIN FREUND, FELDVEBEL GOLDMAN? ICH MÖCHTE FELDWEBEL GOLDMAN SEHEN!*"

Aitch whispered to Celestine, "He wants to see his friend Sergeant Goldman."

The Green Mountain Sentinel photographer popped a couple of flashless shots of Horst during the outburst, and one of the news cameramen recorded it as well. Ludwig produced a pill and reached for a water bottle mounted on the walker. He inserted the medication into his grandfather's mouth and helped him chase it down with a drink. Slutnick hoped that it was a very strong sedative. He decided to cut short his blather and vacate the podium, having absorbed more than his fair share of abuse from Horst Von Essen.

"Without further ado, it is my honor and privilege to introduce Simon Goldman, our Horst Von Essen Professor of Mathematics."

Simon entered to applause and popping flashbulbs. Guillermo removed his mike, attached it to Goldman's lapel, and took a seat in the first row. Old Horst could not get up onto his feet because the meds were beginning to kick in, but he could still bellow.

"*ACHTUNG, FELDVEBEL GOLDMAN! ACHTUNG!*"

Goldman covered the microphone and greeted him in the fluent, Rhineland accented German he had learned in his youth.

"Wie Sie sind, Feldvebel Von Essen?"

Aitch whispered, "Horst Von Essen was a sergeant---a *feldvebel*---during the First World War, refusing an officer's commission despite of his aristocratic background. Simon was once a sergeant too, as were Rolf, Ludwig, Simon's father, grandfather, and his Uncle Meinhold. I'll explain it all to you one of these days, Celestine. It's kind of crazy. A blue collar solidarity kind of thing."

"Old Horst von Essen seems to really like Simon Goldman," said Celestine.

Then she pointed out that Mona had not yet taken her reserved seat. Aitch guessed that she was viewing the monitor in the overflow room, unable to watch Simon suffer in the flesh. And she probably also wanted to line up Morty Zeffman to examine him as soon as the show was over.

Simon remained seated on a stool next to the projector, using a pen as a pointer, directly on the transparencies. After three minutes, Guillermo tiptoed to the dais and fiddled with the acoustic controls to increase the volume, because some in the audience were finding it difficult to hear Simon's weak monotone utterings. To Aitch, Simon seemed like an enfeebled automaton compared to the booming braggart who exposited the other day. What saved the talk were the high quality of Simon's transparencies and the earthiness of his pedagogy, which made reference to last week's Il Gruppo outing, the nodes on Morty's map, and the concomitant explanations involving polynomial time. He gave the history of the Traveling Salesman Problem, including some of the algorithms which, for a while, held the record for problem size, mentioning his own 1989 procedure, this time with appropriate modesty. Aitch was relieved that Simon was less egotistical and self-referential than during his talk in the lounge a few days ago. That was totally nuts, he thought. Goldman flashed a slide.

UNSUCCESSFUL ATTEMPTS AND FALSE PROOFS

"We'll skip that one," he mumbled.

Next he stated his theorem, and gave some heuristics instead of a real explanation of how his proof worked. He concluded with thank-yous, mentioning the Von Essens' great philanthropic generosity and contributions to culture in the Green Mountain State, as well as Chairman Slutnick's visionary qualities and leadership. And as Slutnick had requested, he sucked up to Rector Dr. Friend and Dean Fulton, saying that they provided the facilities and atmosphere at UNV in which important scholarly activity can be conducted.

"Whatever the heck that means," Aitch whispered.

Celestine liked it when he allowed a little academic subversiveness to shine through.

Old Horst turned to see who Feldvebel Goldman was talking about, and his gaze settled on nubile form of the Virgin Queen. He raised his eyebrows and took in a lungful of air.

"ACHTUNG! ACHTUNG! SCHÖNE BRÜSTE!"

"He seems to appreciate Dean Fulton's anatomy," Aitch explained.

-52-

After the talk, the men's room was busy, and Aitch was in line for a urinal. He saw Guillermo twenty feet away, near a sink, engaged in a jovial, animated discussion with the photographer from the Green Mountain Sentinel and one of the TV cameramen---the ones who had recorded Horst's misbehavior.

Guillermo was saying, "And I hope that you edit your material in a way commensurate with our mutual goals of presenting this event in the most positive possible light."

He shook hands with them, and pressed a folded bill into each of their palms. Aitch saw the bearded visage of Ulysses S. Grant---a fifty dollar bribe for each venal journalist.

***

The brunch was held outdoors, on the lawn in front of the Fitch Sciences Building. A beverage trolley was parked under a tent, and next to it there were stacks of fruit, yogurt cups and pastries which Beatrice Beauregard arranged to have delivered from Guillermo's favorite Montreal *patisserie* this morning. The two dozen graduate students in attendance were the first to get at the food, and some stuffed their pockets and knapsacks, even as they gorged. Aitch walked over to Izzy, who was spooning heaps of sugar into his coffee, and handed him a cheese croissant.

"So, Izzy---enjoy the talk?"

They exchanged high-fives, and Aitch sensed that Izzy was less wobbly than usual.

"I didn't attend, Aitch. I was in the lounge, going over Simon's proof some more. I'm convinced that his combinatorics are correct, so now I'm checking every unreferenced fact he used, including things he labeled as 'obvious'. Then I'll be sure."

"Izzy, you really earned that croissant. Take another. Tell me, why are you such a Doubting Thomas about Goldman's theorem?"

"One pastry is plenty for me. My skepticism stems from the fact that his proof is so short. Not a very scientific reason, is it, Aitchie? When it's published in a journal, it'll be what---maybe fifteen, twenty pages? I don't know---a problem that formidable---one that's been around for so many years---you'd expect more."

Aitch thought about it. He knew that the proof of the Four Color Theorem was very long and involved. In fact, it was so complicated that it incorporated computer calculations. He recalled that at first there was some debate in the mathematical community as to whether a proof is really a proof if a machine does part of it, but nowadays little dissent is heard. And he knew that the full version of the proof of Fermat's Last Theorem, in two articles, totalled over a hundred pages. So Izzy had a point, even if it was just visceral. On the other hand, perhaps Simon's insights were so profound that a short proof of the Holy Grail was possible. Aitch was very glad that meticulous old Izzy was taking his time with it.

Celestine was in the shade of a transplanted maple, conversing with the twins and Yu Wong. Aitch waved to her and then walked over to Morty Zeffman, who was standing with his best friend and constant annoyer, Bruce McAllister.

"Hi gruppoids. Morty, you ought to save your map for posterity. It could become a collector's item."

Morty laughed and said that he would stash it somewhere safe and sell it someday so that he could afford to send his three daughters to Ivy League universities. Physicians in Canada don't earn nearly as much as their American counterparts, he reminded Aitch for the fiftieth time. Socialized medicine was to blame.

"Morty, did Mona ask you to look Simon over a few minutes ago?"

"She did, and I did. I'm only seventy percent confident about what I'm saying, because obviously I didn't give him a proper exam in the hallway---just felt some glands, looked at his eyes, tongue, and so on. To me, it looks like his condition is stress induced. I don't think it's toxicity or a bug, or the onset of some major disease. Stress is my guess, combined with its evil cousin, insomnia---a leading cause of insanity, as Bruce can confirm.

Bruce said, "He certainly didn't look very good. Maybe he's overworked, like poor Morty here, who only has enough spare time to exercise eighty hours a week."

He did not mention that Goldman's state reminded him of the insomnia and insanity which he experienced a few years ago, when his proof of the Poincaré Conjecture went south and he tried to end his life.

***

Aitch weaved through the crowd to join Celestine and the three graduate students.

Nathan was saying, "Yes, Professor Sauvage, quantum theory says that randomness is part of nature, but on the other hand, Einstein said that God did not play dice with the universe."

Yu Wong and Ibrahim required an explanation of what playing dice meant, and after Celestine provided it, Ibrahim said, "What you say is true, Finkelstein, but there is no conflict with Einstein here, either in physical models or in religion. Uncertainty is simply part of the Entity's creation and is incorporated into the laws of physics which He designed. This is what Heisenberg tells us."

Yu Wong added, "Yes, I also agree. And this view is consistent with how I understand certain delightful teachings of Confucius."

Celestine was beginning to explain what Thomas Aquinas had to say on the subject, when Aitch decided to bail out before he was required to contribute an opinion. Letting his eyes roam the lawn, he spied a cluster of individuals gathered just outside the Fitch's entrance, consisting of the Goldmans and a few other important personages. He ambled over, and Guillermo seized the opportunity to make a grandiloquent introduction.

"Hear ye, hear ye, here is the great man who first brought Professor Goldman to my attention. I trust that you all know Professor Singleton."

Aitch said hello to the Von Essens and UNV administrators. He stood still and said nothing else, content to scope the Virgin Queen's awesome machinery. She noticed him noticing, and that he was looking much more alive than at the last Faculty Tenure Committee meeting

Longshanks, you appear to be in fine fettle. Methinks the ill kempt French slattern is attending to the demands of your flesh.

Simon was slumped in a chair that Mona had procured for him, and they were both wearing sunglasses. Horst refused to sit and stood on his own, leaning on his walker. Ludwig reached into a sack attached to the device and found a floppy fisherman's hat, which was the only head covering the old man was ever willing to wear. Ludwig said, "*Opa, bitte,*" and placed it on his head, because the sun was strong. Aitch had always liked the Von Essens, and thought that Ludwig was okay for a lawyer.

Carver said, "Long time, no see, Aitch. Yes, we all owe you *huge* thanks for helping us steal Simon Goldman from Harvard" Then to the entire group, "And thanks are due to Dean Fulton, for taking the wise decision to nominate him."

"Why, thank you, James," said Margaret, her accent upper crust Bostonian mixed with British.

My word, what artful, unctuous, groveling. But currying favor. Yes, currying favor on behalf of his sovereign! Stalwart, yeomanlike James!

Rector Dr. Friend proclaimed, "Hear ye, hear ye, all you good people, hear hear!"

Slutnick was standing next to Simon and Mona. Aitch knew that his chairman was about to spew, but Guillermo managed to keep his face frozen in an unflinching politician's smile. A hint of a smirk was working its way onto Mona's cherubic features, but Simon looked serious and distracted. He must really be feeling ill, thought Aitch---neither laughing nor saying something inappropriate here, knowing that he could get away with it because he was the star of the show. Very un-Simon.

Old Horst became restless again, having fought off some of the effects of his pills. With maximum effort, he bumped his walker ten feet across the grass, bringing him to a position facing Dean Fulton. He bellowed into her face.

"*MÖCHTEN SIE BUMSEN? SCHTUPP-SCHTUPP?*"

He rocked on his walker and sprayed spittle, using every ounce of strength to steady himself while staring at the dean's crotch. Margaret did not understand German, but she correctly guessed that decrepit, demented Horst had just invited her to have sex with him. She held her regal smile and said nothing.

Verily, thou art an uncouth Prussian swine. Vile, depraved, bloody Hun.

Rolf said, "Please excuse my father---he is very tired. Poppa, come, sit down, *bitte.*"

Like Horst, Aitch could not take his eyes off Margaret. She looked at him oddly---he could not get a read on it.

You may not visit the royal chambers yet, Longshanks, but one day we may frolic there. Perchance you shall replace the swarthy Israelite under whose banner you serve.

Then Mona declared that it was time for her to take Simon home and put him to bed. This signalled the end of the cluster as a conversational unit.

***

At 11:50, Vito de Bernardi stood in the center of the lawn and whistled his *La Traviata* riff, notifying Il Gruppo that it was time to assemble.

"*Amici*, you can change into your stretchies in the offices of Aitch and Celestine. Then reconvene in the parking lot, and tend to your machines. I hope that we can be underway in thirty minutes time. Today we will cover only eighty kilometers. Most of the road is good, so we will often be in *formazione*---on my signals. We will head south on Route 108 through Bakersfield and on to Cambridge. Apologies to Bao Hoang, because we will pass so close to the site of Chester A. Arthur's nativity, but we cannot visit this sacred shrine today. Try not to get too upset and weepy, okay Bao? No one likes to see a grown man cry, except perhaps Sonya Jorgenson, who is not with us today. Then we stop in Cambridge to absorb *coltura* and *alimenta* if we can find any. If we had started earlier, we might have included the climb up Smuggler's Notch at this juncture, but no, not today---so sorry, Dr. Morty---maybe next week. We head west for two kilometers to Pumpkin Harbor Road, and then swing north. Here is our only real climb, about eight kilometers, so this is Dr. Morty's best opportunity to inflict some moments of pain and humiliation on his masochistic topologist friend, okay Brucie? Then we go through Sheldon, and here Bao Hoang achieves a state of ecstasy because we pass the monument concerning the strange Civil War battle which no one knows about or cares about. Okay Bao? Happy now? Fifteen more kilometers on Route 105 and we are back here in pastoral Enosburg Falls."

CHAPTER 13

How Goldman got endowed and the Alphabet Song: 1997-1998

-53-

Almost six years earlier, on the last Thursday of June, 1997, Dean Margaret Fulton, a.k.a. the Virgin Queen, arranged a ten minute meeting with the six chairmen from her faculty whose disciplines were represented on Horst Von Essen's list of subjects: Biochemistry, European Languages, History, Applied Mathematics, Philosophy and Physics.

She addressed the gathering in her British-lite patter.

"The candidates that you choose are to be of the *highest* academic repute. And of course, you should also possess a high level of confidence that they will actually *accept* a Horst Von Essen Professorship, should such be offered."

Margaret's chamberlain, James Carver, added, "Yes, Dean Fulton, that is a very salient point---we don't want to be used as a lever by some arrogant, ambitious academic seeking a better offer elsewhere."

The six chairmen nodded their agreement like bobble-heads. The dean had no intention of being played for a fool, spurned and left at the altar. The Baronet Mumford did it to her once, and the lesson was well learned.

"I would like to receive the names of your suggested candidates in two months time. Then I shall convene a meeting of my Arts and Science Advisory Committee in order to rank the proposed individuals. The results of these deliberations shall be made extant in October. Of course, in order to maintain a proper perspective on fairness, the committee members belonging to the departments here presently shall not participate in the consultative process."

The committee to which she referred consisted of five elected representatives from the nineteen departments under her aegis. The dean was an *ex-officio* member, but she could vote in a tie-breaking capacity. Slutnick did some quick figuring. What the Virgin Queen was actually implying was that besides her, the ranking committee would consist only of that pipe smoking chinless putz Neville Willows, the poseur who chaired Political Science, and an airhead named Gretchen Maybee from Exercise Science.

Science, Schmience---a yes-man and a yes-woman. She will decide this thing on her own.

Slutnick felt a warm glow and smiled to himself. He had to hand it to her---this woman knew how to run an empire. He found himself curiously aroused.

"Guillermo, I want to remind you that your candidate is to be from the *applied* domain."

To the chairperson of European languages, she said, "And Svetlana, your candidate is to be a scholar of *German* literature. Otherwise, there are no restrictions. I will now ask James to say a few words about our selection criteria, a subject upon which he has pondered mightily."

"Why, thank you, Dean Fulton. Of course, Dean Fulton is giving you *complete* freedom to generate your candidates as you see fit, but there are certain factors you may wish to consider."

Guillermo could never tell if Carver's sinister tone was deliberate or if it was just in his chromosomes. Either way, it was well known that noncompliance with Carver was the kiss of death.

"As you all are all aware, Dean Fulton has been given *carte blanche* by the Board of Governors in appointing one Von Essen Professor from the Faculty of Arts and Science, but this individual will be the candidate we rank *second.* Our *strongest* candidate will be the one we put into competition against the University of Burlington for the extra endowed position---the one to be chosen by the Von Essen family."

Of the half dozen departmental chairs in the room, only Slutnick was Machiavellian enough to intuit where Carver was going. The Virgin Queen noticed this, because Slutnick was nodding and smiling in a knowing way. She found herself curiously aroused too.

Yes, methinks my schedule would allow for a clever, olive skinned Israelite to entertain me on Midweek afternoons.

Carver said, "While academic excellence will of course be the advisory committee's paramount criterion in its deliberations, Dean Fulton asks that certain non-academic intangibles be taken into account as well."

Margaret took over.

"The candidate we put in play against our foes at Burlington should not only be capable of giving a top notch public interest lecture, but also be able to handle him or herself in social and interview situations with the Von Essens. So like it or not, expository skills, showmanship, and personality are likely to be of great import. And I will ask my advisory committee to keep this very much in mind."

I seek another Francis Drake---a man who could navigate in the royal court as well as at sea.

Slutnick ruminated. It would be a huge feather in his cap if the Department of Mathematics acquired a Horst Von Essen professorship, and he intended to put some effort into it. He understood that he needed to produce a candidate who was not only a crackerjack applied mathematician, but someone who would be able to suck up to old Horst. And he would have to convince the Virgin Queen that his choice was correct. He resolved to learn all that he could about Horst Von Essen and his family. Slutnick would start by reading that long, detailed and boring article about Horst's life written by his great-granddaughter Brunhilde, which appeared in the Green Mountain Sentinel last week. Esmeralda must have put it in the recycling bin, so it was still in the house.

-54-

Driving home from the meeting, Guillermo did some advance strategizing. He thought about the applied mathematics group. The best of them was Singleton, who was a fifty year old full professor, as were Felspar and Greenspoon, who were both past sixty. Felspar specialized in numerical analysis, and Greenspoon in catastrophe theory. In their heyday they were both pretty good and even got some grant funding, but neither had published anything for at least five years, and were well on their way to deadwood-hood. Slutnick had been trying to cajole them into taking early retirement to allow for an infusion of new blood, but they were allied and holding out for favorable terms. Each wanted a $50,000 lump sum included in their severance deal, which the Virgin Queen was unwilling to recommend. Guillermo was thinking about how he might sway her to support a figure of $25,000, which he knew they would both accept.

Besides Singleton, Felspar and Greenspoon, there were two junior people in the applied mathematics group---nontenured assistant professors toiling in mathematical biology and chaos theory, both working hard to establish their reputations. So it appeared that Singleton would have to be Slutnick's point-man when it came to generating a candidate. Aitch had good contacts in the fluid dynamics community, but another possibility intrigued Guillermo. He had met Simon Goldman and his cute little musicologist wife several times over the years, when they came up to Vermont from Harvard to spend time with the Singletons. Aitch brought Goldman to the campus during some of these visits, and arranged for him give talks in the departmental colloquium series. Very, very, good talks, Slutnick recalled---Goldman could really strut his stuff. The department paid its guest speakers a $300 honorarium, and whenever Goldman was a spoke, he insisted upon blowing the money by taking the Singletons and Slutnicks out for dinner. And on each occasion, he deferred to Guillermo when it came to choosing the restaurant and selecting the wine. Last time they went to a terrific little bistro in Old Montreal, and when Goldman picked up the tab, he refused to share it or even let the others know what the total was. It surely exceeded the honorarium, considering all the wine that was consumed. Slutnick liked the cut of Goldman's jib. And he had no doubt that Goldman had the mathematical stature to compete for a Von

Essen Professorship. But would he be willing to leave Harvard? And could he appeal to Horst Von Essen in those nonacademic 'intangible' ways alluded to by Carver? Maybe, just maybe.

When Slutnick got home, he ordered Esmeralda to rummage through the paper bin and find Brunhilde Von Essen's bio-piece. He bade her to bring it and his supper of boeuf *bourguignon* to his study, and asked her to keep the brats quiet. No wine tonight, he told her---just Perrier with a slice of lime, if she would be so kind. He had some serious reading and scheming to do. He would page her on the intercom when he was ready for his cheese plate, and after that, for *flan* and a double espresso. She could bring his cognac later.

***

At 11:40 p.m., after digesting both the Von Essen saga and his dinner, Guillermo phoned Aitch Singleton, and Maureen answered. Letterman was speaking in the background, complaining about the hot weather in New York City, saying that the hookers on Seventh Avenue were walking around with battery powered electric fans, offering a blow for ten dollars. Slutnick apologized for the lateness of the call and asked for Aitch.

"Let me see if I can rouse him," said Maureen. "He is laying here, arms splayed and snoring, with a cat named Newton on his solar plexus. But he will be very happy to speak with you, I am quite sure."

Decent looking Englishwoman, thought Slutnick---a turkey like Singleton didn't deserve her. She must have covered the mouthpiece, because he could hear nothing until Aitch gave a hoarse hello, dropped the phone with a clatter and recovered.

"Singleton, it's Guillermo Slutnick. Tell your wife that I'm sorry to be calling at this hour."

Aitch was still half-asleep, but he understood that Slutnick meant he was not sorry in the least, because this was important.

"I'll keep it brief, so that you can resume doing whatever you were doing with your cat. I know they have sandpaper-like tongues, so I am sympathetic to your bestial perversion. Gay sex with animals is the last frontier---Singleton, you are a pioneer. On a slightly different subject---you of course know that we have a shot at an endowed Von Essen Professorship in Mathematics, right?"

"Well, Applied Mathematics is on Horst Von Essen's topics list, so I'd be surprised if we weren't in the running. Funny you called. I was going to look for you tomorrow morning to tell you that I know a top-notch, grade A, number one mathematical scientist who is interested."

"Temporarily please forget about any of your fucking bubble formation cronies. I've been doing a little thinking, and I am asking you to first try to recruit Simon Goldman."

"Guillermo, it was Simon Goldman that I had in mind."

Slutnick laughed so hard that Aitch's eardrum felt like it might pop.

Aitch said, "Honestly, Guillermo, I didn't really think he would nibble. But Simon is both an outstanding mathematician as well as my oldest, dearest friend, so I thought I should give it a shot. A very long longshot."

"Wait, let me guess. He just turned fifty and decided that he's sick of the Boston area, and wants to lead a more bucolic existence. And have very little teaching, very high pay, supplemental research and travel money, and lots of other goodies."

"Guillermo, you've hit the nail on the head."

"Singleton, I got onto Goldman's personal website an hour ago. Impressive. Several honors, consistent federal funding for twenty years, over eighty publications, two graduate level textbooks, major editorships, and he's supervised ten doctoral students. This guy has done so much fundamental work in game theory and complexity that even if he never does another fucking thing, we still ought to get him that endowed position, know what I mean?"

"Agreed. But Guillermo, there's one small complication. It's a two-body problem. Recall that Mona Goldman is an Associate Professor of Music at Boston College. Simon won't consider jumping ship unless she can get a tenured position at UNV as well."

Slutnick stared at a wall and pondered for twenty seconds. Then he felt a delicate tingling in the left parietal lobe of his brain---specifically, in an overdeveloped cluster of neurons dedicated to bullshitting. A vision formed, and he came to realize that he could manipulate the Virgin Queen, and that she could in turn manipulate the BOG.

"It can be finessed," said Slutnick. "Suppose Goldman gets one of the endowed positions---either the guaranteed one or the one up for grabs against UB. Then belatedly, *ex post facto*, he springs his fucking two-body demand. The deanette shits a brick initially, but then I help her realize that she will have no trouble convincing the BOG to create a new associate professorship in the Department of Music, in order to meet Goldman's needs. They will have no fucking choice but to do it. And even though Goldman withheld information from the Virgin Queen and we played her, she will be smoothed over because she gets an extra position for her Faculty of Arts and Science, adding to her fucking empire. All we have to do is tell Goldman not to make his demand until *after* he is formally and publicly told that he won an endowment. If he asks for too much up front, she might not bite. Better to risk causing a little temporary fuss later."

Aitch knew that he was in the presence of an expert---a black belt in university politics.

"Okay, I feel uneasy about any deception, but I won't upset the applecart."

"Give me Goldman's home phone number. I'm going to call him tomorrow. If he's willing to do things my way, we'll invite him up here and I'll give the two of you a bit of coaching."

-55-

In his phone conversation with Slutnick the following morning, Goldman agreed to the idea of forestalling his two-body demand until his nomination was announced, and he expressed willingness to submit to other advice as well, because he knew that Slutnick was a Metternichian mastermind. And there was an e-mail exchange between the two of them later in the day. Slutnick asked twenty strange, offbeat questions concerning Simon's personal background. Simon could not fathom where Slutnick was going with his inquiries, but provided the answers nevertheless.

***

The Goldmans drove up to UNV from Massachusetts on a sunny Monday morning in July, 1997 for a one week holiday with the Singletons. During past summer visits, Aitch and Simon played squash and did some biking in the Greens, and Simon would ride with Il Gruppo on the weekends too. The Music Sisters would play Mozart and Vivaldi on the porch for hours on end---a duet with Maureen on violin and Mona on cello, and often an audience of ecstatic neighbors would gather in the front yard on lawn chairs to revel in the sweet sounds. Always the foursome would do their standard hike to the top of Jay Peak for a picnic, and every night they would eat and drink themselves into a contented stupor.

During the present visit, these pleasures would all be indulged, but there was also business to attend to. Simon and Aitch were required to learn what further deceptions had crystallized in Guillermo Slutnick's labyrinthine mind. Aitch phoned him on Monday evening, and it was agreed that the three of them would meet on campus in the morning.

"It is imperative that we get our shit together," said Slutnick.

***

The next morning, Guillermo expressed his hope that the gourmet Costa Rican coffee and Montreal croissants he was plying them with would make up for the stiffness of their wooden chairs. It became clear at the outset that this meeting was really between Slutnick and Goldman, with Aitch participating only as an observer. But Chairman Slutnick said it was essential that he attend, because he needed to be familiar with all the details of the conspiracy, in case he was ever interrogated under torture.

Slutnick said, "Before we start, let me say a few things. Horst

Von Essen's life story is laid bare in this newspaper article by his great-granddaughter, and it will be our main tool in reforging your identity, Goldman, so as to make you irresistible to him."

He passed copies of Brunhilde's bio-piece to the two of them.

"Reforge my identity? Why? I like my identity," said Simon. "Even if no one else does."

"Okay Goldman, maybe 'reforge' is too strong a term. What I really meant is, we're just going to tweak a few things. And when we're done tweaking, I will write your slightly modified personal history---say two or three pages---and have Beatrice type it up. We'll attach it to your CV. Needless to say, none of this bullshit will be necessary if you get the guaranteed Von Essen Professorship, but it might prove fucking crucial if you wind up vying for the competitive one against UB, in which case we will formally incorporate it into the 'personal statement and family history' that those fucking Nazis demand. We'll show it to the Virgin Queen as soon as possible, however. It ought to convince her to put you forward."

Guillermo reached for some notes he had prepared, a kind of checklist, which would give structure to the tweaking process. Clipped to it was a printout of Simon's e-mail responses to Slutnick's strange list of questions.

"Goldman, let's get started on the metaphysics of this crap. Do you know what a *Yekke* is, and that you are one?"

Simon's eyes saucered.

"Actually, Guillermo, not only am I a Yekke, but I have been emphatically and repeatedly told that I am a Yekke of the highest order---a *Yekke-putz,* in fact."

Then, even though he was seated, Goldman clicked his heels and gave a Nazi salute. Guillermo slapped his desk and laughed, with poor Aitch having no idea what was going on. Simon took pity and clued him in.

"Bumpkin, the word 'yekke' means 'jacket' in Yiddish, the language of the Jewish lower classes, and in Israel it is a highly derisive term used to describe German Jews, who are regarded as very formal, haughty, arrogant, rigid, and regimented. The idea is that they wear their formal jackets even in hot weather, and as you know, Israel is a very informal place, and it can get goddam hot there. So during my sabbatical at the Technion in Haifa in 1984, I learned my true identity. I am not an American Jew to the average Israeli. No! I'm a Yekke-putz! Often, when I expressed displeasure at someone's tardiness or rudeness, or objected to some illogical, levantine bureaucratic procedure, or yelled at a crazy driver to ask if he'd bought his permit in a supermarket, I was reminded that I was a Yekke-putz. Even Mona started calling me a Yekke-putz, and she's not even Jewish."

"I didn't know that. Jeez, Simon---you sound like my colleague Volkemar Volkmann after he returned from his sabbatical in Athens."

"Good analogy, Singleton," said Guillermo. "*That's exactly the fucking point!* Poor Goldman here was a victim of prejudice, just like Volkmann was, because the Jews, like the Greeks, have this little grudge against the Krauts. Possibly something to do with blitzkrieg and genocide. Goldman, in the bio-blurb we are manufacturing, we will say that you left Israel because you were made uncomfortable due to your sensitivities concerning your German identity. We'll say that you ended your sabbatical there a month earlier than planned, and subtly hint that the sabras made you feel shitty about your being a German. The idea is to get those fucking Von Essen Nazis to overlook your Jewishness by convincing them to think of you as a flag waving, dyed in the wool, German-American patriot."

Goldman nodded and grinned in admiration of the man's creativity and brilliance. Aitch fought to keep his jaw from dropping and said,

"Guillermo, they're hardly Nazis. And it says here in Brunhilde's article that when Horst Von Essen immigrated in the 1920's, he worked for and then partnered with a guy named Abie Cohen in Far Rockaway. He's no anti-Semite. Maybe just the opposite."

"I'm playing it safe," said Slutnick. "You can never be too paranoid in this business. Goldman, according to your answers to my previous queries, both your grandfathers served in the German Army in World War I. Let's just concentrate on your paternal grandfather, Hugo Goldman. You wrote that you think he was a supply clerk, working at a train yard in Düsseldorf for the entire war, because he couldn't hear out of one ear since birth."

Simon nodded, grinning so broadly that it looked as though his face might crack. Aitch thought about trying to keep up by making a lame joke about being witness to a Jewish conspiracy, but he held his tongue as Slutnick continued spinning his wanton bullshit.

"Goldman, let me re-educate you as to your family history. Grandpa Hugo was in the Kaiser's Army on the Marne. He won an Iron Cross for killing heaps of Frenchmen before being knocked silly and deafened by a shellburst. And he was a *feldwebel*."

"Why, I never knew that," said Goldman, realizing that Slutnick was a true artist, and probably a genius. "But it must be true, if you say so, Guillermo. I hope none of those Frenchmen was Jewish."

"Right," said Slutnick, who felt a warm glow because he was sure that Simon Goldman had the right stuff to pull this off. "You see, there are some amazing coincidences. Truly amazing. According to Brunhilde Von Essen's article, old Horst was also a *Feldvebel* at the Marne, where he won an Iron Cross. And he steadfastly refused an officer's commission, despite his *Junker* pedigree. Also, the Nazis didn't work your Grandpa Hugo to death at Dachau in 1940 as a reward for being a loyal German and not emigrating early enough. No, he died of natural causes, a patriotic German to the end."

And so it went. It was a nice coincidence that Horst Von Essen and his young family resided in Simon's old neighborhood, Washington Heights, from 1930 to 1938 before moving to Vermont. Slutnick built on this. For example, Simon was a shitpicker in Far Rockaway and not Coney Island any more, because this would resonate with old Horst, who started his rags-to-riches climb working in Abie Cohen's garage in Far Rockaway. And Goldman would now say that when he was a student at Cooper Union, he lived on St. Mark's Place, because according to Brunhilde, Horst lived there for a few months after arriving in America, which Brunhilde said was "the real beginning of my great-grandfather's life." Actually, Goldman lived with his mother in Washington Heights in his Cooper days, but Aitch lived on St. Mark's, so Simon was now Aitch's ex-roommate. The fact that Simon's father Gustav was a sergeant in the Second World War was useful, but the fact that he was chairborne would be omitted. And Sergeant Meinhold Mannheimer was sent from heaven. Slutnick did not even have to embellish him---and he resonated nicely with Rolf Von Essen, who served as a sergeant with the Marines in the South Pacific, earning a silver star at Tarawa. The fact that Goldman came out of Vietnam with three stripes, a Bronze Star and a Purple Heart was another nice riff that needed no modification---and he had a lot in common with Ludwig Von Essen, who did a Vietnam tour of his own, finishing as a sergeant.

"Goldman, Beatrice will type up this version of your biography in Microsoft Word, and I'll send the file to Singleton as an e-mail attachment this evening. Both of you, please gain familiarity with all the fucking details. Also, I'll try to set up a meeting between the three of us and the Virgin Queen for tomorrow, so that we can show Goldman off, and tell her that he's our nominee. Stay tuned for the arrangements."

***

That evening, after a barbecue dinner with the Music Sisters, Aitch and Simon went to the attic to check their e-mail. Simon had no messages, but Aitch received the one which Guillermo had promised.

> Dear fellow gentlemen-scholars:
>
> The file is attached. I am appending it to your CV,
> Simon. A few months from now, the material
> will be incorporated in the 'personal statement
> and family history' that the VonEssens will request.

We shall be taken to lunch by Dean Fulton tomorrow at 12:30 p.m., at the Faculty Club, and we will give her the documents.

Be on time and on your best behaviors. Also, casual but neat dress. No T-shirts, no shorts, and no sandals.

GS

Simon pointed out that Slutnick practiced safe e-mail---there was no mention of the conspiracy in the wording of the message. Then they headed down to the front porch, where their wives treated them to some Mozart

-56-

The UNV Faculty Club was on the third floor of the eighty year old, ivy covered stone building, which housed the university's main offices. Officially, it was the Administration Building, but everyone called it 'The Castle' because that is what is resembled, complete with a battlement, corner watchtowers, bulwarks, slits for archers, and hideous gargoyles. There also were stone spouts for pouring boiling oil, should the need arise.

Simon, Aitch and Guillermo were early and already seated at the table reserved by one of Margaret's secretaries, when she and James Carver strode in. The three mathematicians rose, and Slutnick introduced Simon Goldman, explaining that he was on a social visit. Goldman shook the austere looking dean's hand, and was surprised at how warm and moist it felt. He gave her a serious scoping. She was wearing a sleeveless black dress, and her long red hair was pulled back, held in place by a golden comb which matched her jewelry. Great rack, shapely legs, and no stockings. Nice perfume too. Not bad for dean, thought Goldman. Cate Blanchett on steroids.

She said, "It is an honor and a pleasure to receive such an esteemed visitor from Harvard."

Simon also shook with Carver, who nodded with what looked like forced smugness, his usual expression. Simon recognized his type instantly---an academic zero who becomes an administrator, and then shows scorn towards the faculty. Every university has them.

Slutnick said, "Dean Fulton, thank you very much for taking time with us today, and for the luncheon invitation, which we greatly appreciate."

Aitch and Simon expressed concurrence, and Guillermo continued. He knew that they had a limited amount of time, so he spoke rapidly as he outlined Simon's CV, detailing his record of accomplishment in game theory, combinatorics, and complexity theory, as well as the prizes awarded to him by scientific societies. Then he got to the main point.

"I would like to give you these copies of Professor Goldman's CV as well as a brief summary of his personal history---the sort of material that the Von Essens require of the candidate to be put into competition against the University of Burlington. I have also taken the liberty to attach a copy of Brunhilde Von Essen's rather lengthy biography of her great-grandfather, Horst."

Margaret straightened with interest.

"I saw it, and I must admit, its sheer bulk intimidated me."

The waiter came and told them today's menu. The Virgin Queen chose the poached salmon, and they all ordered the same. Carver selected a California chardonnay.

Guillermo said, "I will get straight to the point, Dean Fulton. There is an *amazing* interweaving of the lives of Horst Von Essen and Simon Goldman---an incredible confluence of events, with several odd coincidences and parallels."

That raised their eyebrows, as Slutnick knew it would. He went through his well rehearsed litany of items in Simon's background that he hoped had resonance with the history of Horst and his family, including allusions to Goldman's Yekke experiences. These were mentioned in the written history only in an indirect and suggestive way, but the desired point was made---Slutnick's spin was an antidote, and more, to any objection the Von Essens might have to Goldman's Jewishness.

The Virgin Queen was not fooled.

Methinks this is artful contrivance. But truly, truly superb artful contrivance. Clever, clever, sons of Abraham.

Carver saw it more or less the same way.

This is bullshit---but very, very good bullshit. Two fucking Hebes sticking together---no surprise there.

Aitch was gaining an appreciation of the epistemology of this thing. Everyone understood that Slutnick was not trying to flimflam the dean---he just wanted to show her how he could present Goldman, should she decide that he would compete against the University of Burlington. She did not need or want to know what in Goldman's history was real and what was massaged. The Virgin Queen would be part of the conspiracy, but at arm's length, with complete deniability. Slutnick knew that these attributes of the scheme were of paramount importance to her, and she knew that he was crafty enough to know it. Once again, she felt sexually aroused because of Slutnick's acumen and deviousness. The salads and wine arrived.

Margaret said, "The process demands that I await the

promulgation of candidacies from all the relevant departments, and then there is to be a selection process involving my advisory committee. So it is still very early, and of course, I am only one voice---and what is more, I do not vote. But I must say, Professor Goldman, my instinct is to argue that you be the candidate placed in competition against our rivals in Burlington."

Carver concurred by producing one of his all-knowing nods. Guillermo's scheme was working perfectly, and the conversation shifted to more mundane topics after the main courses arrived---the weather, the Boston Red Sox's chances this year, and whether or not Howard Dean was a closet fiscal conservative out to screw the universities. They were on their coffee and tapioca pudding when Margaret raised a question.

"Professor Goldman, please forgive my asking something which you have undoubtedly answered in your documents---but are you married? Children?"

Guillermo felt a hot needle of pain in his stomach, and doubled over. He managed to camouflage his spasm as a cough, but felt that he was staring a humiliating death in the face.

Lofas! I'm a fucking idiot! I forgot to coach Goldman on the possibility that his wife would be discussed. The whole fucking thing could go down the toilet! Fuck! Fuck! Fuck!

Goldman's nod communicated that he thought the question was reasonable.

"Please, Dean Fulton, call me Simon. My wife on I are planning to separate and then, in all likelihood, divorce. And fortunately, no children."

Slutnick's feet felt cold, and then a wave of heat traversed his body, the adrenalin induced sensation a motorist feels in the seconds following a near collision. Aitch's Adam's apple was twitching as he stared at the wall and tried to regularize his breathing.

Margaret rose and so did Carver.

"I'm sorry to hear that, Professor Goldman---I mean, Simon. Well, it was pleasurable meeting you, but alas, I must return to my duties. I anticipate that we will have further contact. Oh yes---Guillermo, if you would be so kind, can I admit you to my chambers at 3:30? I have a free half-hour before a meeting with Professor Willows, and I hope that we might discuss the monetary issues involving Professors Felspar and Greenspoon."

Come to me, Robert Dudley, Earl of Leicester, come to me.

***

The three mathematicians made their way back to the Fitch, on the other side of the campus.

Guillermo said, "That was some impressive ad libbing, Goldman. Fucking formidable. I see that you have talents beyond mathematics."

Simon smiled in appreciation of the compliment. Aitch just shook his head.

"You know, Goldman," Guillermo continued, "with that divorce crap you laid out, it plays even better. In a few months, when you spring your two-body demand on her, you will appear less disingenuous."

Simon said, "Right. After they make me the offer, I'll simply tell them that Mona and I have reconciled."

Slutnick said, "All huggy-bear and kissy-pie. Well, I think there is no further business to attend to at present, so the two of you can fuck off and play squash or bike or do whatever the fuck else you do instead of sex. We'll have to wait until October to find out whether or not today's little propaganda exercise succeeded, and needless to say, I will keep you both perfectly posted."

He went on to complain about Dean Fulton.

"She's busting my balls about Felspar and Greenspoon. By simply recommending that they be given a few dollars, she could help me clear those useless deadwood schmucks out of my department. But no, and I'll probably have to sell my soul to get it done."

Guillermo had never before used that phrase in describing his dealings with the dean, but after today, it would become a regular part of his lexicon. Goldman suggested that Slutnick grab a nap before he returned to the Castle, because it appeared that he might be slipping into a bad mood.

-57-

Guillermo slept for an hour in his recliner. He had a private washroom adjacent to his office, and after Beatrice roused him on the intercom, he brushed his teeth, splashed on some cologne, and slicked back his dark, oily hair. He knew that if the dean said she had a half-hour for him at half past three, then that was exactly what she meant, because she had a well earned reputation as a stickler for punctuality and time management.

He put on his Oakley sunglasses and walked back across the campus. At 3:25 he took the elevator to the top floor of the Castle, and entered the Virgin Queen's outer defences---an open area shared by six secretaries, one of whom functioned as a receptionist. A lute recording of *Greensleeves* was playing softly in the background, and there were four comfortable matched armchairs for visitors. Slutnick had an expert's eye for antiques and noted that the chairs and other pieces were excellent replicas of sixteenth century British furniture.

At precisely 3:30 p.m., the receptionist acknowledged his existence and escorted him down a carpeted hallway. There were three doors, one leading to an anteroom used for meetings of small groups, another to Carver's office, while the third was the portal through which one entered the dean's private chambers. Carver's door was ajar, and Slutnick noticed that the associate dean looked more agitated and hostile than usual. The receptionist gently pushed Guillermo through the third door, and the heavy lock clicked behind him.

He scanned Dean Fulton's office, but she was not in sight. Her majestic desk was bare except for in-out trays and a telephone. No computer, Guillermo noticed. He recalled that a year ago, at a Christmas party and after several cups of punch, she mentioned that she was a Luddite, and that all her e-mail communication went through a secretary who did the actual button pushing. Dean Fulton said then that she dwelt in the late 16th century, and the paintings on the walls bore it out. There were three portraits of Queen Elizabeth I in different stages of her life, as well as framed posters of Bette Davis and Cate Blanchett in their turns as the greatest monarch England ever produced. Images of Elizabeth's parents were on display as well---corpulent King Henry VIII and beautiful Anne Boleyn, whom Henry murdered because she did not bear him a son.

The Virgin Queen's complex was, in effect, a fortified penthouse. There was an outdoor perimeter walkway between the offices and a high wall. No one had access to this outside area but the dean, and this was via a curtained door, which had been left open. Slutnick hesitated but then stepped through, onto the battlement path, and was not prepared for the sight which greeted him.

Margaret was lying face down on an inflatable mat, taking the afternoon sun. Her long, red hair was loose, and her clothes were draped over a wicker chair. All she was wearing was a green thong, and her skin was glistening with suntan lotion which smelled of sweet fruit. Slutnick was in shock, but in a pleasant kind of way. He calmed down by force of will, and began to scrutinize. She had a fantastic ass, he realized---a truly Rabelaisian, *zaftig* ass. He took a step closer. Margaret lifted her eyes and propped herself on her elbows, bringing her perfect breasts into full view.

"Greetings, Guillermo Slutnick. You are very prompt, and promptness is a virtue that I value in a man, among other ones. And alas, promptness demands that I bid you adieu in twenty-six minutes. I must not be tardy for my next meeting, which fortunately is to be here."

"I have virtues beyond promptness," he said in as steady a tone as he could manage.

"I am sure that you do, Guillermo Slutnick. Do you know what constituted the greatest danger to Queen Elizabeth?"

"Obviously it was Lady Di."

"Perhaps you are in jest. I am of course referring to Elizabeth I."

"The Spanish Armada?" guessed Guillermo.

She smiled and nodded no, that was not it.

"Okay, wait a minute. It had to be a possible French invasion threatening to put Mary Queen of Scots on her throne. Right?"

She nodded no again, but Slutnick's feel for British history made her moist.

"No, Guillermo Slutnick. In my view, the greatest danger to Elizabeth was her illicit affair with Robert Dudley, the Earl of Leicester, a man many felt was a consummate schemer. Take off your clothes."

He was doing as he was told, hopping on one foot while pulling off a sock, when she came to her feet, swirled her tongue in his ear, and whispered,

"You will be my Earl of Leicester, will you not?"

Her warm breath aroused him instantly---she kneeled and took him into her mouth. He snuck a glance at his Rolex as he gripped her ears.

Lofas! Only twenty-three minutes.

He intended to give this his very best effort. For openers, fearing that he would lose control and pop the weasel too soon, he stopped her and helped her out of her thong. She really *was* a redhead. Guillermo decided to repay her oral stimulation in kind. In this endeavor, he followed the advice of the late, great Sam Kinison, whose cult following included Slutnick in its ranks. According to the former evangelical preacher turned stand-up comedian, the trick is to write all twenty-six letters of the alphabet with the tip of one's tongue---upper case and then lower, dotting the i's and j's, and crossing the t's. Margaret went into a delirium of ecstasy, and the upper case 'E' seemed to devastate her more than the other letters, so he repeated it a few times. She moaned, "Dudley! Dudley!" but muted it, for fear of being heard by her staff.

Why does this randy knave hum the Alphabet Song while pleasuring his sovereign?

He relaxed his grip on her gyrating buttocks and glanced at his watch while doing the lower case 'z'.

Thirteen minutes left!

When he came up for air, she got on all fours and presented him with the canine option. Slutnick did not require an engraved invitation.

Thrust thy stout sword, noble Leicester---I am thy scabbard! Thrust! Thrust!

***

Ten minutes and many muffled grunts later, he was dressing.

She said, "You *shall* be my Earl of Leicester on midweek afternoons, my schedule permitting. I will see you in a week's time---a tryst."

He bowed, kissed her hand, and made for the door.

This anachronistic crap is going to drive me fucking crazy.

To his retreating back, Margaret said, "I do believe we had a bit of business to clear up regarding your Professors Felspar and Greenspoon, did we not?"

He stopped in his tracks, gave his forehead a burlesque *oy vey* slap, and turned to hear her out.

"I have decided to follow your suggestion regarding this matter, and I shall recommend twenty-five thousand dollars severance for each. I have concluded that this would be in the best longterm interests of my Faculty of Arts and Science. But you must understand that the eventual replacements for Professors Felspar and Greenspoon will be at the junior level, due to budgetary constraints."

He bowed again even though he knew she was screwing him. She should be offering senior level replacements, regardless of the severance deal. But he kept smiling, pivoted, and made his escape.

As Slutnick walked down the hallway, Carver directed a murderous, sulking glare at him, looking even more sullen and malevolent than before. And as he passed through the reception area, Guillermo said hello to Neville Willows, the chairman of the Department of Political Science and a member of the Arts and Science Advisory Committee. He was sitting in one of the antique replica armchairs, waiting for his four o'clock appointment with the dean.

-58-

Slutnick was Robert Dudley, the Earl of Leicester, only during their first two trysts, because the Virgin Queen was, by her own admission, quite fickle. The third encounter was devoted to a Tower of London theme. After having him hum the Alphabet Song, she bade him don a black executioner's hood and a kind of pubic wig called a 'merkin', which for some unknown reason was all the rage in Elizabethan England. Margaret kept items of this nature in an antique wooden chest which she called her 'toybox'. "My fellow Merkins," said Slutnick in a bad but enthusiastic Lyndon B. Johnson imitation, while velcroing the plastic chains on her. But Margaret did not see the humor in it and told him to shut up and get on with making her serve her sentence.

During their fourth session, he was required to adopt the persona of William Shakespeare---she called him the Bard, had him wear a codpiece, and quoted with passion from *Much Ado About Nothing* while riding him to bliss.

"*If thou dost love, my kindness shall incite thee.*"

But Guillermo was not quite ready to ask for kindness or concrete favors yet, such as a firm promise that she would push Goldman forward---better to wait a bit longer.

***

The following week he took his family down to Cape May for a shore holiday. Esmeralda was eight months pregnant with their third brat, and on her gynecologist's orders, she had been out of commission for over a month. So Guillermo really missed selling his soul to Margaret while he was on vacation. But it was not all bad. Because he was useless as a father, Esmeralda did not complain when he abandoned her on the beach every day, so that could spend his time playing live stud poker at The Sands in Atlantic City, just up the road along the Jersey Shore. He won five thousand untaxable dollars, even though he was in a continual state of distraction thinking about Dean Fulton.

***

After each visit, as he left Margaret's chambers, Slutnick would say hi to chinless Neville Willows, waiting in the reception area for his appointment and sucking on his unlit Meerschaum. And every time, he would spy James Carver in his office, looking steamed enough to drive an icepick through someone's heart. Slutnick guessed that Margaret controlled her associate dean not with sex but with the mere possibility of sex---and depraved nymphomaniacal sex at that---something that Carver was made acutely aware of every time one of her paramours passed his door. Slutnick surprised himself by actually feeling pity for the poor cock-teased bastard. Carver's balls had probably turned blue by now, he mused.

***

One time, Margaret opted for a variation on the Shakespearian theme. She called Slutnick her Shylock, her swarthy son of Abraham, her clever hirsute Hebrew, her circumcised satyr, before and during her moment of Old Testament truth. Afterwards, she asked if he knew any of Shylock's lines. Now Slutnick, although he was a major culture vulture and extremely well read, always considered Shakespeare overrated, attributing his popularity to some sort of 'Emperor's New Clothes' effect which has miraculously persisted for four centuries, and kept Monarch Notes in business to boot. Slutnick's aversion to Shakespeare was due at least in part to the fact that when he was a plump and precocious tenth grader in the exclusive Venezuelan boarding school his parents shipped him off to, he had the role of Shylock forced upon him in a production of *The Merchant of Venice* by an anti-Semitic drama teacher.

"Why of course, Majesty---I even recall a line which seems particularly apt."

"Pray let us hear it," said the Virgin Queen.

"*Well then, it now appears you need my help.*"

"Ah, very good. And pray tell, what help is it that you are

offering?"

Slutnick believed that he was currently her favorite visitor, thanks to Sam Kinison, and decided that it was a good time to seek advantage.

"My Lady, Your Eminence," said Slutnick, because he had learned that is the manner in which she liked to be addressed. "I have been giving the Von Essen matter considerable thought, and I believe that I have discerned a very advantageous strategy for the Faculty of Arts and Science to pursue. A queen's gambit, if you will."

"And advantageous also to your fifedom in Mathematics, I daresay."

There shall be but one mistress here and no master.

Guillermo performed a courtier's flourished bow, something he had been practicing in front of a mirror when Esmeralda was not watching.

"You know me all too well, Luminescence."

"Pray continue."

"Excellency, do you have a credible candidate in the field of German literature, or any German cultural study, for that matter? Preferably a candidate who is of the genuine Teutonic persuasion?"

Slutnick already knew the answer, because he had friends among UNV's philosophers.

"Why, yes," she breezed. She knew that he was manipulating her, and was excited by his disingenuous sliminess. "We actually *do* have such a candidate in German Philosophy---Professor Dieter Dueppmann of Stuttgart, arguably the world's leading authority on Schopenhauer's Theory of Pessimism."

Slutnick said this sounded perfect and he proceeded to lay it out for her. He said that Dieter Dueppmann should be given a Von Essen Professorship *jointly* in the Departments of Philosophy, European Languages, and History. Let them share the joy, because this way they all would owe her and she could bask in the gratitude of all three units. Screw the biochemists, he told her in so many words, because they were disloyal--- many of them were sympathetic to the biologists during her purge of their department. And screw the physicists too, because their department's research profile was an embarrassment to the university, and she should protect her empire by not building on weakness. Also, the choice of a German cultural type like Dieter Dueppmann, who was a bona fide Kraut, would please and flatter the Von Essens, Slutnick theorized. Hence, the Von Essens would be favorably predisposed to UNV when it came to the competitive position. And Simon Goldman should be the candidate put forward to compete against the University of Burlington. He said that he believed she could sway the advisory committee to do her bidding and nominate him. Guillermo knew that with her schtupping Neville Willows, it was a lock, even in the unlikely event that Gretchen Maybee refused to go along---because the dean could vote to break a tie.

"My Noble Lady, we are engaged in a momentous battle against the knaves at Burlington, and one that we can win. I am sure that you attach a very high priority to it. Glory would rain upon your faculty and the university should you emerge triumphant. If you would honor me by allowing me to be your general, I can and will present you with a great victory. Queen Elizabeth once said *'We are not interested in the possibilities of defeat.'* Luminescence, rejoice---no such possibility exists!"

Margaret reached for the telephone.

"Please ask Professor Willows to be patient. I shall be occupied with Professor Slutnick for another ten minutes."

-59-

Slutnick's plan unfolded without a hitch. In late September, 1997, Dean Fulton explained her choices of Professors Dueppmann and Goldman to the Arts and Science Advisory Committee. Neville Willows was Margaret's hand puppet, and went along. Gretchen Maybee could not understand all the vocabulary in the dean's remarks, so she went along too, because she did not want to seem stupid---a lifetime preoccupation of hers. So Dieter Dueppmann would become a Horst Von Essen Professor of the Humanities, and Simon Goldman would be trotted out by the Virgin Queen as the University of Northern Vermont's competing candidate.

Our Ivanhoe! Our champion! He will joust against Burlington's best man at arms!

***

At the University of Burlington, the candidate put forward was Professor of Electrical Engineering Hishi Yamaguchi from the University of Tokyo, who was a contender for a Nobel Prize because of his world leading work on nanotechnology. Next month, the Von Essens would choose between Yamaguchi and Goldman. When Slutnick heard about this, he was elated. He explained why on a Wednesday afternoon in October, after satisfying his monarch's needs on the carpet. He was wearing a court jester's hat with little bells on the tassles, and the noise they made during his last, hard strokes caused Margaret tremendous excitement and brought her to an even madder climax than usual.

"Eminence, in my estimation, Burlington has blundered."

He put the hat back in Margaret's toybox and pulled up his trousers.

"How so?" asked the breathless Virgin Queen, leaning on an

elbow, enjoying the afterglow.

"Radiance, one of Burlington's guaranteed Von Essen professorships, in Physics, went to a cosmologist from the University of Lyon. After I was informed of this choice last week, I made a few inquiries. Majesty, it emerges that although the Von Essens do much business in Europe, purchasing equipment and selling services, one country is conspicuously omitted from their list of European suppliers and customers. And that country, Madame, is France. I suspect that for some reason, possibly related to the Treaty of Versailles, old Horst Von Essen reviles the French, and refuses to deal with them."

"Pity, that."

"Now, in Hishi Yamaguchi, they did put forward a very strong candidate to compete against Simon Goldman. A world class scientist, to be sure. But they obviously did not study the Von Essen family history as I did. If they had, I doubt that Yamaguchi would have been their choice. Pray recall Rolf's tale, My Lady."

She did not remember the salient biographical facts made plain in Brunhilde's article, so Guillermo reminded her.

"Magnificence, Rolf spent the years 1942 through 1945 as a sergeant in the U.S. Marine Corps in the Pacific, killing all the Japanese he could lay his beefy hands on. And it is well known that most marines and soldiers who fought on those filthy little islands still harbor great animosity toward the sons of Nippon, regarding them as less than human, evil, cruel, maniacal, and party poopers in general. Any vestige of the chivalry and romanticism in war that was present in the European theater was utterly absent in the Pacific. Over the years, I have done some casual reading on this subject, by writers who fought there. Norman Mailer, James Jones, William Manchester and others. Herman Wouk for example, who was as gentle a soul as can be found on this orb and never abused the English tongue, said that Guadalcanal '...was and remains, that fucking island'---and in polite company. No quarter was asked in those battles and none was given. I conjecture that in the Von Essen household, the Japanese are despised even more than the French. I therefore believe that victory is in our grasp!"

The Virgin Queen said, "That is encouraging, but there can be many a slip 'twixt cup and lip, many a slip."

***

Margaret need not have been concerned. The BOG rubber-stamped her choices in February, 1998, and Guillermo's political analysis was spot on. If the brain trust at University of Burlington had done their homework, they would have discovered that the Von Essens eschewed business contacts not only with France, but with Japan as well, even though they had undertaken major construction projects in other parts of Asia.

The following month, a coin flip between Rector Dr. Friend and his counterpart at the University of Burlington determined that the first candidate to be scrutinized by the Von Essens would be Hishi Yamaguchi. Rolf boycotted his talk on nanotechnolgy, which was very high tech, including animations of tiny insect-like robots cleaning clogged arteries, nor did he attend the dinner interview which followed in a Burlington sushi restaurant. Horst and Ludwig took part in these events, but Yamaguchi was dead in the water. Small wonder. Rolf kept a footlocker of souvenirs from the war at his mansion. Among other things, it contained the incisors of some thirty-five Nips he had personally dispatched on Tarawa, Iwo Jima and Okinawa, along with the rusty pair of pliers he used for the extractions.

Goldman's seminar was given the next day, and it was a chalk-talk. His original intention was to use glitzy, colorful slides, but after attending Yamaguchi's talk, Slutnick urged him to go primitive. In his retro-style lecture, Simon explained his current field of research on networks in terms of industrial models. He kept the Von Essens' business interests in the crosshairs throughout, and used buzzwords to which they could relate. They lapped it up.

-60-

For feting and interviewing Simon Goldman, Ludwig Von Essen reserved a private room in the St. Albans Bavarian Brauhaus. The attendees, besides Goldman and the three Von Essens, were Guillermo Slutnick, Dean Fulton and Rector Dr. Friend. The Von Essens had two of their private limousines pick up the guests at their homes and chauffer them to the restaurant. No family members were invited.

Horst Von Essen was still quite spry at ninety-nine, and he set the tone of the gathering by ordering the lederhosen clad waiter to bring six pitchers of varied German beers. No one in the UNV entourage shied away from the guzzling being forced upon them, for fear of offending old Horst. Margaret kept up without difficulty, having done a fair bit of pub crawling with her former lover, the Baronet Mumford, during her graduate student days---before she lost her mind because he jilted her.

"*Prosit! Prosit!*" they all called out while hoisting their steins. Margaret said "Chug-a-lug," and "Down the hatch," a few times too. No one was in position to object to the periodic refills.

Old Horst had read Goldman's 'personal statement and family history', and wanted very much to meet him. So while everyone got plastered on beer and stuffed on schnitzel and bratwurst, they were entertained by a long conversation between Simon and Horst---a fascinating string of reminiscences. The two of them were at opposite ends of the table, so their words passed all ears.

With enthusiastic nostalgia, they shared their memories of New York, recalling street names and other geographic minutia. Simon and Horst discovered that they lived on the same block between Broadway and Fort Washington Avenue, near J. Hood Wright Park. And Rolf played on the same swing-set and monkey-bars there as Simon did, but more than two decades earlier. They both attended P.S. 173, and even had some of the same teachers. Horst mentioned that he left the Heights before the Second World War.

Slutnick thought, *before the Yekkes took over, or they would have fucking hung you upside down from a lamp post.* He was getting so drunk that he almost blurted it out loud.

It enthralled Horst that the locale of Simon's shitpicking career, now altered to be in Far Rockaway, was so near his dear friend Abie Cohen's garage. Another coincidence was that they both once lived on St. Mark's Place in the East Village, although again, not as contemporaries. Then the talk turned to soldiering. Simon observed that his *opa* Hugo Goldman and old Horst must have shared many experiences in the trenches, serving the Kaiser in battles against the detested Garlic Eaters. It was unfortunate that Hugo had passed on, because he and Horst would have had much to reminisce about.

Then Horst asked Simon about Vietnam and how he got the medals mentioned in his personal history, and Simon, who was by now half-soused, rose and answered in German.

"Soldier to soldier, Herr Von Essen, I ask you to forgive me, but I have promised myself to never speak about these matters."

Horst jumped to his feet, clicked his heels, and raised his stein in a grave salute, before draining it and sitting back down. Slutnick sat in silence through the exchange, smiling like a composer hearing his music played to perfection.

Horst told Goldman that he was perplexed about something in his written statement, concerning how his German background led to his feeling ill at ease in Israel during a sabbatical. That was all it said, and the old man was curious.

"*Feldwebel* Goldman, I have visited Israel many times, for both business and touristic purposes, and I never was made to feel uncomfortable because of my origins."

"Herr Von Essen," said Goldman. "I must confess, my first impulse is to say that this is because your visits to the Holy Land were shorter than mine."

He hung his head in self-reproach and switched to his perfect *Rhine-Deutsch* again.

"But I feel compelled to be completely honest with you, Herr Von Essen. In Israel my problems were entirely my own fault. I suppose that I am too formal, inflexible and demanding in some ways, and perhaps I desire order in things too much. *Ordnungsliebe* is simply part of my nature, and in my blood. I deeply regret including that remark about Israel in my personal statement."

There was a moment of silence, and Slutnick had a start when he realized that Goldman was handing the ball off to him. So he spoke up, and in a genteel, good humored and breezy way explained to everyone what the term 'Yekke' connoted, and that Goldman had a typical Yekke experience, which he took too seriously. But he stopped short of relating any of the vicious Yekke-putz jokes that a visiting mathematician from the Hebrew University once told him.

Old Horst bade Ludwig give him a refill. He stood again, unsteady this time, and raised his stein. He burped and wiped his mouth on his sleeve.

"I will tell you something, *Feldwebel* Goldman, before I piss myself and fall on my ass. I want everyone here to relax and enjoy the rest of the evening, so I will announce it right now. *You* are my choice for the endowment. *Prosit, Feldvebel Goldman. Prosit!*"

The old man chugged his beer, belched again, and sat. Simon came to his feet and steadied himself with one hand on the table. He raised his stein in a return salute.

"Herr Von Essen, thank you for this great honor. The honor of a lifetime. I will try to be worthy of it."

Simon burped as well, quaffed his steinfull and sat. There was applause all around, and Rector Dr. Friend appeared ready to burst with joy. The University of Northern Vermont had dealt the University of Burlington a major defeat---a humiliating blow. He toasted Horst Von Essen and thanked him on behalf of the entire university and the state of Vermont. Slutnick and Margaret were sober enough to exchange self-congratulatory glances.

***

The Von Essens arranged for the same limousines which brought their guests to the Bavarian Brauhaus to also bring them home---a good thing too, because they were all much too besotted to have driven. One limo departed with Dr. Friend, while Simon, Guillermo and Margaret boarded the other, which was piloted by a gigantic seventy year old uniformed East German immigrant named Lothar. He opened a door for Margaret, who opted to sit in the rear. Simon and Guillermo entered on their own and shared the seats in front of her, while Lothar ensconced himself behind a pane of tinted glass. Simon was to be taken to Montgomery where he was staying with the Singletons, and Guillermo's home was nearby, in Enosburg Falls. The mathematicians' destinations were twenty minutes away, but Margaret lived in a luxury condo just north of St. Albans, so she had only five minutes to make her point.

"Well played, gentlemen---well played indeed. Brilliantly

executed. A great victory. The tapestry of lies and half-truths which the two of you wove functioned magnificently."

Simon and Guillermo uttered beery thanks, and Margaret went on.

"Come now, Guillermo Slutnick. Tell me true. Precisely *when* were you planning on informing me that Simon and Mona Goldman were reconciling, and that suddenly there arose the necessity of obtaining a faculty position for her? Perhaps in a week or two? Tut-tut, gentlemen, tut-tut."

Guillermo slid down in his seat. It crossed his mind that she might be intending to garrote him---it would be easy enough. Goldman smirked. He knew that Dean Fulton would vent only on Slutnick, the mastermind.

"Guillermo Slutnick, surely you know that I have family and other contacts in Boston, and that ascertaining the state of Simon Goldman's marriage would be a trivial undertaking for me, yes?"

Obeying a mischievous impulse, Simon emitted a long, high-pitched whistle, the kind Uncle Meinhold used when something profound or serious happened, like when The Miracle Mets won the World Series in 1969.

Guillermo gathered what little dignity remained.

"Forgive me, Margaret. It was the only way we could play it. Was it not Queen Elizabeth I of England who said,

'Cowards falter, but danger is often overcome by those who nobly dare'?"

He was saving that one for the right occasion. Margaret laughed.

"You cram these words into mine ears against the stomach of my sense."

"*The Tempest*?" guessed Goldman.

"Ah, very good," she said. "Very good, indeed. You are an afficionado of the Bard, Simon Goldman?"

"Nah," said Goldman. "We had it kind of shoved down our throats at Cooper Union by Professor Klein. It just sounded familiar---I think I remember it from the Monarch Notes. Forsooth, methinks the Bard doth suck the big one. Verily."

Guillermo agreed with this literary assessment, but lacked the courage to voice his concurrence. He slid still lower.

"Do not fret, gentlemen. I shall not banish you from the realm. I have already spoken to Rector Dr. Friend about this contingency, and an associate professorship for Mona Goldman in the Department of Music shall be arranged. Truth be told, an expert on Late Renaissance and Tudor music would be a welcome addition to my Division of Arts and Science. You need not have sought to deceive me."

The limo pulled up in front of Margaret's condo, and Lothar helped her out. Guillermo spoke through the window.

"Margaret, again, my apologies for not being completely forthright. And thank you from the bottom of my heart for your generosity of spirit."

She smiled at him.

"Guillermo Slutnick, we shall discuss this matter further during our midweek rendezvous."

Though God hath raised me high, yet this I count the glory of my crown---that I have reigned with your love.

CHAPTER 14

Counterexample: Monday, June 2, 2003

-61-

At 9 a.m., Yu Wong was seated at his desk, with the twins looking over his shoulder as he corrupted their responses to the *American Psychoanalytical and Psychological Society Basic Personality Assessment Protocol.*

"Lucky you gentlemen used pencil," said Yu Wong, who had been giving his pink rubber eraser a serious workout. If Ibrahim had ticked 'yes' to a question where Nathan ticked 'no', then Yu Wong erased these answers and reversed them. If the twins had both chosen 'yes', then Yu Wong changed both to 'no', and vice-versa. On the sliding scale questions, Yu Wong left odd numbered questions unaltered, but reversed the twins' answers for the even ones. He called his method the 'Han people's semi-random averaging process'.

He was just finishing this subversion when there was a faint rapping. Ibrahim gave Yu Wong a few seconds to stash the forms in his desk, and then opened the door. It was Isidore Fleck

"Hello boys. You know, I've never been down here. I hope I'm not interrupting anything important."

Yu Wong said, "Hello Professor Fleck, no, nothing important. Please sit. Would you like some coffee or tea? We still have muffins in the fridge from delightful brunch on Saturday. Would you like?"

"I'm not a professor, you know. Just Izzy, if you please. Yeah, coffee would be great."

He smiled at Ibrahim from under his long, stringy beard.

"Especially extra sweet Arab coffee with cardamom, prepared in a rusty *kum-kum*. And sure, a muffin would be nice too."

"Of course, Izzy, of course," said Ibrahim, and he began preparing coffee for them all.

The three grad students knew that they were in the presence of a great and venerable mathematician, one who had the respect of Albert Einstein when he was their age. Izzy's title or lack of one meant nothing to them. Nathan got him a blueberry muffin from the fridge and sat him down.

"Boys, I bet you're wondering why I'm here in your subterranean lair. Well, for the better part of a week I've been studying Goldman's proof. I spent most of my time slogging through the combinatorics, and I'm sure that's all okay, and actually quite innovative. Then I looked at every known result he referred to and relied on, checked how he applied them and so on and so forth, and that stuff all looked okay too. So finally, having checked all the big and medium ideas over and over, I started inspecting every supposedly obvious fact that he used---you know, things he mentioned just in passing. And late last night I was looking at the part of his proof where he casually mentions some routine properties of a certain geometric object he constructed---the vector sum of two closed convex cones living in a finite dimensional space."

The three students' faces contorted in concentration as they remembered that Goldman's exposition involved such an object---a 'conical sum' he called it. One cone was polyhedral, meaning that it had faces and edges. The other was a limit of polyhedral cones.

"The people who checked Goldman's proof were all top class combinatorists, but maybe they got fooled by something out of their sphere of interest---something geometric and counterintuitive that I bet other people know as mathematical folklore. It was all too much of a rush to judgement, and there's a bandwagon effect operating here too, I'm sure. What surprises me is that it is something Goldman himself should have caught---it's completely elementary. He was just careless, I guess. Or hurrying, perhaps. Take a look at what it says in his notes, on the bottom of page 27---the very last line, inside the parentheses."

Nathan Finkelstein already had his set of notes in hand, and read Goldman's remark out loud.

Of course, since C^1 and C^2 are closed convex cones, then so is their vector sum, $C^1 + C^2$.

"Boys, I think that sum *need not be closed.* I believe I remember a nice counterexample in three-dimensional space. Maybe I saw it in a journal article or as an exercise in some textbook somewhere, a million years ago. If you guys have a few minutes, can we go up to the lounge where the blackboard is bigger? I'd like you to help me check things. It won't take long."

-62-

Ibrahim's *kum-kum* worked its magic, and they found an extra mug for Izzy. The four of them sipped their coffees as the elevator took them up to the second floor.

"Elixir of the gods," said Izzy, as the doors opened.

They entered the lounge, and the only person present was black clad Phil Schwartz, nursing a brew of his own. He was there in hopes of catching Izzy and putting the squeeze on his brain for a few hours.

Izzy said, "Phil, you punk, we have to put a hold on spatial ripping for a half hour or so. We're checking something in Goldman's proof. I fear there is a grievous error."

Phil closed his eyes and ran his fingers through his mullet.

"You know I'm not in Simon's fan club, but I hope nothing is wrong. I wouldn't wish that on any mathematician, not even a Simon Goldman."

"Come off it Phil," said Izzy. "You wouldn't feel so bad if it had happened to the Unabomber."

For the first time in anyone's memory, Phil Schwartz laughed.

"Izzy, if his proof is wrong, Goldman might *become* a Unabomber!"

Phil's attitude warmed Izzy---he never would have expected it. And Phil was right. An error would be devastating---crushing and humiliating. Izzy had to proceed with caution---but he was already sure.

"I don't want to start a new mideast conflict, so I'll ask Yu Wong to go to the board, and the rest of us can sit and be his puppeteers."

The twins grabbed erasers, cleaned the board for Yu Wong, and found a few decent pieces of chalk for him. Izzy told Yu Wong to draw a three-dimensional coordinate system---the *(x,y,z)*-axes.

"Okay, Yu Wong. Now sketch a Minkowki cone with its vertex at the origin, lying on the positive *x*-axis---above the *(x,y)*-plane."

Yu Wong drew it. It was an infinite ice-cream cone without any ice-cream in it. Izzy asked the three students to write down a formula describing the Minkowski cone, because he was too lazy, he said. Phil preempted them. He was intimately familiar with Minkowski cones, and dictated a descriptive formula which Yu Wong wrote next to the picture.

Izzy said, "Okay, call that sucker C^1, and let C^2 be the negative *x*-axis."

Yu Wong added the labels to the picture. Now the infinite ice-cream cone had an infinite spike coming out of its tip.

"Okay, Yu Wong. Try to prove that the vector sum of C^1 and C^2 is closed. We'll follow along."

An object is topologically closed if it contains its own boundary---an apple is closed if it possesses all its skin. Proving closedness of a geometric object is a rote exercise, and Yu Wong stuck to the usual rubric, with all the others following his steps. And then he got stuck. Izzy sat expressionless as Yu Wong, the twins and Phil huddled at the board for five minutes, trying to make the closedness argument work.

"Does everyone see that it's not closed?" said Izzy. "Take a point like (-1,-1,0). There are points in $C^1 + C^2$ which are arbitrarily close to it, but that point clearly is *not* in the sum of the two cones. Not closed. Case closed."

Yu Wong said, "Yes, I see," and he wrote down a sequence of points in $C^1 + C^2$ which approached the limit (-1,-1,0), which was itself not in the sum.

"Yes, this is good counterexample, Izzy," said Yu Wong.

The twins and Phil nodded their agreement.

"Oh shit," said Phil, still exhibiting the humanity no one suspected he possessed. "Izzy, is it fatal? You know Goldman's proof better than anyone."

"Oh, it's fatal, all right. A proof it ain't. You can prove it's true if *both* cones are finitely generated---you know, polyhedral cones or simple rays---but it fails if one of them is rotund, as we see here in this goddam example. And Goldman's proof---specifically, where he does what he calls 'G-interpolation'---completely falls apart if he has to restrict himself to the polyhedral case, because it's the *limit* of polyhedral cones which he absolutely needs to work with. And such limit cones can be rotund, like the Minkowski cone. This is very, very bad. A disaster. I'm going upstairs to look for Aitch Singleton."

-63-

Izzy's knock distracted Celestine, who was at the small blackboard expounding on the Clarke generalized derivative of nonsmooth calculus. He saw that Aitch was happy, and back to his old self after three years of mourning and numbness.

"Hi, kids," he said, and high-fived them both. "I hate to be the bearer of bad news, but there's something I have to tell you."

He asked Celestine if he could use the board, and she erased it for him. The old man drew the ice-cream cone with a spike, and spent five minutes explaining the flaw in Goldman's proof. And that he was certain it was fatal.

Aitch felt the room spin.

"Oh dear. Oh dear. Not what I need to hear."

Celestine hung her head.

"I feel guilty for not catching this. I am so sorry."

Aitch said, "It's not your fault, Celestine. You made it clear that you weren't intending to check the proof. You quite correctly left it to the combinatorist's---we all did. It's unfortunate that the error is so mundane---simple finite dimensional point-set topology. Any of us could have caught it, had we thought about it."

Izzy said, "That's right. You'd think that if there was a flaw, it would be in the combinatorics. Anyway, my work here is done, as Batman would say. Phil's waiting for me in the lounge, and I don't want him to slip into one of his moods. Such a punk."

***

After Fleck left, Aitch and Celestine double-checked the counterexample and perused Simon's notes. And even though they were not complexity theorists, it was clear to them that the error was a killer, just as Izzy claimed. The polyhedral case was not general enough. The Titanic had hit an iceberg.

"Poor Simon," said Aitch. "He must have known and been freaking, trying to make repairs. Poor, poor Simon."

"Maybe a miracle will happen and he can straighten it out," said Celestine.

"Simon is an atheist," said Aitch. "But he once told me, long ago, that he believes in miracles---something he picked up from his uncle. But Izzy seemed certain that no miracle could save the proof. We should trust him."

"So what will you do?"

"Well, for openers, I'd just like to speak to Simon or Mona."

Yesterday he tried to phone the Goldmans twice, with the intention of inviting them over for a dinner of venison provided by Chinnie, but there was no answer. He had left two voice messages, stating his sociable aim, but got no return call. There was no answer again this time.

***

By noon, the twins were back at their desks in the sub-sub-basement of the Fitch, after dropping off their completed forms at the Department of Psychology. Yu Wong entered the cubicle, carrying today's feast. There were two small envelopes on his desk.

Nathan said, "Yu Wong, please take this money---sixty dollars ---an advance payment to the Han People's Take-Out for our next fifteen lunches, including this one."

Yu Wong put the envelopes in his top drawer and grinned. He was in a good mood, because yesterday team Bigballs won over a thousand dollars.

"So you gentlemen not starve at least two more weeks. Delightful."

The twins did not laugh---they were morose in the wake of the implosion of Goldman's theorem. After a minute of silence, they began making ready for their devotions. Ibrahim knelt on his rug, facing east, and Nathan was at his desk, thumbing through his small black prayer book, turning to today's passage.

As he set the table, Yu Wong looked down, feeling guilty for his attempt at levity.

"Maybe good idea if you gentlemen say prayer today for Professor Simon Goldman."

-64-

When Celestine and Aitch got to Montgomery, they were disappointed that there was no offering on the doorstep from the catamount, which had not missed a day since first making his presence known. Newton and

Minipod were perched on the window sill of the shed, gazing into the darkening forest, missing him as well.

Aitch dialed the Goldmans' number one more time, in hopes of having them over for an impromptu meal. He did not have a notion about how to broach the subject of the cataclysmic counterexample, but he felt that doing so here and in person would make it easier. But again there was no answer.

"Cherie, there is no use in worrying. Try to relax while I fix supper."

He did as he was told, parked himself in front of the TV in the living room, and began flicking through the channels. Normally he would have gravitated to CNN, but world events did not interest him at the moment, and in fact repelled him. Aitch wanted distraction of a more gentle nature, and in hopes of finding some, went to GMPTV. He was disappointed because the station was on a fundraising break, so he closed his eyes, leaned back on the sofa, and drifted.

He was jolted awake by a popping sound from the kitchen---Celestine pulling the cork from a bottle of chablis. He looked back at the set. The announcer was the chairperson of the Department of Music at UNV, and she was asking for contributions in the usual enervating way, as the camera panned the bank of four volunteer telephone operators behind her.

"Hey Celestine. Come look. There's Mona."

She brought his wine. Mona was not speaking to a potential donor at the moment, but she had both hands on her phone, focusing on it, ready to snatch it up if it rang.

"Aitch, look at the folded card on her table."

WB – PLEASE CALL

Celestine made sense of it before he did.

"Mona Goldman wants Wonder Boy to contact her. Aitch, she looks so scared. I don't think she knows where he is."

-65-

By midnight, Aitch had been parked in the Goldmans' driveway for over three hours. He was sitting in the Honda, listening to a Duke Ellington CD and studying the Nonsmooth Analysis reference by rooflight, during those intervals when he could suppress his worries enough to concentrate on mathematics.

He stepped out, leaned his back against the car and gazed at the Milky Way, which looked like a floating fogbank tonight. Over the years, as he grew older and gained more and more scientific knowledge, his sense of wonder about the universe only deepened. He had absorbed a lot of physics during his mathematical life, but gravity and magnetism still seemed magical to him, like when he was a child. And he was always spooked by the fact that he did not see the stars as they presently were---only images from the distant past could be discerned, because it took so long for their light to reach him. Many did not even exist any more, he reminded himself. Gazing at those distant sparklers, many of which were galaxies larger than the Milky Way itself, he felt that he really knew nothing about the cosmos---nothing at all. He only knew some of the equations.

His contemplation of the unknowable was interrupted when he saw the headlights of Mona's Mercedes. She pulled in next to him and sat stone still as he reached a long arm through the window to cut the engine. She remained frozen for a moment more, then leaned forward, rested her forehead on the wheel, and wept---first soft murmurs, then groans.

"Bloody hell. Aitch, what am I to do?"

"Let's go inside, sweetest Mona. I'll fix you a nice cup of tea."

He pried her hand from the wheel, pocketed the keys, and led her to the house. As they walked the thirty steps, two deer bounded across their path, not five yards from them. Their beauty and grace brought her back a bit.

"Yes, I suppose a spot of tea couldn't hurt."

***

He left her on the porch. Waiting for the water to boil, he shuffled through the dozen coffee splattered looseleaf sheets strewn on the kitchen counter. Most bore the same sketch---Minkowski's cone with a spike---Izzy's counterexample---along with calculations scrawled in frustration and panic. Some were attempts to find an error in the counterexample. Others, later ones no doubt, were futile attempts to dance around the example and fix G-interpolation. Aitch felt his heart sink. Poor Simon. The kettle whistled and he fixed a pot of hibiscus tea, the kind he knew Mona preferred in the evening. He came back and sat with his arm around her while it steeped, and she opened up.

"It all started again when Mathilda died---two years before we moved up here. I thought that the suddenness of it was a small mercy---it was a massive stroke, you know. It's how we should all go, I daresay. Lights out. No lingering or degeneration---just close the switch. But it shocked him, and I suppose he didn't get to say goodbye properly. Perhaps he could not have done so under under any circumstances---they were so tied. Whatever the reason, that's when it started again. Bloody hell."

"When *what* started, Mona?"

"I don't know what to call it." Her voice quavered. "Simon is so strong and stubborn---he managed to hide it from everyone. And now I don't know where in bloody hell he is."

Her little body was again racked by sobs. She rested her head on his shoulder.

"Mona, there was an error in his proof---you probably know."

She said nothing, but he felt her nod of agreement tickle his shoulder.

"It's completely understandable that he's upset," said Aitch. "This isn't the first time that a great mathematician had a major theorem break down."

He regretted the choice of words even as they spilled from him, but he babbled on.

"Simon will get over this just like the rest of them did. He'll come home. He's a tough cookie. Resilient. He'll come around. Of course he's upset. Jeez, after all those years of effort."

She sat up, breaking the contact.

"Ha! *All those years*, indeed! Is *that* what he had you believing, Aitch? The truth is that the entire gestation period of Goldman's Theorem was at most three weeks. Until last month, he hadn't done a stich of mathematics for *seven bloody years*."

Aitch became lightheaded and fought to retain his focus as she went on.

"Couldn't get his brain to work since 1996, after his mother passed away. Barely could read anything. Stared at the bloody walls and fidgeted. Still horny as Tony Blair, however. Then that beastly Guillermo Slutnick started putting pressure on him, and the past few weeks have been a mad mathematical scramble. And no more Tony Blair."

"Mona, you say the trouble started two years before you came here?"

"Yes. After a year of mathematical paralysis at Harvard, he told me that he needed a change of scene---perhaps find a place where we could eventually retire---so the offer from UNV was heaven sent. But after we relocated, he remained blocked---that's how he referred to his mental state. And he became more and more frightened. Then a few weeks ago, shortly after he initiated his quest for the Holy Grail, he started having the dreams again."

"The *dreams*? What dreams?"

"After Simon returned from Vietnam, for about a year he had symptoms consistent with post-traumatic stress disorder, although that terminology was not in vogue then---it wasn't called PTSD in 1971. The doctors I forced him to visit either labeled it shell shock, nervous or adrenal exhaustion, or nothing at all. He couldn't sit still. Never slept more than two hours at a stretch. And those dreams, Aitch---many nights he'd throw himself around on the bed and scream like a demon. He wouldn't sit for therapy, and refused sedatives because in spite of everything, he was doing big things in his dissertation at Northwestern, and he wanted to stay sharp. He finally came out of it after a year---he was twenty-five. He said that talking to Meinhold was the therapy that finally worked. As far as I know, that old man is the only person Simon ever told about Vietnam."

"Yes," said Aitch. "Meinhold would have understood things of that nature."

So would the Von Essens, he was certain.

"Thank God and thank Meinhold, Aitch. I had an exit strategy. I was prepared to leave him. Wound up marrying the bugger instead."

Aitch was best man at their wedding in 1973. He never had an inkling about any of this, and now he felt like a dolt.

Mona said, "But during the past few weeks, both the insomnia and the bloody dreams have returned, and with a vengeance."

"Well, I know Simon was wound up tight for the past few weeks. I thought it was just the effects of working hard. Mona, maybe he reached out to Meinhold again. Let's call him---if you think he can handle being told this kind of stuff."

"*Meinhold?* He'd be angry with me if I *didn't* tell him."

Mona glanced at her wristwatch.

"It's 12:30, but the Mannheimers are night owls."

***

She put the phone on speaker and dialed the number. Lotte picked up on the first ring and sang her accented hello. Her voice was that of a younger woman, and when Aitch heard it, he closed his eyes and recalled the aromas of her cooking, wishing that he could go back in time and have a meal in the Mannheimers' apartment overlooking the Hudson.

"Why should we move," they would say whenever they were asked if the suburbs enticed them. "We have everything we need here---this is paradise. And look at that view. Better than the Rhine. You can't buy a view like that."

After hellos, Lotte said, "*Schatz*, today Meinie and I walked up Fort Washington Avenue to Fort Tryon Park, all the way to The Cloisters, where we had a nice lunch, and then we walked all the way back home. Wait while I get him to come to the phone."

Meinhold picked it up.

"Hi Sweetheart. My wife is like a drill sergeant---she keeps me in shape to make up for overfeeding me. You probably want to talk to my nephew, but the *schmendrick* isn't here at the moment. When he comes in, I'll have him phone you."

Meinhold's English was flawless and he was well read, but his accent was thick, even though he had been an American for sixty-five years. He sounded like he had just gotten off the boat, which Aitch suspected was common among the aging Yekkes of this neighborhood..

"He's with *you*, Uncle Meinhold?" Mona asked, fighting tears.

"It sounds like you have the speaker on," said Meinhold.

"Yes, Aitch is with me. We're both worried about Simon."

Meinhold and Aitch had not seen each other since Maureen's funeral, three years ago. It meant a lot to Aitch that the Mannheimers had made the trip.

Meinhold said, "Simon phoned late last night from the Ramapo rest stop on the Thruway, and asked if he could spend a few nights. I had to remind him that he has a key and that this is his home in New York. He got here at midnight and looked like hell. Said he needed to talk to me, but only after he got some rest."

Mona tried to thank him, but he talked over her.

"Sweetheart, we got up at six this morning, but he already left,"

"And no breakfast," said Lotte.

"We haven't seen him since," said Meinhold. "But his bag and his briefcase are still in his room. It looks like he worked all night, judging from the way mathematics books and papers are laying around. He's been drawing the same picture over and over---like an ice-cream cone with a hair growing out of it. His car is parked around the corner on 173rd Street, so it looks like he will be back soon, I hope tonight. And I will be sure that he calls you."

Mona started to thank him for his kindness, but the old man cut her off again.

"Mona, tell me if you think I'm wrong, but I've seen this happen to some of my best friends. Guys who took a year or two after 1945 to readjust their nervous systems to civilian life. After that initial period, they were happy and normal and went on with their lives. But twenty, thirty, even forty years later, there is a relapse. I'm not talking about losers or winos, but doctors, lawyers and businessmen."

"Yes," said Mona. "Now you can add a mathematician to the list, Uncle Meinhold. What you suspect is true."

"Well, it makes sense. With my friends, there was always a trigger---sometimes more than one. With Simon, my sister's death might be contributing. Mona, they recover in time. Simon will be okay. And we'll get him to see a headshrinker this time around. They understand this kind of stuff better nowadays. Don't worry. I will make him promise to go."

Mona said, "Uncle Meinhold, since Mathilda passed away, Simon was very upset, it's true. But it wasn't really a repeat of his post-Vietnam behavior. That started again only a few weeks ago---because now there is also something else."

She went on to describe Simon's seven year mathematical funk, the recent pressurized mathematical flurry, and the humiliating implosion of Goldman's theorem.

"He just wasn't ready to do mathematics," she said, and began to weep again.

Aitch put his arm around her and spoke into the mike.

"It doesn't look like it can be fixed, Meinhold. He must be terribly upset."

Meinhold took a moment to process it all.

"Yes. He is wounded, but if I recovered from a hole in my head, then he can recover from a hole in his proof. Piece of cake. He owes it to himself. I'll phone you as soon as he comes in."

***

The Goldmans had a guest room, and Aitch insisted that he spend the night. Mona did not argue about it and announced that she was going upstairs to have a hot bath. When Aitch heard the water running, he dialed Annie's number in Boston, and gave her a high speed rendition of the whole sad story.

"Daddy, I bet you already understand the psychodynamics of this very well. Let me hear what *you* think."

He realized that this must be a technique his daughter employed with certain kinds of patients.

"Okay. Simon had an unwholesomely close relationship with his mother. That's always been obvious."

Annie said, "Probably an incestuous relationship, psychologically speaking. Not physical incest, mind you, but something nearly as bad. Go on."

"Well," said Aitch, "She was very demanding of him---he felt that he had to be Wonder Boy to keep her happy. I remember her well, Annie. She was a very sad, lonely lady who seemed to get joy only through Simon's successes. I think Simon always hid the fact that he worried about her."

"Yes," said Annie. "He was her main reason for living---she lost everyone else. Refugee-survivor complex---quite common. With her emotional dependency and depression, she inadvertently made him feel responsible for her well being, and then she up and died. I once attended a workshop concerning children of holocaust survivors, with emphasis on ones who have no siblings---not rare in this group. Simon's problems fit the general pattern. And the fact that he had only one parent probably only made things worse."

"So when his mom passed on, he must have gone a bit haywire."

"He's in a severe depression, Daddy. Seven years is a long time to have your brain chemistry out of whack, and to be hiding it from the world. He needs to get some help. The sooner the better."

He gave her details about the past few weeks---the pressure from Slutnick, the Holy Grail, and the displays of cockiness, extreme even for Simon Goldman. He told her about the return of PTSD symptoms, the self-medication with cannabis and alcohol, and then the horror of Goldman's theorem falling apart.

"Oh dear," said Annie. "It sounds like his desperation to get some mathematics done triggered an PTSD relapse when his defenses were down. Then when his proof failed, he suffered what we call a 'narcissistic injury', and it sounds like a very bad one. Daddy, he may be having a breakdown, and no one can predict what he'll do if he snaps and slips into a psychotic state. There is a high risk that he will try to hurt himself. Simon has to be found as soon as possible."

Aitch thanked her, said his affectionate goodnight, and trembled. Mona was still in the tub, so he phoned Celestine, who told him there was no contact with either Simon or Chinnie. He gave her a briefing, reminded her to feed Newton in the morning, and told her that he loved her.

Ten minutes later, Mona came down in her pajamas, and poured them each a snifter of Grand Marnier.

"I'll probably lie awake all night waiting for the phone to ring even after I drink this." She raised her glass. "Cheerio, Aitch. Stiff upper lip and all that."

Aitch clinked.

"To your husband's health. May he live to be one hundred and twenty."

***

The bed was comfortable, and he managed to get some sleep. If Mona wept or was restless during the night, he did not hear her. Now it was eight o'clock on a muggy Tuesday morning, and neither Simon nor Meinhold had phoned. He followed the aroma of coffee to the kitchen, where he found Mona standing by the stove, flipping french toast. Her expression was frozen---she refused to give in to tears again. Stiff upper lip, thought Aitch. He hugged her from behind and planted a kiss on the top of her head.

"Sweet Mona, I'm going to New York, and I'm going to find Simon."

***

He got home before nine, and surprised Celestine by joining her in the shower. She shrieked like Janet Leigh in *Psycho*.

"Now we're even," he said, as she coiled herself around him. Aitch staggered, but found his balance by gripping her thighs and lifting, pressing her back against the wall. "Please...no scratching", he whispered, but a kiss interrupted him---she wanted him to stop reminding her. Their coalescence was tender, which was what he craved. They peaked within seconds of each other in the spray, and remained glued together until the hot water ran out, jolting them back into the world.

As she towelled his spiky hair, he told her what Annie thought ---and that he was embarking upon a quest to find Goldman.

"I want to get going within the hour, after I make some calls. The D-Day talk has to be cancelled immediately, before people make travel plans and we have a major fiasco on our hands. And I have to tell Guillermo Slutnick what is happening."

She hugged him with her ear over his heart, and felt it racing.

"Aitch, listen to me, *s'il vous plait.* Go ahead and do what you must do to find Simon Goldman. I can handle all the rest---don't worry about anything. I will call Joe Malone and explain the situation, and he will contact all the others. And I will take care of Chairman Slutnick. Cherie, you might need some help. Why don't you call Vito?"

Aitch saw the wisdom in it and dialed Vito's home number in Montreal, and then his office at the Université de Montréal, but both times got only his gravelly recorded declaration in French, English and Italian that he was not available. But when he tried the de Bernardi chalet at Lac Kelly, Vito answered on the first ring, and listened in stony silence as Aitch told him everything.

"*Mio amico,* I will be at your door in my Maserati in thirty minutes time. You will let me drive, okay?"

Aitch said, "I'm grateful, Vito."

"You were wise to ask for my help, Aitch. As you know, I have some *famiglia* in New York. They will help us locate our friend."

After Vito rang off, Aitch dialed the Mannheimers' number. Lotte picked it up, sounding anxious this time. Simon was still missing, and Meinhold was out on a dawn patrol, searching.

CHAPTER 15

The Green Machine: 1970

-66-

On a snow-blown Tuesday morning in February, twenty-two year old Simon Goldman pulled into the parking lot behind the Army National Guard armory in Indiana City, Indiana---Company B, 3rd Battalion, 141st Infantry Division. It was in a desolate industrial neighborhood, with weedy vacant lots and ruined warehouses interspersed between a few functioning enterprises. The drive from Chicago's Rogers Park neighborhood in Mona's Beetle took over three hours on account of the bad weather. Simon was glad he left home before sunrise, because he was desperate.

Today there was only a skeleton crew guarding the armory and its wares. But for one weekend every month, the entire contingent of over two hundred men came here for a drill. These gatherings involved rote maintenance chores as well as mind numbing, repetitive training sessions dealing with subjects such as riot control and the intricacies of the gas mask. Nevertheless, there was always a lot of dead time, and many of the troops engaged in prodigious amounts of drinking during the lulls. Brown paper bags provided cover so that the officers and noncoms, many of whom were boozers themselves, could in good conscience not take notice. There was also a fair amount of even more clandestine pot smoking in the nooks and crannies of the armory. For both vices, the unwritten rule was to not stink the place out too much, bag your empties, and field-strip your roaches. Every July, they trucked up to Camp Grayling in Michigan's piney woods for 'summer camp'---two weeks of even more enthusiastic guzzling and toking. 'Weekend warriors' and 'summertime soldiers' they called themselves, except for the handful of John Waynes who were serious about things and disgusted by the lax standards and rampant substance abuse in Company B. But they dared not raise their voices in protest, for fear of retribution from boozers and stoners of all ranks.

Simon circumnavigated the cavernous armory and entered by the main door. The SPC-4 on guard duty recognized him from his visit six days earlier, and waved him through without a fuss to see Captain Morozievicz, the commanding officer. Simon made his way across the glossy drill floor, climbed the metal stairs to the CO's office, and pressed the buzzer.

***

The captain was wearing starched, pressed olive-drab fatigues. He was seated behind a tidy, polished oak desk, and held Simon in his porcine gaze for a moment.

Bell-bottoms and a flower shirt just like the last time he was here, but he cut his hair since then. Another goddam cheesedick wire-rimmed hippie looking to stay stateside.

Captain Morozievicz was a career soldier who did a tour as a supply officer in Pleiku and now ran this bullshit National Guard unit, the majority of whose members were from Chicago and draft dodgers at heart. It was the crappiest dead-end command an officer could get---the West Pointers got all the good ones, the captain knew. But at least he was stationed in his home town. He planned to retire in two years, after he put in his twenty. Then he and the wife would buy a trailer and travel.

"What the fuck do you want, Goldberg? You were here just last week. Nothing has changed. You're still number eleven on the list. Go the fuck home."

"It's Goldman, sir. Simon Goldman. I'm here because I got my greetings yesterday."

In other words, he received his induction notice in the mail from his New York City draft board, ordering him to report to the induction center in Chicago in one week's time---the same seedy place where he took his physical last November, along with hundreds of other fearful, agitated young men. Many were graduate students like himself, who no longer could obtain deferments from military service and were now potential cannon fodder. Two months ago the Selective Service held a national draft lottery, and Simon's birthday got him unlucky number thirteen---a sure ticket to Vietnam, and maybe only one way. Adding to his desperation to avoid returning from Southeast Asia in a body bag was the fear that he would have to interrupt his graduate studies at Northwestern for two years. So he put his name on the waiting list of every Army National Guard unit within two hundred miles of Chicago.

Simon was paying a visit to Captain Morozievicz today because one of his fellow grad students told him that a friend of a friend heard a rumor from another friend that the commanding officer of this company could be bribed. Two hundred dollars got you into the Guard, Goldman was told---and this was a very desirable unit. There was little chance that the governor of Indiana would demonstrate his patriotism by activating this detachment for duty in Vietnam, as happened to other companies downstate. This was because Indiana City, like Gary and Michigan City, had a restive racial atmosphere, and troops might be needed to quell a riot. Simon brought three hundred just in case the price went up after the Tet Offensive.

"Well Goldman, it sounds like you are truly fucked. You should have put a glass eyeball in your ass at the physical and gone for a 4-F on psychological grounds. I heard it really impresses the shrinks."

Actually, Simon did consider faking some serious mental

disability to avoid service, but Uncle Meinhold would have disapproved if he found out. Besides, at his physical he learned that the Army did not fall for that kind of stuff. There was a weeping ninety pound black kid with needle marks in his arm, but they passed him with flying colors. And he saw two latinos sprinkle some mysterious powder into their urine samples, and was incredulous when they too were pronounced fit to serve.

"Sir," said Simon, who felt a glimmer of hope because the captain got his name right in his last utterance. "I was thinking that you could admit me to your unit today, and inform my draft board in a pre-dated letter."

Pushy little Yid bastard, thought the captain, who was not really an anti-Semite per se. He hated all ethnic groups more or less equally, except for his fellow Poles, who were dominant in the grimy steel towns of northern Indiana, along with other Slavic groups.

"Why the fuck should I jump you up on the list? There's ten guys ahead of you and they all have pretty good sob stories. Some of them are even true."

Goldman knew that he was in the universe of *Catch-22* and *The Good Soldier Svejk,* but this was real. He pointed to the typewriter in a corner of the hyper-neat office. It was a shiny black Smith-Corona, vintage 1945.

"Captain Morozievicz, sir, I'm an excellent typist. I could be your clerk. The best clerk in the entire Indiana Army National Guard."

The captain thought about it and saw the potential upside.

"Get behind that fucking typewriter, Goodstein, put in a sheet of paper, and get ready to take dictation."

Simon did as he was told with alacrity, and as he got into position and loaded the paper, he thought of Mrs. O'Connell, his strict and demanding eighth grade typing teacher. He felt a pang of guilt about the time he and his classmates trampled her in a stairwell during a fire drill. She might wind up being the one person most responsible for keeping him out of Vietnam. Maybe he would look her up one day and thank her.

"Prepare to type what I say," said the captain, who had put his boots up on the desk and clasped his hands behind his neck, the posture accentuating his paunch. Simon held his hands above the Smith-Corona's keys, poised to demonstrate his virtuosity on the instrument.

"I am a lowlife unpatriotic cocksucking dope smoking hippie bastard cheesedick asshole scumbag dingleberry draft dodger chickenshit coward and I would sell my syphilitic whore mother to avoid duty in the beautiful Republic of South Vietnam."

Simon's fingers were flying and he finished only a split second after the captain ceased yammering. The machine's bell pinged loudly as he pulled out the sheet and in the same motion handed it over for inspection. Captain Morozievicz perused it and his eyes lit up.

"Out-STANDING, Goodman. OUT-FUCKING-STANDING! But isn't 'cock sucking' *two* words?"

"Yes *sir*. If you say so, *sir*."

"Okay, cut the shit---you passed. I can get you into my company and your draft board can go fuck itself. They'll ship some fucking Puerto Rican to Vietnam in your place---you approve, right? You'll attend this month's drill in civvies, and you'll be working for me here in the company HQ. Then in mid-March, you're off to regular army basic training at Fort Leonard Wood in the Missouri Ozarks, and God help your sorry kike ass when the drill niggers get ahold of you. After that, if you survive, it's straight into MOS school---your Military Occupational Specialty. Unless you decide during basic that you'd prefer to do a three year hitch because you want to live a life of danger as an airborne fucking ranger. I will earmark your file with 'Heavy Equipment' as your MOS, because no clerk slots are available. Learning to drive a bulldozer will be good for an effete Jew asshole like yourself. But don't worry---you'll clerk for me no matter what when you return, because we don't even have any heavy fucking equipment."

Simon thought of Meinhold and knew that he was not capable of measuring up to the high standard of patriotism set by his beloved ex-paratrooper uncle and surrogate father. The National Guard looked like an honorable alternative to Canada or self-inflicted physical damage like chopping off his left pinky, a strategy he had once considered.

"Twenty-four weeks in the Green Machine," said the captain. "It'll make a man of you."

"Yes sir. Thank you, sir."

He knew that he was committing himself to almost half a year of hell, to be followed by five and a half more years of being a weekend warrior and summertime soldier.

"Sir, is there something I need to sign?"

Captain Morozievicz said, "You better fucking believe it. But first you have to provide me with two hundred and fifty reasons why I should admit a cheesedick like you into Company B."

Simon counted out twenty-five tens on the desk, and Captain Morozievicz counted them again.

-67-

Simon attended the weekend drill at the end of February, and it was not as bad as he had feared. Captain Morozievicz did not have much for him to do in the office on Saturday---just filling out some requisition forms, which took twenty minutes, and manning the telephone, which never rang. And he never had to take dictation. In fact, the captain left Goldman alone in the office and spent most of his time in the back room of the motor pool garage, drinking boilermakers while watching college basketball on the tube with First Sergeant Kowalski and the truck mechanics, who were the only members of the company he felt he needed to be nice to. The standing order for Private Goldman was to summon the captain "...only in case of an absolute fucking emergency, like gooks in the perimeter or a phone call from the Battalion Commander down in Valparaiso." He told Goldman to go for a half-hour feed in the mess hall at noon. Today's lunch budget would be spent on delivery pizza like last month, the captain said before vanishing, because one of the fucking cooks sabotaged the main oven again. Donuts and coffee were available in the mess hall too, all day long. The captain also told Simon that he could have a ten minute break every hour, but to take the phone off the hook whenever he left the office.

Simon occupied himself by spreading out his math books on the captain's desk and writing up the proofs of some theorems on pursuit-evasion games, for his doctoral dissertation. Here in the armory, he mused, there was no pursuit---only evasion, and in this regard, he had it made in the shade. The only visitor who ever knocked or buzzed was Captain Morozievicz himself. Apparently some vestigial sense of duty compelled him to come upstairs and check in with Private Goldman every hour or so. During one such visit, after not returning Simon's crisp salute, the captain thumbed through one of his mathematical reference texts.

"You're one weird cheesedick, Goldenberg. What the fuck is an *ordinary* differential equation? What makes it ordinary? Jesus H. Fucking Christ."

He tossed the book back on the desk, farted, and left before Simon could formulate a response that did not sound condescending or arrogant. He was beginning to like his CO, and felt something akin to loyalty towards him. This was going to work out okay, and tomorrow would be even easier. Most of Company B was going to truck down to Camp Atterbury for practice on the rifle range, and Simon would be left alone in the HQ.

***

He discovered that he had some natural talent for functioning in this military milieu, which was a pleasant surprise because he was an utter failure as a Boy Scout---he lacked respect for authority, the troop leader had told his mother.

Simon reasoned that since he was the only member of the company in civilian clothes, he would be very conspicuous if he wandered around. There was the danger that some officer or noncom would try to grab him for an unpleasant detail, or some John Wayne might report him for malingering. Simon knew that he could always invoke the fact that he was the captain's personal clerk and therefore under his protection, but he preferred to avoid the hassle. He wanted to saunter in peace to stretch his legs every few hours. It helped the mathematical process, and besides, he was curious about what was going on in the armory. So in order to protect himself from being waylaid, he adopted the stratagem of carrying a clipboard, parking a pencil behind an ear, and looking as officious as possible. He was a man on a mission and it worked like a charm---no one harassed him.

***

Simon made his final exploratory foray at 4 p.m., an hour before dismissal. He went down a dim stairwell to the dingy basement, and was making his way along a poorly lit corridor when he detected the unmistakable aroma of marijuana smoke. He followed his nose, and the trail ended at a door marked 'WEAPONS SECTION', which someone had left open a crack. It was in this large, moldy room that over two hundred M-16 assault rifles were stored in lock-down racks. In addition, ammo, tear gas grenades, gas masks, and sidearms for the officers were secured in a vault at the back. Second Lieutenant Nathaniel Mills and the seven men under him staffed this place. All were seated in beach chairs, passing around a fat joint worthy of Cheech and Chong, and grooving to a Chicago rock station. One-hit-wonder Norman Greenbaum was singing *Spirit in the Sky.*

Lieutenant Mills was a lanky black from Gary who had received a field commission during his combat tour in Vietnam. He got out of the regulars eight months before, and the bit of pay from the Guard helped cover his tuition at the University of Indiana, where he was a studying law. Mills exhaled a deep lungful of blue smoke and held Private Goldman in a red-eyed stare. Simon snapped off a crisp salute, and the entire weapons section cracked up.

Lieutenant Mills yelped, "Troop, close that fucking door, would you? Which one of you incompetent nincompoop motherfuckers left it open?"

Simon closed it, and no one responded to the question, because none of them knew the answer. He sensed that he was among kindred spirits.

One of them said, "Excuse me, sir, but you're bogarting again."

They all laughed and the lieutenant passed the doobie along.

"Smells like pretty good shit," said Simon, craving acceptance, which was granted on the spot.

Mills said, "You're fucking A right, my man. Acapulco Gold. Nothing but the finest for the troops under my command. But the shit in Nam is way stronger, especially the Cambodian Red. You can hallucinate on it---totally available and dirt cheap. I theorize that Ho Chi

Minh is behind its distribution, the clever gook fucker. I hope he runs for Governor of Indiana one day so I can vote for him. Tell us a bit about yourself and plop your ass down. You can partake."

Simon laid a one minute life history on them as he unfolded a spare beach chair and sat. Another fattie began circulating as Norman Greenbaum gave way to the Jefferson Airplane.

Lieutenant Mills said, "Well, Private Acapulco Goldman, I did sense that you are an erudite, educated, sophisticated motherfucker, and very likely engaged in advanced studies, just like the rest of this assemblage of highly cultured, sociopathic graduate student assholes. Right, guys?"

"Fucking A," they all grunted in unison.

Mills said, "Shitty lottery number, huh Goldman? What's the price of life, liberty and the pursuit of happiness these days?"

Simon blew out a cloud of smoke, and felt the powerful buzz right away. It was the strongest stuff he had ever tried, and he could not imagine the potency of the Vietnam weed that Mills had spoken of. He told them about his unlucky number, and that he had to shell out two hundred and fifty smackers in order to join up They all felt sorry for him---they had no idea the price had gotten that steep. "Fucking Morozievicz," one of them muttered. "Fucking Tet offensive," said another. As the joint circulated, Simon proceeded to get more wasted than ever before in his life. After ten minutes, he thanked them and excused himself, explaining that he was paranoid about Captain Morozievicz showing up in the HQ office.

As Simon started folding his beach chair, Lieutenant Mills offered his insight into the true ethos of the Army National Guard.

"Troop, don't listen to the naysayers and doubters who'll tell you that the Indiana Army National Guard is anything less than an elite military unit. Only the bravest of the brave join up. The best and the brightest. Right guys?"

"Fucking A," they all concurred.

"We pity the poor draftee or volunteer motherfuckers, such as yours truly, who got suckered into boring Vietnam assignments like humping the boonies in the Ashau Valley, hunting for Charlie and getting hunted back, and having our asses shot at. Yeah, we pity the poor assholes, with nothing to keep them busy, and plagued by ennui. We, on the other hand, have lots of excitement here, manning the very ramparts of democracy and defending Indiana against communist domination. And we're doing one hell of an out-fucking-standing job, aren't we, boys? Why, the *espirit de corps* of this spit and polish outfit is so intense that there's a waiting list to get in and even an entry fee. Isn't that so?"

The members of the Weapons Section indicated their complete

agreement by hooting like chimpanzees and stomping their feet. Fucking A.

***

Simon went back up to the office, where he sat stone still and went into a trance, staring at a disturbing photograph of the Commander in Chief hanging on the wall. Nixon's features seemed to be moving, and Simon began to worry that some sort of weird Dorian Gray thing might be happening. He snapped out of his paranoid funk at 5 p.m. when a shrill whistle called the company to dismissal formation on the drill floor. He had no idea where to line up, so he stood with his new friends in the Weapons Section. They accounted for one of the three rows comprising Second Platoon, which also included the truck drivers and cooks. Simon could tell how those squads had spent their day. The cooks were drunk and the truckers were drunk and stoned.

It was a curious thing to Simon that in dismissal formation, everyone made an effort to look serious, even Lieutenant Mills, who was at the left end of his section's row and peering down it critically, ordering his people to take half a step forward or back, so as to dress the line and make it look straight. Captain Morozievicz and his exec, a John Wayne first lieutenant, were at the front of the formation, staring at it with stern, disapproving expressions. Until everyone in the company was lined up just right, they could not go home and melt back into civilian life for the evening. After a few minutes of fussing, the John Wayne blew his whistle and turned them loose.

Simon was much too blitzed and tired to make the long drive back to the north side of Chicago, so in the parking lot he intercepted Lieutenant Mills and asked him if he knew of a cheap place to stay for the night. Mills told him about a flea-bag motel nearby, and then pulled an M-16 magazine from a pocket in his field jacket. He worked the spring-slide of the little box, and pulled out a joint.

"Too bad you're not going to Atterbury with us tomorrow, troop, but this ammo will help you get through your busy day. And when we see you again in half a year, you try to bring some. This shit is expensive."

***

The motel was on a commercial strip near a McDonald's, where he ate. He watched TV in bed for a while, and at eight o'clock, phoned his beautiful sweet Mona to tell her that he loved her, that he was very sorry for kidnapping the Beetle, and that he needed to pass out immediately. He had been awake since 4 a.m. and was incapable of fighting his fatigue.

***

A few weeks later, at 5 a.m. on a dismal Tuesday in March, Simon reported to the U.S. Army induction center, located in a grimy part of downtown Chicago. It was the same somber, spirit sapping place where he took his physical some months before. Mona drove him down from Rogers Park, and now she kept her eyes on him from a parking spot across the street. There was a cold drizzle coming down, so she kept the Beetle's motor running for warmth, with the wipers slapping.

Forty-four soaked, shivering inductees were herded into a tight group in the parking lot next to the facility, near an olive-drab army bus. Each man had a suitcase at his feet---only one was permitted. There was a drill sergeant near the door of the bus---a huge, muscular black wearing a poncho and Smokey the Bear hat, reading from a list of names. When a man's name was bellowed, he was required to run to the cargo bay of the bus, throw in his valise and hustle to the door at the front, with the big noncom screaming obscenities nonstop. Mona saw Simon react when he was summoned, and as he made his dash, she called out his name and waved through the window. He lifted his eyes towards her, tossed in his suitcase, and vanished from view.

CHAPTER 16

Finding Goldman

-68-

Vito was wearing his Sicilia-Italia biking cap when he picked Aitch up---for luck, he said. It was already hot, but they drove with the windows open, both favoring fresh air over air conditioning. After half an hour on local roads, they were on the interstate, heading south along the eastern side of Lake Champlain. Most of the way, the lake was hidden in the trough of its valley, but for one stretch, the opposite shore was in view. Aitch kept his gaze fixed on it and the hazy Adirondacks beyond, dangling a long arm out the window, letting his hand buffet in the wind, lost in memories of sailing on the big lake with his dad.

"*Mio amico,*" said Vito, "You are looking towards Schroon, your boyhood home, yes? We all wish to go back to visit the places of our youth, do we not? To soothe our souls."

Vito's own thoughts sent him back over half a century to Palermo, to the time his father gave him his first bicycle for his seventh birthday. Normally they would have talked about fluid dynamics or partial differential equations, but today they kept silent, content to watch Vermont's greenery slipping by. After an hour, Vito cut west past the southern end of the lake and hooked into the New York State Thruway. By noon they were past Albany, over the Mohawk and into the Catskills. Vito loved to drive his Maserati, and never allowed Aitch a turn behind the wheel. And he refused Aitch's repeated offers to share expenses. If you were his passenger, then you were his guest.

Instead of crossing the Hudson at Tappan Zee, Vito paid the thruway exit toll and entered New Jersey. The Maserati hummed down the Palisades Parkway towards the city, with the Hudson River and Westchester County in view to the east. There was little traffic, and soon the George Washington Bridge loomed. Aitch looked to his left. Westchester had given way to the Riverdale section of the Bronx, and soon he saw Spuyten Duyvil---Spitting Devil to the Dutch---where the Harlem and Hudson Rivers have their foamy confluence at the northern tip of Manhattan. This narrow part of the island is high ground, much of it occupied by Fort Tryon Park. Aitch saw The Cloisters, set like a jewel in the green hillside, and so evocative of a medieval monastery. Lotte Mannheimer once told Aitch that much of the gothic structure was transported stone by stone from Europe, and rebuilt, "...like we were," she had said. He caught a glimpse of the basketball courts where he and Simon used to team up against Norbert and Vinnie, and a few minutes later they were in Fort Lee, on the approaches to the bridge. A fee is charged only when entering New York City---there is none for leaving. Vito paid the toll.

The George Washington Bridge is the third longest suspension bridge in the world, surpassed only by the Golden Gate and Verazanno spans, but in its youth it was number one. It is old and bulky, and some people say it looks as though God constructed it with a giant Erector Set. But Aitch always found it more beautiful than all others except for the Brooklyn Bridge, which he felt was more a work of art than a route across the East River. They were on the upper deck of the GW now, high above the Hudson, gazing toward the Chrysler and Empire State Buildings in the distance to the south. And like countless others taking in this view, they thought of the Twin Towers, no longer part of the panorama. As they neared the Manhattan side, Aitch glimpsed the Mannheimers' apartment building near J. Hood Wright Park and P.S. 173, where Rolf Von Essen and Simon Goldman played and attended school, separated only in time. Most of the bridge traffic would spill onto the Cross Bronx Expressway or access one of the highways flanking Manhattan, but Vito zipped to the right and took the local exit, which plunged them into Washington Heights at 178th Street.

Aitch could see that the population of the neighborhood had changed quite a bit since he hung out here with Simon in his undergraduate days. The old ethnic groups were all still represented---aging Yekkes and other Jews, Greeks, Italians, Irish and Blacks. Now Latinos---mainly Dominicans---were the plurality. But the Heights was in demographic flux yet again, because many buildings, like the Mannheimers', had gone condo and yuppies were moving in. They took Fort Washington Avenue down to 173rd Street and found a parking spot just off Haven. A miracle.

Vito said, "Is that not our friend's car across the street?"

They walked over and checked that Simon's Volvo was locked, even though they knew Meinhold must have already done so. Through the windows they saw the detritus of his drive---empty coffee cups on the passenger seat, a half eaten muffin, a note pad and a dozen crumpled sheets of paper wadded on the floor. Simon was usually fastidious about his car, but not during his last trip.

***

Lotte Mannheimer buzzed them up from the lobby, and hugged them at the door of the sixth floor apartment. Meinhold shook their hands and patted their backs. The Mannheimers first met Vito three years ago at Maureen's funeral, and reconnected with him instantly. Aitch saw that Meinhold's hair was a bit thinner and whiter than it was then, with the scar on his scalp becoming more visible as the years went by.

After settling her visitors in, Lotte sat them all down in the dining room for supper---knackwurst and sauerkraut---Aitch's favorite.

"Still so skinny," she said as she began piling a mountain of food on his plate. "And little Vito, the same goes for you, only more."

Meinhold said, "I keep reminding her that I'm a grandfather four times over and my metabolism is slowing down, but she keeps trying to stuff me and everyone else. Go figure. I have to walk ten miles a day just to not *plotz* and have a heart attack."

He reached up and pinched her cheek.

After coffee and plum pie, she refused offers to help clean up, and dispatched the three men to the living room.

***

They sat in plush armchairs, the same ones Aitch remembered from the 60's. The view out the window was to the west, across the Hudson, with the big bridge very near and the lights of Fort Lee coming on in the distance. He saw that the old cabinet was still in the room, with Meinhold's medals behind the glass, along with the menorah and stack of cards from John Clemons. He retired from Congress eight years earlier, but the cards never stopped coming. The pile was now fifty-six deep.

Meinhold poured three huge snifters of schnapps, and took a healthy swig.

"I've worn out my shoes looking for my nephew. I just got back from the little red lighthouse under the bridge, where he used to play. And I repeatedly checked all his old hangouts, but no sign."

Vito said, "It is probably too late to do more today, Meinhold. Aitch and I should rise early and begin looking for Simon in certain possible locations which Aitch has identified, while also keeping a watchful eye on the local places you have been searching. To aid us in this endeavor, my brother Santino will lend us two of his sons. With your permission, I would like to telephone him this evening and make arrangements."

Meinhold rocked forward, placed his elbows on his knees, and looked straight at Vito.

"Of course, Vito. And make yourself completely at home. Vito, I want to make sure that I heard you correctly. Did you just tell me that Santino de Bernardi is your *brother*? Is he the Santino de Bernardi who I occasionally read about in the newspapers?"

"Yes," said Vito. "And he is a man of honor. I assure you."

Meinhold raised his eyes to the chandelier, grinned, and emitted one of his long surprise whistles. He looked into his schnapp*s* for a long time, and saw Riley and Clemons in the swirls. Then he raised his glass.

"To men of honor everywhere. *Salute!*"

It was repeated by Vito and Aitch, and the three of them quaffed their liquor. Meinhold refilled them in an instant.

Vito said, "May your nephew, Simon Goldman, live to the age of one hundred and twenty. *L'Chaim!*"

They all repeated it, and Meinhold fixed his gaze on the Palisades.

"When we find my nephew, I plan to force him to rejoin the human race. Time for him to stop standing on the outside, looking in."

They drained their glasses like a synchronized drinking team, and Meinhold refilled them again.

***

Aitch called home and Celestine answered on the first ring. Mona was with her, and she called out a hello from the background, as cheery a one as she could manage. Celestine told him that they dined on venison, drank too much Bordeaux, and that there were plenty of leftovers. Newton was home, and Minipod was his only visitor. In other words, no catamount. Aitch was relieved that she was being discreet about Chinnie.

"Cherie, I phoned Joe Malone this morning, and told him about Simon. He was great---a real friend. He contacted the experts who were invited to the D-Day talk and explained the error to them. All got word of the cancellation, so we can relax about that. Aitch, listen. Joe called me an hour ago. He conferred with Chen and Bertoli at length. All three of them are sure that Simon's results on the structure of class-G TSP's are very important on their own, as is the G-interpolation method, even though the density argument failed. Chen says that Simon *did* succeed in proving a property that Bertoli has already labeled the 'near density' of class-G in the space of all TSP's. They all say it will be tremendously important in the design of efficient, near-optimal algorithms, and that his results will stimulate further research. Chen wants to set up a workshop at Yale in August, where Simon could present a series of talks. Chen says that a resolution of P vs. NP might be closer now, because of his recent results. Simon Goldman should hold his head up---he did great work."

"I'll tell him as soon as we find him. Thank you so much, Celestine, for everything."

"One more thing, Aitch. I saw Madame Beauregard and arranged some face-time with Guillermo Slutnick, because I think it's best that I inform him about things in person. I will see him tomorrow afternoon, after he returns from a meeting with Dean Fulton."

Aitch remembered Celestine's fist banging the table in Kerouac's.

"Celestine, you be sure to remain calm and sweet when you meet with him, no matter what. Calm and sweet. This is always the right strategy with Guillermo. Promise me."

"Cherie, you have my solemn promise. Calm and sweet."

-69-

It was 8:15 a.m. when Aitch, Vito, and Meinhold emerged from the lobby. Meinhold had his ponderous vintage binoculars dangling from his his neck, and in the elevator, Vito chided the old man for stealing U.S. Army property.

"Stealing, *shmealing,"* said Meinhold. "You want real stealing, go to Wall Street."

A white Corvette was double-parked outside the building. Two serious looking fellows emerged---swarthy, stocky six footers wearing open collar shirts, lightweight dark suits and pointy black shoes. Each sported multiple gold crucifixes and other jewelry, including heavy knuckle rings. Vito introduced them. They were Carlo and Fabrizio de Bernardi, his nephews and godsons, both in their early thirties. They only nodded towards Aitch and Meinhold, but both kissed Vito's right hand.

"*Benvenuto a Nuovo York, Zio Vito.*"

Vito said, "While looking for Simon Goldman, we will all stay in contact via cellphone. I have asked my godsons to each bring one, as well as extras."

He gestured to Carlo, who reached through the open window of the Corvette and produced two phones from the glove compartment.

"Meinhold, please continue to search the immediate neighborhood. Aitch and I will work together, elsewhere."

Carlo handed one of the phones to Meinhold, and the other to Aitch. Affixed to each was a strip of white medical tape upon which the numbers of all four cells were written.

Vito said, "Carlo, you will go to Coney Island and patrol the beach and boardwalk there. Simon Goldman has an attachment to this area, and it is important to search it well. Show this to people. Perhaps someone has seen him."

He handed pictures of Simon to his nephews---copies of the photo on the poster advertising his talk last Saturday.

Carlo said, "*Ciao*," to the rest of the team, got into the Corvette, and roared off.

"Fabrizio, you will head uptown to the top end of Fort Washington Avenue, near the entrance to Fort Tryon Park. Pay particular attention to the basketball courts there, but check as much of the area as you can. *Buona fortuna.*"

Fabrizio began walking towards Broadway to catch a cab.

"Meinhold, Aitch and I will head downtown to Cooper Union. Good hunting."

"*Buona fortuna*," said Meinhold, who would again scour the neighborhood, energized by the thought of cuffing Simon behind the ear when he found him.

-70-

Aitch and Vito walked to the 175th Street station of the IND line, paid for their tokens, and did not have to wait long before wedging themselves into a southbound A-train. Aitch knew that Simon took the A for seven years when he was young----four while attending Cooper Union, and three years before that when he was a student at Stuyvesant High School down on East Fifteenth Street. As he hung from a strap, Aitch let his eyes scan the subway car, in the silly hope that he would see Simon. He saw faces belonging to people of all ages and races---interesting faces---Manhattanites as well as white collars commuting from New Jersey or Westchester. But no Simon Goldman.

***

They got off at Fourth Street and Eighth Avenue, at the edge of of Greenwich Village, and soon they were passing through Washington Square and the New York University campus, Aitch's old stomping ground when he was a graduate student here. Five minutes later they reached the tiny campus of The Cooper Union for the Advancement of Science and Art.

Vito suggested that they split up. He would do a loop of the engineering school, and Aitch would patrol the perimeter of the Foundation Building. They intended to show Simon's picture to anyone who might be helpful. Aitch thought it was a good plan and agreed to meet Vito in ten minutes, at the corner of Eigth Street and Third Avenue.

Aitch strode along the front of the massive old brownstone, where Lincoln spoke in 1860 while campaigning for the presidency. There were some students around---mainly undergraduates starting a summer term. In Aitch's days here, it was easy to tell the artsies from the weenies, because the artsies were a few years ahead of their academic cousins in adopting the mores and dress of the 60's. But now he was unable to tell who was who. He turned south onto the Bowery, and stood below the big clock at the back of the building, facing the statue of Peter Cooper, the man to whom he owed his undergraduate education. It was in a small fenced off enclosure, which generations of Cooper Union students referred to as Pigeon-shit Park. A large gull lit upon Cooper's head, spread its wings, shrieked, and did its business with gusto. Perhaps this is the fate of all great men, thought Aitch. A statue erected in your honor is eventually splattered with bird excrement.

Turning up Third Avenue, he saw McSorley's Old Ale House to his right, down Seventh Street, and recalled the day he joined Simon Goldman and Tommy Matsumoto in carving their initials on a table, after graduation. Back at Eighth and Third, he spent five minutes leaning on a lamp post before he saw Vito emerge from the front door of the engineering building across the street, waving goodbye to a security guard and on his way over.

"Aitch, our friend was here yesterday in the late afternoon. The guard remembers him standing in front for a while, doing nothing. Like you, just looking around."

Aitch said, "That's good to hear. Vito, I'd like to check a pub where we used to hang out. Meet you back here in ten minutes."

"Okay *mio amico*, you do that and I will talk to security in the Foundation Building."

***

McSorley's was founded in 1854, and for the remainder of the 19th century, when this downtown neighborhood was uptown, the bar was the classiest and ritziest in the city. Now it was just a neighborhood pub, albeit a living landmark. Aitch remembered the wooden tables, the draught beer, and plates stacked with onions, cheddar and crackers. The door was open and he stepped through a time-warp---the place had not changed. It was only 10 a.m. and there were no patrons yet, but a ruddy faced codger in a white apron was sweeping the floor with a straw broom, getting ready for the midday rush. He looked to be over ninety. Aitch fumbled for his picture of Simon.

"Your pal was here yesterday evening," the old man said in his Irish brogue, without looking at the photo. Now Aitch remembered him ---it was surly Mick, who waited on tables in the old days when he was about Aitch's present age. Mick shuffled over to a table in the back and rapped on it with the handle of his broom.

"He had a few pints and spent a half-hour looking for his initials. Everybody wants to find their initials. They all come back, especially you artsies and weenies."

Mick rapped the table again, indicating the spot, and Aitch went over. The letters were as deep and clear as if they were carved yesterday.

SG + TM + HMS
1968

Aitch closed his eyes and ran his fingers over the grooves like a blind man reading braille. Then he forced his mind back to the present, thanked Mick, and hit the pavement. The old man said nothing, and resumed his rhythmic sweeping.

***

After hearing Aitch's report, Vito said, "It is clear that our optimal strategy is to remain in this area and hope that Simon passes through again---subject of course to any information we get from my nephews or Meinhold. Let us obtain some cappuccino. There is a Starbucks adjacent to the engineering building."

"I'm buying," said Aitch.

***

It was past 11 a.m., and the place was crowded with caffeine addicts seeking their late morning fix. Aitch scanned it with a binary search in case Simon might be there, but he was not. They got their cappuccinos and biscottis and sat outside, from where they could maintain a vigil on both the entrance and the street.

A bell pinged at the next table. There were two old men playing speed chess, and one of them had just hit the timer after moving a rook. Vito was a serious player, and was already engrossed in their game. Aitch's mind shimmered as a bolt of recognition struck. The chess players were Professors Emeritus Leibgott and Klein. Leibgott still looked a lot like Jack Benny---had Jack Benny lived that long. And Klein still smelled from pipe tobacco. Aitch guessed that they must have retired fifteen or twenty years ago.

Leibgott pushed a pawn forward and slapped the timer.

"Check. And time out, Harry."

He pointed a finger at Aitch.

"I remember you," said Professor Leibgott. "Physics major. They all called you Bumpkin."

Aitch nodded in amazement bordering on suspended animation.

"Oh yes, of course," said Professor Klein, sucking on his unlit pipe. "You were friends with the arch-weenie, Simon Goldman. Tell me, do you know---is he still a royal pain in the ass?"

"You couldn't possibly even begin to imagine," said Aitch.

Leibgott said, "Bumpkin, next time you see Goldman, you tell him that I always knew he was behind that blackboard business. And that the spelling error was deliberate."

The cell phone in Aitch's shirt pocket began vibrating and playing The William Tell Overture. Vito said "*Scusi*," and extracted it before Aitch could react.

"*Sì, sì*, okay. We will meet you there as soon as we can. *Grazie,* Fabrizio." He turned to Aitch. "Simon Goldman was seen at the basketball courts in Washington Heights not half an hour ago. We must go there immediately."

"*La Nostalgie n'est plus ce qu'elle étai,*" Klein sighed.

Leibgott said, "Don't you try to out-culture me, Harry. Simone Signoret said it, probably while she was schtupping Yves Montand and thinking of someone else. Nostalgia is not what it used to be."

-71-

They walked out of the café and Vito flagged a cab within seconds. The driver was a turbaned, fifty-ish Sikh.

"Top end of Fort Washington Avenue," said Aitch.

You never have to tell a New York cabbie to step on it. They were on the East Side, so they took the FDR Drive uptown along the East River. The United Nations and Yorkville slid by on their left, and soon Yankee Stadium came into view---the Roman Colosseum in Fort Apache, The Bronx. Vito hated the mixed imagery, and hoped that one day the Yankees would move to New Jersey, as football's New York Giants did. They climbed the hill to Highbridge Park, crossed Broadway, and took Fort Washington Avenue uptown to Margaret Corbin Circle. Aitch paid the fare and gave the cabbie a fat tip.

***

Fabrizio was waiting for them at the gate of the basketball court enclosure. He pointed out four Latino boys playing two-on-two. Aitch wondered if he and Simon were ever as good.

"*Zio* Vito, I showed those Spics your friend's picture, and they told me they saw him here, maybe an hour ago."

Fabrizio called one of them over. The kid was happy to give them a minute of his time. Vito knew that his nephew had already paid the boys to stick around.

"Pedro, tell these gentlemen what you told me, *por favor*."

Pedro was a skinny fourteen year old second generation Dominican, born and bred in the Heights.

"Well, the old dude in the picture comes over and asks us, can he borrow our spare ball and shoot some hoops by himself at the next basket over. He looks like a bum so we say no, fuck off, so he says he'll let us hold his Timex for security, and he'll give us five bucks when he's done, so we say okay, and he starts to shoot his hoops. And then he starts to shoot Goldies, so I go over and I ask him how come he knows how to shoot Goldies. He says to me he *invented* the Goldie move thirty-seven years ago, right here---and I say bullshit and he laughs and gives me back the ball with *ten* bucks, and I give him back his Timex. He laughs some more and he says I should go over to Ricci's Grocery and ask Fat Vinnie about it. Then he leaves and I don't know where the fuck he went. Weird dude, man---carries a clipboard with an ice-cream cone picture on it. Looks like he sleeps on the sidewalk, if you ask me."

***

Meinhold was working a stretch of Broadway, visiting every location he could think of which was connected to Simon's youth---a bowling alley, a pool hall, and the Yekke synagogue where he had his bar-mitzvah. He checked a courtyard on 180th Street where Simon and his friends played stoop-ball, a couple of bodega*s* which used to be soda fountains, and the Loew's cinema which was now Reverend Ike's church. At each location he showed Simon's picture to people, but there were no nibbles. When he got to 168th Street, in sight of the Audubon Ballroom where Malcolm X was assassinated and near the hospital where Simon, Rutie and Eva-Leah were born, he felt a pang of hunger. So he turned the corner and headed up Haven Avenue towards home, where Lotte would fix him something.

Meinhold was about to enter his building but stopped---one more visual scan before lunch, he told himself. He put the field glasses to his eyes and began sweeping to the north in a slow, steady motion. A traverse of the GW bridge's pedestrian walkway revealed only a mother pushing a pram towards the Manhattan side---and a bolt of intuition struck. He shifted his view three blocks down Haven to a terrace in the park---to Mathilda's bench, where she spent so much time gazing at the river, lost in thoughts of the past. A slumped, hooded figure was seated there. Meinhold lowered the binoculars and dialed Aitch's cell phone.

***

When Aitch and Vito got there, Simon was rocking back and forth, and Meinhold had an arm around him. They were atop an outcrop known to countless generations of Heights kids as the 'Danger Rocks', a forbidden obstacle climbed by only the most intrepid. Goldman was unshaven and wearing a soiled Harvard tracksuit with the hood up, despite the warmth of the day. He was hunched, looking down at the clipboard between his feet. Aitch sensed that his friend was at last resigned to the death of his theorem, and opened his mouth to attempt a greeting. But Meinhold waved him off and directed Aitch and Vito to seat themselves on the grass.

"Simon, I'm your one and only uncle, so you listen to me and you listen good. Thirty years ago you told me what happened over there, and you were better for a long time. Now it's time to tell your friends, and later, your wife. Then this theorem crap will look a lot less grim."

Aitch said, "It looks a lot less grim already. Chen and Bertoli are saying that what you did is very important, even if G-interpolation failed, and..."

Simon cut Aitch off before he could go on.

"Thanks. I'll get over it. Piece of cake."

"Not unless you spill your guts, you won't," Meinhold persisted. "Tell them what happened and then the world will start getting right again. You owe it to yourself."

Meinhold took his arm off his nephew and moved over, to give him space. Simon never looked up.

-72-

"My National Guard company was activated and sent to Vietnam in September, 1970. No one expected it---Indiana City was a racial hotbed and we thought we were indispensable. But the governor of Indiana thought otherwise. The upside was that a tour in Vietnam would kill off my commitment to the Guard---no more drills and summer camps after that. An all expenses paid vacation in Southeast Asia---right, Uncle Meinhold? My unit was designated as a supply company, and we were stationed at a big base twenty miles north of Saigon. Our job was to organize supply convoys to nearby firebases. Shipping clerks, that's what we were---probably because it was all we were capable of. It was a job that two sub-cretins could do, so they sent two-hundred drunks and stoner's from the Guard to do it. That's the army for you---right again, Uncle Meinhold?"

***

Company B, 3rd Battalion, 141st Infantry Division, had been in the Saigon suburbs for two weeks. None of them had acclimatized except for the few veterans like Lieutenant Mills and Captain Morozievicz. The shock of their activation, the jetlag, and the unrelenting wet heat combined to induce mass insomnia. But even though the men were stuporous, they knew that they had it good. Made in the shade and in the rear with the gear. They were still divided into sections such as weapons, cooks, mechanics and drivers, but only for organizational purposes, because all those functions were handled at the battalion level. The nineteen officers of the company were each assigned a driver, even though there were only five jeeps, and little need for those. So the drivers doubled as gofers for the officers. Lieutenant Mills had asked for Private Goldman. "Because I value intellectual discourse," was what Mills told Captain Morozievicz in explaining his request. The captain agreed to part with the trooper he said was the best goddam typist in the entire United States Army, because Mills laid a bottle of Cutty Sark on him and offered up one of his own Weapons Section dickwads to replace Goldman---a Ph.D. candidate in Sociology at the University of Chicago who could type almost as well, not that there was much typing to do.

Being Mills' driver protected Goldman from inspections and make-work projects created by the John Waynes. Stoned conversation was how Goldman and Mills kept themselves out of the doldrums, at the depot or in Mills' hooch, where they could also listen to rock.

"Goldman, enough Cambodian Red and you can hallucinate your ass out of here," Mills would say. "Roll us another one just like the other one."

Sometimes their discussions were held during aimless drives around the base, when a jeep could be wangled. They usually spoke about history or literature, but all topics were allowed except for law and mathematics, their individual fields of expertise. One infernal, humid evening, after Captain Morozievicz had given him the green light, Mills ordered Goldman to drive him to downtown Saigon so he could visit his favorite whorehouse, one familiar to him from his first tour.

"My treat, Acapulco," said Lieutenant Mills, as Goldman parked the jeep in front of the rundown building, once a French hotel. "Give Ngo the Ho a try. She's the mama-san, and she can suck a grapefruit down a garden hose."

Mills offered to pay the ten dollars, but Simon could not be convinced because Mona would take a dim view of his getting the clap. So he waited in the jeep, sweating and observing the cacophonous Saigon nightlife through a purple haze, while Mills was inside, getting it off. A ten year old street vendor came by and sold him a small teak box with a water buffalo image fashioned from seashells. At five dollars he could not resist it---a gift for his sweet Mona.

***

During the drive back to the base, as they were nearing the outer ring of barbed wire and sandbagged guard posts, they heard three explosions off in the distance. Simon braked and Mills grinned. He held up a hand and counted off 5-4-3-2-1 on his fingers, and as if on cue, there were another pair of blasts in close succession.

"You know what that was, Acapulco?"

Simon shook his head yes, pretending to be calm. It was the first angry fire he had ever heard.

"Yes, Acapulco, that's right---there are nasty, highly motivated little motherfuckers out there who want you dead. Fucking A. You just heard three mortar rounds landing at Firebase Alpha, maybe six kliks from here, and then another two rounds five seconds later. Probably that ninety millimeter Russian crap. The second salvo had a dud, or maybe they only had five rounds total to start with. Charlie set himself up a little mortar battery, maybe a half a dozen men for three tubes. But they've already dismantled and on the move---and split up, if they're smart. Some of our specials will go out hunting for them in a few minutes---that's for sure. Could be this sector's heating up. That's the way it goes here. Lulls punctuated by flying shit and hide-n-seek."

-73-

"Every war is different," said Meinhold. "But some things never change. Tell them the rest."

Simon was sitting up straight now, his gaze riveted on the bridge.

"There was no further fire that night, but the next morning my commanding officer came up to Lieutenant Mills and me, with orders."

***

Their jeep was parked near the battalion mess tent, and they had just consumed an after-breakfast doobie. The lieutenant was dozing in the passenger seat, and when Private Goldman saw Captain Morozievicz approaching, he jumped out, opened the hood, and began to fuss with the battery cables. It was the first time Simon had ever observed the captain wearing his helmet. A .45 Colt automatic was on his hip, an M-16 was slung across his shoulder along with a bandolier of ammunition, and four grenades were dangling from his web gear.

"Wake your ass up, Mills---we got orders. And Goldberg, you can stop fucking around. Your busy act won't work this time."

Mills said, "I wasn't asleep sir. Just meditating on the vagaries of life and the unfairness of my being sent back to the Nam."

Captain Morozievicz said, "Well, things just got more vague and unfair, Mills. You can tell your fucking congressman about it when you're back in the world. Apparently, Charlie's potshots fucked up the dirt road leading into Firebase Alpha, and I have to deliver a road grader pronto to level it. Goldstein, you're the only man in the company qualified, so your ass is mine. And yours too, Mills. I want you along in case we run into something out there."

Simon began to tremble, and struggled to keep his voice in a manly register.

"Sir, I don't know if I remember how to start the motor, let alone drive or operate a grader. And I'm really bad at it, sir. Totally incompetent. My MOS training was shit, and besides, the main concentration at Fort Leonard Wood was on Caterpillar bulldozers. I never really learned to level a road, sir. I bet there are guys in the motor pool section or some farmers among the cooks with lots more experience than me."

"Well, you should have paid more attention. You're the only officially qualified cheesedick in my company, so shut the fuck up."

Simon knew that it was pointless to suggest that the captain go up the ladder to battalion or division and find someone else. Perhaps he could somehow float through this.

"Yes, sir," he said.

Lieutenant Mills asked, "What's the deal?"

"The two of your arm up and meet me back here in ten minutes. We will take this jeep over to the battalion motor pool, pick up the grader and rendezvous with our ARVN escort. Goldbaum, you will drive the fucking grader with me and Lieutenant Mills behind you in the jeep and Marvin the ARVN up front."

Mills did not like it. He never trusted the Army of the Republic of Vietnam. In his experience, they were often disloyal and you could count on them to bug out if things got hot. And he thought that many of them were ready to turn VC if they were not VC already.

"Shit, sir. Why Marvins? Can't we get a better escort? There's Rangers and Green Berets on this base, for Christ's sake. And a battalion of regulars too."

"I feel the same way," said Captain Morozievicz, "I tried, but there isn't a fucking thing I can do about it. The ass-kickers are out sweeping the boonies for little people and the grunts are doubled up on the perimeter. We get Marvins."

The universe was spinning out of control for Simon, who knew that he must be losing his mind, because he was more fearful of screwing up the roadwork at Firebase Alpha than of getting shot on the way there.

***

When the three vehicle convoy was set to leave the motor pool, Simon was at the controls of the grader, weighted with dread and sweating in the wet heat, with his M-16 and a bandolier at his feet. Staring at the myriad controls, he recalled which lever raised and lowered the leveling blade, but was at a loss when it came to setting its many possible angles and pitches. Like the captain said, he should have paid more attention. When he tilted his aching head back to take a drink of water from his canteen, his helmet felt heavier than ever before.

The jeep in front was occupied by a sullen ARVN captain named Tran and his driver, a Corporal Nguyen. Lieutenant Mills would drive the jeep behind the grader, with Captain Morozievicz riding shotgun. After conferring with Tran, Morozievicz informed Private Goldman that the trip to Firebase Alpha would take about thirty minutes, and that they were to maintain bowling alley following distances. Morozievicz took his seat, Mills honked, and they headed through the gate.

The bumpy dirt road was built by army engineers five years earlier. The jungle was kept clear thirty feet on either side, and in places there were ditches for runoff. The behemoth of a grader was slow and difficult to control as Simon rumbled it behind the Marvins. It bothered him that neither Tran nor Nguyen ever turned around to check on the rest of the party. He looked back now and then, because Mills' calm, stoned-out demeanor gave him hope that he would survive. The lieutenant would grin and flip the bird or give a thumbs-up every now and then. And Simon was comforted by the fact that Captain Morozievicz was so unworried that he fell asleep in the passenger seat, despite the heavy jostling.

Twenty minutes into the trip, at a spot where the jungle to their left gave way to a broad rice paddy, Simon saw Captain Tran slap his driver on the shoulder and point forward. Corporal Nguyen nodded and the ARVN jeep accelerated, its tires screeching and splattering mud as it disappeared around a bend. Simon was more confused than afraid---his instincts kicked in and he braked the grader. As it idled in the heat, he heard a metallic pinging from the chassis and smiled. He thought there might be a problem with the engine---maybe the valves were blown and the misson would be aborted. Then he heard what sounded like a jackhammer in the jungle to his right. As if in a dream and with time distending, Simon came to the realization that he was under automatic weapons fire. He ducked low in his seat and turned back to Lieutenant Mills, who was crouched beside his jeep alongside Captain Morozievicz. Mills was shouting and pointing.

"AMBUSH! DITCH! MAKE FOR THE DITCH!"

Simon jumped off and dove into the shallow drainage ditch between the grader and the paddy. As he made his dash, he heard more rounds impacting near him and thought he saw muzzle flashes in the jungle about fifty yards away. Hugging the mud, he cursed himself for leaving his M-16 behind. Mills and Morozievicz were also cursing as they grabbed their weapons and headed his way. Mills got there first, and rolled more than dove into the ditch. Captain Morozievicz was slower and interrupted his sprint by pausing behind one of the grader's huge tires.

"Where's your fucking weapon, Acapulco?" asked Mills, as he peeked over the lip of the ditch.

Goldman shrugged and pointed at the grader.

Mills said, "Shit." He popped up and fired a full magazine into the jungle, on automatic. Goldman covered his ears and put his face to the ground again.

The lieutenant roared, "CAPTAIN---INTO THE DITCH---ON MY NEXT BURST!"

He crawled five feet to a new firing point and put another twenty rounds into the brush. When Mills' magazine was spent, the captain dove in, and the full weight of his body slammed onto Simon, who felt something crack, high on his left side. He was pinned under the big man's weight and felt a warm wetness seeping onto his shoulders. Then the searing pain from three cracked ribs knifed into him.

"Ah, shit," said Lieutenant Mills. Simon functioned on adrenalin only and extricated himself from under the captain's bulk. He rolled him over and recoiled at the gaping wound in his throat. The captain was dead and it was all happening too fast, yet liminally, Simon felt as though he were watching a movie in slow motion.

Mills said, "Fucking Marvins. It was a setup. Are you hit?"

He fired a burst, then rolled onto his back. He dropped the spent magazine, inserted a full one from his bandolier and yanked on the M-16's charging handle.

"I think the captain broke my ribs," said Simon.

"The fat fuck. Acapulco! Think! Grab his weapon and lay some fire on those fuckers! Short bursts---displace in between."

Simon was in shock, but did as he was ordered. He could not see a target and his injury precluded taking decent aim, so he sprayed his rounds into the same general area Mills was raking. When his weapon was spent, he pulled at Captain Morozievicz's bandolier, but with use of only his right arm, it was a struggle to take it off him. Mills pulled his trench knife from its leg scabbard and tossed it over. Kalashnikov rounds stitched the lip of the ditch.

"Cut the strap! Get his grenades too."

Simon did as he was ordered, and tossed the bandolier and four grenades between himself and the lieutenant. Mills' *sang froid* kept him together, at least enough to pay attention.

"Can you run?" asked Mills, and Goldman shook his head no.

"Listen up. There are three of them across the road---and they're stupid---clustered and not maneuvering. But they picked a good spot---we've got no bush to jump into, and we can't bug out across the paddy. But they can't get behind us either. We've got decent enfilade here and they've only got AK-47's. We're going to pull some shit I learned from the NVA in the Ashau. Fucking A."

Mills seemed to be enjoying this in some atavistic way, as only a true warrior could. Goldman did not fathom it at all.

"I'm going back to the grader and you're going to scream your fucking head off because I am a coward who is deserting you. When I take off down the road, you be convincing, and put a few high rounds in my general direction. They'll buy it because they'll want to. After I'm out of sight, I'll work my way behind them and waste their sorry gook asses. And you keep their heads down for me, okay?"

Simon's mind was swirling into a black hole.

"Sir, maybe I should try to run. Why don't we both take off together? "

"Because you can't move fast enough and you'll get shot. And also because I just gave you a direct fucking order."

He stuffed two magazines into his pants pocket, patted Simon on his good side, scrambled to the grader, and took cover behind one of its giant tires. As rounds began to ping on the machine, Lieutenant Mills turned towards Goldman, grinned, and took off down the road in a hunched sprint. He went straight for twenty yards, and then began to weave, with bullet impacts raising small explosions of mud near his feet. Simon did as he was told---screaming, cursing like a banshee and shooting over Mills' head. Then he put his fire back on the VC.

***

Aitch said, "Simon, I had no idea you went through anything like that. I wish you had told me."

"He's telling you now," said Meinhold. "Nephew, tell them the rest."

***

Simon saw Mills disappear around a bend, seventy-five yards away.

Now he was alone, hugging the bottom of the ditch, wet with the captain's blood, and he was the sole target. The three VC trained their weapons on him, and he fired blind over the lip of the ditch, not exposing himself and not aiming. His movements tore at his fractured ribs, and the pain was giving way to paralysis by the time he was down to his last two magazines. Then he heard shrieks in Vietnamese followed by the popping of an M-16 and more AK-47 fire.

***

"I convinced myself that they got Lieutenant Mills and that soon they were going to get me. I just lay in the mud next to the captain's body. It was quiet, but after a few minutes I thought I heard movement in the brush across the road. So I threw a grenade blind---just pulled the pin and lobbed it. After that, I lay in the ooze for an hour, and I didn't hear a thing. Eventually a Ranger patrol came looking for us, and I was home free."

"Sweet Jesus," said Aitch. "You should have told me."

"Couldn't. See, Mills wiped out the three VC just like he said he would, but not before they shot him up. None of them looked older than sixteen, the Rangers said. Mills was hit, but it was shrapnel that killed him---that's what they told me. No one knew it was from the grenade I threw when he came out, hurting and needing help. I should have looked, but I didn't. He told me to think, and I didn't. I killed him after he saved my life, and for that they gave me two medals and three stripes. What do you think of that? Enough to piss you off, isn't it?"

He looked out at them from under his hood, eyes ablaze.

-74-

Aitch got up, stared at his feet and kept silent, afraid that he might say something inane. Vito rose as well and gazed towards the river, focusing on a tight pack of cyclists spinning north along the shore path.

The spell was broken by the shrill dismissal bell from P.S. 173, on the other side of the park. Still on the bench next to Simon, Meinhold looked towards the school through his field glasses.

"Boys, our position is about to be overrun."

A minute later, a dozen noisy fifth graders charged to the terrace, dropped their knapsacks and clambered over the railing. Their undeclared game was Follow the Leader, and today's leader was the wiry little black who lived on Meinhold's floor.

"Watch this, Mr. Mannheimer!" the boy cried, as he jumped from one boulder to another, asserting his mastery of the Danger Rocks.

"Piece of cake, Billy!" called Meinhold, whistling with approval and clapping his hands. "Don't let your mom catch you doing that!"

Billy climbed to the top of the largest boulder and eyed his rivals queueing below, awaiting their turns to emulate or outdo him. It was a six foot leap across empty space to the safety of the terrace, and the boy looked towards Meinhold just before taking flight. But he fell short, and for a long five seconds he hung onto the lowest strut of the railing, dangling over the thirty foot chasm like a trapeze artist with a problem.

Simon got to him first. He reached over the barrier, extending himself as he grabbed the boy's T-shirt at the scruff. Aitch and Vito each seized one of Simon's legs, and together they reeled him and Billy in.

Aitch gathered his courage and said "Jeez, Vito, we wouldn't want to lose Simon now, would we?"

"No," growled Vito, "Not after all that effort."

Simon did not react and seemed to be retreating back into his funk, when Meinhold placed a hand on Billy's shoulder.

"You know, my nephew here used to climb those rocks, about forty-five years ago. How old are you?"

"Almost ten and three quarters," said Billy, so awed by the time warp that he forgot about his near death experience.

Simon was leaning on the rail and looking down, over the precipice.

"Kid, that maneuver you tried---I was eleven the first time I made that jump. But I was the first one in my gang who could do it. And that's what counts. Right?"

"Yes," said Meinhold. "Billy will do it next year, when he's ready. Piece of cake."

"Something for him to look forward to," said Vito.

The Good Humor man was ringing his bell at the corner of 173rd and Haven. Heeding the call, Billy's friends rushed back to the terrace via a safe route, grabbed their bags and ran off in a pack. A girl called out, "Silly Billy!" as she led the charge to the ice-cream.

Meinhold produced a twenty from his pocket, pressed it into the boy's hand, and made sure his fist closed around it.

"Tell everyone to have an ice-cream cone. Or whatever they want. My treat."

The kid expressed his gratitude like a ten year old anticipating a sugar rush and took off, catching the others before they reached the small white truck.

Meinhold bent and picked up the clipboard as Vito, Aitch and Simon watched the Good Humor man get swamped with extravagant requests. The old man looked at the smudged Minkowski cone and then at Simon, shaking his head, acknowledging that there were some things that would forever be beyond his comprehension.

"Nephew, maybe you or your friends can explain to me how abstract mathematics connects to anything in the real world." He held the clipboard high. "Here is my problem. I understand how mathematicians turn food into mathematics, but how you do the reverse ---that I do *not* understand."

Aitch and Vito only grinned, as if they were guardians of secret knowledge. Simon forced himself to produce a shrug.

"What a way to make a living," said Meinhold.

He rapped the top of Simon's head with the clipboard.

"Let's get some food into you."

-75-

Celestine glanced at her sports wristwatch and saw that it was time for her 4:45 appointment with Guillermo Slutnick. As Beatrice waved her into the chairman's office, Aitch's advice to remain calm and sweet echoed in her mind.

Calm and sweet, Celestine repeated to herself as she took a seat on a rigid wooden chair. Slutnick was leaning back in his padded recliner, holding a mug of coffee on his belly as he checked her out. Margaret had it right, he thought---Celestine Sauvage must be schtupping Singleton. Never worth a head-turn before, had she recently metamorphosed from a wild-haired, four-eyed math geekette into the lithe, curvaceous creature seated before him. His observations were more aesthetic than sexual, because the Virgin Queen had drained him of his last drop of testosterone thirty minutes earlier. She had cast him as Macbeth during today's tryst, and the chain mail hauberk she forced him to wear while humming the Alphabet Song was heavy, making his manly exertions more exhausting than usual.

"That watercolor is very lovely, Professor Slutnick. And that Esmeralda obelisk is quite interesting. It looks like it was once alive."

Guillermo did not know why Celestine Sauvage requested this meeting. Perhaps she had an offer from another university in hand, and now wanted to pressure him for early promotion with tenure and a pay raise. No fucking way, he thought---he would call her bluff. Or maybe she wanted to duck being czarina of MATH 101 next year because it would interfere with her research. He would not give in to that either. But he sat in incredulous, stony silence as she delivered her rehearsed statement about Goldman's mental breakdown, the implosion of his theorem, and his subsequent disappearance. Slutnick's temples were banging by the time she finished, and his stomach made loud gurgling noises as it filled with acid. He popped in two Rolaids.

"Let me get this straight. You're fucking telling me that Goldman was full of crap and now instead of pimping him for honors and prizes I have to go into damage control mode, eat endless buckets of shit, and kiss ass from here to fucking eternity? Is that about it?"

Slutnick had turned deep crimson. Calm and sweet, Celestine

reminded herself. She went on to explain what Chen and the others were saying---that Goldman's work was very significant in spite of the error, and worthy of a Yale workshop.

"I don't give a hairy rat's ass. What the fuck do I tell the Virgin Queen and the Von Essens---'Sorry, hope you enjoyed the pastries and crumpets after Goldman's talk, and oh---by the way, it was a crock of shit? And he made an error that even a fucking undergraduate wouldn't make?' We will be a laughing stock and UNV will never get another goddam *pfenig* from the Von Essens."

"Professor Slutnick, surely the Von Essens will understand---all three know firsthand what war can do to someone's mind. And the truth will mitigate any embarrassment---it will all be a plus in the end---you'll see. The truth is that Simon Goldman's results represent a significant advance in complexity theory, and may eventually lead to a solution of P vs. NP. That's what Chen's people and Bertoli are saying. Please Professor Slutnick, look at the bright side."

Slutnick's hands were trembling and he had to put his coffee on the desk. He gripped the armrests of his recliner and leaned toward her, spraying spittle.

"The truth? The bright side? I'll tell you what the fucking truth and bright side are. I can't touch Goldman because of his endowment deal, but I can give Singleton a reaming he will never forget. This whole fucking mess is his fault---he should have known---Goldman is his friend. I'll double his teaching load. He'll never get a another sabbatical. I won't approve his travel requests. I'll..."

Celestine banged her fist on Slutnick's desk.

"*Tabarnouche!* You will do nothing---do you hear me? *Nothing!*"

She reached for Slutnick's mug and threw it past him, splattering his shirt and staining the carpet.

"How dare you?" he said. "Are you out of your mind?"

Celestine took two steps towards the easel and seized the watercolor. Slutnick did not have time to form words of protest as she impaled the painting on the pointy tip of the Esmeralda obelisk. He reached for the telephone, eyes wide with fear.

"I'm calling Campus Security!"

As he started to dial, Celestine kicked the sculpture. It snapped in two when it hit the edge of the desk.

"Go ahead, Chairman Slutnick. Make your call. When Security gets here, I will report that you were harassing me sexually. I had to defend myself."

She crossed her arms and smiled. Calm and sweet.

***

At the precise moment that Celestine was laying waste to Guillermo's mind and artwork, Sonya Jorgenson was in her office, looking over the twins' data in joyous disbelief. She was useless at statistics, so she had one of her graduate students crunch the numbers for her. The results were startling. All her predictions based upon Hoffer Theory were borne out in the analysis of variance. The levels of statistical significance in the data were higher than she could have hoped, and there were amazing correlations as well. Nathan Finkelstein and Ibrahim Ibrahim had answered many questions differently, with measurable variability in their responses. Yet their overall scores on the personality markers relevant in Hoffer Theory were virtually identical---the twins were equal in traits such as paranoia, magical thinking, and righteous indignation. Sonya knew that she needed to do another study with a sample group larger than two, but she was emboldened by the powerful data and began writing up a preliminary announcement of her findings for the *Journal of Group Behavior.*

-76-

Aitch was at the wheel of the Volvo as they crossed the big bridge, heading home, with Vito already miles ahead. Simon turned in his seat to get a parting glimpse of upper Manhattan's lights, and then buried himself under the quilt which Tante Lotte had provided. They were entering the Palisades Parkway when he spoke from under the cover.

"Bumpkin, you never finished telling me what Chen and Bertoli were saying."

Aitch told him everything---that in the opinion of the experts, Goldman's results on the Traveling Salesman were profound, and that the near density of class-G was the greatest thing in complexity theory since God invented π, even though the density proof failed. And he told him that Chen wanted to set up a workshop at Yale in August, with Goldman being the main speaker.

Twenty minutes passed, and Aitch thought that Simon had fallen asleep. But he had not.

"Bumpkin," he mumbled. "I bet I can repair that density argument before August. Piece of cake."

He wrapped the blanket around himself more tightly, and drifted off.

***

It was past midnight when Aitch pulled into the big rest stop near Burlington, less than an hour from home, because he wanted to phone Celestine. Simon could not move and would wait, cocooned in the passenger seat. He had spoken to Mona earlier, and returned to the sweet dream he was having about her.

Celestine was all joy and giggles upon accepting the charges, because Mona had already informed her that the Math Brothers were on their way home.

"Cherie, I have the most wonderful news. Chinnie has returned from the forest! Little Newton taught him how to climb the oak tree in the backyard and invited him to come in through the attic window, and he left a beautiful pheasant on your desk. They are both here with me in bed, and we will stay awake until you come home. Won't we, Chinnie? Won't we, Newton?"

She held up the phone, and he could hear them purring.

****

ACKNOWLEDGEMENTS

First and last, I want to thank my beautiful wife, Judith Baylin-Stern, for her unwavering love and patience, as well as for her editorial help. I have no doubt that without her kindness and affection, I would not have been able to see this project through. My sons Sach and Adam also shared in the adventure, and never faltered in their loyalty and support.

Many friends offered me encouragement, even if they thought it strange that a mathematician would dabble in fiction. I am eternally grateful for their kind words, pats on the back, and interest in what I was doing. There are far too many such individuals to mention, but I will name those who perused early drafts of *Goldman's Theorem* or provided other forms of tangible support.

These kindhearted souls include Ed, Eva, Frank, Karen and Leah Baylin, Adi Ben-Israel, Marco Bertola, Abraham Boyarski, Francis Clarke, Jean Courcelles, Jacques Duval, Manuela Franzo, Luigi Fraquelli, Ken Hague, Judith Herz, Mel and Neomi Kronish, Helena and Jeff Leibgott, Mimi Liu, John McKay, Steve Nahmias, Hal Proppe, Yvon Provencal, Moti Sherer, Brenda Shestowsky, Mireille Silcoff, Rich Stern, Henry Wolkowicz, Dawn and Greg Yates, and Michael Zigman.

One friend deserves special mention (and possibly blame). Ian Irvine, Professor of Economics, runner, cyclist and squash player extraordinaire, is the creator of the demented Dean Margaret Fulton, a.k.a the Virgin Queen, although I must take responsibility for some of her more extreme excesses.

Finally, I want to express my gratitude to Ruth M. Thompson, Editor-in-Chief of Saga Books, for her editorial and publishing expertise.